FEARFUL FATHOMS

COLLECTED TALES OF AQUATIC TERROR
SEAS AND OCEANS

EDITED BY MARK PARKER

ILLUSTRATIONS BY LUKE SPOONER

SCARLET GALLEON PUBLICATIONS, LLC
BOSTON

FEARFUL FATHOMS: Collected Tales of Aquatic Terror (Vol. I – Seas & Oceans)
Copyright © 2017 Mark Parker
Published by Scarlet Galleon Publications LLC
FIRST EDITION
Edited by Mark Parker
Cover design by David Mickolas
Illustrations by Luke Spooner

"Abandon" used by permission – copyright © 2017 Brad P. Christy

ISBN – 13: 978-1974213023
ISBN – 10: 1974213021
Printed in the U.S.A.

This publisher acknowledges the copyright holders of the original (or reprinted) works as follows:

"Widow's Point" copyright © 2017 by Richard Chizmar and Billy Chizmar
"The Gray Man" copyright © 2017 Mark Parker
"Fear Sun" copyright © 2017 by Laird Barron (originally published in *Innsmouth Nightmares*, PS Publishing, 2015)
"Carnacki: The Lusitania" copyright © 2017 by William Meikle (originally published in *Carnacki: Heaven and Hell*, by Dark Regions Press, 2013)
"Floodland" copyright © 2017 by Cameron Pierce
"Sirens" copyright © 2017 by Dallas Mullican
"Draugar" copyright © 2017 by Bryan Clark
"Old Bogey" copyright © 2017 by Lori R. Lopez
"The Lighthouse" copyright © 2017 by Annie Neugebauer
"Port of Call" copyright © 2017 by W.D. Gagliani (originally published in *Extremes 3: Terror on the High Seas*, Lone Wolf Publications, 2001)

ACKNOWLEDGMENTS

Many thanks go to:

Richard and Billy Chizmar, father and son, for entering into a landmark collaboration to write a wonderfully haunting story for this project.

Jack Ketchum, for sharing his talent with us in a story that has been out of print for nearly a decade—and for permitting us to bring it back for readers within this volume.

Luke Spooner, for offering his incredible talent, once again, by creating original artwork for each story (and for surprising me by creating *color* versions for the digital eBook).

David Mickolas, for once again creating an incredible cover design—but this time for *two* books!

Jim Braswell, for a wonderful job of interior book design and layout.

Doug Rinaldi, for offering his reading skills to this project early on.

To each contributor, for their support and patience throughout.

DEDICATION

For my mother, who first introduced me to the wonders of the sea, and taught me the importance of respecting her many mysteries.

CONTENTS

O abandon!
Lost is the promise of childhood's dreams
The kiss of ocean spray on my lips
And the feel of the trade winds
Ushering me into the vastness of possibility
How I craved the freedom of the open sea
To discover the exotic, the taboo

O wretched, ruinous abandon!
Lost is the promise of a life well-lived
Helplessly, I reach up toward the sun
Its rays breaking through the wavering surface
Sparkling ghosts that I cannot grasp
Blue fades to crushing black
Dragged down into these fearful fathoms.

—Brad P. Christy

INTRODUCTION

The sea has always called to me.

I don't know about you, but it both fascinates and terrifies me in equal measure. When I was fourteen years old, JAWS was released into theaters and I must've seen that particular film at least twenty-five times that summer—each trip to the movie theater funded by the hundred-customer paper route I had at the time. JAWS changed everything for me. I don't know why it held such power over me, but it did. Spielberg and his crew hit the shores of Martha's Vineyard, and turned a tiny island community into the backdrop for one of the most iconic films of all time. Of course as soon as it hit bookstore shelves, I ran into my local Waldenbooks to purchase a copy of THE JAWS LOG, wanting to know every secret behind the making of the film. But I think it was the chord of inexplicable fear that the story itself planted deep within me that affected me most, and kept me obsessed.

After my marathon summer of movie watching, I remember taking a friend's skiff out for an afternoon of sun and spray, only to be haunted by memories of those shark-shadows—and, of course, that terrifying dud-dum…dud-dum…dud-dum music that continued to play over and over again inside my head. It was the same music, you might remember, that swelled each time another appearance from the shark took place in the movie. Even if 'Bruce' was merely a mechanized stand-in for the real thing, I was chilled to the bone every time its dorsal fin cut the surface of the ocean.

I suppose it was seeing that movie all those many years ago, that had me wanting to do an anthology like Fearful Fathoms. I thought it was a cool concept—one that had teeth, I guess you could say. But mostly it was about that chord of fear.

That inexplicable spear of terror that rose up in me each and every time I permitted my thoughts to turn to whatever might be lurking beneath the water's surface. I mean, any number of truly horrible things could swim up to greet me, tug at my leg, or, hell, even bite it off, if I allowed my thoughts to drift deeply enough.

What about you? How deep does your fear go?

I know that's been a question I've asked myself many times over while compiling the stories for this collection. Sometimes, the answer comes back: Not too deep. While, other times, it's a resounding: All-the-way-down deep!

Contained here are stories that will touch on almost every experience a reader might have had on—or in—the sea. Hopefully the stories selected will chill you, some subtly, and some a bit more directly, but all in ways that are as cold and fearful as memory allows. Enjoy!

Mark Parker, Editor
July 2017

WIDOW'S POINT

Richard Chizmar & Billy Chizmar

Video/audio footage #1A (5:49pm, Friday, July 11, 2017)

The man holds the video camera in his left hand and grips the steering wheel with his right. The road, and calling it a road is charitable at best, is unpaved dirt and gravel, and the camera POV is unsteady. Mostly we see bouncing images of the interior dashboard of the car and snippets of blue sky through a dirty windshield. The Rolling Stones' "Sympathy for the Devil" plays at low volume on the car radio.

After another thirty seconds of this, we hear the squeal of brakes in need of repair and the car swings in a wide circle—giving us a shaky glimpse of a stone lighthouse standing atop a grassy point of land—and comes to a stop facing rocky cliffs that drop perilously to the Atlantic Ocean below. The ocean here is dark and rough and foreboding, even on a clear day like today.

The man turns off the engine and we immediately hear the whine of the wind through his open window. Off in the foreground, an old man, thinning gray hair, glasses, and a wrinkled apple of a face, shuffles into view.

The man exits the car, still pointing the camera at the old man, and we see his hand enter the top corner of the screen, as the driver flips the old man a wave.

"Hello," he yells above the wind, walking toward the old man.

Up ahead, we watch the old man shuffling his way toward us through the blowing grass. It appears as if the wind might

1

steal him away and send him kiting over the distant cliffs. At first, we believe he is smiling. As we draw closer, we realize we are wrong, and the old man is scowling. It's not a pretty sight; like a skeletal corpse grinning from inside a moldy coffin.

"Turn that damn camera off," the old man growls.

The picture is immediately replaced with a blurry patch of brown and green grass, as the man lowers the camera.

"Okayyy, we'll just edit that out later," the man says to himself off-camera.

And then in a louder voice: "Sorry, I didn't think it would—"

The screen goes blank.

Video/audio footage #2A [6:01PM, Friday, July 11, 2017]

The screen comes to life and we see the stone lighthouse off in the distance and hear the muffled crash of waves pounding the shoreline off-screen. It's evident from the swaying view of the lighthouse and the intense howl of the wind that the camera is now affixed to a tripod somewhere close to the edge of the cliffs.

The man walks on-screen, carrying a knapsack and what looks like a remote control for the camera. He appears to be in his mid-forties, shaggy blonde hair, neat dark-framed glasses, artfully scuffed boots, pressed jeans, and a gray sweatshirt. He stares directly at the camera, green eyes squinting in the wind, and sidesteps back and forth, searching for the proper positioning.

He settles on a spot just in time to witness a particularly violent gust of wind defeat the tripod.

"Shit," the man blurts, and sprints toward the camera—as it leans hard to the left and crashes to the ground.

There is a squawk of static and the screen goes blank.

Video/audio footage #3A [6:04PM, Friday, July 11, 2017]

The video switches on again, and we see the man standing in the foreground of the lighthouse, pointing the remote at the camera. The image is much steadier this time around. The man slides the remote in the back pocket of his jeans and clears his throat.

"Okay, only have a few minutes, folks. Mr. Parker is in quite the hurry to get out of here. He's either playing the role of hesitant and anxious lighthouse owner to the extreme and faking his discomfort, or he's genuinely unnerved and wants to be pretty much anywhere else but here on the property his family has owned for over a century now."

The man leans over, his hands disappearing just off-screen, and returns holding the knapsack, which he places close on the ground at his side. He stands with an erect but relaxed posture and folds his hands together in front of him.

"My name is Thomas Livingston, bestselling author of *Shattered Dreams, Ashes to Ashes*, and eleven other bestselling non-fiction volumes of the supernatural. I'm here today on the windswept coast of Harper's Cove at the far northern tip of Nova Scotia standing at the foot of the legendary Widow's Point Lighthouse.

"According to historical records, the Widow's Point Lighthouse, originally named for the large number of ships that crashed in the rocky shallows below before its existence, was erected in the summer of 1838 by Franklin Washburn II, the proprietor of the largest fishing and gaming company in Nova Scotia."

Livingston's face grows somber.

"There is little doubt that the Widow's Point Lighthouse led to a sharp decrease in the number of nautical accidents off her shoreline—but at what cost? Legend and literally centuries of first-hand accounts seem to reinforce the belief that the Widow's Point Lighthouse is cursed...or perhaps an even more apt description...*haunted*.

"The legend was born when three workers were killed during the lighthouse's construction, including the young nephew of Mr. Washburn II, who plunged to his death from the lighthouse catwalk during the final week of work. The weather was clear that day, the winds offshore and light. All safety precautions were in place. The tragic accident was never explained.

"The dark fortunes continued when the lighthouse's first keeper, a by-all-accounts 'steadfast individual' went inexplicably mad during one historically violent storm and strangled his wife to death before taking his own life.

"In the decades that followed, nearly two dozen other mysterious deaths occurred within the confines—or on the nearby grounds—of the Widow's Point Lighthouse, including cold-blooded murder, suicide, unexplained accidents, the mass-slaughter of an entire family in 1933, and even rumors of devil worship and human sacrifice.

"There have been many other detailed accounts of additional mysterious and supernatural incidents, not only inside the lighthouse, but outside on the grounds and even upon the stormy waters below.

"After the final abomination in 1933, in which the murderer of the Collins' family left behind a letter claiming he was 'instructed' to kill by a ghostly visitor, the most recent owner of the Widow's Point Lighthouse, seafood tycoon Robert James Parker—yes, the grandfather of Mr. Ronald Parker, the camera-shy gentleman you glimpsed earlier—decided to cease operations and shutter the lighthouse permanently.

"Or so he believed...

"Because in 1985, Parker's eldest son, Ronald's father, entered into an agreement with the United Artists film studio from Hollywood, California to allow the studio to film a movie both inside the lighthouse and on the surrounding acreage. The movie, a gothic thriller entitled *Rosemary's Spirit*, was filmed over a period of six weeks from mid-September to the first week of November. Despite the lighthouse's menacing reputation, the filming went off without a hitch...until the final week of shooting, that is...when supporting actress Lydia Pearl hanged herself from one of the catwalk guard railings atop the lighthouse.

"Trade publications reported that Ms. Pearl was despondent following a recent break-up with her professional baseball playing fiancé, Roger Barthelme. But believed differently. They believed with great con\ after all those long years of silent slumber, the Wic curse had reawakened and claimed another victim.

"Regardless of the reasoning, the lighthouse was once again shuttered tight against the elements three years later in 1988 and for the first time, a security fence was erected around the property, making the lighthouse accessible only by scaling the over one-hundred-and-fifty-foot high cliffs that line its eastern border along the Atlantic.

"In other words, no human being has been inside the Widow's Point Lighthouse in nearly thirty years…"

Livingston takes a dramatic pause, then steps closer to the camera, his face clenched and square-jawed.

"…until now. Until *today*.

"That's right—tonight, for the first time in over three decades, someone will spend the night in the dark heart of the Widow's Point Lighthouse. That someone is *me*, Thomas Livingston.

"After months of spirited—pardon the pun—discussion and negotiation, I have been able to secure arrangements to spend an entire weekend inside the legendary lighthouse. The ground rules are simple. Today is Friday, July 11, in the year of 2017. It is…"

Livingston checks his wristwatch.

"…6:09pm Eastern Standard Time on Friday evening. In a matter of minutes, Mr. Ronald Parker, current proprietor of the Widow's Point Lighthouse, will escort me through the only entrance or exit to the lighthouse, and once I am safely inside, he will close and lock the door behind me…"

Livingston bends down and comes back fully into view holding a heavy chain and padlock.

"…using these."

He holds the chain and padlock up to the camera for another dramatic beat, and then drops them unseen to the ground below.

"I will be permitted to take inside only enough food and

...er to last me three days and three nights, as well as a lantern, flashlight, sanitary supplies, two notebooks and pens, along with this video camera and tripod, and several extra batteries. In addition, this…"

Livingston backs up a couple steps, reaches down into his knapsack, and quickly comes up with a small machine in his right hand.

"…Sony Digital Voice Recorder, capable of recording over one thousand hours of memory with a battery life of nearly ninety-six hours without a single charging. And, yes, please consider that an official product placement for the Sony Corporation."

Livingston laughs—and we get a glimpse of the handsome and charming author pictured on the dust jacket of one of his books—and then he returns the voice recorder to his knapsack.

"I will not be allowed a cell phone or a computer of any kind. Absolutely no Internet access. No way to communicate, or should anything go wrong, no way to request assistance of any kind. I will be completely cut off from the outside world for three long and hopefully peaceful nights."

We hear a car horn blare from off-screen, and a startled Livingston's eyes flash in that direction. He looks back at the camera, shaking his head, a bemused expression on his face.

"Okay, folks, it's time to begin my journey, or shall I say, *our* journey, as I will be recording all of my innermost thoughts and observations in an effort to take you, my readers, along with me. The next time I appear on camera, I will be entering the legendary—some say, *haunted*—Widow's Point Lighthouse. Wish me luck. I may need it.

"And cut…"

The screen goes blank.

VIDEO/AUDIO FOOTAGE #4A (6:04PM, FRIDAY, JULY 11, 2017)

Livingston is carrying the video camera in his hand again, and we share his shaky POV as he slowly approaches the lighthouse.

Mr. Parker remains off-screen, but we hear his voice nearby: "Eight o'clock Monday morning. I'll be here not a minute later."

"That will be perfect. Thank you."

The lighthouse door draws nearer. The door is large and weathered and constructed of heavy beams of scarred wood, most likely from an ancient ship, as Livingston had once unearthed in his research. The men stop when they reach the entrance.

"And you're certain you cannot be convinced otherwise?" the old man asks.

Livingston turns to him—and we finally get a close-up of the reclusive Mr. Parker, an antique crone of a man, his knobby head framed by the blue-gray sea behind him—and Livingston laughs. "No, no. Everything will be fine, I promise."

The old man merely grunts in reply.

The camera swings back toward the lighthouse and is lowered, and we catch a fleeting glimpse of Livingston's knapsack hanging from his shoulder and then, resting on the ground at the foot of the entrance, a dirty white cooler with handles by which to carry or drag it. Livingston leans down and takes it by one plastic handle.

"Then I wish you Godspeed," the old man says.

The camera is lifted once again and focused on the heavy wooden door. A wrinkled, liver-spotted hand swims into view holding a key. The key is inserted into an impossible-to-see keyhole directly beneath an oversized, ornate doorknob and, with much effort, turned.

The heavy door opens with a loud *sigh*, and we can practically hear the ancient air escaping.

"Whew, musty," Livingston says with a cough, and we watch his hand reach on-screen and push the door all the way open with a loud *creak*—into total darkness.

"Aye. She's been breathing thirty years of dead air."

Livingston pauses—perhaps it's the mention of "dead air" that slows his pace—before re-gripping the cooler's plastic handle and stepping inside.

At the exact moment in time that Livingston crosses the threshold into the lighthouse, unbeknownst to him, the video goes blank. Entirely blank—with the exception of a time code in the lower left corner of the screen, which at that moment reads: 6:07pm.

"I'll see you Monday morning," Livingston says.

The old man doesn't respond, simply nods and closes the door in Livingston's face. The screen is already dark, so we do not see this; instead, we hear it with perfect clarity and finality.

Then, we listen as the key is once again turned in the lock, and the heavy chain is wrestled into place. After a brief moment of silence, the *click* of a padlock being snapped shut is heard, followed by a final tug on the chain.

Then, there is only silence...

...until a rustle of clothing whispers in the darkness and there comes the *thud* of the cooler being set down at Livingston's feet.

"And so it begins, ladies and gentlemen, our journey into the heart of the Widow's Point Lighthouse. I will now climb the two hundred and sixty-eight spiraling stairs to the living quarters of the lighthouse, lantern in one hand, camera in the other. I will return a short time later this evening for food and water supplies, after some initial exploration."

We hear the sound of ascending footsteps and:

"Originally built in 1838, the Widow's Point Lighthouse is two hundred and seven feet tall, constructed of stone, mostly granite taken from a nearby quarry, and positioned some seventy-five yards from the sheer cliffs which tower above the stormy Atlantic..."

Video/audio footage #5A (6:14pm, Friday, July 11, 2017)

We hear Livingston's heavy breathing and then notice the time code—6:14pm—appear in the lower left hand corner. Once again, the rest of the screen remains dark.

"Two hundred-sixty-six...two hundred-sixty-seven... two hundred-sixty-eight. And with that, we have reached the pinnacle, ladies and gents, and just in time, too. Your faithful host is feeling rather…spent, I have to admit."

Even without a video feed, we can almost picture Livingston dropping his knapsack and holding up the lantern to survey his home for the next three nights.

"Well, as you can certainly see for yourselves, Mr. Parker spoke the truth when he claimed this place was in a state of severe ill repair. In fact, he may have managed to actually underestimate the pathetic condition of the Widow's Point living quarters."

A deep sigh.

"I believe I shall now rest for a few moments, and then venture upward and explore the lantern room and perhaps even the catwalk if it appears sturdy enough before returning downstairs for my food and water supplies. Once I've straightened up a bit and established proper housekeeping, I will return to you with a further update.

"I also promise to discuss the mysterious incidents I referenced earlier—and many more—in greater and more graphic detail once I have made myself at home."

The sound of shuffling footsteps.

"But, first, before I go…lord in heaven…just gaze upon this magnificent sight for a moment with me."

Livingston's voice takes on a tone of genuine awe. The phony theatrics are gone; he means every word of what he is saying now.

"Resplendent mother ocean as far as the eye can see…and beyond. The vision is almost enough to render me speechless." A chuckle. "Almost."

The time code disappears—and the video ends.

Voice recorder entry #1B (7:17pm, Friday, July 11, 2017)

Well, this is rather strange and unfortunate. After I last left you, I returned downstairs and brought up a day's ration of food and water, then spent considerable time cleaning and straightening in preparation for the weekend. Once these tasks were completed to my satisfaction, I settled down for some rest and to double-check the video footage I had shot earlier.

The first several videos were fine, if a little rough around the edges, but then I came to the fourth video…and discovered a problem. I was shocked to find that while the audio portion of the recording worked just fine, the video portion seemed to have somehow malfunctioned once I entered the lighthouse. And I do mean as soon as I stepped inside the lighthouse.

I proceeded to check the camera lens and conduct several test videos, all with the same result—the audio function appears to be operating in perfect order, while video capabilities are disabled. I admit I find the whole matter more puzzling than troubling or unsettling, even with the rather bizarre timing of the issue.

Perhaps, something inside the camera was broken when the wind knocked it down earlier by the cliffs. Or…perhaps the otherworldly influence that dwells here inside the Widow's Point Lighthouse has already made its presence known. I suppose only time will tell.

In the meantime, this Sony—hear that, folks, Sony—digital voice recorder will serve my purpose here just fine.

VOICE RECORDER ENTRY #2B (9:03PM, FRIDAY, JULY 11, 2017)

Good evening. I've just taken my first dinner here in Widow's Point—a simple affair; a ham-and-Swiss sandwich slathered with mustard, side of fresh fruit, and for dessert, a thin slice of homemade carrot cake—and finished organizing my copious notes.

Now it's time for another brief history lesson.

Earlier, I referenced more than a handful of disturbing incidents that have taken place in and around the Widow's Point Lighthouse. I also promised to discuss in further detail many of the lesser-known tragedies and unexplained occurrences that have become part of the lighthouse's checkered history. In time, I will do exactly that.

However, for the sake of simplicity, I will first discuss

the three most recent and widely-known stories involving the Widow's Point Lighthouse. I will do so in chronological order.

I referenced earlier the 1933 mass murder of the entire Collins' family. What I did not mention were the gory details. On the night of September 4, 1933, lighthouse keeper Patrick Collins invited his brother-in-law and three local men to the lighthouse for an evening of card-playing and whiskey. This was a nearly monthly occurrence, so it did not prove particularly troublesome to Patrick's wife, Abigail, or their two children, Stephen, age nine, and Delaney, age six.

One of the men whom Patrick invited was a close friend of his brother-in-law's, a worker from the nearby docks. Joseph O'Leary was, by all accounts, a quiet man. A lifelong bachelor, O'Leary was perhaps best known in town as the man who had once single-handedly foiled a bank robbery when the would-be robber ran out of the bank and directly into O'Leary's formidable chest. O'Leary simply wrapped up the thug in a suffocating bear hug until the authorities arrived.

According to Collins' brother-in-law and the other two surviving card players—Joshua Tempe, bookkeeper and Donald Garland, fisherman—the night of September 4 was fairly typical of one of their get-togethers. Collins and Tempe both drank too much and their games became sloppy and their voices slurred and loud as the night wore on. On the other hand, the brother-in-law ate too many peanuts and strips of spicy jerky, and as usual, there were many complaints voiced about his equally spicy flatulence. O'Leary was his quiet, affable self throughout the evening, and if any one observation could be made regarding the man, it was agreed by the others that O'Leary experienced a stunning run of good luck throughout the second half of the game.

By evening's end, a short time after midnight, the vast majority of the coins on the table were stacked in front of O'Leary, with a grumbling Donald Garland finishing a distant second. The men shrugged on their coats, bid each other goodnight, descended the winding staircase in a slow, staggered parade, and returned to their respective homes and beds.

All except Joseph O'Leary.

When he reached his rented flat on Westbury Avenue, O'Leary went directly to his kitchen table, where he sat for just over an hour and composed the now-infamous, lengthy, rambling, handwritten letter explaining that earlier in the night while taking a break from card-playing to visit the bathroom, he had experienced an unsettling—thou admittedly, thrilling and liberating—supernatural occurrence.

To relieve yourself in 1933 in the Widow's Point Lighthouse, you had to descend to what was commonly (albeit crudely) referred to as the Shit Room. Once you found yourself in this isolated and dimly-lit chamber, you tended to do your business as quickly as possible for it was a genuinely eerie setting and not designed for one's comfort.

It was here, inside the Shit Room, that O'Leary claims the ghostly, transparent image of a young beautiful woman wearing a flowing white bed-robe appeared before him—at first frightening him with her spectral whisperings before ultimately seducing him with both words and embrace.

Afterward, O'Leary returned to his friends and the card game in a daze. He claimed it felt as if he had dreamt the entire incident.

Dreamlike or not, once O'Leary finished composing his letter, he rose from the kitchen table, took down the heaviest hammer from his workbench, returned to the Widow's Point Lighthouse, where earlier he had purposely failed to lock the door behind him as was the custom, ascended the two hundred-and-sixty-eight steps—and bludgeoned the Collins' family to death in their beds.

Once the slaughter was complete, O'Leary strolled outside onto the catwalk—perhaps to rendezvous with his ghostly lover now that the task she had burdened him with was complete—and climbed over the iron railing and simply stepped off into the starless night.

O'Leary's body was found early the next morning by a local fisherman, shattered on the rocky ground below. Shortly after, the authorities arrived and a much more gruesome discovery was made inside the lighthouse.

VOICE RECORDER ENTRY #3B (10:59PM, FRIDAY, JULY 11, 2017)

It's late and I can barely keep my eyes open. I'm rather exhausted from the day's events, so I bid you all a fair goodnight and pleasant dreams. I pray my own slumber passes uninterrupted, as I am planning for an early start in the morning. Exciting times lay ahead.

VOICE RECORDER ENTRY #4B (4:51AM, SATURDAY, JULY 11, 2017)

(Mumbling)

I can't. I don't want to. They're...my friends.

VOICE RECORDER ENTRY #5B (7:14AM, SATURDAY, JULY 12, 2017)

Good morning and what a splendid morning it is!

If I sound particularly rested and cheerful for a man who has just spent the night in a filthy, abandoned, and reputedly haunted lighthouse, it's because indeed I am. Rested and cheerful, that is.

Trust me, folks, I'm as surprised as you are.

My night didn't begin in very promising fashion. Although I tucked myself into my sleeping bag and dimmed the lantern shortly after eleven o'clock, I found myself still wide-awake at half past midnight. Why? I'm not exactly certain. Perhaps excitement. Perhaps trepidation. Or perhaps simply the surprising coldness of the lighthouse floor, felt deep in my bones even through my overpriced sleeping bag.

I lay there all that time and listened to the lighthouse whisper its secrets to me and a singular thought echoed inside my exhausted brain: *what was I hoping to find here?*

It's a question I had been asked many times in the days leading up to this adventure—by Mr. Ronald Parker and my literary agent and even my ex-wife, just to name a few—and never once had I been able to come up with a response that rang with any measure of authenticity.

Until last night, that is, when—in the midst of my unexpected bout of insomnia, as I lay there on the cold floor in the shadows, wondering if what I was hearing…the distant hollow clanking of heavy metal chains somewhere below me and the uneven scuffling of stealthy footfalls on the dusty staircase…were reality or imagination—the answer to the question occurred to me with startling clarity.

What was I hoping to find here?

Inarguable proof that the Widow's Point Lighthouse was haunted? Incontrovertible evidence that nothing supernatural had ever dwelled within the structure, all the stories and legends nothing more than centuries-old campfire tales and superstition?

The answer that occurred to me was none of the above—and all of the above.

I didn't care what I found here in the Widow's Point Lighthouse. For once, I wasn't looking for a book deal or a movie option. I wasn't looking for fame or fortune.

I was simply looking for the *truth.*

And with that liberating revelation caressing my conscience, my eyes slid closed and I fell into a deep and peaceful sleep.

Voice recorder entry #6B (8:39am, Saturday, July 12, 2017)

Now that I've completed my morning exercises and eaten a bit of breakfast, it's time for another history lesson.

As I already noted in my opening segment—and I'll try not to repeat myself too much here—Hollywood came to the town of Harper's Cove in September of 1985. More specifically, Hollywood came to the Widow's Point Lighthouse.

Although town officials and a handful of local merchants were enthusiastic about the financial rewards Harper's Cove stood to gain from the production, the vast majority of the townspeople expressed extreme unease—and even anger—

when they learned that the subject matter of the film so closely paralleled the lighthouse's tragic history. It was one thing to rent out the lighthouse for a motion picture production, but a horror film? And a ghost story at that? It felt morally wrong to the residents of Harper's Cove. It felt *dangerous*. A handful of women from the Harper's Cove Library Association even gathered and picketed outside the movie set, but they gave up after a week of particularly harsh weather drove them inside.

Rosemary's Spirit was budgeted at just over eight million dollars. The film starred Garrett Utley and Britney Longshire, both coming off modest hits for the United Artists studio. Popular daytime television actress, Lydia Pearl, appeared in a supporting role, and by many accounts, stole the movie with her inspired and daring performance.

The film's director, Henry Rothchild, was quoted as saying, "Lydia was such a lovely young woman and she turned in the performance of a lifetime. She showed up on set each day full of energy and wonderfully prepared, and I have no doubt that she would have gone on to amazing things. The whole thing is unimaginable and tragic."

Executive producer, Doug Sharretts, of *Gunsmoke* fame, added: "There were no signs of distress. I had breakfast with Lydia the day it happened. We sat outside and watched the sunlight sparkle across the ocean. She was enchanted. She loved it here. She was in fine spirits and excited to shoot her final scenes later that evening. And she was confident that she and Roger would work out their problems and be married. There were no signs. Nothing."

The rest of the cast and crew are on record with similar statements regarding Miss Pearl and the events of the night of November 3, 1985. Lydia was, by all accounts, in fine spirits, well liked and respected, and her death came as a shock to everyone involved in the film.

However, there was one dissenting voice and it belonged to Carlos Pena, *Rosemary's Spirit's* renowned director of photography. At the time of Lydia Pearl's death, Pena was one of the few members of the crew to never comment on record.

Most people attributed this to Pena's reticent nature. He was that rare individual in Hollywood: a private man in a very public business.

Fifteen years later, dying of lung cancer at his home in Mexico, it was a different story, as Pena told a reporter from *Variety*: "I've worked on over a hundred films and I've never witnessed anything like it. It still haunts me to this day.

"The rest of the cast and crew were on lunch break and I thought I was alone in the lighthouse. I was going over the next scene, pacing out camera shots and thinking about changing the angle on camera number two when I heard someone whispering from the level below me. I was surprised but I figured it was just one of the actors running their lines. After a few minutes, the whispering grew in volume and intensity, to the point where I couldn't concentrate any longer, so I went to investigate.

"Some of the crew had constructed a makeshift break room on the next level down. It was cramped quarters but there was enough room for a small refrigerator and a handful of uncomfortable chairs.

"I was surprised to find the room in total darkness when I reached the doorway. The lights had been on not ten minutes earlier when I'd passed it on my way up to the set. I figured once the person heard my footfalls, they would stop running lines and call out to me, but they didn't. The whispering continued unabated. It was a woman's voice, and now that I could make out the words she was saying, it chilled me. Whoever this was, hidden here in the darkness, she wasn't running lines; she was having a conversation—with herself.

"Uneasy, I reached inside the doorway and turned on the light, and I was shocked to see Lydia Pearl standing very close to and facing the far wall. The whispering continued despite my intrusion.

"I called out to her: 'Lydia? I'm sorry to interrupt.'

"She didn't respond. I walked closer, my heart beating faster in my chest. Something wasn't right here.

"'Is everything okay?' I asked, almost upon her now.

"Again, there was no response. Just that frenzied whispering, almost a hissing, as though she were arguing with herself. She stood with a rigid posture, arms limp at her sides.

"Once I was close enough, being careful not to startle her, I softly called her name and reached out and placed a hand gently on her shoulder—and she whirled on me, one rattlesnake-quick hand lunging out to claw at my face. I backstepped in shock, blocking her advance.

"Her face is what I best remember, even now in my dreams. It was twisted in rage. Spittle hanging from her drawn lips. Teeth bared. Her eyes were the worst. They were impossibly large and unlike any human eyes I had ever seen. They were feral and burning with unimaginable hatred. This woman I barely knew wanted to kill me, wanted to devour me.

"And then, as quickly as it had begun, it was over. Her face relaxed, arms lowered, and she drew back, blinking rapidly, as if awakening from a dream. Her eyes seemed to regain focus and she saw me standing there in front of her, quite a sight, I am sure. She sobbed, 'I'm sorry' and ran from the room, brushing against me as she fled. I remember her body was ice cold where she had touched me.

"Later that evening, when news of her suicide reached me at my hotel, I was not surprised. I was sad, but not surprised.

"I've never spoken of this before and I never will again."

According to William McClernan, the reporter from *Variety,* Carlos Pena had grasped his rosary in his hands and crossed himself numerous times while recounting this unsettling story.

Voice recorder entry #7B (11:44AM, Saturday, July 12, 2017)

Hello there, again. I've spent the past hour scribbling in my notebook, thoughts and observations to look back upon once this experience is over. I've learned not to rely too heavily on memory. Memory is a tricky beast, as I have learned the hard way over the years. It's not to be trusted.

Lunch soon and then another history lesson, this one even

more scandalous than the last.

Voice recorder entry #8B (11:49am, Saturday, July 12, 2017)

Did I mention that several times now I've heard the echo of footsteps in this lonely place? Last night and twice this morning. I'm convinced that it's not my imagination, but then what is it? The Widow's Point Lighthouse, all these years later, still settling into the rocky earth below? The harsh Atlantic wind searching for entry and creeping its way inside these heavy stone walls? Rats scavenging for food? Ghosts?

Voice recorder entry #9B (1:01pm, Saturday, July 12, 2017)

Despite the highly-publicized and controversial death of actress Lydia Pearl in the fall of 1985, the Widow's Point Lighthouse—save for a handful of NO TRESPASSING signs set about the perimeter—remained unguarded and largely accessible to the general public. It wasn't until almost three years later, during the late summer of 1988, that the razor-topped security fence was erected and local authorities began patrolling the area.

This is the reason why:

In the spring of 1988, fifteen-year-old Michael Risley had just finished his freshman year at Harper's Cove High School. Michael wasn't considered particularly popular or unpopular. In fact, he wasn't considered much at all. Even in a school as small as Harper's Cove, he was largely invisible.

Because of this fact, no one knew of Michael Risley's fascination—his obsession—with the occult and the Widow's Point Lighthouse. No one knew that he had spent countless hours in the local library doing research and talking to the old-timers down at the docks about the turn-of-the-century legends regarding devil worship taking place in the woods surrounding the lighthouse.

And, because of this, no one knew that Michael Risley had spent much of his freshman year performing his own satanic rituals in those same woods just outside of the Widow's Point

Lighthouse, sacrificing dozens of small animals, on several occasions even going so far as to drink their blood.

By the time July rolled around that summer, Michael was ready to move on from small animals. On the night of a Thursday full moon, he snuck out of his house after bedtime, leaving a note for his parents on the foyer table, and met two younger kids—Tabitha Froehling, age 14, and Benjamin Lawrence, age 13—at the end of his street. Earlier in the day, Michael had promised them beer and cigarettes and dared them to accompany him to the old lighthouse at midnight. Every small town has a haunted house and for the children of Harper's Point, it had always been—and always would be— the Widow's Point Lighthouse.

The three of them walked side-by side down the middle of First Street, their shadows from the bright moonlight trailing behind them. They walked slowly and silently, their backpacks slung across their shoulders. It was an idyllic scene, full of youthful promise and innocence.

Early the next morning, Michael Risley's mother read the note her son had left on the foyer table the night before. She managed to call out to her husband once before fainting to the hardwood floor. A frantic Mr. Risley bound down the stairs, carried his wife to the living room sofa, read the note grasped in her right hand, and then immediately called 911.

The police found Michael and the other two children exactly where the note had told them they would be. A break in the thick forest formed a natural, circular clearing. A fire pit ringed in small stones was still smoldering at the center of the clearing. Tabitha and Benjamin lay sprawled on their backs not far from the fire. Strange symbols, matching the symbols adorning many nearby trees, had been carved into their foreheads with a very sharp knife. Both of their throats had been cut and their chests had been sliced open. Their hearts were missing. Deep, ragged bite marks lined the length of their exposed legs.

Michael was discovered several hundred yards away— at the base of the Widow's Point Lighthouse. Naked and incoherent, the officer in charge claimed in his written report that it was like looking at "a devil on earth." Michael had used the other children's blood to paint every inch of his body red. Then, he had consumed portions of both hearts.

According to the note he had left, Michael believed that once this final ritual was completed, he would be "taken in by the Dark Lord and spirited away to a better place."

Instead, at some point during the long and bloody night, Michael Risley's sanity had snapped, and the only place he was spirited away to was the mental hospital in nearby Coffman's Corner.

A week later, the security fence was in place.

Voice recorder entry #10B (3:15pm, Saturday, July 12, 2017)

On a whim, I took the video camera out onto the catwalk a short time ago and gave it another try. It's such a gorgeous afternoon, the sun high in a cloudless sky, the ocean, unusually calm for this time of year, sparkling like a crush of fine emeralds scattered across a tabletop. I spotted a pair of cruise ships steaming south on the horizon. Later, a parade of fishing vessels hauling the day's catch will journey past on their way home to port.

I filmed the entirety of this spectacle and tested the footage when I returned below. Alas, the screen remained blank.

Voice recorder entry #11B (4:56pm, Saturday, July 12, 2017)

You'll have to excuse my labored breathing, as you are kindly accompanying me to the bottom of the Widow's Point Lighthouse to retrieve additional water supplies, traversing the same spiral staircase once climbed by killer and actress alike. I can feel history here with each step I take. In a way, the atmosphere feels similar to a leisurely stroll through the grassy hills of Gettysburg, another haunted place where history and death lock arms and dance for all to see. A spectacle of names flittering through your conscience while you construct a façade of mournful respect, all while secretly wishing to have bared witness to the ancient slaughter. Macabre, most certainly, but also an undeniable truth. Interstate rubberneckers don't clog traffic due to frivolous curiosity, but rather they can't help themselves, hoping to be fortunate enough to see a splash of scarlet blood on the roadside or a glimpse of mangled flesh. After all, the scores of spectators that crowded into the ancient coliseums didn't come for the popcorn.

Navigating these endless stairs, I must admit I feel a closer kinship with Lydia Pearl and Joseph O'Leary than I ever have with any fallen soldier of the Civil War. Why is this? Perhaps it is simply the nature of time and urban legend…or perhaps it is just the nature of the Widow's Point Lighthouse. Ghosts surround me here.

VOICE RECORDER ENTRY #12B (5:10PM, SATURDAY, JULY 12, 2017)

I've tested several bottles of water from the cooler and discovered something mildly alarming. The water has a salty tang to it. Subtle, but present nonetheless. The bottles were purchased from a grocery store just yesterday afternoon, and the water I consumed last night and earlier today suffered no such issue. Perhaps I'm a victim of my own overgrown imagination, or perhaps it's just an unexpected effect of the salty air here on the coast. Regardless, I can't help but wonder and I can't help but tell you all about it. After all, my own voice is—*(chuckles)*—and always has been, my greatest companion.

VOICE RECORDER ENTRY #13B (5:29PM, SATURDAY, JULY 12, 2017)

Ninety-one, ninety-two, ninety-three…

VOICE RECORDER ENTRY #14B (5:53PM, SATURDAY, JULY 12, 2017)

My goodness, I am winded. The journey down these twisting stairs felt endless, but the journey back up feels like forever-and-a-half, as my late father was wont to say. I tried counting the two-hundred-and-sixty-eight steps, as I did during my summit just yesterday, but I kept losing count. I swear to you I have climbed over five hundred stairs by now.

To add to my sense of displacement, I can hear the unmistakable rumblings of a storm approaching outside. Odd, as the skies were crystal clear just hours ago. I had been particularly meticulous about checking the local weather reports in the days leading up to this adventure. Each and every online report called for clear days and pleasant nights. Oh, well, no matter, a storm will just add to the mounting atmosphere.

Voice recorder entry #15B (6:01pm, Saturday, July 12, 2017)

Many of the historical volumes I read about the Widow's Point Lighthouse discussed the frequent storms that hit this particular section of the Nova Scotia coastline. More than one author claimed that during the most violent of these storms, you could actually feel the old stone lighthouse trembling on its foundation. I chalked this observation up to showmanship and hyperbole, but boy was I mistaken.

When I finally reached the lighthouse living quarters after what felt like an eternity of climbing, I was stunned at the vision that greeted me outside. Heavy rain lashed the lighthouse windows. The once-crystal skies were now boiling with fast-moving, dark, roiling clouds. Jagged shards of lightning stabbed at the horizon. Angry whitecaps danced across the churning sea. The wind was howling and I could feel in the very bones of the lighthouse the surging waves crashing onto the rocky shoreline at the base of the cliffs.

I stared in awe—and yes, I admit, a sliver of encroaching fear. I had never seen the sea in such a state.

Voice recorder entry #16B (7:15pm, Saturday, July 12, 2017)

I've somehow lost my flashlight. I carried it with me during my earlier journey on the staircase and I know I placed it near my sleeping bag while I ate my dinner. Now it's gone. I've looked everywhere. Puzzling to say the least.

Voice recorder entry #17B (8:12pm, Saturday, July 12, 2017)

First my flashlight, and now I'm hearing things again. Twice in the past hour, I could've sworn I heard the faint strains of a child singing somewhere below me. I know this isn't possible, of course. The ghosts of Widow's Point and the storm are playing tricks on this old boy. Despite my initial sense of unease, I'm grateful for the experience. It will make a fine addition to these entries.

Still no sign of that blasted flashlight.

Voice recorder entry #18B (8:24pm, Saturday, July 12, 2017)

There! Can you hear it? A banging, like someone knocking on the floor right underneath me, and—

There it is again!

I'm not imagining it.

Can you hear it?

Voice recorder entry #19B (9:57pm, Saturday, July 12, 2017)

What a night it has been! First, the unexpected arrival of the storm and the disappearance of my flashlight. Then, the mysterious singing and knocking sounds. Perhaps worst of all, and I know precisely how trite this sounds, I now feel certain that someone is watching me. Several times I have sensed something…a *presence*…directly behind me. I have felt it. Yet each time I've turned to find nothing but shadows. I'm sure my colleagues would find great pleasure at my skittish behavior.

I've talked and written ad nauseam about the energy that is often trapped inside houses of haunted repute, especially those places where violent crimes have occurred. I feel that energy here in the Widow's Point Lighthouse. And it's getting stronger.

It's not yet ten o'clock and I'm already tucked inside my sleeping bag, hoping for an early night of it. I can hardly see the floor in front of me. The lantern, although in fine working order last night, has proven a sad replacement for my flashlight, as the flame tends to extinguish within minutes of each lighting. Whether this is the result of a malicious gust or 'geist, I cannot say, but my temporary home certainly has a draft that I hadn't noticed at any time before. And it's cold draft at that. I had been told that the summer heat would be retained in this old stone monolith, but it seems as if the ocean winds blow colder inside the lighthouse than outside.

Speaking of outside, the storm continues to rage. If anything, it's grown stronger as the night has progressed. Every few moments, lightning slashes the sky, illuminating the room around me with a startling brilliance before plunging it back into darkness. I can't help but wonder if—

(A long, silent beat followed by a beeping sound)

Ladies and gentlemen, the video camera appears to have come back to life.

Video/audio footage #6A (10:06pm, Saturday, July 12, 2017)

The video switches on and the screen is flooded with murky shadows. Only the time-code can be clearly seen. Then, we hear a muted crash of thunder and a flash of lightning illuminates the lighthouse living quarters. A few seconds later, the lightning is gone and we are greeted again by mostly darkness.

"Initially, I dismissed what I was seeing as a trick of the lightning, but then I realized that the blinking red light at my feet was coming from the video camera. When I heard the beep of the battery, I immediately picked up the camera and ran a quick test. For whatever reason, it seems to be working fine now.

"I'm thinking perhaps I jarred something when I moved the camera after dinner or—JESUS, WHAT WAS THAT?!"

The video shifts and we hear heavy breathing growing more rapid by the moment. Then, the rustle of footsteps, moving cautiously at first, but soon gaining urgency. The echo of boots slapping pavement transitions to boots clanging against metal as Livingston ascends the stairs to the lighthouse's catwalk.

We hear a door being yanked open and are overpowered by the cacophony of the storm. Wind howls. Rain lashes. Thunder roars. Skeletal fingers of lightning dance across the violent sea.

Livingston moves closer to the iron railing and points the camera at the ocean below. Enormous swells crash on the rocks below. The camera zooms closer—and Livingston gasps.

"My God, do you see it?!" he yells, his voice swallowed by the wind. "Someone needs to help them!"

The screen goes blank.

Video/Audio Footage #7A (10:50pm, Saturday, July 12, 2017)

We see Thomas Livingston's haggard face staring back at us. His hair is wet and he's shivering. His bloodshot eyes dart nervously around the room. For the moment, the lantern is lit, bathing his skin in an orange glow.

Livingston looks at the camera for maybe thirty seconds but doesn't say anything. We can see him searching for his words. Finally:

"I know what I heard. And I know what I saw."

He sounds as if he might break into tears.

"I heard it crashing upon the rocks."

He glances down at the ground, steels himself, then looks back at the camera and continues.

"It was a massive ship. At least two hundred feet long. And it broke into a thousand pieces. It was an awful sound. Dozens of men…thrashed and tossed upon the rocks…impaled on splintered planks…drowning in the waves. I can still hear their screams.

"I recorded all of it, I'm certain of that. I knew what I was witnessing wasn't possible, but I saw what I saw and I kept the camera rolling…"

A deep breath.

"But there's nothing there now. I checked the video after I returned inside and changed into dry clothes. I checked it a dozen times. There's nothing there."

He looks up at the camera and the brash showman we saw earlier is gone.

"You can hear the thunder and the crash of the waves. You can see the lightning flash and the ocean below...but there's no ship anywhere to be seen. No bodies."

Livingston rubs his eyes with his fists.

"I offer no explanation, ladies and gentlemen, because I have none."

VIDEO/AUDIO FOOTAGE #8A (11:16PM, SATURDAY, JULY 12, 2017)

The video turns on and once again we see a shaky image of the churning ocean at the base of the cliffs. The rain has slowed, but the wind is still gusting and shards of lightning still decorate the sky.

"It's taken me the better part of an hour to summon the courage to come out here again."

The camera zooms in for a closer view. Waves crash onto an empty shoreline.

"The ship is gone."

The camera zooms back out.

"I know what I saw."

After a moment, the camera lowers and we hear footsteps on the catwalk, and then a loud clanging sound.

"What the...?"

The camera shifts, as Livingston bends down, and steadies on the object he almost just tripped on.

It's the missing flashlight.

"Jesus," he whispers and picks it up.

VOICE RECORDER ENTRY #20B (11:33PM, SATURDAY, JULY 12, 2017)

I must sleep now, if that is even possible. I've had enough for one day. Do you remember earlier when I said I was only here for the truth? Well, that was a fucking lie.

VOICE RECORDER ENTRY #21B (1:12AM, SUNDAY, JULY 13, 2017)

(The sound of footsteps descending the stairway)

Sixty-eight, sixty-nine, seventy, seventy-one, seventy-two, seventy-three…

VOICE RECORDER ENTRY #22B (1:35AM, SUNDAY, JULY 13, 2017)

Two-sixty-six, two-sixty-seven, two-sixty-eight.

(The shuffling of footsteps as Livingston reaches the bottom of the stairway, turns around, and immediately starts climbing)

One, two, three, four, five, six, seven, eight, nine, ten, eleven, twelve, thirteen…

VOICE RECORDER ENTRY #23B (2:09AM, SUNDAY, JULY 13, 2017)

Two-hundred-and-ninety-nine, three-hundred, three-hundred-and-one, three-hundred-and-two, three-hundred-and-three, three-hundred-and-four, three-hundred-and-five…

(Livingston's voice is pointedly deliberate, almost as if he has been hypnotized)

VOICE RECORDER ENTRY #24B (6:42AM, SUNDAY, JULY 13, 2017)

The night was endless, a nightmare. If I slept at all, I don't remember. The hours passed like a fever dream. At one point, I heard someone crying, a woman, but was too frightened to get up and investigate. A little later I thought I saw something moving in the doorway, the pale outline of a person, but it vanished when I switched on the flashlight. And it's so cold in here I can't stop shivering, even inside my sleeping bag. My entire body aches, and my feet are filthy and tattered, as if I've walked a great distance without shoes.

I need to eat and drink, but I'm too exhausted to move.

VOICE RECORDER ENTRY #25B (7:29AM, SUNDAY, JULY 13, 2017)

It occurs to me now that someone might be playing a cruel joke. Either that old bastard Parker or perhaps my bitch of an ex-wife. To what end, I haven't the slightest idea, but I don't know what else it could be.

All of the water bottles I brought up with me last night are empty. And I certainly didn't drink them. I was too frazzled to even take a sip after the storm last night. And the crackers and the cheese I carried up, all stale. The apples and the one remaining pear rotten to the core. I need to somehow summon the energy to walk downstairs to the cooler. My mouth is so dry I can barely spit. My stomach is growling.

Voice recorder entry #26B (8:17am, Sunday, July 13, 2017)

I've nearly reached the bottom, thank God. Just another couple dozen stairs.

(Labored breathing)

The video camera is once again not working. It was my intention to bring it with me to chronicle what I found below, but the camera wouldn't even turn on. I tried several times to no avail, leaving me with this crummy voice recorder—sorry, Sony, and go fuck yourself while you're at it.

(A deep breath and the sound of heavy footsteps on the stairway ceases)

Thank God, after everything else, I almost expected the cooler to be gone.

(The cooler lid is lifted. A rustling of ice as a bottle is lifted out. The snap of the cap being loosened and a loud gulp of water being swallowed, then—a chorus of violent gagging and vomiting)

Voice recorder entry #27B (9:09am, Sunday, July 13, 2017)

All of the water is contaminated. Pure salt water. Every goddam bottle. The caps were all sealed tight. This isn't a joke. This is…something else.

All of the food has gone bad too. There are maggots in the lunchmeat. The fruit is rotten. The bread is brittle and spotted with mold.

I'm so tired. I feel like I'm losing my mind.

Voice recorder entry #28B (9:48ᴀᴍ, Sunday, July 13, 2017)

I tried pounding on the front door, but no one answered. Of course. The security gate is locked tight and won't be opened again until tomorrow morning when old man Parker arrives. Next, I tried prying the door open with a piece of scrap metal but it wouldn't budge. I'm considering bringing down my sleeping bag, lantern, and the rest of my supplies and holing up down here until tomorrow morning. It somehow feels safer here on ground level.

(A chortle of muffled laughter in the background)
Now that I've calmed down a bit, I've given the situation a lot of thought. I can survive just fine until tomorrow morning without food and water. I've done it before.

(Another burst of laughter that Livingston obviously doesn't hear)

I just have to keep my wits about me.

(More laughter and then: 'I'm coming, darling. I'm coming.' The voice belongs to a man, deep and tinged with an Irish accent. A loud, wet cracking sound is followed by guttural cries. The man laughs again and there are several more wet cracking sounds)

Whether this is all somehow an elaborate ruse designed to make a fool of me or truly the work of whatever spirits inhabit the lighthouse, I don't care anymore. The videos and audiotapes I've made are pure gold. My recollection of the shipwreck is enough to seal a book deal all on its own. Toss in the other things I've seen and heard, and we most likely have a movie, as well. It's pay day, and just in time for me. Hell, I don't even have to embellish that much this time around. The only thing I truly wonder about is—

(Livingston gasps)

Get off of me! Get the fuck off of me!

(Frantic footsteps pounding their way up the stairs, finally slowing after a number of minutes. Heavy breathing)

Something grabbed me down there. I felt it on my shoulder… squeezing. Then I watched as a lank of my hair was pulled away from my head. But there was nothing there. My goddam hair was moving by itself.

(The footsteps pick up the pace again)
How in God's name have I not reached the top yet?

(More footsteps)

One, two, three, four…thirty-three, thirty-four…fifty-two, fifty-three…one-hundred-and-seventeen, one-hundred-and-eighteen, one-hundred-and-nineteen…two-hundred-and-sixty-six, two-hundred-and sixty-seven, two-hundred-and-sixty-eight, two-hundred-and-sixty-nine, two-hundred-and-seventy…
Dear God, how is this happening?

VOICE RECORDER ENTRY #29B (TIME UNKNOWN, SUNDAY, JULY 13, 2017)

(Note: from this point forward, the voice recorder's time-code is corrupted for reasons unknown)

There are things occurring here clearly beyond my comprehension. Forget the hundreds of impossibly extra stairs I just climbed to reach the living quarters. Forget the fact that I witnessed an ancient fishing vessel crash upon the rocks below last night or watched my hair floating in mid-air right in front of my eyes this morning. Forget the cooler full of contaminated water and rotten food.

However, the bloody fucking hammer with the initials J.O. carved into its polished wooden handle I just found laying atop my sleeping bag is another story entirely.

Now get me the fuck out of here!

VOICE RECORDER ENTRY #30B (TIME UNKNOWN, SUNDAY, JULY 13, 2017)

I'm sitting with my back against the wall. The lantern is lit for now. I can see the entire room and the doorway from this position. All I have to do is make it until eight o'clock tomorrow morning. I would tell you what time it is now, but my motherfucking watch has stopped working.

VOICE RECORDER ENTRY #31B (TIME UNKNOWN, SUNDAY, JULY 13, 2017)

How is this storm still raging? How is it possible? It's so dark outside, it feels like the end of the world.

VOICE RECORDER ENTRY #32B (TIME UNKNOWN, SUNDAY, JULY 13, 2017)

(Defeated whisper)

I came here for the money. Of course, I did. It's always been about the money.

VOICE RECORDER ENTRY #33B (TIME UNKNOWN, SUNDAY, JULY 13, 2017)

Late last night and the night before, Tommyknockers, Tommyknockers, knocking at the door. I want to go out, don't know if I can, 'cause I'm so afraid of the Tommyknocker man.

VOICE RECORDER ENTRY #34B (TIME UNKNOWN, SUNDAY, JULY 13, 2017)

It shouldn't be night already. It can't be. It wasn't even ten in the morning when I was downstairs at the cooler. There's no way that much time has passed. It's not possible.

VOICE RECORDER ENTRY #35B [TIME UNKNOWN, SUNDAY, JULY 13, 2017]

Get off of me! Stop touching me!

VOICE RECORDER ENTRY #36B [TIME UNKNOWN, SUNDAY, JULY 13, 2017]

(Crying)

Something keeps touching my face. I can feel its breath on my neck.

VOICE RECORDER ENTRY #37B [TIME UNKNOWN, SUNDAY, JULY 13, 2017]

(Sobbing)

Please just leave me alone…

VOICE RECORDER ENTRY #38B [TIME UNKNOWN, SUNDAY, JULY 13, 2017]

Can you hear her singing? It's a little girl. I think she's getting closer.

VOICE RECORDER ENTRY #39B [TIME UNKNOWN, SUNDAY, JULY 13, 2017]

Everything's gonna be okay. Everything's gonna be okay.

VOICE RECORDER ENTRY #40B [TIME UNKNOWN, SUNDAY, JULY 13, 2017]

(The deep Irish voice we heard earlier)

Yes, love, it's done. Each one's nothing but a bloody carcass on a bed sheet. Oh yes, darlin', very bloody.
What's that? You want this one, too?

VOICE RECORDER ENTRY #41B [TIME UNKNOWN, SUNDAY, JULY 13, 2017]

There's evil in this place. I can feel it inside my head. It wants to show me something…something terrible.

VOICE RECORDER ENTRY #42B [TIME UNKNOWN, SUNDAY, JULY 13, 2017]

(Screaming)

Oh my God, it hurts!

(Sobbing)

I dozed off and woke up with the most awful pain shooting through my leg. I rolled up my pant's leg and found fucking teeth marks! Something bit me while I was sleeping! Oh Jesus, I have to stop the bleeding!

VOICE RECORDER ENTRY #43B [TIME UNKNOWN, SUNDAY, JULY 13, 2017]

(Unintelligible)

VOICE RECORDER ENTRY #44B [TIME UNKNOWN, SUNDAY, JULY 13, 2017]

Our father who art in heaven, hallow be thy name, thy kingdom come, thy will be done…

VOICE RECORDER ENTRY #45B [TIME UNKNOWN, SUNDAY, JULY 13, 2017]

(The following is spoken by Livingston in Hebrew, and has since been translated)

For rebellion is like the sin of divination, and arrogance like the evil of idolatry. Because I have rejected the word of the Lord, he has rejected me as king.

We know that we are children of God, and that the whole world is under the control of the evil one.

VOICE RECORDER ENTRY #46B [TIME UNKNOWN, SUNDAY, JULY 13, 2017]

(Frantic footsteps)

I'm going out on the catwalk. It's my last hope.

(The sound of a door opening, then hard wind and rain)

I can't stop my leg from bleeding. I can't stop the voices. They're getting closer.

(Thunder crashes)

The bloody hammer disappeared from atop my sleeping bag. That means he's coming for me now. Joseph O'Leary is still here. He never left. If I can make it until morning, I can—

***

OFFICIAL POLICE REPORT

FILE #173449-C-34
DATE: July 13, 2017
REPORTING OFFICER(S): Sgt. Carl Blevins; Sgt. Reginald Scales

At 8:37am on Monday, July 14, 2017, the Harper's Cove Police Department received a phone call from Mr. Ronald Parker, age eighty-one, reporting a missing person and summoning them to the Widow's Point Lighthouse.

Sgt. Scales and I arrived at the lighthouse grounds at approximately 8:56am. Mr. Parker greeted us at the security gate and directed us to park next to a red Ford pick-up and a gray Mercedes sedan.

Mr. Parker showed us identification and explained that the Mercedes belonged to a male in his mid-forties named Thomas Livingston. Mr. Livingston, a well-known author, had rented the lighthouse from Mr. Parker's company for the purpose of paranormal research. The dates of the agreement ran from Friday evening, July 11 to Monday morning, July 14. Mr. Parker was contracted to return to the Widow's Point

Lighthouse at precisely 8am on Monday to unlock the front door and escort Mr. Livingston from the property.

According to Mr. Parker, he arrived on Monday morning at approximately 7:50am and waited inside his truck until 8am. At that time, he unlocked the front door and called out for Mr. Livingston. When there was no response, he returned to his truck for a flashlight and entered the lighthouse.

On the lower level, he found Mr. Livingston's cooler still mostly full of food and water. He also noticed a puddle of vomit nearby on the floor.

After repeatedly calling out to Mr. Livingston and receiving no response, Mr. Parker climbed the spiral staircase to the lighthouse's living quarters. There he found a blood-soaked sleeping bag, a video camera, a lantern, and several other items belonging to Mr. Livingston. He also noticed a series of strange symbols had been scrawled on the walls in what appeared to be blood.

Before returning to the lower level, Mr. Parker searched the catwalk for Mr. Livingston. He found no sign of him, save for a Sony tape recorder located on the metal walkway. Mr. Parker left it there for the responding officers.

After Sgt. Scales and I finished interviewing Mr. Parker, we searched the lighthouse in tandem. Failing to locate Mr. Livingston, we proceeded to search his unlocked vehicle, before searching the surrounding grounds and woods.

At 9:31am, I summoned the Crime Lab, and Sgt. Scales and I begin establishing a perimeter.

As of today, thirty-one (31) items have been logged into Evidence, including the video camera and audio recorder. Additional analysis of the digital files found within the camera and dozens of audio files is underway.

Weather conditions remain sunny and clear, and additional searching of the lighthouse grounds is currently underway.

Sgt. Carl Blevins
Badge 3B71925

THE GRAY MAN

Mark Parker

I suppose I should've been fraught with fear, traveling to one of the most reputedly haunted places in America. But I wasn't. In truth, I looked forward to spending my would've been wedding day on Pawleys Island, South Carolina—home of the legendary Gray Man—a ghost whose legend factored heavily into my next paranormal mystery novel, set in the oldest seaside resort in America.

My ex-fiancé, Derek, often rebuked me for what he liked to call my 'unhealthy fascination' with the paranormal, wondering why I'd want to spend a career writing Gothic-styled mysteries instead of working hard to become a real writer, whatever that meant. He scoffed upon learning that I planned to center my new novel on the legend of the Gray Man, from the early 1800's, and the dark history that surrounded him. Derek thought my pursuit of such things was silly, preferring his beloved Science Channel over my go-to Haunted America.

So be it! I thought. Honestly, I'm not sure what I ever saw in Derek. We couldn't have been anymore different in our likes or dislikes.

So much for making a lifetime of memories together...

We'd certainly made our share of memories in the time we were together. Most of them bad—some of them really bad. Derek had a short fuse and saw no problem with using his hands, or fists, in making a point whenever he felt I'd missed something he tried to impart. Thank God I'd seen him for what he was before we went through with the wedding.

Ghost or no ghost, it was a welcomed relief to be here on

Pawleys, enjoying the calming rush of the tide, the sunbaked, salty sea air, and spending leisurely hours hunting through history to make sure I got all my fictional details as accurate as possible with this new novel.

By comparison, even the most vengeful of spirits—in the Gray Man's case, dating back before Sumter and the Revolutionary War—was a welcomed departure from the nastiness Derek could wield whenever the mood suited him. And, in hindsight, I now realized that it suited him quite often. I'd much rather contend with fictional relationships over real-life ones, especially one wracked with abuse.

Pushing open the door to Turtle Bay Books where I was scheduled to do a book signing for my latest release, Sea Specters, Violet DeMarco's warm, smiling face welcomed me. The shop's owner was always kind and inviting. No wonder her business thrived, when others boarded up for the winter.

"Sarah, honey, I have you all set up in front." Violet led me over to a whitewashed plank table, piled high with large stacks of my novels. A beautiful display surrounded the books, set off by a nautical themed flower arrangement of sea-blue flowers, moss, seagrass, and laced with bone-white sand dollars, brick-red starfish, all held in place by a large square glass vase filled with multicolored shards of opaque sea glass. The floral array was a nice contrast to the stormy graphic of the Specters cover, which featured a clifftop manor house with ghosts floating mist-like across a turbulent sea below.

Violet had taken the time to have the cover art blown up to poster size and mounted to use on an easel next to the table where I'd be doing the signing. "You're the best!" I told her, hugging her tightly. "You always go above and beyond to make my events truly special. You'll have to let me pay for the poster, at least. It's a real beauty. I appreciate all the effort you put into my signings. You've outdone yourself once again."

Violet shook her head. "Don't you dare think you're paying me for a single thing, young lady! I love your books. Besides, I can't wait for the next one to come out. Maybe I can get one of those ARCs when it publishes; that would surely be payment enough. You said you're doing research on it during this trip, right?"

"Yes." I nodded, momentarily distracted by a shadow passing by the shop's large, single-pane front display window. "You-know-who's going to be featured in this one," I said with a conspiratorial wink.

"The Gray Man?" Violet asked, her chubby cheeks flushing red at the thought.

"The one and only," I said, pouring a glass of water from the pitcher she'd provided. I had an hour of meeting-and-greeting ahead of me and was already parched.

***

After nearly two hours of signing books and talking with readers, I asked Violet if she'd like to join me for an early dinner at Percival's, the restaurant located on the main floor of the plantation manor house that had been restored and named in honor of the town's founder—Percival Pawley. The place was like a second home to me, now that I'd stayed there a number of times on past trips to the area. Derek had always sulked when I insisted on making these research trips from Boston alone. Although he had no interest in sharing in the research of any of these historical paranormal accounts, he still felt slighted for some reason, even if it was clearly all a joke to him.

The staff at Pawleys Inn always reserved my favorite room on the top floor, looking out over the Atlantic. It was a beautiful spot, no matter the time of year. I was one of those people who actually preferred visiting seaside locales off-season, when only the locals were in town. To me, I found it gave more of a flavor for the scenic life, when the rest of the world wasn't looking. The locals were all too willing to join in conversations about the numerous ghosts said to haunt the area. The Gray Man being one of the most popular ones.

The legend of the Gray Man was quite a tragic one. Allegedly, he was a soldier in the Revolutionary War, who, upon traveling home from Charleston to reunite with his beloved fiancé, became mired in rain-soaked marshlands that had turned to quicksand and literally got sucked into the ground, along with his steed, never to be heard from again.

Of course, his bride-to-be thought he'd chosen not to return home to her and her family and died of a broken heart. The legend held that the ghost of the Gray Man continued to walk the barrier island of Pawleys, using his lantern to stave off incoming ships in danger of being thrashed against the rocks, in the throes of an oncoming hurricane. The locals considered the ghost a guardian angel, doing his best to protect the home of his beloved by watching over its people with his timely warnings. Of course, not all have heeded his warnings throughout the centuries, which supposedly resulted in numerous deaths and immeasurable destruction.

***

When I walked Violet out after sharing a meal together, I decided to take a stroll down to the beach to work off the crab cakes, clam chowder, and fried okra we'd split. The local cuisine was incredible, but laden with buttery calories that demanded at least a bit of metabolism-boosting exercise before turning in for the evening.

The night air was warm, but laced with a thread of moisture due to the rain that fell earlier. I welcomed it. The dampness felt good on my face as I made my way down to the water's edge. The clouds overhead splayed volcanic gray, churning with patches of greenish-blue peeking through. When I reached the short, weather-worn pier that stretched out into the shifting surf, I heard a scream from further down the beach. A young boy waved his arms frantically, pointing toward a curved jetty that always reminded me of the unmistakable shape of Cape Cod.

"What is it, honey?" I yelled to him, as he ran up the beach to meet me.

"I saw—him—" the boy stammered.

"Saw who, sweetheart?" I asked, shading my eyes from the rays of the setting sun that pierced through the parting clouds.

"The Gray Man!" The boy's voice grew tense with fear.

I followed his gaze out toward the jetty, where a man dressed in a long dark-gray coat and wide-brimmed hat stood gazing out at the whitecaps. A passenger ship headed toward port, venturing dangerously close to shore. I could make out its shape against the gloom because of its bright white exterior. I couldn't remember ever seeing a cruise ship come so close to land before, unless of course it was docking.

Catching glimpse of the man in the long gray coat, I realized that he did look a great deal like all the images I'd seen in my research of the Gray Man. Even though I knew it couldn't possibly be the legendary ghost, I didn't contradict the boy by saying as much. Instead, I bent down and took his trembling hands into my own.

"Honey, I don't think that man on the jetty is the Gray Man. I know he looks similar, but I think he's just dressed in rain gear. He must've been out in the downpour earlier and just walked out onto the jetty to watch the cruise ship coming into port."

"No!" the boy insisted, shaking his sweat-dampened head. "I wasn't talking about that guy. That's Gary. He's a local fisherman who likes wearing that getup. He says it makes him look more like an old salt, whatever that is. The Gray Man was further down the beach, down by the North Inlet. He was dressed like Gary, but his clothes were older, more ragged. And he was a lot paler. Gary's tanned like my mom gets in the summer. He was kinda serious looking, too. Like he was upset about something—or worried. He walked toward me, holding a lantern out in front of him. I remember my mom telling me stories about the Gray Man that always included a lantern. It's gotta be him!"

Feeling a chill run up my spine, I reached out and took the boy into my arms. "Honey, where are your parents?"

He didn't say anything at first, but then shot a look up toward the western bluff of the island, his face turning red like he was going to cry. "My dad left us, and my mom is on her third wine cooler of the day. Usually, when she gets to the fourth one she passes out in front of the television. I'm guessing she's already passed out, because she hasn't called me in for dinner yet. She's gonna freak out when I tell her we've gotta leave."

"Leave?" I asked. "What do you mean...why would you have to leave?"

"You know the legend, don't you? Whenever the Gray Man appears, a deadly storm follows. He's here to warn us, so we can all get out before the storm hits."

"You've really done your homework, haven't you, honey?" I rustled his head and smiled in an attempt to ease his nerves. "I'll bet your mom is really proud of you. You seem like a very smart, special boy."

"I doubt it," he said, pushing away from me. "She doesn't seem to notice anyone but that new boyfriend of hers. If you ask me, he's a real loser. I know my dad isn't perfect, but he's certainly better than this new jerk. He's a stupid guy if you ask me. He's always putting his hands on her, even when she tells him to leave her alone."

"C'mon, let me walk you home," I said, taking him by the hand. "I want to make sure you get home safely, and I'll tell your mom where you've been, so she isn't worried. Do you have your dad's phone number? If you're mom's passed out in front of the TV, we will need to call her dad to come and get you."

The boy pulled a small flip-phone from his pants pocket and held it up, looking far more mature than his age would suggest. "It's in here," the boys said, holding the phone out to me. "Mom programmed him as number two. She's number one."

***

It was a short walk to the boy's house. He and his mom lived in a small weather-beaten cottage that, if you craned your neck in just the right direction and stood on your tippy toes, you could see a sliver of beach and water and some of the rooftops of the shops on Alabaster Avenue.

Still holding tightly to the boy's sweaty hand, I knocked on the door. In no time at all, I heard footsteps approaching, which I took as a good sign, thinking I may not have to call the boy's father after all.

When the door opened, I gasped. It was like seeing a ghost. A real one.

Derek's lumbering frame took up much of the doorway. He appeared just as surprised to see me, as I was to find him there.

"What the hell are you doing here?" I asked, my mouth no doubt gaping. "And what on earth are you wearing?" He was dressed head-to-toe in all gray. His clothes were ragged and worn, even tattered in some spots. At seeing me, his face went ashen.

The boy tugged at my arm frantically. "That's him! That's my mom's new boyfriend, but I've never seen him dressed like that. That's the guy I saw down on the beach the Gray Man!" The boy looked confused.

"Honey, can you give me a minute. Go in inside and see how your mom's doing, and I'll be in to speak to her in a minute."

He slipped past Derek, and I could hear him explaining to his mom—who must've passed on having a fourth wine cooler—where he'd been, and what he'd been doing.

"I came here to bring you home," Derek said, reaching for my hand. "You came here looking for your Gray Man—and you've found him. Now let's get outta here."

"Hold on a second," I said, feeling a noxious chord of anger rise inside myself. "What are you doing here? I mean, at this woman's house. The boy said you're her new boyfriend. You sure don't take long before moving onto your next conquest!"

"Julia and I are friends. She's been helping me try to find you."

"Friends, huh? Where did you meet her? At some bar, no doubt."

"She's a very nice woman, Sarah. And her son's a great

kid."

I shook my head. "Well, he didn't have such great things to say about you. He said you put your hands all over his mom. Even after she's told you not to. Sounds familiar…"

***

Trying my best to discourage him, Derek insisted on walking me back to Pawleys Inn when I refused to 'get outta here' with him. I couldn't believe he'd followed me all the way to South Carolina, in some hair-brained scheme to dress like the Gray Man to force my return to Boston with him.

My head was swimming with everything that'd transpired in the last hour. It was all pretty crazy. He was crazy. I had no trouble standing my ground when he'd asked me to leave with him. But I also didn't want to provoke him, or get his ire up. I couldn't tell if he'd been drinking, so I didn't want to do anything that might provoke him or result in an argument. From experience, I knew all too well how things could go from one extreme to another with Derek in a matter of seconds. Which usually ended with him laying his hands on me, like he apparently did with this Julia woman.

I'd be damned if he was ever going to lay his hands on me again! Least of all after we'd ended everything between us and called off the wedding.

Walking back to Pawleys Inn, as we passed by Violet's bookstore, in the lamplight that glowed from the large window at the front of her shop, I watched as our reflections rose up in front of me. In the window, I saw myself clearly—even the anger on my face when Derek kept trying to take my hand, like we were still a couple.

But something with Derek's reflection seemed off. The face staring back at me beneath the large, wide-brimmed hat, was somehow stronger, more angular, and the sideburns were much more accentuated, like muttonchops from a bygone era. Instead of seeing Derek looking back at me, it was the face I'd always pictured when I tried to imagine what the Gray Man might look like—had he really lived, and died, in the early

1800s.

Even in the surrounding twilight, I could see the blood drain from my face in the window's dark reflection of me. I jumped back from the pane of glass noticing a menacing glint spark in the eyes of Derek's reflection. There was something wild about the glimmer in his stare.

Derek bent over and began to cough, quietly at first, and then more pronounced. A throaty, gurgling sound rose from within him as he heaved.

At first, I thought he was coughing up blood, but soon realized it must be something else. It had a briny, sea-sour smell so it could only be one thing. Seawater. A full stream of water gushed forth, filled with long, slimy tangles of seaweed, clotted with broken shards of glass and seashells. Fixed to the spot where I was standing, I was terrified by what I was witnessing. I watched in horror as a rush of fist-shaped hermit crabs dropped out of his widely opened mouth, each clattering to the pavement before scuttling off.

I couldn't believe Derek could be vomiting up such a gruesome rush of sea castoff. The air grew thick and warm and even more humid than it'd been during the brief deluge of rain from earlier. Soon, everything around us ground down to an absolute sea of black nothingness. A tinkling of bells interrupted the silence, and then a hand touched my shoulder.

"Honey, who's this man?" It was Violet. "Is everything okay? Do I need to call an ambulance or the police?" Her face creased with concern, a calming light shining out at me through the sudden veil of putrid darkness.

"This is Derek..." In a state of utter shock, I could barely find words to tell Violet what was happening. In truth, I didn't really know myself.

Beside me, Derek's whole body began to tremble, and then thrash as he fell to his knees, vomiting up another solid stream of the sea's salty waste.

Despite my near hatred for the man, I found my senses firing again, propelling me to grab him by the wrist in an attempt to help stabilize him. As I grasped onto him tightly, I realized there was no pulse beneath my slime-slick fingertips.

"Oh, my God!" I shouted. "I think he's either dead...or dying!"

Violet crouched down next to us and wrapped her ample arms around me.

"Honey, do you have your cell phone with you? Or should I go inside to call 911?"

"I can't believe this is happening—" I barely whispered. And everything around me devolved into a queasy sea of black.

***

When I came to, amid a swirling staccato of flashing blue and red lights, Violet still knelt next to me, holding me tightly with a mother's care. "Sweetheart, everything's been taken care of. I called the coroner's office, and they already came to get Derek—and the EMTs are here now to take you to the hospital. Tidelands Georgetown Memorial is less than fifteen minutes from here, so you'll see a doctor in no time!"

I wanted to say that I didn't need a doctor or to go the hospital, but I didn't have the energy to put up a fight. So I just remained where I was, until two tall men dressed in blue came over with a sheet-covered gurney, lifted me onto it, and into an ambulance that idled a few feet away.

Even in the subtle chaos of the moment, I couldn't help but notice something needling at the back of my mind. Wasn't it said a hurricane or tornado always followed an appearance from the Gray Man? As the thought occurred to me, I smelled something drifting in on the incoming tide. A strange odor, dark and menacing. I'd lived through a number of hurricanes and knew intimately their potential for terrible destruction.

After I was secured into the ambulance, one of the EMTs helped Violet up into the vehicle beside me. With the worrisome smell coming in off the tide, I found myself thinking, if I was going to ride out a hurricane over the next couple of hours, no better place to do it than in a hospital. After all, hospitals were constructed of some of the strongest, most impenetrable walls possible.

Once my vitals were taken, a nurse came into the examination room and handed me a blue bottle of Gatorade, instructing me to drink it all so my electrolytes could replenish. Grateful for the beverage, I drank it down a few deep gulps. My mouth was dry and scratchy. After I finished, I put the empty bottle on the bedside table and let my aching head rest against the pillow behind me.

Violet's smiling face was off to my right, where she sat in a chair in front of the room's only window. Her presence reassured me. She had proven herself much more than a bookstore owner who hosted my occasional book signing events. Over the trips I'd made to the area, she'd more than demonstrated herself a good and lasting friend, as well.

"Honey, are you feeling any better?" she asked, glancing up from her cell phone. "You had me worried there for a while. At least you're getting your color back. And that's a good sign."

After a few moments of answering Vi's questions, I felt myself drifting off. The overwhelming drama of the day finally caught up with me. Soon my head swam with spectral images. There was the Gray Man in all his legendary creepiness…my countless fictional characters…and then Derek. I still couldn't believe he was gone. It was difficult to think he hadn't at least in some way brought most of this on himself. I began to believe the reciprocal nature of karma. What went around came around. In his case, it seemed as if Derek paid his debt with his very life.

Within minutes, I slipped into a kind of shallow sleep. Laying there with my eyes closed, I could gradually see the plotline of my next book knitting together inside my head. I saw how the legend of the Gray Man would factor in, and even sensed a title developing: Storm Surge. It fit the direction I considered taking the book in. I could almost see the cover illustration coalescing in my head as I let myself drift further into sleep.

I woke with a start to the sound of a loud alarm going off. Violet sprang to her feet, running out of the room to call for a nurse. I looked up at the TV mounted to the wall over the foot of my bed. It was muted, but the screen came to life with dazzling graphics. A WEATHER ALERT message scrolled across the screen in bright red, backed by a large stream of color-blocked red, black, and white flags signifying a hurricane. It would seem the Gray Man's warning had come just in the nick of time. Here I lay, in an emergency room with a severe weather event quickly approaching. Those who subscribed to the 'life being stranger than fiction' thing, sure knew what they were talking about. Especially on a night like this!

When she returned, Violet was the picture of calm. She said the hospital staff was evacuating everyone to the lower levels for everyone's safety. Probably an unnecessary precaution, I thought, but one we would heed. Until we heard from the sheriff's office or fire department, hospital officials naturally wanted us to take whatever measures necessary to insure our safety, which I found reassuring.

Violet said that we would be moved to the lower levels and notified as soon as the requisite authorities arrived onsite and had a chance to inspect the situation.

I couldn't help thinking Violet should be home with her family on a night like this. I knew it was too late for her to leave at this point, but I hoped her family would be safe without her there to reassure and guide them.

After the Gatorade, and the few moments of rest, I felt well enough to take the stairs down to the lower level. I knew they wouldn't want us to clog the elevators, especially should a power outage occur.

Once on the basement level, it wasn't long before the authorities arrived and informed us of those medically cleared to leave, to do so, as each patient's care was appropriately triaged and swiftly administered.

Outside, I was thankful to breathe fresh air again. Hurricane or no hurricane, I felt energized by the gusting wind.

I'd forgotten that neither of us had a car since we'd arrived in an ambulance.

Sensing my momentary apprehension. Violet grabbed my arm and smiled. "Honey, my husband's on his way. Don't you worry, he'll get us in out of the storm in no time!"

***

When I woke the next morning in my bed at Pawleys Inn, I was surprised to hear people outside my door anxiously discussing an approaching hurricane, especially after we'd been cleared to leave the hospital the previous night, only after the weather services deemed everything safe—that the storm had all but passed us by. Georgetown Memorial had only released some of us, so that we could beat the hurricane and get to safety in as timely a manner.

Instead of taking the time to shower, I cleaned off in the room's sink before getting dressed, and heading out into the hallway. As I pulled on my jacket, my cell phone began trilling on the room's only dresser. The caller ID displayed Violet's number at the store.

"Hi, hon. I know you've probably already heard there's another hurricane on our doorstep. Ron and I would like you to come stay with us, so we can ride out the storm together. If you haven't already made other plans, of course."

I took a moment to think about it, and knew immediately what I wanted to do.

I pushed the TALK button and spoke into the phone.

"At some point I'll need to go back to Boston to get all my belongings, but I've decided to relocate to Pawleys. This place feels more like home than Boston ever did, especially now with Derek gone, and with you and Ron here I won't feel quite so alone. Derek was always the one who wanted us to stay in the Boston area, near his family. That was never my desire. I just wanted to make him happy, so I went along with everything. But that's no longer an issue. I'd love to ride out the storm with you and your family, and then make more permanent changes once the storm's passed."

I could sense Violet smiling on the other end of the line. "Well, isn't that wonderful news, honey!" she said. "I know I shouldn't want you to be here during a hurricane, but if Pawleys is going to be your new home, I suppose there's no time like the present to get yourself accustomed to such things. We get our share of seasonal storms. And we have ghosts. Plenty of those!"

When she and Ron arrived a few minutes later, I felt happier than I had in a very long time. Derek was dead, and I knew I should feel bad about that. But instead I felt free. In some ways, freer than I'd ever felt before.

FEAR SUN

Laird Barron

Click.

Wow, this is exciting.

BOO-ooom! *goes the green-black surf against green-black rocks that jut crookedy-wookedy as the teeth of an English grand-uncle of mine.* FAH-whoom! Ba-room! *go the torpedoes bored into the reef like bullets from God's six-shooter (in this case a borrowed nuclear submarine). Then the dockside warehouses on stilt legs fold into the churning drink. Fire, smoke, death. On schedule and more to come in act two of Innsmouth's destruction. Daddy would have a hard-on for this action. Perhaps, in his frigid semi-after life, he does. I bet he does.*

The red light means it's on, lady. Let's hurry this along. All hell is breaking loose as you can see on the monitors. You don't need the gun, I'll speak into the mike. We've never met, but I know who you are, and why you've come. I like you, chick, you've got balls. My advice, run. This won't lead anywhere pleasant. The Black Dog is loping closer. Gonna bite you, babe. Smoke on the water hides worse. Okay, okay, ease back on the hammer, girlfriend. I'll satisfy your curiosity even though you'll be sorry.

Speaking of, mind if I have a cigarette? Judging from your expression, it'll be my last.

***

Okay, let's start with last night and go from there.

Last evening went much the same as most of my nocturnal expeditions among the locals do—cocktails and appetizers at the *Harpy's Nest*. Bucket of blood on the Innsmouth docks and the closest thing to a lounge within fifty miles. Lobster entrée, ice cream dessert cake. Karaoke night with the locals, oh Jesus. I totally abhor karaoke. I made fat ass Mantooth get up on the dais and sweat his way through "Dang Me." Not bad, not bad. Andi told me that Mantooth graduated from Julliard's drama division before he got into the muscle business. Huh. That goon has opened doors and twisted the arms of my stalkers since I escaped college. Surprising that I never knew.

My dress, a Dior original, cut low as sin. Better believe I danced with a whole bevy of rustic lads. The clodhoppers stood in line. Before the bar closed, my ass was bruised from all those clutching oafs, and I got a rash from the beards rubbing my neck and tits.

For an encore, I balled a sailor in a shanty. A grizzled character actor named Zed, whom the project team recruited from a St. Francis shelter and planted here in 2003. We shared a smoke, and he recited the lore of this hapless burg and its doomed inhabitants.

"That's not the script I gave you." I stroked his dead white chest hair in warning. My nails alternated between red and black.

"It's the truth, missy. The devil's own." His tone made it evident he hadn't a clue with whom he conversed. Not a shocker—I eschew the public eye like nobody's business. It's also possible the drunken fool believed that theater had become life.

Zed's perversion of the project script offended me. Granted, I'd done the equivalent of visiting Disney World, fucking Mickey Mouse, and getting offended when the dude in the costume refused to break character. Call me fickle. I whistled, the boys waltzed in, and beat him with a pipe. Got bored watching him crawl around like a crab with three legs broken. They pinned his arms while I exorcised a few of my demons with a stiletto heel. The actor gurgled and cussed, but he won't tell. Know why? Because I stuffed a personal check covered in my bloody fingerprints into his shirt pocket. What was on that check? Plenty, although not nearly as much as you'd think.

That's it for last night. Oh, oh, I had a Technicolor dream. Dream may be the wrong word—I seldom do and anyway, I was awake at the time and staring at the motel ceiling, trying to connect the water stain dots, and I closed my eyes for a few seconds and had a vision. I got shrunk to three inches or so tall. and Dad's head loomed above me with the enormity of a Mount Rushmore bust. Icicles dangled from his ears and his flesh cycled from blinding white, to crimson, to midnight blue as the filament sun downshifted through the color spectrum. Dad said I made him proud and to keep on with the project. *The seas will swallow the earth!* And *All the lights are going out! Beware the ants!* His lips were frozen in place. He boomed is visions telepathically. Reminded me of my childhood.

***

Oh, Daddy.

Unless you're a well-connected investor or an FBI special agent, you probably haven't heard of my father. His personal wealth exceeded eighty billion before I got my hooks into it as sole beneficiary. Super!

Most of his projects weren't glamorous, and the sexy radio-ready ones have always operated through charismatic figureheads. Tooms? What etymological pedigree does that connote? We've got relatives all over the place, from East India to Alaska--don't get me started on those North Pole, hillbilly assholes, my idiot cousin Zane especially. Anyway, he's dead. The Mexican Army shot him full of holes and good riddance, says I.

Daddy dwelt in an exalted state that transcended mere wealth; he was supreme. He created worlds: futuristic amusement parks, intercontinental ballistic missile systems, and designer panties. He also destroyed worlds: rival companies and rivals; he hunted tame lions in special preserves for dudes too smart to let it all hang out on safari. He aced a few hookers and possibly his first wife, I am convinced. The earth trembled when he walked. Cancer ate him up. All the money in the world couldn't, etcetera, etcetera. Per his request, the board froze his head and stored it in a vault at a Tooms-owned cryogenics lab—like Ted Williams and Walt Disney! Everybody thinks it's an urban legend. Joke's on them; I've seen that Folger's freeze-dried melon with my own two eyes—the hazel and the brown. What's more, he's merely the ninth severed cranium to adorn the techno ice cave. Every Tooms patriarch has gotten the treatment since the 1890s.

Come Doomsday, Daddy and his cohort will return with a vengeance, heads bolted atop weaponized fifteen-story robot bodies to make the Antichrist wee his pants. For now, he dreams upon a baking rack throne beneath a filament that blazes frozen white light. This private sun blazes cold *and* emits fear. His favorite drug of them all.

Yes, Daddy was a true mogul.

Mother came from Laos. A firebrand. Nobody ever copped to how she hooked up with Daddy. Some say *ambitious courtesan* and those some may be as correct as they are eviscerated and scattered fish food. Not sure if she was one hundred percent Laotian, but I'm a gorgeous puree of whatever plus whatever else. She hated English, hated Daddy, and virulently hated my older brother Increase (the get of the mysteriously late first Mrs. Tooms). She called him Decrease. Doted on yours truly. Taught me how to be an all pro bitch. Love ya, Moms. Mr. Tooms passed when I was sixteen. Mom died in a mysterious limo fire that same winter. Very traumatic for me, although splitting a fortune with my brothers eased the pain.

The family business putters on under the tyrannical thumb of Increase. He knows what's good for him and leaves me to do as I please. No business woman am I.

My talents lie elsewhere. I revel with the merciless ferocity of a blood goddess. I settle for filthy rich, impossibly rich, which means *anything* is possible. Rich enough to buy a tropical island is rich enough to get a hold of a bag of Moon rocks on the black market is rich enough to turn this dying (dead) Massachusetts port town that time forgot into whatever I want. The people: sailors, peasants, moribund gentry, and their slothful cops, alder persons, zoning commissions, and chamber of commerce bureaucrats, mini moguls who measure up to Dad's shoe laces, if I'm generous. I own them too.

***

Let's step farther back to my vorpal teens.

Time was I aspired to be better than I am. Kinder, if not cleaner. Were I in the mood to justify a career of evil, I'd cite the head games (snicker) Daddy played with me and Increase, and that other one, the one who got away, the one we never speak of. I'd tell you about the Alsatian, Cheops, my best and only friend during adolescence, and how he drowned himself in the swan pond in a fit of despair. Took him three tries. I fished that waterlogged doggy corpse out myself because the gardener got shitfaced and fell asleep in the shed.

Mostly, though, I'm the way I am because I like it, love it, can't get enough of it. Nature versus nurture? Why not some of both? It's impossible to ever truly know the truth. You have to dig extra deep to churn the real muck. You have to afford a person an opportunity to sell her soul. Gods above and below, did I have opportunity to aggrandize an overheated imagination!

The idea for the Innsmouth Project has incubated in my brain since I laid up with pneumonia at age twelve, and somebody left a stack of moldy-oldies by the bed. The pinch-lipped ghost of HPL and his genteel madness made a new girl of me.

Great Granddad put ships in bottles. Dad made exquisite dioramas and model cities. Increase enjoyed ant farms. I read Lovecraft and a lot of history. Marie Antoinette's little fake villages captivated me. It all coalesced in my imagination. A vast fortune helped make the dream someone else's nightmare. Frankly, the US government, or a shady subdivision of the government, deserves most of the credit.

Six months after my father passed away, I graduated from

high school, with honors, and treated myself to a weekend at a Catskill resort that had been a favorite of the Toomses since the Empire State came into existence. No ID required for booze; handsome servants kept the margaritas coming all the livelong day for me and a half-dozen girlfriends I'd flown in for company. Andromeda kept a watch on us. With Daddy out of the picture, there was no telling if Increase or some other wolf might try to erase me from the equation. Ahem, *Andrew.* Andromeda was Andrew then, and not too far removed from his own youth. I read his, *her*, dossier on a whim. She'd majored in paleontology. When I asked why she'd thrown away the chance to unearth dino bones for a security gig, she smiled and told me to mind my business. Most intelligent bodyguard I've ever had, although not necessarily smart.

A guy approached me in the salon, and Andi almost broke his arm as I signaled. The dude, nondescript in a polo shirt and cargo pants, introduced himself as Rembrandt Tallen. He bought me a drink. I should have known from the ramrod posture and buzz cut that he was military. The next morning, upon coming to in a dungeon, blindfolded, chained to a wall, I also deduced that he was a spook. He removed the blindfold and made me an omelet. Pretty snazzy dungeon—it had a wet bar, plasma television, and the walls and ceiling were covered in crimson leather cushions.

Tallen kept mum regarding his team. The game was for me to assume CIA or NSA, and that's what I figured at first since our family was frenemies with those organizations. Black holes in the ocean was a topic I vaguely recalled. R&D at one of Daddy's lesser known companies looked into this decades before it became kinda-sorta news on a backwater science news site. The military and commercial implications were astounding.

My captor turned on the TV and played a highlight reel of various improbable atrocities that no citizen, plump and secure in his or her suburban nest, had the first inkling.

"Oh, my, goodness," I said as in crystal clear wide-screen glory, a giant hydrocephalic baby jammed a man in a suit into its mouth and chewed. Tiny rifles popped and tinier bullets made scarcely a pinprick on the kid's spongey hide. The action shifted to a satellite image of a village in a jungle. Streams of blackness surrounded the village as its inhabitants huddled at the center or atop the roofs of huts. The camera zoomed in as the flood poured over the village and the figures dispersed in apparent panic. Not that panicking or fleeing helped—the black rivulets pursued everywhere, into huts, onto roofs, up trees, and engulfed them.

"Beetles of an Ur species unknown to our entomologists until 2006. Vicious bastards. Although they refer to themselves as preservationists." Tallen smiled and his ordinary, bland face transfigured in the jittery blue glow. "Bad things are happening out there, Skylark. How would you like to help us make them worse?"

Would I!

The seduction progressed over the course of a couple of years and numerous clandestine rendezvouses. He quizzed me about Majestic 12, MKULTRA, and Project Tallhat. Had I ever met Toshi Ryoko or Howard Campbell? Amanda Bole? No, no, and no, I'd never even heard of any of these persons or things. That pleased Tallen, and seemed to relax him. He confided his secrets.

"It's not important, kiddo. Ryoko and Campbell are flakes. I'd love to see them erased, zero-one, zero-one. They have powerful friends, unfortunately. Forget I mentioned them. Servants of our enemies. Ms. Bole is open to an introduction, assuming you and I reach an accord. We think you're exactly the person to help us with a project."

"You mean my money can help with your project."

"Money, honey. You funnel the cash, we supply the technical know-how and the cannon fodder. You have a vision. We have a vision. It's a can't miss proposition."

Tallen was so smooth and charming. I crushed on him. That corn-fed blandness really grew on me, or the Satan-light dancing in his eyes grew on me, or the fact he believed in elaborate conspiracies excited me (he claimed insects were poised to overrun civilization and that the Apollo explorers found a cairn of bones on the Moon). At any rate, he broke out the maps, diagrams, and the slideshow prospectus. My jaw hit the floor.

His organization (I never did learn its name) had, sometime during the winter of 1975, allegedly established contact with an intelligence residing in a trench off the Atlantic shelf. As in an extraterrestrial intelligence that burrowed into the sediment around the time trilobites were the voting majority.

He laughed when I, unabashed Lovecraft enthusiast, blurted *Dagon! Mother Hydra!* and told me not to be stupid, this verged on Clark Ashton Smith weirdness. His associate in the deep requested some Grand Guignol theater in return for certain considerations that only an immortal terror of unconscionable power can offer.

Tallen, having researched my various childish predilections, proposed that we build and staff a life-model replica of Lovecraft's Innsmouth. Inscrutable alien intelligences enjoy ant farms and aquariums too. Some of them also quite enjoy our trashiest dead white pulp authors. He claimed that this sort of behind the scenes activity was nothing new. In fact, his superiors had been in frequent contact with my father regarding unrelated, yet similar, undertakings.

"Let me consider your proposition," I said. "Who is Bole? Why do I dislike her already?"

His smile thinned. "Mandy is the devil we know. It's tricky, you see. She came to us from across the street, on loan from her people. Her people are overseas, so she's here for the duration." Later , I learned that *across the street* was code for a foreigner who hailed from an extraordinarily far flung location. Off-planet, say, but within a few dozen light years. *Overseas* meant something else that I decided was best left unclear.

I did ask once if Bole bore some familial relationship with the "intelligence." I was high on endorphins and bud.

So was Tallen. That didn't keep him from slapping my mouth. "Are you trying to be funny? That's asinine." He relaxed and kissed away the bits of blood on my lip. "Let's not do that again, eh?"

I smiled, wanting him to believe I liked it, no hard feelings while I privately reviewed all the ways to kill him slowly.

***

Surviving to majority as a Tooms heiress tempered my enthusiasm with a grain or two of skepticism. I hired world-class detectives—the best of the best. My bloodhounds tracked down scientists and sources within and without the government and from foreign countries. Results from this intelligence gathering dragnet convinced me of Tallen's sincerity. Numerous reports indicated covert activity of unparalleled secrecy off the New England coast. The veracity of his most staggering claim would require personal investigation.

Meanwhile, my detectives, and the scores of unfortunate people they contacted, died in mysterious accidents or vanished. I did the math one day. Okay, Mantooth did it on the back of a napkin. Four hundred and sixty-three. That's how many went *poof* because I asked the wrong questions. The number might be bigger; we were in the car on the way to a stockholder meeting.

"You gonna do it?" Only Andi would dare to ask.

Pointless question. She knew my capabilities. She knew I had to do it, because beneath the caviar slurping, bubblegum popping, jet setting façade throbbed a black hole that didn't want to eat the light; it needed to.

***

This town had a different name when Protestant fisherman Jedidiah Marshal founded it in 1809. Always off the beaten path, always cloistered and clannish, even by New England standards, afflicted by economic vagaries and the consolidation of the fishing industry into mega corporations, this town proved easy to divide and conquer. I retain an army of lackeys to orchestrate these sorts of stunts. Corporate raiders, lawyers, feds on the take, blackmail specialists and assassins.

First, we drove out the monied and the learned. The

peasants were reeducated, or, as Tallen preferred, made to vanish. Gradually more actors were introduced and the infrastructure perfected. Necessary elements within the US government made the paperwork right. All it required was a nudge here and a bribe there from Tallen's operatives. The town was wiped from road signs, maps, from the very record. With the groundwork laid, Innsmouth, my own private economy-sized diorama, raised its curtain.

Assuming you're a casual observer, it's a humdrum routine on the surface.

Children ride the bus to school. Housewives tidy and cook while soap operas numb the pain. Husbands toil in the factories or seek their fortune aboard fishing boats. Come dusk, men in suits, or coveralls or raincoats and galoshes, trudge into the taverns and lounges and slap down a goodly portion of the day's wages on booze. At the lone strip club on the waterfront on the north edge of town, bored college girls and older women from trailer parks dance sluggishly. *The House of the Revived Lord* sees brisk trade Wednesday, Black Mass Friday, and by the numbers kiddie-friendly Sunday. I cherish the reactions of the occasional lost soul who accidentally detours through town: Some bluff day trader or officer worker tooling along Main Street with his uptight wife riding shotgun, her face scrunched in annoyance as she comes to grips with the lies the pocket map has fed her; and two point five kids in the back, overheated and embroiled in child warfare.

Annoyance gives way to confusion, which yields to revulsion at the decrepitude of the architecture and physiognomy of the locals, and ultimately, if the visitors prove sufficiently unwise as to partake of the diner, or gods help them, layover at one of Innsmouth's fine hotels, horror will engulf the remainder of their brief existence.

Even I, maestro and chief benefactor, can see but the tip of this iceberg. Scientists and men in black lurk behind the grimy façades of Victorian row houses—the scientists' purpose is to experiment upon the civilian populace as they might lab rats. Green lights flash through the murky windows, screams drift with the wind off the Atlantic. Ships and submarines come and go in the foggy dark. Andromeda and Mantooth worry about what they can't detect. I don't bother to order them to relax. Worrying is in their job description.

I acquired an estate in the hills. Fifteen minutes leisurely drive from town square. The gates are electrified, the house is locked tight, and guys with automatic weapons pace the grounds.

My first encounter with Miss Bole came when she wandered into my rec room unannounced. I sprawled across a giant beanbag while the news anchor recited his nightly soporific. I knew Bole to the core at first sight—kind of tall, black hair in a bob from the '50s, narrow shoulders, wide hips and thunder thighs. Pale and sickly, yet morbidly robust. Eyebrows too heavy, face too basic, too plastic, yet grotesquely alluring like a Celt fertility goddess cast from lumpen clay. She wore a green smock, yoga pants, and sandals. Sweat dripped from her, although she seemed relaxed.

"Hey there, Skylark Tooms. The Gray Eminence loves your style. I'm Amanda Bole. Call me Mandy." Her voice was androgynous. She gripped my small hand in her large, damp hand and brushed my cheek with cool, overripe lips.

"Gray Eminence. Is that what you call…him?" Pleasure and terror made my heart skip, skip, skip. Sorry, Agent Tallen, but I think I'm in love.

"It, Skylark. *It.* I usually call it G.E. Confuses anybody at the NSA we haven't bought." Her wide smile revealed white, formidable teeth.

I'm usually an ice bitch during introductions. Feels good to keep the opposition on the defensive. Her? I looked into her sparkling frigid eyes and couldn't stop. Nothing in those shiny pebbles but my dopey face in stereoscope. "When will I meet it?"

"Assuming your luck holds? Never, my girl. G.E. has big plans for you."

Mandy pulled me to my feet. We had tea on the front deck by the swimming pool. The deck has a view of the ocean, hazy and smudged in the twilight distance. Lights of town came on in twinkling clusters.

"I think I've seen enough," she said, setting aside her cup.

She stripped and dove into the water. Reflections are funny—she kicked into the deeper end, her odd form elongating as it submerged. Ripples distorted my perspective and made her the length and width of a great white shark, gliding downward and gone as the tiles of the pool dilated to reveal a sinkhole.

Tallen called later. "I'm glad you're all right."

"Any reason I wouldn't be?"

"Ms. Bole told me that she'd decided to terminate your involvement. That would involve being shaken from a fish food can over the Atlantic. It seems she changed her mind."

"Uh, good, then?"

"Convenient! Now we can begin."

***

Some of what comes next, you already know. The cold death mask of rage, the pistol in your hand, what comes next is why you've returned and looked me up. Here's some context, some behind-the scenes magic:

"Who gets to escape?" Mandy and I were revolving in the sex swing in the rumpus room. Mantooth hadn't seemed completely comfortable installing the equipment. I love that repressed New England prudishness about him.

"The narrator." Mandy's obsidian eyes reflected the light over my shoulder, or trapped it. Her eyes glazed, or shuttered (happened so fast), and reflected nothing from a patina of broken black vessels, a thousand scratches from infinitesimal webbed claws. "Our girl works for an amateur filmmaker. The source material is a trifle staid. Tallen made sure the filmmaker brought a camera crew, per G.E's request. Bubbly blonde, sensible, tough as nails brunette, strapping cinematographer, a weasel tech guy. That way there's a bit of sex and murder to spice up the proceedings. Our heroine, the sensible brunette, will escape by the skin of her teeth. Over the next couple of years, we'll shadow her, dangle the clues, and, ultimately, lure her back in for the explosive finale. Should be fun."

Hard to tell whether Mandy actually relished the impending climax. She remained disinterested regardless the circumstances. I relished it for the two of us.

Earlier, she'd given me a tour of a factory that covered for a subterranean medical complex. Her scientists were busily splicing human and amphibian DNA with genetic material from the Gray Eminence and subjecting that simmering, somatically nucleated mess to electromagnetic waves generated by some kind of Tesla-inspired machine. They'd been at it since the '70s, moving the operation from South Sea lagoons to secret bunkers such as this one. According to the chief researcher, Dr. Shrike, the resultant test tube offspring teemed in the frigid waters along the coast. Allegedly, G.E. found them pleasing. It absorbed more and more fry every spawning cycle. That had to be a positive sign.

A few days later, I received an email. Man, I watched the footage of the pursuit and slaughter of that film crew (all but one) like a jillion times. The only downer, little miss tough as nails brunette stabbed the clerk at the wine shop through the eyeball. Too bad; he was sort of cute, and my god, what exquisite taste.

Point of fact, our heroine stabbed three guys, blew two major buildings to shit (with a few of our drone mercs inside), and steamrolled the Constable as she roared out of town in a wrecker. According to the goon in charge of the affair, at the end his minions weren't even pulling their punches, they were trying to get the hell out of the chick's way.

I was tempted to tell Mandy, sorry, babe, I've got the hots for another woman. Two reasons I kept my mouth shut—one, Mandy scared me oodles and oodles, and two, I suspected she didn't give a damn, which scared me worse.

***

How do we arrive at this junction? The explosions, the chatter of machine guns, screams, and death? Innsmouth crashing into the sea in a ball of fire? All according to the master plan, the Punch and Judy show demanded by the torpid overlord in the deep. This is what happened in the infamous story that HP wrote. I often wonder if he had help, a muse from the hadal zone, maybe.

Who can say where art ends and reality asserts primacy? Mandy's script, our script, called for you, our dark-haired girl, to return at the van of a fleet of black government SUVs. I hired a mercenary company to dress in federal suits and Army camo and swoop in here and blow the town and the reef to smithereens. Much as you did your first time through, except big enough to warm the heart of a Hollywood exec.

And here we are, you and I.

Certainly I believed my privilege would shield me, that I could gleefully observe the immolation of Innsmouth from the comfort of my mansion's control room. I figured when the smoke cleared and the cry was over, I'd pack my designer bags and flit off to the Caribbean for a change of scenery. Fun as it has been, nine months of cold salt air a year has murdered my complexion and my mood.

Guess you could say I was surprised when my guards were shot to pieces and an armor-piercing rocket blasted the front door. That's what Mantooth said they hit us with before you waltzed in here and capped him. Through the eyeball, no less. Don't you get it? All this destruction, Mandy and Tallen's betrayal, you glowering down at me, poised to ram a dagger through my black little heart? A mix of prep and improve. Somewhere a dark god is laughing in delight, rapping his knuckles on the aquarium glass to get the fishies spinning.

The question is, do you want to live to see a curtain call. You're the heroine and if we're following the original plot, you have an unpleasant reckoning in your near future. I don't think this version of the tale will see you transforming into a fish-woman and paddling into the sunset. No, this is major league awful. G.E. awaits your pleasure. I doubt even God knows what's going to happen in the monster's lair. Got to be boring, lying there and emoting telepathically eon after eon.

You'll make a pretty dolly, for a while.

Or, you could play it smart. My jet is fueled and idling at a strip just down the road. With my money, we can go damned near anywhere. Take your time and think it over. I'll give you until I finish this cigarette.

BANG! from a gun. A body thuds on the floor off-screen.

GODDAMNIT, *Andi! Why the fuck did you do that to the broad? It was under control. I had her in the palm of my hand. Shit. What do we do now? Mandy is gonna go nuclear. G.E. surely won't be amused. Where do we find a metaphorical virgin sacrifice at this hour? Andi..? Andi!*

You bitch. You almost had me going. No, I'm not sure if anywhere is beyond the reach of our friends. But let's hit the friendly skies and see, huh? Shut that down. I want to watch it later.

Click.

CARNACKI: THE LUSITANIA

William Meikle

I arrived in Cheyne Walk that winter evening in response to an unexpected card from Carnacki. It had been several weeks since our last supper together, and I thought him off on his travels. It was a foul night outside, with a snell wind howling up the Thames, sending rain lashing in my face as I scuttled along the Embankment. But Carnacki had a hot toddy waiting for me as he took my coat, and I was soon as warm as toast, both inside and out.

The others had arrived before me, and Carnacki wasted no time in showing us through to the dining room where we had a hearty meal of a thick lamb stew and roasted potatoes—and plenty of it. By the time we retired to the parlour, our bellies were as tight as drums, and I was looking forward to sitting by the fire and listening to a tale to aid my digestion.

Carnacki waited until we had charged our glasses. We were settled in our seats and lit our smokes before he started.

***

"It began with a telegram," he said. "It came two weeks ago yesterday from the Second Officer on the RMS. Lusitania, and was short and to the point."

"'Something is screaming on the Lusitania. We shall be docked in Liverpool until it can be stopped. Please help.'"

"Now you chaps can see how this immediately caught my attention. Two things in particular persuaded me to book the first train available to the Northwest. One was the fact that I was most eager to see the inside of such a fine cruise-liner, and the other was in the wording of the note itself.

"It said *something*...not someone.

"That same day I was on my way, with my defences accompanying me in a crate in the baggage car. I had a very good steak and some fine claret for lunch before disembarking at Liverpool, ready and eager for action.

"A short carriage journey took myself and my luggage to Albert Dock, where I was left on the quayside to marvel at the magnificence of the liner which loomed above me. It exuded an air of solidity and modernity that seemed to brook no argument as to its status. As I stood there, I was at a loss as to what could possibly be wrong with such a fine piece of Twentieth Century engineering and craftsmanship.

"The Second Officer, a very proper Scottish gentleman by the name of McAllister, led a small group of men off the boat and met me at the bottom of the gangplank. He ordered the men to work, ensuring that my luggage, and my defences, would be stowed in the cabin allocated to me. Once he was sure his orders would be followed, he led me up onto the great ship.

"It was immediately apparent that the craft was even more opulent than I had imagined. It seemed to be built from mahogany, brass and mirrors, enhanced with chandeliers of the finest crystal, and carpets of the deepest pile. I was led to a room that would have graced any club in London and sat in an armchair that threatened to swaddle me with comfort. I was given a Cuban cigar and a glass of the finest brandy. Then I was told a story that chilled me to the bone.

"'It began off the southern tip of Ireland,'" McAllister said. "'Up until that point, it had been an uneventful trip across the Atlantic after our protracted stay in New York for the Hudson-Fulton Celebration. We were all starting to look forward to some shore leave and family visits. It was not to be. The first sign there was anything amiss came from The Ballroom. The night's festivities were over and the guests back asleep in their cabins. But several of the crew heard cries echoing along the corridors. When they went to investigate, they discovered not late revellers as they had expected, but an empty room.

Nevertheless the cries continued. They were screams—but not of joy. There in that empty echoing Ballroom something *howled*, like a beast in rage.'"

"As you can imagine, I checked all the men for signs of drinking. But, to a man they were all sober. Sober, and badly frightened. The night went downhill rapidly after that. More screaming was reported in the engine room, quiet at first, beneath the noise of the turbines, but growing steadily. And all too soon the mania had spread. Shouts and cries began to rise along the corridors and even out on the decks. Soon the whole ship was in an uproar, with passengers and crew alike running hither and tither, either away from, or in search of, the source of the shouting.

"It was the longest night of my life—of all our lives. I doubt that a single wink of sleep was had by any person on board. I had the band play on deck, as loud as was possible, but even that was insufficient to drown out those screams. They seemed to come straight from Hell, and blasted a chill through the hearts of even the stoutest of us.

"We made full steam for port here in Liverpool, and I do believe we may have set several speed records in the process. The screams persisted all the way. When we arrived, the passengers—and, I must say, most of the crew—disembarked as soon as the gangplanks were lowered. It will be a cold day in Hell before any of them return."

"'We have been in dock six days now," McAllister continued. "The screams have died down. But they still persist, particularly around the Ballroom, which no one will go near. We cannot in all good faith take another trip, for a repeat of the last one would bring ruin, possibly for the whole fleet. We need your help, Mr. Carnacki.'"

***

Carnacki paused to refill his pipe, and we took our cue to refill our glasses and get fresh smokes of our own lit.

"I say Carnacki," Arkwright piped up. "Did you know that when the Lusitania took the Blue Riband for eastbound crossing from the Kaiser Wilhelm, she averaged twenty four knots westbound and twenty three knots eastbound? But they say that a certain Mr. Wright in New York is promising that the days of the liner are over and that flying machines will be making the trip in two days or less in the next few years. Did you know—"

Carnacki now had his pipe lit to his satisfaction. All it took to quiet Arkwright was a glower through the fog.

Once more, we settled as Carnacki continued.

***

"As you chaps can see," he continued. "This was just the sort of thing I could get my teeth into, although I must admit the sheer scale of the *activities* had me somewhat daunted at the task to come.

"McAllister showed me to a most sumptuous cabin, and I was solely tempted to succumb to its luxury. But duty called and besides, my curiosity had been piqued. I considered setting up immediate defences, but decided that a closer look at the lay of the land was required before committing myself to a course of action.

"McAllister led me to the Ballroom entrance, but refused to go inside, blanching at the very prospect.

"'You will think me an awful coward, Mr. Carnacki. But I have had my fill for the moment. And you will understand yourself soon enough, once you encounter what waits for you.'"

"He took his leave, with the promise of more brandy for me in the Club Room when I was ready for it. I waited until he had gone down the corridor, then approached the tall door to the Ballroom.

"I stood for long seconds, listening. The ship's engines were quiet, and the only sound was a far off whistle of a train. I summoned up what courage I had, opened the door and stepped inside.

"The Ballroom seemed to double as a dining room, and was as expensive and opulent as you chaps would imagine, occupying a space two decks high and topped by a huge ornate dome. Corinthian columns and potted palms defined the seating areas, with a dance area and bandstand dominating the lower floor, and tables on the upper deck. My footsteps echoed on hardwood flooring as I walked across the space.

"Now I will freely admit I was ready to run almost as soon as I reached the dance area, for there was a feeling about the place that raised the hairs at the back of my neck. My first thought was that it was cold—cold and clammy—as if I walked through thick fog. I tasted salt spray on my lips, and that in itself nearly sent me back to the door. But it would be a dashed bad show to have come all this way just to flee within a minute of arrival, so I stiffened my back and strode into the center of the dancefloor.

"I stood, hands at my side, just waiting. McAllister had been right; I did not have to wait long. It started as little more than a whisper, but like a train rushing down the line, it grew and grew until it filled the whole Ballroom with a shriek the likes of which I have never before encountered.

"I don't mind telling you that my knees were like jelly, and I was sorely tempted to leave that place and never return. But I forced myself to endure, to try to discern the nature of what was around me.

"The scream rose, sending the chandeliers high above rattling, grating on the nerves like fingernails on a blackboard.

"I thought I might be able to discern patterns in the noise, but by this time my heart pounded high in my chest and in my ears, and my legs would brook it no further. I backed away, slowly at first, then faster as the sound seemed to follow me, intent on driving all rational thought from my mind.

"In a blue funk, I fled."

***

Carnacki paused and took a long swig from his whisky, as if he needed a stiffener just to erase the memory of the experience. When he put the glass down he was once more composed as he continued.

"McAllister was true to his word. He had a large snifter of brandy waiting for me when I reached the Club Room. That, and a pipeful of his fine tobacco, settled me somewhat, enabling me to look back more dispassionately at my experience.

"It was my belief that some denizen from the Outer Realms had taken hold in this liner, and that only by expulsion would its effects be mitigated.

"I told McAllister as much over a smoke. He seemed relieved that I at least had a plan, and I got the impression that he was a man close to the end of his tether, holding it together only by the compelling force of his duty. I resolved to do whatever I could to ease his fears. I had him return with me to my cabin and together we carried my defences back to the ballroom.

"As soon as we got there the officer showed every sign of wanting to be somewhere else, despite the fact that our own voices were all that could be heard, echoing around the vast empty space. He hovered near the door, torn between being courteous to me and an obvious urge to go. I waved him away.

"I shall find you if I need you," I said. "Besides, I rather prefer to be alone on these occasions.

"He had gone almost before I completed the sentence.

"I set to building my defences.

"I started by drawing a circle of chalk, taking care never to smudge the line. Beyond this, I rubbed a broken garlic clove in a second circle around the first.

"When this was done, I took a small jar of water that had been blessed by a priest and went round the circle again just inside the line of chalk, leaving a wet trail that dried quickly behind me. Within this inner circle, I made my pentacle using the signs of the Saaamaaa Ritual, and joined each Sign most carefully to the edges of the lines I had already made.

"In the points of the pentacle I placed five portions of bread wrapped in linen, and in the valleys five phials of the holy water. Now I had my first protective barrier and with this first stage complete the circle, now protected as it was by the most basic of spells, already felt more secure.

"I set my electric pentacle to overlay the drawn pentagram upon the floor. When I connected up the battery, an azure glare shone from the intertwining vacuum tubes.

"I was as ready as I was ever going to be.

"As it turns out, all my defences were to be to no avail. I had hardly lit up a pipe when the noises started again, a whistling howl, like a tortured cat mewling in the wind. The noise rose and rose to a crescendo. And all the time, the valves on the pentacle maintained a steady soft glow, showing no reaction to the *manifestations*.

"Once again the fear gripped at me, like ice in my bones. I tasted salt on my lips and suddenly I felt wet, soaked through to the skin and spluttering to keep my breath under a sudden flood of water.

"Avaunt!" I cried. "*ADJÚRO ergo te, omnis immundíssime spíritus, omne phantásma, omnis incúrsio sátanæ, in nómini Jesu Christ.*"

"There was no discernible slackening of the onslaught on my senses. Now you chaps know that I've been in some dashed tight spots and come out unscathed. But never before have my defences proved so entirely useless against my adversary. And as the sound rose once more to a raging howl, I'm afraid to say that my own mental defences also proved equally limited. I could take it no more. I rolled across the floor, my legs refusing to support me, destroying the circles in the process. With screams still wailing like a banshee in my ears, I *crawled* out of that ballroom, a defeated man."

***

Carnacki stopped suddenly. His face had gone white, the memory quite overcoming him. He drained a glass of whisky that would have floored a lesser man and puffed urgently at his pipe.

We took the opportunity to recharge our own glasses. Arkwright, with his usual lack of tact, chose to press Carnacki on particulars.

"So, when you say *defeated*, Carnacki, do you mean

that you never got to the bottom of the wretched matter? It's just that I had a hankering for a cruise myself and if there's something on that liner, I might just have to change my plans. I hear there's a new, larger ship being built in Belfast. I may wait for that one. Although I must say—"

Carnacki waved him quiet with a weary waft of a hand.

"I would put off any thought of sea cruises if I were you," Carnacki said, and there was such a sadness in his voice that we were all moved to complete silence. "I fear the seas may not be safe for some time." He would say no more. "The reason will become clearer as our story continues."

He took his time filling his pipe again, giving us all plenty of opportunity for reflection on what he had already told us.

"I have thought long and hard as to whether to tell this tale at all," he said. "I have delved deep in places where mortal man should not tread. But in this case I have gone even further than ever before. And I have not yet come to terms with all that the story portends, for either myself, or all of you chaps. Mayhap it will become clearer in the telling.

"Now, are we all settled?"

***

"I only have the vaguest recollection of making my way back to the Club Room. McAllister was three sheets to the wind by now, and I was sorely tempted to join him. Indeed, I may well have done so, had it not been for the arrival of a worker from the engine room, face and hands covered in dark oil, eyes like white saucers staring at me wildly.

"'They say you are here to help?'" he said to me without preamble. "'If that is the case, you need to come with me.'"

"Without another word he turned on his heels and left. I followed, my mind whirling. I don't mind telling you that a large snifter of brandy was uppermost in my thoughts—that and a pipeful of tobacco—in my own armchair in front of my own fireplace.

"All thoughts of comfort were wiped from my mind as he led me out onto a promenade deck high above the dark waters of Albert Dock. Lights twinkled on the far side of the Mersey, but it was as if my eyes were blurred and unfocussed, a haze hovering in front of me like heat from a hot road.

"'Listen,'" the man who had brought me said.

"Then I heard it. This was no scream. It may well have come straight from the Outer Regions, but this time it was a wail so soft, so piteous that I felt sudden tears form in my eyes. A desolate sadness threatened to overwhelm me, a sense of the utter futility of life and the smallness of my place in the *Macrocosm*. The man beside me sunk to his knees, weeping like a lost child. I will admit to considering doing the same, but once more, my curiosity was piqued. I realized that the sound and the blurred movements were synchronized and seemed to coincide in a dance that was happening just too fast for my eyes to follow.

"The noise grew to a steady whine. And that is when I had my epiphany. I remembered my experiences in the Larkhall Barrow, where my defences had proved inadequate against a *noise*. But something else had proved most efficacious.

"I dragged the poor man at my feet away, back inside the adjoining corridor, where he finally pulled himself together. He was apologetic, somewhat sheepish, and showed a willingness to help when I told him what I required.

"'It's a big boat, sir,'" he said. "'I'll find what you need, even if I have to look in every cabin.'"

"While I waited on his return I went back to the Club Room where, to my surprise, McAllister was still upright and working his way down the brandy decanter, although somewhat slower than previously.

"As I strode across the carpet toward him, the whole ship *rang*, twice in rapid succession, as if hit by a mighty hammer. I must have looked surprised, but McAllister laughed hollowly.

"'Aye,'" he said, his brogue starting to show as the drink took hold. "'It does that as well.'"

"I joined him in a snifter, but only a small one, for I knew that the night was by no means done. I tried to engage the officer in my growing theory, and in the principles of sonic vibration and how it might relate to the Outer Entities. I told him of my adventures at Larkhall, and how I had prevailed through the manipulation of tonal acoustics. I also explained how I thought I might be able to *dampen* the aural assault on the Lusitania, but by then it was too much for the poor man, and I am afraid I bored him into a drunken slumber.

"The brandy was starting to look very enticing, but I contented myself with a fresh pipe as I waited for the engineer to return.

"The ship lay quiet around me. Although we were perched on the edge of one of the largest cities in the country, I felt like we could be anywhere on the Seven Seas, lost and adrift at the whim of current and tide. I tasted salt at my lips again and had to wash it away with some brandy.

"The engineer returned as I was lighting my second pipe. He went straight to the liquor and took a long slug that made him cough and splutter.

"'I found what you wanted, Mr. Carnacki, sir,'" he said when he recovered. "'I have left it in the Ballroom as you requested. But, if it's all the same to you, I think I shall stay here and get on the outside of more of this brandy?'"

"My walk back to the Ballroom was a slow and lonely one. If truth be told, I was on the verge of fleeing, for I had no desire to face the wailing shriek for a third time that night. But I was bolstered by remembering my triumph in that barrow on Salisbury Plain, and although I was by no means certain of success, I was no longer considering the possibility of failure."

***

At that point, Carnacki stopped again. He looked pensive as he tapped fresh tobacco into his pipe.

"I find I am loath to continue," he said after a moment. "We are reaching the climax of the tale, and in the telling, I may have to divulge things that you will not be able to talk of save to each other."

"Come man," Taylor said. "We have kept your confidences in the past, and gladly. You cannot leave us high and dry at this stage of proceedings."

"Dashed bad show, Carnacki," Arkwright said. "Do you not trust us?"

"With my life," Carnacki said quietly. "You are the best friends a man could have. But trust is not the issue. Once I tell you what must be told, you will not be able to forget it. And the thoughts that will accompany the tale's conclusion may lead you to question many of the tenets you hold dear. Indeed, it may even lead you to question the very nature of reality itself."

Arkwright guffawed.

"You always were the one for melodrama, Carnacki. Come, tell us your tale, and we shall discuss it afterward as usual. It cannot be any more outrageous than some of your other stories."

Carnacki smiled, but it didn't reach his eyes.

"My dreams are haunted now," he said. "I had hoped not to inflict the same on you. But if you insist..."

Taylor and Arkwright spoke almost simultaneously.

"I insist."

Carnacki lit his pipe.

"Very well. Let us rush on to the conclusion. But do not tell me you were not warned."

***

"The Ballroom was as cold and clammy as before," he continued. "The equipment lay in the middle of the floor near what remained of my circles. Although my defences had proved of no use so far, I did not want to abandon them completely—more for my own peace of mind than from any feeling of confidence in their efficacy. I spent five minutes repairing the damage I had done before turning to investigate what the engineer had brought.

"He had been as good as his word. Not one, but two new phonographs lay on the hardwood floor. They looked to be the latest models, and I guessed that they had been raided from the first class cabins. Arkwright here would have spent hours poring over the technical specifications of these fine boxes, indeed as would I, given the time. But for now, I was aware that the aural onslaught could return at any moment.

"I wound up both machines and waited.

"The whispering that signalled the start of the *manifestation* started almost immediately after I'd lit up a pipe. I set the wax discs recording, clamped my teeth on the stem of the pipe, and prepared to endure whatever was coming.

"I must tell you chaps, I never again wish to be exposed to such sheer *terror* as that which engulfed me. It lasted mere minutes, but felt like I had been tossed in a shrieking, howling maelstrom for hours. Sweat poured from every pore, and I believe that had my pipe not been made of stern stuff, I might well have bitten it in two. The noise swelled and rang through the huge empty space, filling every nook and cranny with fear and panic.

"Then, as quickly as it had come, it was gone.

"It took me long seconds to realize that silence had fallen. My every muscle trembled, as if I'd undertaken many hours of strenuous activity, and my heart pounded so loud in my ears, that I was afraid I might *burst* with the tension. It was noticing that the cylinders were still recording that got me moving.

"I switched both off and started one replaying, realizing, too late, that I had forgotten to wind up the machine. That proved to be a blessing in disguise. The playback started at a very slow speed, and that's when I realized that what I had been listening to all along were voices, human voices raised in terror, but speeded up to an unnatural degree.

"I have the cylinder in a drawer in my library, and someday I may play it for you chaps, but trust me, you never want to hear it as I did, in that empty liner, in the midst of the dark empty ballroom. People screamed, and footsteps rang on the hardwood, as if fleeing from some unseen terror.

"I tasted salt in my mouth again, and I realized that the manifestation was returning, but this time it came as images. No—more than that—almost solid figures. The people who made the sounds appeared in front of me, as if in a stage play, running and screaming with no hint that my presence had in any way been noted.

"Even when I stepped outside my defences, they ignored me. But their terror was real enough. I watched as the initially full ballroom emptied, people climbing over each other in their frenzy to escape, grown men leaving weeping woman and children in their wake, in their rush.

"I followed the throng out into the corridor where the fleeing crowd was joined by vast numbers of guests in their nightclothes and panicked crew members, all trying to reach the outside. The taste of salt grew stronger, and the boat lurched underfoot.

"Suddenly, I knew I had to find out what might have caused such a manifestation, which was surely a message of some kind from the Outer Regions. I waited until the corridor had cleared and made my way slowly toward the bridge.

"There was a curious overlap in my vision, with the current ship which I inhabited *overlaid* on the one where the terror was being played out. I considered that I might be seeing a previous emergency on the boat, but I had not read of such a thing occurring in the vessel's relatively short history, and surely an event of such a magnitude would have been reported.

"My puzzlement did not last long. I arrived at the bridge to see a worried Captain dictate a telegraph. His voice came to me as if from a great distance, but the words are stuck in my memory.

"*'Mayday! RMS Lusitania struck by German torpedo thirty miles west of Cape Clear Island. Taking on water and listing badly. Estimate ten minutes until capsize. Many dead. Mayday!'*"

"There is more, but I want to stop here, and consider something."

***

Carnacki paused and puffed at his pipe.

"German torpedoes," he said softly. "We all know such a thing, although *possible*, has not happened. But hearing the rest of the telegraph got me thinking—about free will, and destiny. I have never been a believer in fate, cleaving to the principle that I always have a choice in the direction of my future.

"But what I heard next gave me pause, for you see there was a date spoken, a date I could scarcely believe.

"*'Dictated by Captain Turner...Fourteen-twenty hours... May Eleventh...Nineteen hundred and fifteen.'*"

There was a moment's uproar in Carnacki's parlour as we came to understand the import.

Carnacki gave us a second, then waved us into silence.

"Now you see what has caused me to anguish over this telling," he said. "I always believed that time was an arrow, that the past was gone and the future still to come. But what if everything in the *Macrocosm* exists simultaneously? Are we all mere pawns, forever destined to walk pre-ordained paths? I admit that thought depresses me mightily. What I have seen makes me wonder at the purpose of my very existence.

"But to return for a moment to the tale. The figures around me began to fade as they reached the end of a cycle. The bridge emptied and, although the boat on which I stood was firm enough, the one in the *vision* lurched alarmingly and once again I felt as if I had got a soaking. I was buffeted as if by a strong current, and I swallowed the taste of salt water.

"But I had an idea...one born back in the barrow in Larkhall.

"I returned to the ballroom and began experimenting with different speeds of playing the cylinders I had recorded. I knew that different sounds, being as they are at source mere vibrations, can interact with other sounds. In extreme circumstances, one set of noises can act as a dampener for another, in effect cancelling themselves out to produce silence. It was this, which I was attempting to do now.

"I had to force myself to endure three full cycles of the howling and screaming, spending the best part of the night watching over again as frantic passengers crushed themselves into too small an exit. I was an emotional and physical ruin by the end, but finally I had it. I cranked up both phonographs and replayed them back, one at full speed and one two seconds ahead on starting, but timed to finish at the same instant. The resulting noise was an unholy cacophony. But it did the job asked of it. While the phonograms were playing, the howling manifestation faded and died until the phantom images stopped moving, and not even a whisper of a scream could be heard. When the phonograms stopped there was only a deep silence in the Ballroom, which already seemed warmer and more inviting.

"I stayed there for two more days, but there was no recurrence of anything untoward. McAllister was sober now, and most thankful for what I had done. But as I left, I saw the same fear in his eyes as I feel in my own heart. I did not tell him of the date I overheard the doomed Captain dictate, but I think he knows that one day, perhaps soon, there will be a major problem with the Lusitania. McAllister is a stout fellow. I do believe he means to stay with the boat, and endeavor to mitigate the severity of what may come.

"I wish him well.

"As for me, I have been to the Admiralty, trying to impress on them the danger that is, or will be caused by German U Boats. But you chaps can see their problem, can't you? They cannot in all faith accuse the Germans of something that hasn't happened yet, and they cannot ask Cunard to keep the Lusitania in dock in Liverpool, for it would bankrupt that great company.

"No, life shall go on...or rather, life *always* goes on. I have seen a new manifestation of the Outer Realms during this case, one that I wish I had not. I find at the moment that I cannot look ahead to the future with any great confidence, not for my own part in my own destiny, or for this country's part in what I fear *must* come to pass in little more than five years."

***

It was a somber Carnacki who looked up as his tale finished.

"Well, chaps, have I dented your view of what is right and

proper in the world?"

None of us spoke. We had sat and listened to many of Carnacki's tales, reveling vicariously in his adventures. I believe we all now realized that with the adventure comes a realization that we were privy to things we might not be *meant* to know, or even understand.

"Those dashed Huns," Arkwright said. "Someone should make them pay for what they've done."

Carnacki smiled wanly.

"Will do," my dear Arkwright. "Will do. And I have no doubt that what I saw will come to pass, no matter what we here might do to try to prevent it. All I can say is that I, for one, do not intend to ever take a sea cruise. And I suggest all here refrain, for many years to come."

We were all still quiet as Carnacki herded us onto the porch with a soft *"Out you go..."*

Jessop accompanied me along the Embankment for a time. We were lost in our own thoughts, neither of us in the mood for conversation. It was only as we parted at the bridge that he spoke.

"I say old chap," he said, taking a newspaper from his coat pocket. "I did not want to bring this up in front of the others, but I cannot keep it to myself. I think it is pertinent."

Indeed it was, and it has haunted my dreams for many a night since.

The newspaper was the Daily Mail, and the headline seemed to leap out of the page at me: *GERMANY PREPARING FOR WAR ON THE BRITISH EMPIRE*

FLOODLAND

Cameron Pierce

Doug Marsh, proprietor of Hawthorne Bait and Tackle, was updating the catch report bulletin when a stranger entered the shop. Doug ground the chalk between his calloused fingers. "We don't open till six," he said to the young man, whose eyes were bloodshot, his clothes soaked.

"I think you'll want to see this," the man said.

Doug pocketed the chalk and took up his mug of steaming coffee, then followed the man—a teenager, really—out to the parking lot. He grumbled to himself about forgetting to lock the door again. Anglers, eager to hit the river, were always trying the door as early as four in the morning, even though the posted hours said Hawthorne Bait and Tackle opened at six sharp. Sometimes Doug found sleep troublesome. Nightmares awoke him, or else, the dread of experiencing such nightmares resulted in him working through the night, repairing tackle, tying flies, molding lead weights, reading, sweeping, drinking coffee, drinking bourbon, shuffling up and down the musty aisles of the shop, gazing through his thick-framed glasses at the trophy fish mounted on the walls. With increasing frequency, owing either to his sleeplessness or age, Doug forgot to lock the shop door after smoking a cigarette out front. That was how the Eager Earls, as he referred to these non-store-hour-abiding folks, got in. But sometimes he let them buy what they needed anyhow. After all, he was awake, and if he turned them away, they would just wait out in the parking lot until opening hour.

Never in his thirty-seven years running the bait shop had anyone ever barged in before six with a fresh catch to show him. At that hour, the night fishermen were heading home, too exhausted to pay Doug a visit, although they'd later bring in photos of any notable catches to tack on the bait shop walls. Most other diehard fishermen had either launched their boats by six or else they were swinging by Doug's to pick up some essential item before hitting the water. This young man, with his claims of an extraordinary catch, had piqued Doug's interest. He was probably some out-of-towner who'd caught a big sturgeon.

Doug sipped his coffee and approached the Dodge truck where the man stood, waving him over with frantic gestures.

"Well, what've you got?" Doug said.

The kid lifted the lid on a big red ice chest, and Doug peered inside. The cigarette fell from his mouth when he saw what was in there. A blue-eyed fish with human-like arms and legs, a mouth full of jagged teeth like a shark's, and a crimson dorsal fin that looked as if it were meant to cut through steel.

"Thought you'd want a look," the kid said.

"Where in hell did you catch this?"

"The Harbor. Between Burnside and Steel Bridge. That hole where the water drops to ninety feet. I was fishing for sturgeon off the floating walkway there, the Esplanade."

Night fishing for sturgeon was prohibited but never mind that. This was one weird-ass fish.

"So what do you think," the man said.

Doug lit another cigarette and studied the young man, seeking any sign of a ruse, but the kid appeared to be telling the truth. He'd caught a weird-ass fish, and he'd taken it to Doug. That was the beginning and the end of his story.

"So…"

"Odds are, this thing is one of a kind. Just another superfund mutation. Then again, maybe not. Maybe there's more of them. So we're gonna go inside and call ODFW. They won't open for another couple hours, and it likely won't be a couple hours after that before an officer swings by. In the meantime, you're gonna take me out and show me exactly how you caught this thing."

The kid looked like a deer in the headlights. "I ain't going out there again. I told you where I caught it. I'll give you the rest of my bait if you want. I was just fishing a whole squid off the bottom, the way I always do for sturgeon. Nothing different." He shook his head insistently. "I'm done fishing that goddamn river." He pointed to the creature in the ice chest. "When I pulled it up—it spoke."

"What do you mean it spoke?"

"Before I bonked it, the damned thing spoke to me."

Doug scoffed, lit another cigarette.

And then, as if on cue, the creature raised its head from the bed of ice and spoke in perfect English.

Doug felt a hand on his elbow, and he knew it belonged to the fish.

The fish with hands.

"Excuse me, sir?" So, it was a polite fish. "Sir, are you all right?"

The young man was talking. The fish remained lifeless in the ice chest. Doug slammed the lid down and flipped the latch, sick of looking at the hideous thing.

"Are you okay?" the kid said.

"I'm fine," Doug said, forcing a distant grin. The pain splintered his left arm like lightning, spreading up into his neck. His heart felt like it lay outside his chest, heavy as if ready to give birth, and the air surrounding it was made of pins and needles. His knees went wobbly. "Better call an ambulance," he said.

As he plummeted to the cold gravel, he felt certain he caught a glimpse of the creature popping out of the ice chest like a jack in the box.

It's not so bad, he thought. Whether he referred to death, or the fish, or the pain within, he did not know.

After the pain broke, Doug found himself as someone else. He was driving on a strange road in an unfamiliar town. The truck was a Chevy with a good engine. He glanced in the rearview mirror and saw leathery skin, wavy gray hair, and piercing blue eyes that scared even him. He did not look at himself again.

He turned on the radio to see what kind of music he listened to.

Old blues.

Hellhounds and shit.

Beside him on the bench seat, a cellphone rang. The screen said 'Wife,' and he felt an involuntary flutter in his heart, though he could not definitively trace the sensation back to himself, Doug, who might be excited to see 'Wife' calling because he had never been married, only fantasized about the married life, or maybe this other person, whoever he had become, felt deep and abiding feelings for this 'Wife.' Whatever the source, he realized that he missed her.

He picked up the phone and said, "Hey, honey. I'm on my way home."

As if this were normal.

As if he knew where home was.

The wife asked him to pick up something for dinner on the way home. She didn't feel like cooking. He told her that he would stop at Los Hermanos.

They said 'I love you,' and they said 'goodbye,' but in the clipped, fast-forward way of people who are used to saying such things.

Loveyoubye.

When he stepped out of the truck outside the Mexican food restaurant, the heat took him by surprise. A tumbleweed rolled into traffic. On the other side of the four-lane street, a kit fox stared at him from a field that had recently been razed to make way for a new housing development. The air was the color of Earl Grey tea. It smelled like cow shit and exhaust fumes. He went inside the restaurant and tried not to think about where he was, let alone why. He ordered some of his favorite dishes. He ordered some of his wife's favorite dishes. He instinctively went to order some of his son's favorites but stopped himself, found an absence in his chest that resided where his son used to be. *My son is gone*, he told himself, knowing how foolish it was, knowing he had never had a son. He ordered enough food so that he and his wife could take the leftovers to work tomorrow.

The drive home was uneventful except that he got stuck in traffic. He sat there wondering what a man like himself did in the evenings after work. Did he watch television with his wife? Did he go fishing, like he did in his real life? Did he go out to bars and drink beer and play pool with friends? With limited time and money, there were only so many ways a man could occupy his evening hours. He had never conceived of an evening that did not involve fishing. He recalled the pain he'd felt just before ending up here, and it was almost enough to bring it all back.

I'm a different man now, he thought. *Just go with it.*

Eventually, he pulled into the driveway of a ranch-style home in a suburban housing community named Pheasant Creek or Eagle Springs, or some shit like that.

He brought the brown bag holding the Mexican food inside. In the living room, his wife sat on the couch with a laptop on her lap. He leaned over and kissed the top of her head. She appeared to be playing Spider Solitaire, but he thought he'd detected the sudden closure of a browser window as he kissed her. He mined his emotional and experiential database and decided that he trusted her. She had never given him any reason not to.

"Come eat," he said.

On the walls of the living room were photos of a young boy who shared the steely blue eyes he'd seen when he looked at himself in the rearview mirror.

My son is gone.

Certain street and business signs had looked blurry to him as he drove home. At first, he thought something must be wrong with his vision. Sunspots, maybe. After all, he was not used to such a bright place. Then he realized what it was. The name of the town. Whatever brought him here was obscuring from him the name of the town. Wherever it appeared, he saw a blur. He imagined that if he heard someone speak the name, he would hear a blur as well.

The fate of his son also remained a mystery. When he had

absently begun to order his son's favorite food, some new kind of sadness began to eat away at him. He'd experienced loss before, a range of it. The loss of a parent, the loss of a trophy fish. This was different. This hurt worse.

He sensed the same sadness in his wife as they sat down at the kitchen table and began to eat. They spoke about their days. The mundane things, the funny things, the frustrating things, some gossip, the happenings of the impending weekend. He wanted to ask about the son. Where was he? Was he around? Was he coming home soon? Away at college? In prison? Dead? There were only so many places a son might be, and none of them a father couldn't reach.

After dinner, they caught up on their favorite television show. The husband drank beer, and the wife drank boxed red wine. Throughout the evening, she stepped outside three times for a cigarette. The first time, he touched his breast pocket, feeling for the pack of cigarettes he, Doug, kept there. The reassuring hardness of the rectangular pack was gone, and his fingers sank into the flab of his pectorals. He'd asked the wife for a cigarette, and she'd looked at him strangely. He said never mind and told a joke that made no sense in that or any other context, then while she went outside to smoke her cigarette alone, he went into the kitchen to grab another beer. In there he felt dizzy. He found breathing difficult. Each lungful entered him like cotton. He thought of the bad air outside. He pressed a hand to his heart, wondered why its rhythm seemed so wrong, thought he counted off thirty seconds between beats, but his counting must have been wrong. When he heard the front door open, he grabbed a beer from the refrigerator and returned to the living room to continue watching television with his wife. Their favorite show. The second and third time she went outside for a cigarette, he did not ask her for one, and he did not leave the couch. He'd grown afraid there in the kitchen. Afraid of what, he did not know.

In bed that night before they slept, his wife said 'I love you' in the dark. It sounded so much like 'goodbye' that tears welled up in his eyes. He trembled and wept. His wife held him, her body soft beneath loose pajamas. She did not ask what was wrong. She only said kind and tender things. This calmed him, yes, but also worried him. The wife's words and touch confirmed that all his pain was real. He'd wanted so badly for it to be make-believe. He wanted to be done with all this sadness and this fear. Her fingers combed through his hair, and she kissed him on the mouth. Beneath the blankets, she spread her legs, inviting him. He stirred despite himself. They did not make love so much as they applied a salve to their mutual pain.

Afterward, tangled in the sweaty sheets, he felt whole again. He laid a hand on his wife's belly and wondered how long it would last. He opened his mouth to ask her a question, to propose that they try again, buy an RV, go on vacation, eat at that four star steakhouse they'd talked about for years— anything to fuel the calm he felt another mile. Something to look forward to. Something to feel good about. By the time he settled upon the ideal proposal, the wife was already asleep. He stayed up half the night and watched her sleep. Life and love had not been easy for them. Despite all that had transpired, in the gloaming she looked beautiful, happy, and at peace. He could not help but celebrate this quiet victory.

Loveyoubye.

When he awoke in the morning, his wife was already gone. He got out of bed and dressed in the clothes he'd worn the day before. He was late for work. He ate some sort of breakfast bar and left the house. On the highway, he missed his exit. Instead of getting off and turning back, he kept on going. He drove right out of town. When he caught sight of himself in the rearview mirror, he looked a little bit less like the man he'd become. He drove north. He stopped for gas and coffee somewhere, gas and a sandwich somewhere else. He tried to avoid seeing himself, but every couple hours, he couldn't help looking or catching a glimpse by accident. Every time, he looked different. The further north he drove, the more he resembled Doug. He guessed it was only natural to become himself, and left it at that. By the time he arrived in Portland, he'd become Doug again. He drove directly to the bait shop. He did not open up for business. Instead, he locked the door after him and went up to his room above the store. He climbed into bed and fell fast asleep even though his back ached from the miles on the road. He had driven very far.

Doug woke in his bed. The young man who'd caught the strange fish sat in a chair beside him. When the young man noticed Doug was awake, he put the book he was reading aside and asked, "How are you feeling?"

"How do I feel?" Doug said, and laughed painfully. "I feel as shitty as the day I was born."

"You fainted, so I brought you up here."

Doug shook his head, mumbled, "I didn't faint. I became someone else."

"What was that?" the young man said.

"Nothing. You didn't call an ambulance, did you?"

"No."

"Good. I don't have health insurance. What time is it?"

The young man looked at his watch. "It's four in the morning."

"Good," Doug said. He groaned and sat up in bed. "Then it's about time we got started."

"Started with what?"

"Fishing."

"You can't be serious—"

"Look, boy. You showed up here almost twenty-four hours ago with a freak fish in your ice chest. Next thing I know, I've lost a day of my life, and trust me, I ain't got many left. You owe me for that day. You're going fishing with me."

But as soon as he'd said it, Doug realized the young man was not in the room with him. He was alone. He'd no idea how many days had passed, one or ten, or none at all. He'd no idea how he'd managed to get upstairs to his room.

Gray light filtered in, but not enough to tell if it was early morning or late evening. He moved to the window and looked out. The young man's Dodge was still in the parking lot. Now it was nearly submerged. Doug's chest tightened.

A flood had rolled in and swallowed the earth. His car had already gone under. He knew his shop was flooded. He'd lose his fish mounts and so much else. His only phone was down there, so that was gone. No chance of calling anyone. The rain continued falling heavy. Soon the truck would also vanish under the roiling waves. Somewhere in a distant town, a man who wasn't Doug had a wife. Somewhere in this floodwater, the blue-eyed fish with human limbs and such sharp teeth must have dwelled. Maybe it was dead. Maybe not. Maybe a million more like it existed, ready to emerge from the river in this time of flood. Somehow, he knew the creature had gotten the young man who'd caught it.

If only he could will himself to be that other man. But he could not. He locked the bedroom door and retrieved the Smith & Wesson from the safe. He sat in the rocking chair by the window, the revolver on his lap, staring out at the strangely desolate world. No people or rescue crews out there. Only dark water, dark sky.

SIRENS

Dallas Mullican

The sea threw tumultuous waves to crack against the rocks far below. Only a hushed echo rose above the cliff face, blending with the gentle whine of chilled winds, and the weeping of a dozen dark shapes gathered along the graveside—a somber requiem and befitting ambiance. The salty air joined with tears, a bittersweet taste to linger on the tongue long after earth covered her coffin, and her face dimmed in memory.

"Our dear sister, Elizabeth, taken from us too soon…"

The man stood apart from the other mourners, only dimly aware of the reverend's droning platitudes. He didn't belong here. A stranger…even to himself. Eyes veiled in black lace, or shadowed by the brims of top hats, cast furtive glances his way. The words *rogue* and *rake* made it to his hearing, as was the intent of the speakers. Whispers uttered under the breath, yet aimed with deliberation—slings and arrows meant to wound. Their postures seemed to scoff at him, rich with disdain, before regaining their dour expressions, accompanied by the obligatory sniffles and moans.

"Let not your hearts be sadden. Our dear sister finds embrace amongst the angels…"

A clap of thunder out at sea and the scent of rain, caused the horses to stamp and neigh, snapping the reins affixed to the hearse carriage. The stranger shared their restlessness and impatience. He turned and walked away. Gasps from the mourners at this audacious departure followed him from the cemetery—followed him, clung to him, along with so many ghosts.

He wandered into the city, the city of his birth, a place

he had loved once. So many nights with friends, taking in a show, drinking at the pubs, or simply enjoying the sights and sounds allowed only to the affluent. They had ruled the city, lords of their domain. Yet, the past faded and friends drifted. Now the city seemed little more than a duplicate of every city everywhere. Buildings, streets of dirt and cobblestone, finely dressed people bustling along the sidewalks headed to some business or entertainment, and the poor, the refuse of the city, begging for handouts or waiting on the work carts to take them to another all too brief job. Every window and door now held the apparitions of nostalgia. Their appearance sickened him. He waved a hand in the air, hoping to banish their prying stares, their…judgments. Nothing remained for him here. Nothing was unique or special anymore, nothing held him, nothing to call home.

He found his way to the bar just off Essex Street, a place he knew well, though time had been kind to neither of them. The building's façade flaked and splintered, cracks in the windows disfigured reflections. The interior fared no better. Once a home to the well-bred, only the wealthiest clientele had borne claim to this section of the city not so long ago. The depression of the day left few areas safe from vagrant, down-on-their-luck types. The wealthy now kept further north, or better yet, to their countryside mansions and estates, to avoid the filthy teeming masses altogether.

Inside, the stranger took a stool at the counter. A flick of his finger brought the bartender over.

"Whisky," he said, without looking up.

"Sure thing." The bartender returned with the drink and stood appraising his new customer. "Don't get many dandies like you in here. I see a fella in a suit like that one, and I figure he's coming from a wedding or a putting some poor sap in the ground." The bartender chuckled, an ample belly quaking beneath a button down, which like his establishment, had seen better days, stained with splotches of dark ale and cheap red wine.

"Funeral," said the stranger.

"Uh, damnation. I-I'm sorry, Mister." The bartender wiped the counter to busy himself and avoid eye contact with the stranger. "Well, I hope they had a good life."

The stranger glanced up, the minimal gesture taking all his strength. "She had...regrets."

"Uh, I see. Uh...let me know if I can get you anything else." The bartender hurried away, taking up a conversation about the 'damned parliament' with a man at the other end of the bar.

The stranger nursed his drink, gazing into the amber liquor. He thought he heard the call of the sea whispering to him from the bottom of the glass. A quiet summons voiced in the slosh of liquid, side to side. He always felt at home near the sea. Its ominous breadth, its fathomless depths, the mystery of the thing, made him feel both small, insignificant, and welcomed.

Behind him, a couple's laughter intruded on his thoughts. Their merriment seemed an affront to his need for solitude, his need for recrimination.

"You know how I love you," said a male voice.

"Oh, I'm certain you do. I hear you love all the ladies," said a female voice, which sent a twinge of discomfort around the interior of the stranger's skull.

"Lies, all lies. People are simply jealous of the love I have only for you."

"And Betsy Stover? She's simply distraught over you."

"A mere child...and such a bore. She meant nothing to me."

"I will be any different? Am I to be your fashion of the month?" Her voice lost some of its facetiousness, a serious undertone creeping in.

"This city would ruin me. They besmirch my reputation, sullying my good name. Yet, none of it matters. Only how I appear in your eyes matters. A momentary fashion? Bah. Believe me, my love, you will suit me for all of time. I should lop off my arm rather than not have you on it."

She giggled. "Such sweet things you say. Your words are like flowers, you'll dash off before they wilt."

"You wound me. I will never leave your side."

"I want to believe you. I do love you."

"Trust what you feel. I am yours…yours alone. I will never leave you."

"Nor break my heart?" Almost a whisper, a quiet plea.

"I would sooner rip out my own heart than to chance breaking yours."

Wet sounds of the two kissing brought bile into the stranger's throat. He coughed as he stumbled off the barstool, gaining their attention for an instant, nodded an apology and ambled from the building. Though he could hold his liquor, and only indulged in one drink, his head swam as he wandered the streets. Aimless, his legs carried him with a seeming will of their own. He found himself at the docks, the sea like an old friend standing before him with open arms. He gazed into the dark waters for a moment, then closed his eyes, head tilted back. *The cold current washed over him, cradling him in a gentle embrace. It enveloped him, coalescing over his head like easing a door closed. The stranger sank, arms waving back and forth, pulling the waters close. Memory faded and pain dimmed, a life lived grew faint and small as it receded into the darkened depths.*

"What you doing there, lad?"

A gruff voice jarred him out of the daydream. He turned to find a large man staring at him, a mischievous and sinister smirk on the other's face, and a fighter's stance in his deportment. The man, obviously a sailor, wore the customary attire of any one of the dozen or so whaling ships anchored in the harbor. Slops, his loose fitting trousers, flapped lazily in the breeze beneath a gray waistcoat and narrow brimmed black hat. Whaling, a booming industry, always lacked sufficient hands on deck, and the stranger knew well some of the more nefarious means of filling ships' roles.

"Got any coin on you? Loan me a bit?" asked the sailor.

"I'm afraid I don't have any to spare, friend."

"We're friends now, are we? Well, friend, I bet my captain'll give you a coin or two for your hard labor…eventually."

"Your captain?"

"Of course, aboard that ship right there." The big man thumbed toward a rather derelict looking brig. Sailor smiled, a gap-toothed sneer, and darted forward, much more quickly than his bulk would have suggested possible. A cudgel held behind his back whipped upward at an arc and caught the stranger just below his left temple. The world swooned in a grey fog.

Festive music filled his head as the room took shape around him. Portraits of the noble dead stared down from high walls. Crystal chandeliers glowed overhead while crystal glasses, brimming with wine, occupied every hand. Laughter and conversation swelled in a pleasant din from a room full of jovial partygoers. He remembered this night, a ball for some lord or lady. Dressed in his finest tuxedo, he danced with Elizabeth, resplendent in her evening gown. A silver necklace swung like a pendulum beneath her throat and hovered above a plunging bodice hem. She was enthralling, an unmatched beauty. She giggled as he twirled her across the ballroom floor, an expression of pure joy in the glint of her eyes and the radiance of her smile.

The grey fog deepened to a charcoal miasma…

Elizabeth gazed up at him in the quiet of a darkened room. A single candle burned by the bedside, casting ghastly shadows onto the walls. She looked haunted, pale, clothed in her white nightgown. Her eyes demanded his attention, would brook no turning away. There was no hate in her countenance, but instead—hurt, betrayal, disappointment.

The cry of a gull sounded from somewhere near. Then, a single note, a sorrowful sustained note, plucked out on ivory keys. The stranger's mind whorled and went black.

***

An ancient ship rocked to and fro upon ferocious seas. The roar of its fury filled the stranger's ears as he clung to the railing. Above the water's rage—the crack of splintering wood, tearing at a hull near to breaking, the sweetest song entwined with shrieking winds, and a man strapped with heavy rope to the mast who bellowed into the gale.

Violent waves slapped against the deck. Men flung over the railings, cried out into the wailing wind, disappearing in the blackness of the night and the anger of the sea. Awoken to a nightmare, this tempest and the ship's imminent doom, confusion gave way to fear as the stranger struggled to find purchase, desperate to move away from the beast lurking over the railing. Blinding sheets of rain obscured sight, feeling along the planks yielding no assistance.

"You, there!" The man bound to the mast screamed over the roar. "Secure yourself!"

Through the downpour and the squall's near solid walls, the stranger could just make out the man who spoke. He wore antiquated armor, bronze and leather, battered and nicked, as if just out of battle. His long beard and thick brown hair, streaked in gray, flagged outward with the force of the maelstrom. The stranger tightened his hold, palms rubbed raw by cords of thick rope. Yet amidst the violence and panic, again the song, an ever present resonance, called to him—his terror and the melody created a dizzying amalgamation.

"Do not heed the song, only calamity awaits those who listen. Achelous' daughters sing to entice us to our doom. Though beautiful, they are witches or worse still," he yelled to the stranger.

"Who are you?"

"I am Odysseus, King of Ithaca. I return from the Great War with Troy. Though we prevailed against the Trojans, it seems I have angered Poseidon. His wrath will see us at the sea's bottom if we cannot weather this storm."

"And the song? What is it? Where does it come from?" In spite of his fear, the song tugged at the stranger's heart.

"It is the lure of the Sirens. They call to men who happen within range of their song, drawing them to their isle, from which there is no return."

"Why do they hate men so?"

Odysseus contemplated the question, flinging water from

his face. "Perhaps it is not hate they harbor. They search for something that eludes them. Peering into the souls of men is the only means they know which may yield the thing they seek. Men who fall captive to their song are searching to fill some longing within themselves as well I think. The fervor of their desire betrays them. They will not find what they yearn for upon the isle of the Sirens."

Odysseus' warnings and the ferocity of the storm could not dampen the stranger's attraction to the song. He found the sea and the wind, the king and his ship, all dissolving into the soothing strain. The song became his world entire, all his will compelled to seek it out. How he came to be adrift in the sea, fighting the turbulent waves, he could not fathom. Perhaps the ship gave in to the ongoing assault, broke apart, and cast out its occupants. Maybe the waves swept him overboard. Odysseus had vanished. In truth, none of that mattered, only the song mattered and finding its source.

His head bobbed above the surface one last time before he drifted below the roiling waters. He felt life leaving, floating up even as his body sank further and further down. Fear of death did not accompany him, only the regret that the song lay forever lost. Gentle hands grasped him beneath his arms and lifted him high above the raging torrent. He rose up out of the sea into a night sky filled with the sound of music and wings.

A meadow, green and lush, filled with flowers of every kind and color, cradled him as he recovered his bearings. He could still hear the wind and waves, but faint and distant. Dozens of shapes hovered in the air all about him—women with the wings of birds. Their naked bodies, perfect, appeared chiseled from the finest marble. Each shone with a vibrant glow, the moonlight reflecting off supple skin.

The splendor of this place, and its inhabitants, took his breath. Snow-capped peaks towered against the horizon, pools of sparkling blue with surfaces like glass gleamed in the warm glow of the sun. Animals drank from the clear waters, showing no fear, relishing the company of the Sirens. A serene peace overcame the stranger. This place existed in the eye of the storm. A place forever hidden from the world, it shared a forbidden secret with its denizens.

The Sirens floated above him, wings fluttering in rhythmic undulation. They sang to the stranger, only to him, as if in worship. The voices at once distinctive and blended in unison. The song enveloped all. This must be heaven. Surrounded by beauty, he let go…sweet release.

A single note buried somewhere amidst the melody slowly turned sour and rose in pitch and timbre. Its tone rang all wrong, and he knew the song must soon collapse, or change to gain harmony with the new note. A new melody rebelled against the old, discordant, eerie in its mystery, its threat of horror.

His mind filled with this shrill new song. Unbearable pressure built as each voice added to the cacophony. The Sirens sang. They sang with a yearning so deep it made his heart ache and his soul shatter. The stranger knew this song, for he sang it too. He sang it through the tears of an unanswered longing, through the sorrow of loss, and the absence of absolution. A single fleeting hope that's fruition lay forever just on the edge of feeling, its image dim, and its substance like smoke escaping through grasping fingers.

They came close now, dozens of women bearing the wings of eagles, hovering above the meadow floor. Some of their faces he knew well, others only a faint recollection, but he had seen them all in another time and place. Hair of blonde, red, ebony, and brown flowed out in streamers as if the meadow sank beneath the surrounding sea, their bodies now floating amidst cool pure waters.

They encircled him; the song took him to his knees. Their faces changed to reflect the inharmonious choral. Eyes, mirrors consumed with hurt, betrayal, and disappointment, blind and turned a foul grey, stretched from their heads on thin worming stalks. Mouths grimaced with hunger and turned from horizontal to vertical, covering the length of those terrible visages, each lined with shining silver swords. At the apex of each mouth a single bulbous eye fixed into the V where the two lips met. Only this eye possessed sight. Its vision locked onto the stranger seeking to peer beneath his skin. That terrible prescience burned away all that lay inside.

The Sirens converged, each in turn, on wings morphed into those of great bats. Elongated tongues snaked out to taste his flesh. Razor sharp teeth bit down on torso, leg, arm, and neck. A deep and lingering bite. The sickly sweet scent of blood permeated the air, streaks of crimson created macabre masks for each Siren to wear. They reveled in his agony, their song now shrieks of delight and rage, his own anguished cries serving as an ear shattering counterpoint to their hideous lullaby.

Each took a piece of him. What he gave would never sustain them, only momentary in its nourishment. What they gave lasted forever—scars gouged upon his soul. The illusion shattered, all laid bare. The horrible truth of longing, of loneliness, of guilt, made known in screams and pain.

He should have ignored the song and sailed the waves down into the depths of the raging black waters. He should have felt the dreams anchored to him. Dreams he betrayed. So many promises broken. So many hearts…. Yet, if he could somehow have managed to hold onto the beauty, before the note turned bitter, if he could remember the song as it should have been, the scars might fade, and the promise of paradise revealed—one woman with wings like a dove and the stranger, lost in sweet harmony, at home in the bosom of the sea.

DRAUGAR

Bryan Clark

The *Surt* rolled over the waves, its flexible construction allowing it to buck and bend with the rough water. The other ships in the fleet were pulling ahead, while the *knarr* was falling behind and being drawn farther south by powerful storm winds. Not as long as many of the *skeid* in the raiding fleet, but wider and riding higher in the water, and with fewer oar benches to aid the sails in giving speed, the *Surt* was finding difficulty maintaining the pace of the rest of the fleet in the storm. Olaf the Strong had demanded at least one cargo ship join the raid, however, for he predicted massive takings and wanted the extra capacity at hand should it be needed.

The raiding fleet was headed for the Orkneys—a fertile land for pillage, but a brutal journey across hundreds of miles of open sea. Solar compasses were accurate to a point, but although a war-band may have their ships aimed in the right general direction, it was always a game of chance whether they would land next to a fat, rich monastery, or find themselves fighting to keep from being dashed to pieces against walls of stone.

Thorstein Shieldbreaker stood and roared at his crew, "Pull those oars til your bones crack and your skin splits, lest Odin take you for a lot of feeble Englishwomen and laugh when you plead entrance to Valhalla!"

"We're pulling, Thorstein," said a raider named Kark. "But this storm is fighting us like Jormungandr himself!"

"None of the other ships seem to be having the same difficulties, Kark. It is unwise to invoke the name of the Midgard Serpent in these waters. Perhaps we should throw you overboard as a sacrifice, and the lightening of the boat would ease the other men's labor."

"Just shut your mouth and row, Kark," snapped Torben Bent-Leg, the navigator. A dour man, he shared naught of the other raiders' bloodlust. He fought and went a-viking, not for the joy of the thing, but to please the gods, and do his duty as a man of the Vik.

"We've lost the others in this wretched mist. Torben, try to keep us on a straight line. We shall have to wait until the weather clears to catch them up."

Sigurd the Bastard, Thorstein's second in command, stopped rowing and looked around nervously. "Do you feel that?" he said.

"Feel what, Sig?" asked Torben.

"The wind is changing direction, driving the spray and rain ahead of us. Feel it on your face."

Several of the men stopped, lifting their faces to the sky. The wind had indeed changed, and the soaking mist was changing to painful, ice-cold lances of rain, picking up speed. The gray skies, the gray rain, and the gray sea all blended together until the men couldn't tell where one ended and the other began. Then a low moaning insinuated itself into the consciousness of all aboard, rising with alarming speed to a deafening howl. Locks of soaked hair whipped into dripping, freezing faces as they struggled to see.

"You woke Jormungandr, calling his name like that!" said Bjorn the Shipbuilder.

"Nonsense!" said Kark.

The gale parted the condensing mist enough to permit them to see the solid wall of rain just yards away from the boat and approaching faster than any of them had seen weather move.

"Handholds! Find handholds!" roared Thorstein over the storm, and then it slammed into them and the boat was tossed as though they were in the heart of a maelstrom.

For two exhausting hours they rode out the worst storm any of them had ever seen in all their years at sea. Then, as though all their pleas to all their various gods were heard and answered all at once, all was calm. Twenty men looked out from under their tarpaulins and from behind their thwarts. Bjorn was the first to speak.

"What was that? Where is the water?"

"Beneath us, and still as glass," said Torben.

"The storm must have passed," said Kark. "The water is calm, and everything is silent. Not so much as a dripping of water from the oars."

"The fog seems to have stayed. Thick as milk, but at least it's not that damned freezing mist," said Torben. "Something is wrong, though. We're nowhere near the Orkneys, the Vik, the fleet, or anything else any of us has ever known."

"There's nothing but water in all directions, you old fool, how can you tell that?"

"Hah! I've spent more years at sea than you've lived. I know the sea, the sky, the winds, the play of the sun on the waves. You would sail off the edge of the world, or straight into a mountain, were I not with you."

"Very well, where are we then?"

"I think," said Thorstein, "that you are all asking the wrong questions. Our location may be a mystery, but I find myself more curious about the fact that Bjorn seems to have gained a bench mate."

The men turned as one to look at Bjorn, who was staring straight ahead as if frozen, afraid to look beside him. A glutinous, slurping intake of breath, as through a throat clogged by phlegm and rot, made Bjorn jump and drop his oar. It slipped into the perfectly smooth water without a sound and disappeared. Finally, Bjorn summoned up the courage to turn his head, and what he saw almost made him follow his oar over the side.

Next to him was a hunched figure garbed in ragged, decayed clothes and draped in seaweed that pooled in coiling strands at the figure's bare, skeletal feet and traced paths of shining salty slime across the deck when the figure shifted. Its flesh was rotted and mottled blue-gray, hanging here and there in tattered, congealed strips from exposed bone beneath. It turned slightly and looked back at Bjorn cowering against the gunwale, regarding him with eyes that once may have been bright blue, but now were obscured by bone white cataracts. The sense of weary exasperation in its expression was almost palpable.

"Had I wanted to kill you, your life would already be mine," it gurgled. "You men have nothing to fear from me. We are all—" Here the thing stopped to remove a tooth that had come loose and was getting in the way of its tongue as it tried to speak. It examined the tooth for a moment, rolled it between forefinger and thumb, shrugged, threw the tooth over the side, and continued. "We are all in the same boat." The dead man laughed at his own joke, and the sound of his syrupy chuckling sent the men's scalps crawling.

"You are a *draugr*?" said Thorstein.

"As are you all."

"No, we live!" said Kark.

"Do you?" said the *draugr.*

"Of course! We breathe, we speak, we—"

"Am I not breathing and speaking to you?"

Kark opened his mouth to reply again, but found the words had all flown from him.

"I am dead and drowned, and so shall you all be in the fullness of time. Look you, there is shore ahead. Mark well the rocks, and beware."

The men all turned to look ahead where the *draugr* pointed. Just as the shade had said, there was a shadow looming up out of fog that billowed like thick curtains of spider web lofted in a gentle breeze.

"What must we beware?" asked Thorstein, turning back to the *draugr*. But the ghost was already fading away with a rattling, phlegmy sigh. The look on its face as it melted away into the fog was one of sorrow, pity, perhaps even a trace of fear. *What could a ghost have to fear?* Thorstein thought to himself. Then he remembered the warning to mark the rocks, and forgot for the moment what a ghost might fear when there was much for living men to fear while approaching a strange shore in a thick fog.

"Stop gawping, and put your oars back in the water!" Thorstein said. "Row slow, look for rocks, and sing out if you see anything. We don't know what lies ahead, and ghost or no, we must take the *draugr* at his word. I, for one, do not wish to meet my end tearing out the bottom of my boat so close to our goal and see his prophecy fulfilled."

No rocks lurched up out of the sea to tear the hull out from under them. As the boat approached the sandy beach, the men could see a small village of huts huddled miserably around the shore. Several larger buildings, communal structures, no doubt, stood behind like watchful parents tending children at play. No real children played in the village. There was no sign of life at all. At the edge of the water stood a circle of a dozen enormous monoliths, tall as three men standing on each other's shoulders. The sea lapped around the bases of the nearest ones, and one on the village side had toppled onto its side in the sand.

"Those pillars," said Torben. "Do you think perhaps those were the rocks the *draugr* meant?"

"They could be," said Thorstein. "We'll beach the boat next to them. They will save us the trouble of building a palisade, and be far better shelter than a few logs besides."

"We may not need any shelter, Thorstein. The village appears to be deserted."

"Either we've gotten incredibly lucky, or we've sailed to Nifelheim," said Kark.

"Silence," said Thorstein. "This does not appear to be a terribly wealthy place, so luck wouldn't seem to have much to do with it. The place isn't in ruin, so it can't have been abandoned for long. I dislike the fog and the quiet. Keep your wits about you."

The men beached the boat and began to leap into the ankle-deep surf. Thorstein assigned Torben, too lame to be of great use in a fight, and Ufuk, their best archer, to stay back, make the boat fast, and keep her safe. "Perhaps I should stay with the boat as well," said Kark.

"Perhaps you should do as you're damned well told," growled Thorstein. "We may have been saddled with you because you're Olaf's nephew, but that does not mean I trust you with my ship."

The other nineteen men moved cautiously ashore, prepared for any surprises in case the village was not as empty as it appeared. As they neared the first of the dwellings, Thorstein raised a hand in the air and the men stopped behind him, senses heightened to an excruciating level. Almost as one, they heard it—the burble of running water. After several breathless seconds of listening, Thorstein turned to the men. "We'll split into three groups," he said. "Bjorn, take Asmund and Eluf and go beyond the village to find the source of that water. Even if we find nothing of value here, our fresh water supply needs to be replenished. Erling, take half the men and search the eastern part of the village. The rest of you, with me."

Bjorn, Asmund and Eluf walked up the main path through the middle of the village toward a copse of trees that marched up a low hill a short distance beyond the last buildings. The omnipresent mist crept around every corner, obscuring their vision and grasping at their ankles.

"I do not like this mist," said Eluf. "The entire village could be hiding anywhere, ready to spring an ambush."

"Yes," said Bjorn. "Lucky we have those rocks to guard our ship. They'll make a fine redoubt should we find ourselves on the back foot."

"Where is the sound of the water coming from?" said Eluf. "It comes from here one moment, and there the next. It sounds as though it's moving around through the fog. Sometimes it even sounds as though it's coming from inside the dwellings."

"That's impossible. The stream must be farther ahead. Everything sounds strange in a fog like this. It makes your senses play tricks on you. Perhaps it will lighten the farther we get from the sea. Once we get a little way up that hill, we should be able to see well enough to find the stream."

***

"What are you doing, Torben?"

"Just having a look at these stones. They're not rough-hewn, as I first thought. Weather and a skin of slime have done much to obscure them, but there are carvings on them, pictures and a writing that is familiar to me."

"What does it say?"

"I said it was familiar, not that I was fluent. It's a very old language, mostly dead before my great grandfather's time if not before. I remember my father had a few documents with words like these, which he taught me to read. Not all of these are ones I know, but I think I can piece their meaning together from the ones I do."

Erling's group wove stealthily between dwellings. They were mostly made of earth, with thatched roofs. A few were more sturdily constructed of stone. The earthen ones looked soaked through, as though they were about to collapse, and the stone ones were beaded with cold salt sweat. The thatch on all of them drooped under the weight of the moisture.

The babble of running water swirled around them like the fog, ever-present, intensifying, building, dying away only to spring up in another place. The men could feel the relentless sound combining with losing most of their sight to the fog to fray at their nerves and prey on their minds.

"I'm beginning to wonder whether the fog ever goes away around here," grumbled one of the men. "I fear we'll end up taking it back to the Vik with us in our pockets and cursing our homes with it as well."

"It is damnably thick, and moves like an animal, slinking around this village looking for quarry."

"Quit your griping," said Erling. "We did not come here for pleasant sights and the warmth of the sun, we came for plunder, and plunder we shall have or be off to another place. We shall start here, in one of these stone buildings. If there is any treasure to be had at all in this wretched place, it will be in a home whose owner had enough wealth to pay someone to haul the rocks into place."

Erling unlimbered his axe and reached for the door.

Across the village, Thorstein was having much the same discussion with his group of men. "Cowering children, the lot of you. Afraid of a little mist."

"The mist is only the last in a long line of things which have conspired to unnerve us this day, Thorstein," said a man named Erik. "Have you forgotten the *draugr* who hitched a ride on our boat this morning?"

"I have not, but he is no longer here. We are, and there is either plunder to be had, or preparations to be made to put back to sea. In the meantime, we've come to the end of the village and not seen so much as chicken stirring. The villagers may have hidden had they seen us coming, but they would not have had time to hide their livestock as well as themselves far enough from here that we wouldn't hear a cow moo or a goat bleat, let alone set up an ambush for us besides."

"Who knows if we would hear bleats and moos over this infernal stream in any case?" said Kark. "Bjorn couldn't have had to go far for water. It sounds like the water's course is right behind us. Unless it sounds like it is in front of us, or to the side. Who can say when it seems to be constantly moving?"

"I must say I agree with Kark, distasteful as it is," said one called Selvig. "Even in a mist like this, sound should not prowl about so."

"It may prowl, but I doubt sound can pounce," said Thorstein. "I think we're safe for the time being. So let us have some loot or be gone!"

The door of the stone house before them shivered into splinters before Thorstein's mighty hammer, and the men peered forward into the gloom.

***

"Odin protect us!"

"What is it, Torben?"

"These carvings. They tell the story of why these stones came to be here. They were erected generations ago to protect the village..." Torben trailed off, squinting at the carvings. "To protect the village from the sea," he finished in a hushed voice.

"They are certainly stout, but they do not seem to be much of a levee," said Ufuk.

"No, not from waves or flooding. It hardly seems to make sense, but not much has made sense this day. It says the sea claimed victims from the village, and the power held in these stones, and the runes carved on them, holds it in place. It's written as verse. 'Twelve stand watch to calm the sea, twelve must stand or all shall be, taken by the roaming sea'."

"Roaming sea? What does that mean?"

"Twelve must stand. But only eleven stand."

"Yes, and any wave that could knock one of these stones over would take all of them down. Unless..." Ufuk walked over to the sentinel stone that lay on its side. "Torben, look here. There are scraps of rope still looped around it. Someone pulled it down on purpose."

"Why in Odin's name would anyone want to do that? Twelve must stand. Oh gods."

The men looked down at the same time at the erosion marks leading from the beach to the sea. Rills and runnels made in the sand by the action of the water. At the same time, both men realized they had been looking at them wrong. They didn't run from the shore down into the water. They led from the water up to the shore. Then the screaming started.

***

Thorstein and the other men stood in the middle of the room, looking about them with equal parts awe, curiosity, and fear.

"Do you suppose it is this way in every dwelling here?"

"That would explain the sounds of water."

"Did you send Bjorn chasing after echoes?"

"I know not. I hope not. Bjorn is a clever man. He can keep his head in a bad situation. He will not let them get lost, and will bring them back safe if they do not find the stream."

"Do you think there really is a stream, or just more of this *madness*?"

"Hard to say."

Water covered every surface in the building, running up the walls like a waterfall in reverse, to pool in a rippling lake on the ceiling. Much of the soaked thatch had come loose and swayed in the gentle current like seaweed. The sight had a disorientating effect, and several of the men stumbled and nearly lost their balance.

Thorstein turned and saw too late Selvig reaching for the water flowing against nature. He had no chance to bark out a warning before the man's fingertips dipped into the liquid. The reaction was instantaneous. Water flowed rapidly up Selvig's arm, soaking his clothes and gushing into his mouth, nose, eyes and ears. Selvig tried to scream but managed only a deep retching sound.

The men all stared in horror as their comrade bucked and gargled and then stood still, his head and arms drooping, sodden hair hanging down to cover his face. He raised his eyes, slow as a glacier, to glare at them. Bloodshot eyes that bulged under a thin film of constantly moving water, the flesh around them already wrinkled and bloated from soaking.

The sound of running water faded and stopped as the bizarre tableau all around them became still. Thorstein's battle-honed reflexes took over and drove him toward the exit a fraction of a second before he roared the command to retreat.

The water released its grip on the ceiling and crashed down onto the men, whose screams were quickly reduced to the same horrible gargling Selvig had made. Thorstein, Erik, and Kark were closest to the door, and were the only ones who made it out without a drop touching them. They landed in a pile on the ground outside the house and stared back in horror at the sodden shadows moving within.

"Do you think any others made it?" asked Erik.

"We shall see," said Thorstein, standing and taking a firm grip on his hammer. The first of the drenched men shambled into the diseased gray daylight and raised his eyes to the three dry men. They were as Selvig's were. Erik drew his sword. "Do not touch them," said Thorstein. "You may end up just like them."

More drowned men joined the first. They reached out their arms toward the remaining three, and tendrils of the living water poured forth from their fingers and coiled through the air, grasping for more victims.

"To the boat! NOW!" Thorstein bellowed, turning and running for the shore. "Pray that Torben and Ufuk have her ready and have not been made like them."

The sploshing footsteps of pursuit echoed eerily through the fog behind them as the three men pelted through the village, squinting for familiar landmarks. The oppressive gray made the already similar buildings even less distinguishable from each other. It would be all too easy in panicked flight to miss a turn and move further from the boat, or run straight into the arms of the walking drowned men.

"Thorstein, I hear more footsteps before us!" shouted Kark. The men came to a stop and listened.

"I hear them too," said Thorstein. "Who goes there? Bjorn? Erling?"

The footsteps came closer and men took shape out of the fog. Bjorn, Asmund, and Eluf sploshed into view, their hair and clothes plastered to their bodies, writhing tentacles of water surrounding them.

"On to the boat, and don't let those tendrils of water touch you!" said Thorstein, and the men ran on, the sounds of pursuit falling behind step by step.

As the buildings began to thin out, and the soil gave way to sand, Thorstein called out to the watch. "Torben, Ufuk! Are you still with us?"

"Aye, Thorstein!" came the response from several yards to the left of the fleeing men.

"Ready the boat, we must leave at once!"

"Are all the men with you? Your steps don't sound very many!"

"No," said Thorstein as they came into view of each other. "The others of our group and Bjorn's are lost. We must be away from here, and attempt to rescue Erling's group later if we can."

"What in Hel happened?"

"Time enough for explanations once we're away from the village."

"I thought you said they were lost," said Ufuk. "The others are right there."

The men spun around to see a large group of their comrades marching down the beach toward them.

"What's that in the air around them?"

"Water," said Thorstein. "This place is cursed, the water flows of its own will and takes over men, turns them into those things. One touch and you're finished. Ufuk, see if you can take some of them down."

Ufuk was hesitant to loose arrows at men who were his friends an hour ago, but as they got closer, he could see they were no longer the men he knew. While Thorstein and the others hurried to make the boat ready for launch, he knocked and fired, again and again. The arrows' impact slowed the targets down, brought a few to their knees, but they just got up again and continued their relentless, squelching advance.

"Look Thorstein, it's Erling!" Ufuk cried out, then his face fell in dismay as he saw Erling's band join the group of drowned creatures on the beach.

As they stepped forward, runnels of water spilled forth from their feet and poured across the sand toward the men. Kark screamed as one found his leg and flowed up his body and into his mouth. Without thinking, Erik drew and swung his sword in one smooth motion, lifting Kark's head from his shoulders. Instead of gore, a geyser of water sprayed out of the stump of Kark's neck, rushing up the sword before Erik could drop the contaminated weapon, up his arm, his neck, his face, to choke off his terrified scream and pour into his eyes and nose and ears.

Thorstein hoisted Torben into the boat; he and Ufuk slammed their shoulders into the hull, and pushed the keel free of the sand. They hauled themselves over the gunwale and grabbed oars to get as far from the accursed village as their exhausted and burning muscles could take them before they collapsed.

As Thorstein looked back toward the beach to see if their assailants still gave pursuit, he saw them lined up along the surf. As one, they knelt and plunged their hands into the water. "Row! ROW!" he roared, thews bulging as he strained against the ocean.

"Thorstein..." Torben pointed to a spot near the stern where a small trickle of water was beginning to run over the side and pool on the floor.

The men exchanged a glance, the grim defiance and steely determination of their northern blood flashing in their eyes.

They drew their weapons and waited.

OLD BOGEY

Lori R. Lopez

Fog danced and skimmed the surface, a nocturnal ballet accompanied by the rub of piers, the lap of water against pilings. It was a night of dense mists, unfit for man or beast, save one—a legendary creature that prowled and ruled obscurity, hunting for its latest meal, the flesh of humankind.

So they said. Finn Strand McGinney trudged along a street lit by sparse lamps, a fist choking the neck of a bottle. "I'm the luckiest man on the seven seas," his baritone voice crooned, "because I am still alive!" He learned that song on a whaling vessel as a young man. There was a lot of truth to it. Unlike provincial wives' tales; gibberish about leviathans. Made-up nonsense.

A minor splash in the harbor gave him pause. Eyes bleary, the whiskered salt peered into a soupy cold. Tentacles reached for him…wispy arms of vapor. He couldn't see much, vaguely etched details, but he was able to steer blind and remain on his feet. This region of the town was mapped on his psyche. Finn used to set sail from the harbor, until skippers stopped hiring him, fearing he might fall overboard drunk. German and Irish, maybe it was in his blood. Maybe he had no choice.

"Pirates guzzled plenny of rum and nobody tole them it was against policy. Ain't nothin' wrong with a nip to warm a feller's bones. World's gone soft in the head," he griped, stumbling to the pier where his dinghy the *Esmeralda* was tied. She was all the deckhand had left of the ocean since he was resigned to toil as an odd-jobber on land, spading dirt, unloading, mending and mucking. Even the dock master rejected him. His dignity had been robbed with his sea legs.

Finn swayed at the edge of solid ground, a concrete verge dividing soil from water. He sniffed the breeze then squinted. Something was out there, studying him. He could sense it, a chill that prickled nape and spine. No little fishy, either. It was big. Not that he swallowed the yarn about a pale sea-monster dubbed Old Bogey. He knew better. Whatever lurked in the ocean was genuine. He had witnessed all her demons: Giant Squids, Great Whites, Orcas, thick eels half the length of a trawler that some claimed were sea-serpents. He watched shipmates meet death screaming, their blood paint the water red as burgundy wine.

The only thing he was afraid of resided on shore.

A peculiar buzzing. He grunted with confusion. "Ahhh." Remembering, he dug in his trousers for a fold-up gadget. "Speak of the devil." His niece had given him the phone and was the sole person to call its infernal number. "Hullo, Meg."

"What are you doing, Uncle Finn?" Not even a greeting. She was worse than a nagging bride.

"I'm doin' fine, Megan. Thanks for asking."

"I said what, not how. Never mind. I can hear the slurred speech."

"This is the way I talk!"

"If you're plastered."

"Now come on, I just had a few, to wet my whistle. I'm going straight to bed."

"I hope that's true. You're not very reliable."

"Least I'm not a drug addict," he teased.

"I tried pot one time! Don't go near the water, Uncle. You know how you get."

Jeebus, her too! "How do I get? Like I've got half a brain? Quit worrying about me." Finn snapped the device shut. Maybe he should have said goodnight. She meant well.

Annoyed, he jammed the telephone into his pocket. When did he start answering to her? She was only his niece. Make that his only niece. His only family. And him for her. The girl was all he had on this earth.

"Don't matter if she's the queen of England. I dun need to

be henpecked. Or sent to dry-dock," Finn carped. "She needs to keep her shrew's beak where it belongs—out of my affairs." He dredged the gizmo from his britches and pantomimed hurling it to black water beneath the fog, imagining a dull satisfying sploosh. "Goodnight, Niece."

He tucked the phone in its berth, amused, then unscrewed and tipped whiskey to parched lips, taking a swig. Cripes, Meg would kill him if he lost the durn thing. She paid extra for an indestructible waterproof model to shield it from storm, spray, and spilt alcohol. The gal was thorough. He swiped the back of a hand across his mouth and closed the bottle.

An ex-girlfriend once accused him of having more tolerance for liquor than for being loved. Finn chortled. *That* was a fact!

Plodding the brink of the wharf to a ramp, he gingerly descended a walkway with safety ridges a guy could trip on. This ridiculous obstacle course led to a flush expanse. Weathered planks bounced. The pier and he were unsteady dance partners, a perfect match. For some reason, the port seemed agitated. Finn stared into the haze. Perhaps he should do as he promised, stagger to his tiny room over a barbershop and flop onto a squeaking rack.

Heck, I'll be in a casket soon. His liver had to be pickled, his gut rotted by booze. If he was going to shove off, kick the bucket like his niece fretted, he should be in a boat.

"A man must choose his passions. And his poisons." Finn wove to the end of the boards. Stooping, he tugged at a poorly knotted line. The rope slipped his grasp, and the dory began to drift. "Oh no you don't. Wait for me!" Clumsily, Finn hopped, tipping the vessel, banging shins and kneecaps. Reeling to the center, he managed not to capsize. The man clasped a gunwale, pulled himself onto the rowing seat then blinked, baffled. "Why did I untie you? I'm not going anywhere."

Muttering to himself, juggling his bottle, the duffer removed a bench plank toward the bow, stationing it flat. He knelt to loosen the middle seat from slots and position it by the other. Finn awkwardly wriggled out of a garment then stretched himself in the skiff and sighed, wrapping the vintage peacoat around his torso, lulled gently by current. This was his favorite place to relax when weary, not a lumpy mattress in a lonely room. The mariner missed going to sea, missed the camaraderie, the motion of the waves. He couldn't afford a sailboat or motorboat with a cabin, such as those tied or anchored in the harbor.

"I could die like this," he vowed with contentment, his face to the stars twinkling above an oppressive bank of fog. Stars were so clear out on the ocean, so bright.

A mass in the water bumped the dinghy. Finn sat up and fanned a grayish brume with his hand to peep at murky liquid. A white shape glided ghostlike below the choppy texture. His bottle lay seeping an amber puddle. "No!" A croak of anguish. Markets and the pub were battened for the night. He couldn't fetch a substitute 'til morning. He liked going to sleep with a bottle, same as a baby. The man perched his chin on a wood border and brooded at the sea. What was down there, a shark? He had heard of twenty, thirty-footers shooting up to unsettle small crafts and tip the occupants out. *Rubbish*, he spurned. *Stories.* Then the water erupted. An enormous mouth of jagged monstrous teeth rose higher, higher, higher…

A yelp cut off. He jolted awake to the *Esmeralda* rocking in unnatural swells. There was no wind. It was something in the drink—whether the salty or the fermented. He wasn't alone, and he was no longer dreaming. "I can't see you, but I can feel you," Finn murmured into the night, his voice grave as a foghorn.

He fumbled near a thigh. Fingers connected with glass. Whiskey sloshed. He raised the bottle, vastly relieved, and unthreaded the cover. "What a nightmare," he grumbled, thinking of his tonic. Finn smooched the bottle, then took several chugs. It soothed a man's anxious soul…while damaging everything else.

Movement diminished to intense stillness, rapt anticipation. He became aware of a perturbing synchronicity, a pulse drumming with his own. Double heartbeats, eerily similar.

"Go away!" he barked. "This is my harbor! My home!"

A cauldron simmered, brewing a squall. The tar felt it in his marrow and uneasily sealed the liquor.

That instant, decades of denial were shed. A lever had been thrown, diverting the galoot's train of thought to the opposite direction—not reversing but changing track, or tack in nautical jargon. He knew before it happened, in that fraction of a clock's tick, the tale was no myth. If it was, then he himself did not exist!

A tempest poured upward. The brine surged aloft, a sinister form thrusting out of it, cavernous mouth agape, with a narrow under-flap on top. The white phantom, a figment of hysteria or intoxication, loomed for a stupefied interval as he goggled at it.

With a clap of thunder, the harbor vanished. He was engulfed beyond conical teeth that resembled stalactites, dangling overhead. The gigantic menace submerged, its trap closing.

Keep your wits! Men have survived being gulped by whales. It's in the Bible. He wished he had faith, prayers, religion. Lying prone, absorbed by a pool of darkness, a lifelong sinner resolved to give the beast a hell of a struggle. He might go to his maker from chronic insobriety, but he sure in tarnation wasn't going to be dinner for a whale! Especially not a ghost whale.

The behemoth turned, emitting loud clicks, maneuvering a deep natural harbor, righting itself and cruising out to sea. Vapor expelled through a blowhole, audible in the chamber between jaws.

Finn's grizzled aspect lifted to a pocket of air. It couldn't be a ghost, the man argued. *The dead don't breathe.* "So you're not Old Bogey after all," he panted. "Unless Old Bogey is alive."

The goliath's maw imbibed water and oxygen taking him. An orb bobbed next to his ear trailing ribbons of seaweed. Bullwhip Kelp, he identified from touch. "Just you and me,"

Finn told the ball. "I'm the meat, and you're the salad. Wonder what's for dessert."

Torpid faculties grappled with why the juggernaut appeared to be cradling him like a pill too big. A Sperm Whale had the capacity to swallow a person. He'd caught a glimpse of rugged white skin and judged it a Humpback. However, gauging by the square bulky snout that lunged upside down, a slender mandible parted, he surmised it could only be one type. "An albino like Moby Dick," he whispered. Then gruffly pledged, "I'll drink to that."

To his surprise, a fist retained the bottle. Sopping, trembling, he unlidded it for a generous slug. Heat spread at his core. Finn exhaled. "I'm gonna have a helluva fish story to tell." He laughed so hard he coughed. "Who would believe it? They'll assume I was soused to the gills. I reckon I am. Meg's correct. My brain is half-eaten." He capped his bottle with numb digits.

The legend swam forth, carrying him from land. It had to be eighty feet. *Impossible.*

Tendrils of lambent frost enveloped the seafarer's head. *It shouldn't be this icy.* Shivering like a gulag prisoner, he abided in a damp cell, bleak as a cloudy night without moonlight or hope. "Look. Whatever your name is, I know you can hear me. I may be a worthless specimen. I've slain your kind and your cousins. Netted, harpooned, hacked by propellers. I guess this is revenge." The man's words forlornly resonated, sprawled in the coffin-like den. "I don't care if you're intelligent. If you have feelings. Or if the whale-huggers want a piece of me too. I'm not gonna flip over like an expired goldfish. You challenged me. This is a duel. I won't surrender. And that means one of us has to die. Are you prepared for that?" Watery splishes and sploshes amplified. Finn shouted, *"Are you?"*

The cetacean responded, a mournful rather musical horn blast. Finn let go of the bottle to clamp his ears. Vapor gusted from the blowhole, leeward. The cave floor dipped as the creature dove at an angle—a creased submersible.

Finn sputtered, water in his nose. The man's skull struck

one of the huge mammal's treacherous cusps, now jutting like stalagmites along the flanks. Weaponless, defenseless, already in the brute's mouth, he presented a scrawny and feeble adversary. Arms flailed to elevate his chin, replenish the air in his bellows. The whale shifted its trajectory, arcing in a steep ascent, and Finn washed to the throat, his breath bated. He was abruptly wrenched inside a slick opaque tube, entering a cavity with a gush of saltwater, coated by mucous like a newborn. Acid irritated flesh. Eyes stung. He knuckled them and could discern his surroundings. He had been sucked into a holding tank, the first of four bellies that constituted the ogre's digestive system. Pressure from the whale's volume encompassed him, and fluids churned. Comprehension gripped that his plight was dire. He had to get out. This stage would smother him, then begin the process of breaking tissue.

Panicky, Finn thrashed. He booted a limp juvenile hulk with tentacles. The stomach's interior glowed, jittery and macabre, the uncertain gleam of candles, a waning neon bulb. From experience, he knew these titans consumed cephalopods that gave off luminescence. Objects bumped him, flotsam the whale had glugged and couldn't dissolve. A myriad of squid beaks rustled and rattled. Plastic bags, nylon rope and netting entangled him. By the flickers, he detected a doll, the hair nibbled away. And a glass container, his dregs intact. A navy coat. He liked that coat, but it would weigh him down. A plastic gallon jug floated. The whale had an appetite for junk food. Minus the food. He guffawed, lips squeezed together.

The confirmed lush groped to retrieve his bottle. An insufficient quantity to dump out and upset Old Bogey. The whale was an awful lot heavier than a human and may require kegs or barrels to affect. *Cheers. Bottoms up.* He couldn't think of another toast. Uncapped, the bottle emptied. Finn blustered in his head: *Take that, you fat wretch! How dare you try to eat a man while resting in his boat!*

It wasn't enough. He was surely doomed. Nobody could endure these conditions, and he had wasted good whiskey. Finn rued not polishing it off himself. The whale might have ejected him for his alcohol level.

Oxygen deprived, his consciousness winked out. Phosphorescent hues extinguished. Dusk and serenity conveyed him on a stream, reclining dormant in a gondola solemnly ushered by an indifferent ferryman. He didn't care where it was going. This was peace, this was heaven.

A shroud ripped from his cadaver, leaving it exposed to a black acidic rain that drenched him to the bone.

A bleached and bearded soul breathed air through frozen blue lips, flooding his lungs with life. Why was it so cold? Eyelids reluctantly unshuttered. He felt calm, stimulated by the waves of eternity. Finn stared at the depths of the ocean swirling about pupils inkier than the heart of shadows. Who was this man reviving him? *"What do you want?"* The question reverberated. He was both standing and lying. Without a fundament, it was the same.

"I've been confined in this bitter tomb for quite a time." Yellow and black teeth. Sunken cheeks. A pasty complexion. Gray-rimmed eyes. And an ugly gash from his forehead over his crown. *"I was a sailor, the ship and the main my home. I had everything, boy. The sea flowed in me veins. I'd have never traded all that for liquor. A man would have to be a fool."* Unkempt silver hair straggled across his visage. He chuckled. *"I've met your ilk. It was a besotted shipmate on watch, passed out, neglecting to ring the bell. Instinct roused me, then the hull jarred. I rushed to the deck. The monster breached in moonlight, white as a spirit, only he wasn't yet. 'Whale off starboard!' I called. No 'There she blows!' for it weren't a normal hunt. More that we were the hunted. The crew woke, their blood racing. That was adventure! We thrived on it, lived for it, day or night. Swift as a tern's wing, the Dory Anne listed, rammed from beneath. I was knocked off the foc'sle by a rougher hit. Straight down the hatch, into the mouth and belly of the beast. My noggin cracked like a coconut 'gainst a tooth. I've been part of him for ages. Counting the hours and days since my demise. Scoring notches in his gut with a knife fashioned from a squid's beak. Fancied slicing my way*

out. Where would I go? This is home. Ships have chased us. Harpoons would lodge when he was alive. He always escaped, broke lances and towlines till one finally done him in, a slow and painful death, writhing in the deep. Was then I knew I could never be free. Blasted whale and me roamed like a ghostship with a crew of one. But now I've got company!" The ancient mariner slapped Finn's shoulder. *"Jolly Jake's the name. Give ya me last stale breath. I kept it — refused to exhale."*

Finn grew angry. *"I can't stay here. I have a niece!"*

"A niece, you say? And how close would you be to this girl?" The sea-dog growled into his ear, *"I gave you a gift, son. A choice. If you go back, it has to be without this snake juice."* The old sailor clutched Finn's bottle. *"Swear it, on Davy Jones's locker!"*

"Ah! You're not real! You're her, stuck in my head!"

"Don't be an idiot. I'm your conscience. The man you could be. The uncle you should be. Abandon the sauce and live, while you still may. You don't need anything but air, water, food, and love. You have all of that. Appreciate it. Or fester in this purgatory like me. Forever."

"Wrong. I need that knife. Hand it over." Scowling, Finn plunged for the blade in Jake's belt. They wrestled.

"Why should I help a fuddler who won't help himself? You're three sheets to the wind, a waste of effort. Your niece is better off without you," scorned the mariner.

"No!" Swinging a fist, the drunk was alone once again in the stomach of a whale. Frustration and rage filled his heart. Who was the decrepit corpse to give him advice? He would decide how he lived and died, not that seasoned castaway or this creature of midnight fantasies! If he couldn't slash out, he would crawl.

Seared by acid, the man feistily vaulted side to side, contorting the sac, never doubting he could battle the mammoth from within and be the victor—whereas squids had failed to defeat the predator. Men were not by nature the food of whales. Nor were they quitters.

A mature squid would cram this space tightly. A man had

elbow room, and a fighting chance. He tussled and squirmed to the pipe evacuated earlier, then wormed up the esophagus. It was slimy, warm, stifling…yet he gouged and wiggled back to the mouth's pent layers of brine and oxygen. With a cry of exultation, Finn clawed out and flopped over, then drank air like the sweetest gin. There was less water; atmosphere had thinned. The scrappy fellow's head was toward the exit, fenced by ten-inch teeth.

"Open your yap, you overgrown minnow!" snarled the captive. "You're a ghost! This isn't your world. You can no more incarcerate me as eat me. So open your bus of a snout, and I'll be on my way!"

Smooth and encrusted choppers lining the under-jaw separated from sockets in the upper jaw. Air and liquid drained with a quick huff, then the base jaw slammed firmly. A minimal amount of oxygen lingered. Waterlogged, the man sagged on a springy mat, gasping for breath, the kelp stranded beside him. "That wasn't…what I had in mind."

Nerves tingled unpleasantly, burning like his skin, on fire with apprehension. The environment was stuffy and humid. A muggy film of sweat beaded his brow, though the temperature was frigid. He coughed a plume of rimy fog. The laws were dodgy with a paranormal entity. Somehow, he had to bust out, afore the whale transported him to the darkest fathoms.

Anger rekindled, and a thirst for living. He flung himself at the pallid roof of Old Bogey's mouth. Finn rebounded onto the tongue. "If only I had that geezer's blade. Or my bottle." Groaning, expending precious cool air, he conducted another assault with the same result. "I'm getting somewhere," he joked. "That had to bother you."

Finn took a respite to collect his senses, a tender gourd cushioned by spongy tissue. His head ached from colliding with a tooth. Fortunate for him Old Bogey was a relic, grander in size than modern Sperm Whales, or he could have been crushed by a slim and cramped orifice.

"Come on!" Kicking heels like a petulant brat, the man too late realized his mistake. Bogey's tongue smacked him against the ceiling. He collapsed on it, stunned. "Ohhh." Ribs were bruised. His face hurt.

The whale snorted then inhaled.

"Here we go." Finn slid as a dive commenced. Undaunted, he catapulted sturdy legs up, limber and strengthened from laboring. The steel toes of work boots sank into flesh.

Old Bogey released a shockwave of sound underwater. Jaws unlocked. Finn plummeted. A fist latched to a gold ribbon; he and the kelp tumbled in a flurry of sea and bubbles. A radiant white wall of scars, furrows and barnacles passed, bumping him. He ducked to avoid remnants of harpoons, then somersaulted away from a broad tail wagging up and down.

Ripples subsided. Tenebrous shadows embraced. His lungs were splitting.

Briefly disoriented, he followed intuitive bearings and stroked to the surface. The stubbled man devoured air.

An orb emerged, tethered like a preserver. "We made it." Grinning, he liberated the kelp's strand then kissed the tan bulb. "Go on. Roll. Ride the tides. You're free."

Would the monster return? He gazed at the night, paranoid and sober.

A faint keening summoned attention. The pitch seemed visceral, intrinsic. What could it be? His mind was a vacuum, temporarily dazed. Treading water, he frowned. Eventually Finn recognized it as wind howling through a cave on the town's coast. His birthplace was named Whistler's Cove for the anomaly.

In this fog, he couldn't spy the shore, couldn't distinguish harbor lights or the red one blinking on a jetty. But he had two decent ears and could navigate home. Yanking laces, Finn discarded his boots and swam defiantly past a bent metal buoy. The beast's tail swatted it, he appraised. A bell was crumpled. He had seen boats, an entire ship wrecked by whales protecting their pods, struggling to live.

The survivor traversed a distance, alternately paddling and listening for the whistle; tuned for the approach of a cunning phantom.

Sperm Whales were reputed to have the biggest brains of any creature alive or dead. Old Bogey was smart, not to mention hostile. A rogue, hounded and wounded, turned belligerent. Whales were not aggressive unless provoked. The majority were placid. Easy targets. Curious and friendly.

The man unleashed a sob. Tears streaked his countenance, merging with the ocean. How much of the sea was grief and suffering? How much blood? He had spilled his share.

Finn's maiden voyage was aboard a whaler when he was sixteen. Months of despicable slaughter. It was very real. He couldn't stomach the gore of carving, flensing blubber. He saw their eyes in his sleep: staring at him with looks of agony, torment. Pleading for mercy. That was far worse than blame. Guilt-ridden, he jumped ship and sailed with fishing vessels. Then merchant steamers, international freighters. The harbor cruise and whale-watching boats wouldn't accept him. In the end, nobody would. He had whiskey on his breath.

Maybe the guilt drove him to drown his sorrows…caused emotions to harden. Maybe he lost his soul like Jolly Jake; he just didn't know it 'til now.

Had Old Bogey materialized to punish him for his sins? To haunt him?

"Here I am!" yelled Finn, repentant—arms dripping above the water, legs pumping below. "Get it over with. I deserve it!" His voice faded. The ocean was quiet.

An undercurrent of activity and tension frothed, stewing, fomenting a maelstrom as an ornery presence circled. Finn welcomed the specter, convinced he was cursed to decay in a demon whale's paunch.

The sea foamed. A chimera towered, breaching. An eye peered from a mountainous ridge white as snow as the whale flew by, arching downward. Saltwater doused Finn, aggravating patches of scorched leathery skin. He spat and fought for balance, alert, slapped in the face.

The fog dispersed. A disk hovered, casting silver translucence. Finn ogled a familiar aspect in awe. As if it were a sign—or a symptom of mental fatigue—Megan's features beamed at him from the Moon. Jolly Jake's words echoed in his skull: *"Your niece is better off without you."*

It wasn't true. She cared. She gave him this phone, didn't she? Finn patted a trouser pocket. He must have done something right. Did she know that he loved her? That he kept her pictures with him, and a birthday card she made for him? Leaning back, legs fluttering, the man unbuttoned a shirt pouch and unfolded the photographs of a smiling little girl, a teenager, and a woman. A construction-paper heart with childish handwriting, crayon doodles. The treasures were soaked. He refolded them, stowed them in the pocket, then buttoned the soggy fabric.

He couldn't remember if he ever told her that he boasted about her constantly in the tavern where he ate and drank. That she was the daughter he never had.

Meg was the one he wanted to relate this crazy incredible story to…the one who would never believe it without concrete evidence.

Old Bogey leaped behind, saturating him.

Finn delved for the phone in his pants and held it out of the water. Did it still work? It was supposed to be waterproof. This would be a good test. He examined the instrument. A window lit up on the outside; it was functioning. She had instructed him how to shoot pictures, but that was a while ago, and Finn was probably bored, thinking he wouldn't need it. By accident, a button on the side had switched the screen to camera mode. *So that's why it keeps making that clacking noise in my pocket.* He must have numerous dark photos of lint. Which way should it point? He squinted, finding a teeny lens. The guy fiddled with exterior controls, viewing himself on the screen. An experimental clack. A verifying clack. *Got it.* Further monkeying produced a flash.

His hand shook as he aimed the camera-phone, awaiting the spirit.

Glimmers of white. The speed of the whale's orbit increased to a dizzying pace. Finn's legs were tired. The Moon shone without pity, an implacable visage. "This is for you,

Meg. Wherever you are." Would he see her again? He wanted desperately to impress her—to earn the respect of a girl who must regard him as an embarrassment. An eyesore. A public spectacle. She couldn't consider him her uncle, or anything more than a drunk.

Brine eddied around him. An apparition curved airborne, suspended, then plowed into the gurge. Saltwater inundated. Finn clung to the camera, snapping a tardy shot. Patient, the man in the waves persisted. He couldn't see the screen as the lens captured random, potentially blurred, segments. And knew it would not be adequate.

The water yielded before his eyes. A magnificent white gargantuan coursed in front of the lens. His finger jerked. The mechanism clacked.

Finn cheered, "For Meg!"—hoisted the camera in triumph, almost dropped it, and then safeguarded the phone inside a vacant shirt pocket, securing the button.

A cantankerous dickens braked to spiral. Tall swells cascaded over Finn, and he went down with an aura of bubbles, spinning. Old Bogey pursued. The shade's mouth yawned. Pectoral fins stirred eagerly. The man darted, evasive. His lungs could not outlast the whale; he was forced to surface, where he heard the shrill notes of the sea cave.

Finn gave it his personal best, feeling scant hope yet swimming like a champ. He had competed as a kid, won medals at the sport but was seriously out of practice. Now, his life at stake, determined to prove himself to Meg, he sprinted for the finish line.

Water boiled. A dreadnought hustled after him, accelerating in a vindictive up-and-down charge. The surf undulated, pushing the man faster. He spotted harbor lamps at the right, beckoning. Whistler's Cove. A nostalgic pang. It had always been there, no matter how many leagues he sailed. The cave should lie dead ahead.

No clicking, only the fluting wail reached his ears. He had a plan. A wild idea. Ignoring delicate ribs, he focused all of his energy on that insane gambit and lured Old Bogey to the mouth of the tunnel—where Finn scrabbled onto stones, dragging himself from the ocean, scaling a gray slope of rocks. "For Jake!" he vented, a fist uplifted.

Moonlight illuminated inhabitants through holes in the roof. Crabs scurried; a lounging seal by the outlet of the shaft gawped at the disturbance. As a tremendous whale arrived, crashing into the cave, the seal blatted in fright then plopped to the drink and fled.

Wraith or ghastly flesh, Old Bogey's muzzle plugged an entrance of the flue, interrupting a soughing lament.

"Ha!" cackled a fellow crouched amidst the rubble of land, quaking with a blend of terror and exhilaration. "Ha!"

The whale was too startled for some minutes to react.

Finn stood and jigged. His voice boomed, "I'm the luckiest man on the seven seas, because I am still alive!" The merriment halted when his foe threw a tantrum, attempting to extract a prodigious nose from the cave. "You can't," gloated Finn, reassured.

The leviathan furiously bashed its flukes at a cliff. Earth and shale dislodged. Slinging the tail in multiple directions, the sea-beast applied its weight for leverage to pry at the edges of the tunnel.

"We're even." A bold statement. Finn smirked, then tapped the shirt pocket with the camera. "Maybe I'll take one more."

Stretching an arm, his back to Old Bogey, the man grinned at the phone and took a selfie. The cave was dim, but the whale had an occult sheen. Aided by moonshine and flash, the picture didn't look bad. He would explain what the big white blob was. Finn stashed the device.

A pelagian bugaboo flogged and lashed to pummel waves, batter rock in vain. Old Bogey then lay idle, as if spent or debating. Fragments showered from a ceiling adorned by growths and cobwebs.

The vanquisher strode to his conquest like a big-game hunter admiring a kill. "You're no legend. You're a dumb cork."

Liquid washed his stockinged feet. Remorse, chilling as

the ocean, welled in his heart.

Finn confronted the world's largest nose and placed a palm on wrinkled hide. Nostrils twitched. "None of this was your fault. Boats attacked you. They speared you. Repeatedly. You were a victim. A bull in a ring." Tears leaked from his eyes. "I'm sorry, I truly am."

Eyeing the whale, the man devoted himself to shoving with both hands. "For a spook, you're pretty hefty. A little help?"

The creature bucked, flukes pounding. Stone fissured. The tunnel shattered, rumbling. The whale was liberated. Roof and walls tremored. Rocks smashed down. Jaws widened, and Finn was tossed to plunk on his rump in the suds with a leg between two teeth. The mouth closed. Old Bogey retreated, hauling him—angling toward open sea as a bit of stone conked Finn's brow from above.

The stars frolicked on a nether sky. A phantom drew him across a span of velvety glitters.

His leg was relinquished. Finn observed white shimmering balls gathered to assemble a bed of ghost kelp, ribbons knotted. The lucent bulbs wafted to support him.

Fuzzily, the man perceived a massive light-colored form towing his raft, a braid of streamers looped round its stern. Contours of the harbor hove into sight.

He was home.

With a swish of its tail, the spirit let go the raft and spouted crookedly, then immersed.

Was it gone? Finn's throat constricted, a sharp twinge of regret. "We had us an adventure. That we did."

Old Bogey ascended to boost the kelp mattress and nudge the human onto the floor of a stray dinghy. The spectral giant prodded the *Esmeralda* to an empty slot at a pier crowded with dories and launches. Finn sat up, head clanging in dolor, his feet aft, and met the whale's eye.

Luster ebbed; uncanny fumes declined. A grim eidolon melted away.

"Bye, Jake." Finn wiped blood off his brow and hastened

to unbutton a shirt pocket. He extended a hinged gadget, blinked at a glowing window. What were the numbers? The guy thumbed keys, lips pursed, then hummed with the camera-phone to an ear. Luckily, Megan had typed her number into his contacts. He grasped the gunwale as the skiff bobbed. He was going to have one doozy of a hangover. Or concussion. Same thing.

A groggy female replied. "Uncle Finn? Are you okay?"

"Megan! I'm fine, sweetheart. It's good to hear your voice." He clenched the phone and his molars, restraining an urge to giggle.

"Are you sure you're okay? You sound funny. And you never call me."

"I'm terrific! Can I come by?"

"No. It's three in the morning."

"Tomorrow then. Later. As soon as you're up."

"Why? Is it money? How much do you owe?"

"It isn't money. Although it might make us famous!"

"Uh-huh."

"Meg honey, I've got a whopping tale to tell you," he blurted.

"Your voice is weird. You must be blitzed. I'm going back to sleep."

"It isn't the booze. You're never gonna believe this. I saw Old Bogey!"

"You what?"

"I did!"

"Uncle Finn, you told me for years that's a hoax."

"I was wrong. About a lot of things."

"I'm getting concerned. You don't sound like yourself."

"That's because I'm not myself. I'm somebody else. I wanna be dependable."

"I'm taking you to a doctor. First thing."

"Meggy. I know how it seems. You have every right not to listen. Who would believe me? But I have a picture!"

"Of what?"

"Old Bogey!"

"A picture of Old Bogey."

"I took it with my telephone."

"You took a picture? I didn't think you were interested. You had this blank expression."

"I'm not a complete idiot, despite what some think."

"I'll believe it when I see it."

"And you know what else? I was in Old Bogey's stomach," he bragged.

"No you weren't. You were in your boat."

"I was swallowed!"

"It was a dream."

"It wasn't."

"Do you have a picture of that?"

"No."

"Uncle Finn, you told me yourself, the stories of being in a whale's belly are bunk, prattle, dribble and drool. Did I forget anything?"

"They are, but mine isn't."

"Get some rest."

"I don't need to sleep it off," he bristled.

"Okay. Whatever." She yawned drowsily. "I'm going."

A dial tone blared from the receiver. He winced. "Meg?"

Sighing, he pocketed the camera-phone and buttoned a flap. "Can't blame her. She only knows the uncle who reeks of alcohol, whose cheeks and nose look sunburned."

Finn reposed on bare timbers, linking fingers over his abdomen, and scrutinized constellations.

Eyelids drooped, burdened by a sudden exhaustion. He'd show her....

The town lost its whistle.

And so did he.

THE LIGHTHOUSE

Annie Neugebauer

There was always a new candle glowing in the sconce to my right when I woke. I never knew who lit it or when, only that I fell asleep in blackness and woke to the dim, orange glow of a single flame. The light was there to illuminate me, and not my surroundings, casting shadows to my left and further blinding my eyes to the contents of the darkness around me. It lasted a long time, the candle, its profuse drippings coating the metal sconce and stone wall below, hardening into grotesque shapes.

I knew where I was: in the old dungeon under the lighthouse. I knew this not because I had been down here before—as children we weren't allowed down here, and I'd never come back as an adult—but because I could hear the surf slamming into the walls around me. The ocean's desperate attempts to break in made continuous thunder, too loud to ever become background noise. The waves had never been this loud above ground, up in the lighthouse itself. It had never been this dark in the lighthouse either.

I didn't know who kept me here or why, but I kept going back to thoughts of the lightbox. In the decade since I'd last been here, on the summer of my sixteenth birthday, I'd almost convinced myself it had been make-believe. Even now, I wasn't sure.

Cold sank through the thin fabric of my clothes. I had on shorts and a nice blouse now ghastly with lack of washing. I sat against the wall with my arms outstretched like a lazy Christ. Shackles small enough for my wrists dug into my skin.

I was thirsty. God, I was so thirsty that I didn't even feel the pain of hunger anymore. I continuously licked my lips in a compulsive attempt to satisfy my need. My lips had cracked and bled, scabbed over and reopened so many times I couldn't feel them anymore, but I licked them anyway.

My dirty feet stretched before me. I curled my toes, just to make sure they were mine. I never knew what they would take away from me next. They'd cut off my hair, first.

I could never forget the horror of that realization when I awoke to the candlelit dungeon the first time—not knowing who'd done it, when, or why. My hair had been long, almost to my waist, curly and beautiful. I'd tried staying awake after that, even after the candle burned down, but time always won. I always slept.

The first time I saw the greenish glow of eyes in the darkness, I thought I was dreaming. They stayed unwavering for so long, staring so piercingly into my own eyes, that it seemed impossible they could be real, but then, finally, they blinked. Fear quickly overcast hope. The shadow that the eyes peered from was so thick I couldn't determine what height the eyes were at amidst their surroundings, or how far away.

I pulled my feet into my body, tucking my heels as close against my legs as I could and pushing my back more upright against the wall. I tried not to blink, but those eerie green eyes reflected the candlelight so continuously that I began to lose my edge of emotion. It was easy to become numb down here. Afraid of not finding out before the candle burned out, I spoke.

"Who are you?" My voice came out surprisingly loud, echoing against the walls in this chamber of noise.

I couldn't breathe for the hope of a reply. The lack of an answer smothered me.

The eyes blinked, then disappeared.

I cried that night, the first time since they'd cut my hair. I fell asleep well after the candle had burned out. The darkness was so pure I didn't know if my eyes were opened or closed.

***

The inside of my chamber was coated with the dank smell of isolation. The slick stones reflected the light from the candle as if the entire room were the moist insides of some great beast's mouth. I began to fancy that the constant groans of the waves were actually the beast snoring, and that any moment he would wake and swallow me down.

I couldn't understand how I was still alive. I guessed I'd been here more than two weeks, based on the new candles, but I couldn't be sure how long they burned. I didn't know how long I slept. Time meant nothing anymore.

All I wanted was water. And light.

Maybe someone was feeding me in my sleep. Was that possible? How could I be getting food and water without waking up? Yet I passed each sleep soundly, never waking until the candle was lit again. I closed my eyes with a sigh and leaned my head back against the stone. I'd never gone to sleep when the candle was lit. I was too hungry for vision, for light. Too hopeful, still. Just as I finally gave myself permission to sleep, I heard a noise.

My eyes opened wide, pupils adjusting to the familiar gloom, searching. I saw nothing in the blackness. I pushed my shoulders off the wall, straining forward in my shackles, eyes alert. I held my breath. I couldn't hear anything over the surf.

Then I saw them: the green eyes were looking at me again. Silent and still as before, slanted slightly upwards, wide and refracting my candlelight. I forced myself to breathe silently, gentle and slow. I wanted to scream.

What if it's my captors?

I was afraid to speak, afraid of losing contact with those eyes. I needed not to be alone anymore. I needed.

I decided to risk it. I'd smile to let them know I was friendly. I licked my lips and made the effort, but my lips split, and blood spilled over my teeth. I dropped my chin down to my chest, whispering, "Please..."

A soft scuff from the direction of the eyes snapped my head back up. The eyes seemed larger, closer. They blinked twice.

"Please," I tried again. "Who are you?"

A small, furry circle emerged in the outermost edge of

candlelight. It had two pointy ears and a solid black face.

I sat numbly staring at the creature staring back at me with curious, feline eyes. It walked one petite step forward into the reach of the light, sat on its haunches, wrapped its tail around its dainty front paws, and cocked its head to the side in a way that only cats can. I almost laughed.

"Why hello, pretty. You're a nice little thing, aren't you? Your fur is very shiny and nice. Do you want to come over here? I promise I'll be nice to you." *God, I said nice like a dozen times.*

That doesn't matter, idiot. It's a cat.

The cat straightened its head and twitched its tail. I couldn't look away from its green eyes, no longer glowing since the distance between us had changed. I didn't want it to leave again. *Please don't leave me.*

"You're a little thing for a cat, but you're fully grown, aren't you? Just small for your age? I was wondering if you're a boy or a girl. Are you a girl?"

Such brilliant green eyes. They reminded me of lightbox itself, glowing in my memory or imagination.

"A girl. I thought so. Forgive me if I'm wrong. You're welcome to come over here if you want to, sweet thing. Come on over here..."

The cat didn't come, but she did plop on her side and continue watching me as I talked on and on, trying to entice her. I only talked about the cat—nothing else. I finally had a distraction. By the time the candle was low, I'd worn my voice to a hoarse whisper and put the cat to sleep, delicate chin tucked on two soft paws.

I fought sleep harder than ever that night, when the dark had consumed us both, but as always, sleep eventually won.

***

I knew that I dreamed.

I was in the lighthouse, above ground, running around in bare feet despite the chill. I was about ten years old, energetic and already bored. I'd only been here for a few days, and already I felt eager for something new. I sashayed up and down the steep spiral staircases effortlessly, flitting from level to level, my bright blond hair trailing behind me like a banner. I wore an oversized gray sweater to ward off the nip in the air.

The afternoon sun floated specks of radiant dust in the lighthouse, and I sent them dancing when I ran by. I was on the third floor—not counting the old dungeon that was off-limits—and toying with the idea of visiting the lantern room above even though I knew Dad was busy.

The dream flipped like a page in a book: I was sitting in Dad's lap looking out over the sparkling night ocean, dark like black glass. Even then, perfectly content, my feet tapped the air with impatience, and I missed his explanation of the beacon. Something about twenty-four hours a day.

"...and though it looks pretty, Princess, the ocean is a dangerous place. The waves by those big rocks there, that look nearly still right now, are so rough they can drown even a strong swimmer like me in a moment. You are never to go down there without me. It isn't safe. Those are evil waters. Do you understand?"

"Yes, Daddy." Evil waters? I stared at the impenetrable surface, caressed but not penetrated by even by our bright beacon. What sorts of monsters swam down there? What would they want with a girl like me?

The sheer, unknowable terror of it captured me for only an instant before distraction won.

"Daddy, do you like my hair?"

"Yes, Princess, it's gotten much longer since last time you came, and curlier too, I think?" He stroked my head with calloused, gentle hands. "And what's this? Still no flaws on those baby cheeks? I'll roughen them up a bit, I wager!"

He rubbed his scratchy beard against my face until I was pink with glee, hollering for him to stop and loving it.

***

The cat wasn't there when I woke up to the newly lit candle. I waited and waited, searching the dark ahead of me with eager, hopeful eyes for the flash of green that had become my hope. I tried calling to it like a pet, but my voice sounded hollow in the echoes it created. I thought my tears had been used up, but I cried again, harder than ever, sobbing until sleep shouldered my pain.

***

I woke to the exhaustingly familiar glow of candlelight and the coarse, dry feeling of the cat licking my toes. I blinked at her confidence, cracking into a smile that split my face with its unfamiliar joy. I giggled.

"You're not going to start eating me next, are you?"

The cat continued cleaning my feet with an efficiency that bespoke motherhood.

"God," I whispered, "I missed you so much yesterday. How come you didn't come visit me, kitty?"

The cat looked at my face with eerily intelligent eyes. I swallowed and shifted to sit cross-legged, more upright against the wall. She switched to licking her own paws and rubbing them vigorously over her face.

Now that I wasn't making eye contact with her, I could see that she had long, white whiskers and eyebrows. Her ears were big and her face was tiny, and I wanted her. My loneliness drew me to her, and soon she warmed to me as well.

After that, the cat came back every day when the candle was lit and stayed for hours at a time. Sometimes, she was there when I woke up, and other times I'd see her green eyes glow in the candlelight first and call her to me. She would sit in my lap occasionally, and though I couldn't pet her, she'd purr as if I were.

***

I woke, jerking my wrists against the manacles. I groaned in pain, but it came out a raspy, unfamiliar sound. My mouth was parched, my tongue a swollen, dry wad of cotton balls that puffed their way down my throat. I tried to work up saliva but couldn't. My mouth tasted like metal. I needed water so badly. The waves pounded the walls and the inside of my head at the same time. I didn't want to open my eyes.

When I did, even the gloom seemed too bright. Squinting, I looked for the cat, but I couldn't find her within the circle of the sconce's light. I didn't see green eyes glowing back at me, either. Solitude hit me like a punch to the gut.

Weakly I called out "Kitty?" My voice was foreign to me. My tongue felt like a dead animal. "Here kitty-kitty. Come here, kitty-kitty."

The blackness the light couldn't reach seemed even darker in the intensity of the candle this time.

Leaning my head back against the stone, I closed my eyes and sighed, "Please come, little kitty. I need you to come back. Please come..."

"For you? No problem," a deep, male voice purred from the darkness. "Me-ow."

My head snapped up. Two glowing green eyes floated in the black. Fear pinged through me fast and high. I stared at the eyes.

The left one winked.

"Who are you?" I demanded, but it came out scared and weak.

"Well I'm your little pussy—cat," the voice sang in a perfect baritone.

I crossed my shaking legs. The eyes followed that small movement, predatory.

Before I could think, I spoke. "Show yourself."

"Which parts?" he hummed, stepping forward into the light.

I gasped.

He was a large, black, human-sized cat standing on his hind legs. His fur shone in the light, silky smooth. His face was feline with green eyes and white whiskers, but his mouth moved like a human's. He stroked the fur dangerously close to his crotch with paws that functioned as hands. His tail twitched lazily behind him, and he licked his chops with a quick, pink tongue.

"Go away," I tried.

"You're awfully bossy considering you're the one chained up," he cooed, his hands dipping lower. I looked away. "But I've always been a sucker for a girl in cuffs, so I'll let it slide this time."

He stepped closer, looming over me, stroking his belly suggestively. I closed my eyes.

"Are we shy?" he teased, "Now that the candle is lit?"

I didn't know what he was talking about. I wanted him to go away. *I* wanted to go away. *Please God, make it all go away.*

He started purring, a deep contented sound. He was at my level now, probably kneeling or squatting right next to me. He leaned over until his warm breath tickled my ear, and I squeezed my eyes tighter.

"I'm going to eat you," he purred.

His breath smelled human. I opened my eyes wide but the candle was out, leaving me in a darkness truer than I'd ever known.

***

I was dreaming. Again, I ran through the tall, sun-infused spaces of the lighthouse. It was warmer this time, and I wore pink, my hair in a ponytail. I'd been here several weeks now. I was about fourteen, barefoot as usual, and learning to love the melancholy isolation of this feral place. My mother hadn't wanted me to come, hadn't wanted me to spend summers here with my dad, but he'd said, *Darling, it's the safest place she could be.*

Looking out the rows of modern, renovated windows, I could see the chaotic waves thrash lines of white against the rocks below as if they were trying to break them from our little island. As if they were trying to steal our stable base bite by bite.

I hadn't seen my father yet this morning. It was unusual for him not to wake me up early with a big breakfast.

A doorbell rang. There was no doorbell at the lighthouse. I thought to myself that this wasn't quite right, but pranced downstairs anyway to see who it was.

My father called up, "Princess, it's your uncle and Tommy!" *So, that's where he's been*, I thought, *sneaking Tom in to surprise me*. It made no difference to the dream that I would have heard the boat bring them up to the island. No one came to the lighthouse without Dad's clearance.

I sprang down the stairs, suddenly eighteen, my body morphing as I ran. I slowed to see the people in front of me. My cousin Tommy was still fourteen, though he was supposed to be my age, freckled and lanky. He ran up to hug me, tucking his head below my chest as I looked across to see my uncle. All that was left were suitcases, stacks of them piled in the entry that belonged in our regular house back home, not here in the lighthouse.

I tried to step back, but Tommy wouldn't let go of me. "Okay, Tom-Tom," I said, trying to keep my voice light. I wrapped my hands around his wiry arms to pull them away from me. "That's enough."

Tom still hugged me, gripping too tightly.

My dad appeared next to the suitcases, staring at me with hollow eyes, but I was eighteen, and my dad had died on my sixteenth birthday. He'd committed suicide by diving into the sea during a storm.

I gasped. "Dad?"

"Of course, Princess."

"But...Daddy," I pieced together in my confusion. "Dad... you're dead."

I knew after I said it that I shouldn't have. That it made the dream bad. I wanted to wake up.

Tom looked up at me then. My cousin looked up at me with green eyes gone black and cheeks sunken in like grave dirt, and I knew that he was evil – dark and volatile as the sea that took my father.

"Dad?" I begged weakly. "Will you help me?"

His words were as hollow as his eyes. "How can I help you if I'm dead?"

Please let me wake up. Please.

He still had a vice grip around me, pinning my arms to my side. Tom opened his mouth, wide, and it was a dark hole that kept expanding. His jaw unhinged, and it grew, grew, grew impossibly large.

Then he lunged at my face.

***

After the big tomcat, I started keeping my eyes closed even when the candle was lit, and I was awake. I tried sleeping then, too, but every invisible sound brought my head up and my eyes seeking. The little cat never came back, but my mind slipped into an odd sort of hyperawareness that left me numb.

So numb that I wasn't surprised to see a spot of green glowing in the dark again. It was that same eerie shade, like a digital clock. At first, I thought it was the cat—big or little, talking or normal, I didn't know—with its head turned to the side so I could only see one eye, but the spot of green lacked a pupil and moved too much. It flitted around like a glow-in-the-dark bouncy-ball. I couldn't muster the energy to sit up and strain, but I did open my eyes wider and follow the spot.

I heard the humming of insect wings through the surf noise and relaxed, knowing that a glowing bug had somehow managed to sneak into my chamber. *Poor damn bug.* The humming amplified, unreasonably loud, growing into what sounded like high-pitched chatter.

The bug was chittering, nearing.

The glowing ball burst from the black, scattering tiny green flecks of light-refraction into the circle of my vision. I shook my head at my own delirium. I thought I heard real speaking. Too high to distinguish, but it was familiar as English. *Well, what other language do you expect a bug to speak?*

I wasn't asleep. This was no dream. Had I gone crazy?

I tried to see what type of bug it was, but it was too bright. It started darting in and out at me. I figured it was attracted to the candlelight, so I leaned left, away from the sconce. I didn't want to get stung or bitten, but it kept coming at me, not the light. It was breezing dangerously close to my face, and I whipped my head around to hit it with my hair, but that was gone.

It flashed in one final time and landed on my upright knee, in front of my face. I felt the pressure of its small weight on my bare skin. I wanted there to be warmth from the glow, but there wasn't. The bug was colder than I was.

I cringed, waiting for it to bite or sting, but no pain came. When I looked again, it was silent and had stopped glowing. It was larger than I expected, the silhouette coming into focus.

"What are you doing?" asked a small, annoyed voice.

Great. Now the bug talks, too? You're not answering this.

"What do you mean?" *Damn it. Shut up. It's a bug.*

"I'm not a bug," it sighed in exasperation. "And what the hell do you think you're doing?"

I stared at the tiny man that stood on my knee. He had long, iridescent wings, like a cockroach.

"Why haven't you tried to escape?" His high-pitched voice sounded so much like a bug.

"You're a fairy!" I breathed in astonishment. "How did you get in here?" My voice cracked.

"Your voice will come back, eventually," he said. "Once you're off the..." A high-pitched hum and his wings glowed quickly, like an SOS code.

"Off the island? I don't think I'm going to get off the island. Are you real?" My chains rattled as I tried to reach to touch him.

"Don't move your hands, for Christ's sake!" I'd never imagined fairies would be this belligerent. His tiny voice was starting to give me a headache. I shook my head back and forth as he flew up to examine my shackled wrists. "You've already got some serious infection building, despite my best efforts, and maybe ischemia. If it develops into neuropathy, you'll lose the use of your hands. Don't be an idiot."

"I try not to move my hands," I muttered unhappily.

I felt a sharp sting, and I jerked. "Hey! You bit me! You're a bad fairy."

"It's for your own good. The sooner you tell us where the

lightbox is, the sooner this will be over."

"I don't know where the lightbox is. He hid it. He hid it because someone was coming."

"Have you even *tried* to escape?" he berated me as he flitted to my other wrist. His tiny, cold hands pushed my sore skin like I was a big, doughy typewriter.

I hoped he didn't bite me again. I was starting to feel dizzy. Why did the fairy care if I escaped?

"Go away," I mumbled. "The 'cuffs are too tight." I could feel my head drooping to my chest.

"You've got to stay more hydrated than this," he buzzed. "Hold on."

I heard odd noises as I started to fall asleep.

"The waves...are so...loud..." I sighed.

***

I dreamed I was in the lantern room. It was the night before my sixteenth birthday. I stood against the windows, wrapped in a soft fleece blanket. In the glass, I could see my father's reflection, standing behind me in the phosphorescent green of the small lightbox. He looked older than just weeks before. I could see it in the stoop of his upper back, the gray blossoming along his temples, the deep lines leading from the corner of his mouth to his jaw.

I didn't turn around. For the dozenth time, I asked, "What is it, Dad?"

Until then, he'd always told me he'd tell me when I was older. That time he said, "It's love, princess."

"Dad."

"I mean it. It's love. As long as you believe in it, it will keep you safe."

I swallowed a sigh, wondering when he would really tell me.

"Someone is coming," he said. "I'm going to hide it."

I switched my gaze from him in the glass to the view through it. The beacon continuously swept the dark sea, as if it were searching for something. It wasn't searching, though,

I knew. It was warning—warning ships of the danger here, the brutal rocks and dark depts and unknown, unfathomable threats that swam around below our tower of light.

"Where?"

"I'd rather you not know," he said. "You'll be safer if you don't know."

I stared at the violent waves. They were the worst I'd ever seen. Through all of my summers here, the waves had never been like this. They came up over the rocks we stood on, smashing into the round walls that supported us. The impact vibrated through the floors.

"Okay," I said, pulling my blanket tighter. "But I wish there was someone we could trust."

"You can't trust anyone, Princess." I saw another five years stacked on his shoulders when he added, "Not even family."

I didn't know then that it would be the last time I ever saw him, but in the dream, I knew. I knew it'd be my last memory of him as he walked downstairs, up-lit by the eerie glow of the lightbox. I knew that after he hid it, wherever he hid it, he took his last breath and dove into the depths.

***

I opened my eyes to a blurry, black face inches from my own. I started, horrified to see the tomcat squatting before me. His white whiskers seemed to smile, and he purred, "Well if it isn't sleeping beauty! Just in time for your prince charming, sweetheart."

He sat back on his haunches, but then he sat up like a human and pulled his tail between his paws, stroking it languorously.

I suppose my silence annoyed him, because he snapped, "What? No hello kiss? Nothing to say?"

I stared at him with wide eyes, wishing I had enough in my stomach to vomit on him. I didn't reply.

"That's okay, doll. I've missed you. I hope you're hungry, because I know I am." He smiled, showing straight, white teeth, and leaned closer.

My first attempt at a scream didn't work. My throat was too rusty, my tongue too dry. It came out a harsh sigh that grew into squeaky leaks, and finally, the sound caught somewhere deep inside me and I screamed. I screamed as I'd never screamed in my life. Even the echoes of it temporarily drowned out the waves.

The cat lunged at me. I struck out with my feet. My bare soles connected with warm, silky fur. The candle went out in a silent hiss. I froze, straining my ears to detect a sound through the noise of the waves. Any sound.

From my left came a slow, deep chuckle.

Another, from ahead to the right, louder.

A full-bodied laugh from above.

I lost it. I thrashed against my chains and screamed, "Let me out of here! LET ME OUT OF HERE. And turn on some goddamned lights!" I was sobbing, my long-lost body fluids flooding my eyes, nose, and mouth. "Damn cat," I mumbled.

I heard the heavy, metallic flip of a switch, a click, and the humming whir of energy. The chamber was lit in the mind-numbing high-relief of fluorescents.

For one instant, before my pupils shrank to protect me, I saw everything clearly: the rounded, kidney shape of the walls, the empty pair of manacles to my left and the unlit sconce to my right—candle still smoking—the stone stairs at the other side of the room leading to a dark wood door, that I was alone, the rows of sterile lighting hanging down, and finally, the small, metal grate in the cement ceiling above me, with a single pair of green eyes looking down.

***

I felt like I woke, but I couldn't see. I realized that even in my dreams here, I heard the waves pounding the outside of my chamber, but now that repetitive roaring was silent. If I dreamed, I wasn't in the dungeon anymore.

I tried to blink, but I couldn't quite do it—wasn't even sure if my eyes were open or closed. I tried to move, but my limbs were long, heavy strips of meat. I had the thought that I should be terrified, that I might be paralyzed, but my mind was full of gossamer spider webs. My mouth was crammed with them too, dry and fibrous, full of my tongue.

I tuned into voices. They floated to me on a calm wave of masculinity. One of them sounded vaguely familiar. Or both. Did I recognize them?

"Why do I always have to be the fairy?" one of them droned.

"Maybe because you never fuck her," came a gruff reply. This voice was deeper and louder.

"Just hurry up."

"What's the rush?"

"She needs more. Let me inject her again. Her finger's twitching."

"But I like to hear her whimper." *Are they talking about me?* "And if you give her too much, she can't answer."

"You're not even asking the questions anymore."

A slow chuckle, then a voice vibrating right in my ear, "Where's the lightbox, princess?"

I don't know. I don't know. I've gone through every hiding spot I can think of. If it's not in any of them, I don't know.

"This is stupid," the other one hummed. "I'm giving her more."

I heard sounds in a nonsensical jumble. I felt a dark, stinging pressure. An unbearable heat, then nothing.

***

Strong hands gripped my biceps, pushing me forward so I couldn't see the two men at my back, holding me on the edge of the long rock jetty. Out here, the waves were louder but still less overwhelming than in the dungeon. It was the echoes that made the difference, the starlight, the cool salty wind brushing my bare neck. Heavy weights wrapped my ankles.

I had only been out this far twice. The first time in rebellion or curiosity, or some combination of both, shortly after my dad warned me not to. I remembered the feel of the sharp rocks beneath my toes, and how angry my dad had been when he realized I didn't even have on shoes.

The second time, I stood on the edge of ragged rocks with shoes on, but my dad was gone. Really gone. I was stranded at the lighthouse for weeks, unable to give clearance without him for anyone to come get me. I'd contemplated jumping in. I stood still, with my arms crossed under my chest, and I ached to have him back. The wind pushed against my shoulders, urging me to make the dive, but the chaos hidden beneath the surface terrified me. I'd closed my eyes and counted, but I hadn't jumped.

A deep voice said, "Where is the lightbox?"

Above us, the beacon swept in slow, steady circles, lighting the black surface of the waves in gleaming sweeps. What was down there, even now, lurking in those evil waters?

"I don't know," I rasped.

The softer voice said, "This really is your last chance."

I nodded, scanning the water with the beacon, searching. They pushed.

As soon as my arms were free, I dove. I brought my hands above my head and angled for a spot between the rocks jutting from the surface. My weighted legs flopped gracelessly behind me, pulling me upright and dragging me down.

Pitch black. The depths raced by as I plummeted. The salt felt harsh on my wounded wrists and stung my eyes, but I couldn't close them. I searched the dark for danger.

A current brushed past me, heavy and distinct—the movement of something large passing. Again. Circling. Something immense.

I tried to swim up, but I was far too weak, the weights on my ankles too heavy. I continued to sink.

Something slick brushed my calf. Bubbles escaped me in a surprised burst.

Still I descended, almost slower now. I knew it couldn't really be slower, but I was so far suspended in the deep that speed meant little.

A slow, intentional caress on my neck, as if a single long

finger stroked me—or a flexible tongue.

With vague shock, I realized I could see. Not well, but gray outlines against the black. Silhouettes swam all around me, strange, surreal, distorted shapes large and small, darting in and out, circling me down, down, down. It seemed the water itself helped it, helped them, helped them all.

A sharp bite to the back of my arm. I flailed, fighting whatever latched onto me from behind.

The sudden motion twisted me, put me off kilter for a moment, and I saw light coming from below. Green. A perfect square of phosphorescent green up-lighting the hungry, eager things that swarmed me, closing in.

The closer I got, the farther they backed away. Were they afraid of the light? I needed to get to it faster. A long, thin, tentacle traced my ear. I blew out the last of my breath, releasing bubbles so I sank quicker. The feeler slipped away as I dropped the last body-length into the aura of green, feet hitting the ocean floor, squishy between my toes, knees collapsing beneath me.

Three feet from the weights around my ankles, a cigar-box-sized rectangle glowed. The lightbox.

This was the hiding place that no one would find?

Beside it, a few feet away but still inside its glow, pieces of a skeleton rested on the silty muck. My chest clenched, but I smiled. Dad hadn't hidden it then killed himself; he'd died hiding it.

And, I was dying finding it. At least there was that. I was the last person to know, and the knowledge would die with me.

I dragged myself toward it. My head grew light with dizziness, with lack of air, but I managed to grasp it in my fingers, smooth and faintly warm.

I looked up.

All around me, monsters teemed, facing me with ghastly, beady eyes, with toothy, overhung grins, with gaping, yawning mouths, with reaching, greedy appendages. Inward they hovered, over and around me, just outside the brightest reaches of the lightbox's glow.

PORT OF CALL

W.D. Gagliani

No one ever really challenged the official account of the events, which now force me to confess and relate my own role as unwitting accomplice. Perhaps instigator, my blurred memory sometimes nudges. Certainly victim, though it's much too late to care. An inquest was held, of course, but Harding's politician friends somehow smoothed the waters—ha!—even after all these years I see irony and humor in that phrase, and yet I weep for my soul even at the thought.

Harding, we learned, benefitted from highly placed connections I later suspected might have dated back to the War, and his somehow slightly soiled record as first mate aboard a frigate, which may or may not have carried questionable cargo on behalf of powers other than the Naval Secretariat. But such was the War, and men often dabbled in side projects of doubtful ethical natures, given the desperation and huge amounts of cash floating about. Any connections Harding had made in the War were safely left behind until this spot of trouble cropped up, and then the favor was repaid, and that put Closed on the whole deal for every one of us, as well, deserving of such mercy or not.

It is only because I feel the darkness coming that I bother to put to paper this account. I guarantee that it's no balm for my soul, and true sleep has evaded me all these years, so I write only to unburden and not to seek a forgiveness no one can provide.

When Harding stepped from his cabin with the bulbous Mauser pistol gripped in his claw-like hand and pointed at me, I nearly felt the 9mm Parabellum slugs tear through my flesh. His index finger seemed about to caress the trigger but for some modicum of spasm control, while his hand never wavered. I hoped there would be no spasm while the muzzle stared into my gaze like a one-eyed serpent.

"You and your men will stand down, return to your stations, and proceed with supervision of the loading, or I will deal with you myself—and worry about the Admiralty later."

The sweat that constant slick sheen of precious fluids leaving us every moment of the sweltering Indian day, the curry-flavored sweat was in his eyes and it must have stung, but he didn't even blink.

Looking into Harding's eyes, you knew he meant every word. There was little doubt in my mind that his pistol skills would account for a half dozen of us. He'd had the ringleaders pegged thanks to the traitorous Spaniard, Idalgo, who had served as Harding's eyes and ears amongst the crew for the duration of the journey, and whose gaunt frame now stepped from behind Harding's bulk to add another gun barrel aimed at us, his that of a tiny and womanish revolver—a strangely ineffectual weapon—held in a shaky, oily grip.

A cabin door opened behind us, and those who spun to gaze down the shadowy companionway found ourselves now facing the first mate, a Teutonic giant named Gunther, of course, locked in his best SS stance and gripping the black scorpion frame of a Schmeisser MP-40 machine pistol with left hand around the full magazine jutting from the bottom of the receiver.

I heard muttering among the crewmen and smelled their fear, leaking almost visibly from their pores along with the precious sweat. A crossfire would finish us, and the rest of our mates in the bowels of the ship. All the slick faces turned to me, their fear set aside in order to grant me the honor of leadership. I was their spokesman, and I cursed the lot of them for their cowardice and uselessness. I cursed myself for having dared to lead a group of what news accounts would surely call mutineers, when all I wanted to accomplish was the equitable treatment of human beings reduced to a state of mental and physical deterioration by the stalking ego of one man, Captain Voss Harding.

"Well, Second Officer Corelli," said the Captain. "The men await your oratory."

He kept his lip from curling, but only barely.

I summoned my voice.

"Sir, we have been in this port forty-nine days. The loading will take at least three more weeks to finish at this pace. We are down to a cup of water per man per day. The local water is contaminated, or so we are told. Our alcohol rations are running low, as is our food supply. The men have been warned to avoid leaving the ship due to the cholera epidemic. We have dead men in the cold room, and we now number nearly a dozen cases of dysentery in the infirmary. I speak only facts, sir, and I must insist that you cut short our stay and allow us to head for a friendly port where we can recover from the disaster that has been this voyage since we first set out. With all due respect, sir, we implore your humanity."

My ears heard the words, but it was as if someone else had spoken them. They could not have come from my lips, parched as they were, or my brain, mired as it was in the molasses of fear. I awaited the hail of bullets that would greet the end of my speech.

But there was no volley, no explosion of gunfire in that confined space.

For a moment, it seemed as if a cloud pregnant with rain were about to burst overhead. The lamps twitched as if tugged on a single chain pull. I felt the pressure of the heat build up in my head to the point where I thought my plugged ears would collapse outward, release some sort of bile stream, and spew away my life. I could see similar thoughts in the grim faces of the others, and I sensed that if the moment lasted any longer our space would implode and suck us through some sort of cosmic net strainer.

And through it all, Captain Harding's eyes, surveying the landscape of my soul.

***

Though a new coat of paint hid the majority of the rust staining the bow and hull, the *S.S. Caritas* was still an aging mid-size freighter, which had changed hands a dozen times during its life. Now owned by the C Corporation, we officers and men were also made to welcome the new commanding officer, Voss Harding, who carried an American passport but spoke in an accent I decided was either Dutch or German. Perhaps Afrikaans. All of which might have explained the curt superiority with which he treated his crew. Before long, we officers had mostly accepted the fact that he would rarely fraternize with us, taking his meals either alone or in the company of Gunther, a first mate also shipped from Corporation headquarters on Harding's request. Our own first mate was removed when Harding found him drinking with the crew in their mess, amidst much cheering and singing. From then on, we knew that our new captain would tolerate little by way of friendship and camaraderie, and we went about our business grimly and with only clear thoughts of the paychecks to motivate us.

We were a veritable Foreign Legion of a crew, mostly legitimate career men but with a few questionable former criminals or thugs who kept to themselves as much for anonymity as for anti-social tendencies. We numbered a half dozen Americans, several Irishmen, a German or two, some Italians such as I, and a couple each of Frenchies, Russians, Greeks, and Egyptians. On any given day, one could discern conversations in a dozen different tongues and dialects, but mostly everyone settled on English for orders and official communication. We spent two weeks getting to know each other and the ship, scraping off rust and slathering paint in its place, buffing floors and railings, smoothing iron and polishing fittings until the *Caritas* seemed almost presentable. Throughout, Captain Harding deigned to be seen in public only rarely, though the lights in his quarters shone at the most inconsistent times.

The journey had begun as routine as so many before, though the route was new to us, leaving Southampton with small electronics and industrial goods for various stops in the Mediterranean, taking on textiles in Genoa, olive oil in Naples, then off-loading portions of all those goods in Alexandria—especially a large number of sealed containers we all knew hid some sort of contraband labeled MACHINE PARTS—and then wending our way through the Suez Canal, newly widened a year before in 1963, and into the Red Sea. After refueling at Aden, we took a straight course across the Arabian Sea to Goa, a tiny state in India not long ago before a Portuguese protectorate, where our holds would be emptied of all goods and loaded again with silver ore chipped from the mines a day's drive inland. The ore would ride us low in the water throughout our return to Southampton, where the ship's belly would be flushed of its precious cargo and pay the company very well indeed.

This was a scenario well known by every one of us aboard, officers and crew, that our paychecks depended upon the safe and timely completion of the cycle. The monkey wrench could have snagged the works anywhere on the route, but it had chosen the hot Indian west coast—trapped in the hottest summer on record—to lay itself between the gears that had brought us there so smoothly.

Goa was a state of burgeoning importance, thanks to the iron and silver mines, but it had not yet begun to turn the riches into new facilities, and once at anchor in Panaji harbor, in view of the Old City, we learned that our empty holds were to be filled with silver not in crane-loads, but by a constant stream of hundreds of native porters filing onto the ship on foot, each carrying a huge wicker basket on his back and emptying its heavy contents into the yawning maws of the hold. When the process began after vigorous bargaining with the representatives of the mines, we watched in amazed silence. The waiting line of porters stretched as far as the eye could see on the crumbling stone quay, split in two as they came and went side by side, singing or chanting, weighed down by their awesome burdens in the heat of the Indian day and in the humid chill of the nights. It was a sight the likes of which we had never seen, and we spent the first few days gawking at the porters, as young as twelve and as old as my grandfather, who slowly snaked onto and off the deck as if they were the cogs of a living machine.

Captain Harding watched too, with obvious disgust, from the railing around the bridge. His smirk turned to frowns and eventually to a continuously angry set of his thin lips, his eyes radiating hatred of the place and of the porters. And, we soon realized, of us.

At night, the ancient pier and the shoreline were dotted with hundreds of cooking fires as a portion of the porters squatted on their haunches and cooked fragrant curries in tin pots, dipping balls of rice into the rich broth with their fingers and swallowing their dinner amidst the low-voiced chattering of their companions. We learned to make the curries ourselves, our cook stretching the meats in our cold lockers by imitating the locals, whose diet consisted of mostly of the bulk rice spiced with the brown sauces made pungent by spice and flavored with various meats—some of which we chose to avoid thinking about. Later, the porters chanted long into the night. Eventually we would come to despise the sound of it.

After a week or so, boredom had already set in.

"Hey, Corelli, play with us."

Cards had become the pastime of choice as little remained for us to do while the never-ending line of porters slowly, achingly slowly filled the bottom of the hold with ore.

Bentz, a German who boasted of moneyed relatives, sat in the saloon with Sullivan, the ex-IRA bomber with a price on his head, and with an American whose name I've since forgotten. They were playing some crazed version of poker I'd never seen, a dozen beer bottles already arranged in empty ranks between them.

"I'll pass," I said. "I wouldn't last two hands with you ruffians." Then I lectured. "Slow down on the beer. For one thing, the captain wouldn't like to know you're already drunk in the middle of the afternoon. For another thing, we're going to run out of beer—and everything else—if you don't slow down."

"What else is there to do, man?" said Sullivan. "This is the first time I been on a load, and I weren't needed."

The others nodded.

"There's gotta be a better harbor somewhere on this fuckin' coast," piped in the American. "Some place with cranes and modern equipment."

"Well, if there is we aren't there," I pointed out. "We're lucky we were able to dock at all—it's shallow here. Just remember what I said about the captain."

"He ain't likely to visit us, is he?" Sullivan got a laugh for that.

"No, but his goon Gunther might," I said, and they shut up because they knew it was true.

Out on deck, the procession of stooped, sun-wizened old men and brown little boys and strapping lads continued like a life cycle in the heat of the summer sun. And the silver pile at the bottom of the hold climbed slowly, ever so slowly upward.

I opened the porthole in my airless closet of a cabin and wondered how much longer we would be here.

***

The third fight to break out in the month since we had first sighted the low-lying hills of inland Goa turned uglier than the others almost immediately. I was halfway through my afternoon's sleep when the shouting awoke me and, rushing to the deck, I saw that a Greek and one of the Frenchmen were circling each other, slowly, and then rushing closer together in a feint or a thrust, and I saw that they each held knives. The Greek, a long and slightly curved blade right out of the Iliad, and the Frenchman some sort of Bowie knife most likely contributed by one of the encouraging Americans in the throng of sailors who watched, excited. Behind all this, the porters ignored us and continued their life's work, adding ore to our hold in tiny increments.

As I rushed back to my cabin to strap on a sidearm with which I could break up the fight, I caught a glimpse of Harding and Gunther, watching almost approvingly from the bridge. Gunther leaned in to say something to the captain, and they both laughed. I had no time to be sickened, for I heard the men's shouts intensifying. I returned in time to see that blood had been drawn, as the Frenchman held his naked side, and blood streamed over his fingers. But they continued to taunt and challenge each other like children, so I went for my revolver—a burly old .455 Webley—and squeezed a shot off in the air. The hammer fell on an empty chamber, however, and I squeezed again. Again a *click*, and a sickening feeling spread through my guts as I realized that someone had emptied the cylinder of cartridges.

Suddenly there was one tortured scream, and all the men went silent, and I looked up just in time to see the Frenchman on his knees, his belly gaping where the Greek's cutlass had carved him open like a turkey. The skin and flesh were peeled back like sliced lard, and the grotesque mess of his intestines gushed out of him in a curtain of blood and bile. And then, he fell forward on his face, landing in the pool his life made as it left him for good.

I stood, weakly, the empty revolver in my hand. A symbol of the god of futility.

Above us, on the bridge, I saw Gunther lean toward Harding. Paper money changed hands. Paper blood.

***

A month.

The stagnant air stifles us, while the spotlight orb of the sun burns every metal surface to a constant sizzle.

The porters continue to spill ore into the hold.

The beer is gone. Alcohol in the form of British rum, a necessity in the tropics, is dangerously low. Citrus, that preventer of scurvy, is almost finished. Water is rationed. The curries, so delicious at first, now seem to have blocked our every pore, flavoring the insides of our mouths and nostrils with their sickeningly sweet stench, which pervades our lives—our urine and even our bowel movements seem to belch the curry out of our tired and gaunt frames. Feverish eyes follow wherever I go, as I attempt to keep the men on tasks for which they have lost all heart.

Our cold locker now holds three corpses, the Frenchman killed in the fight, another—a Russian—throat slit while he slept, the result of some personal vendetta, and an Egyptian whose penis was severed under mysterious circumstances by an Englishman who refuses to answer questions, even after ten days in lock-up. There is no local police, and Harding would never allow them aboard if there was, so we watch over our own as they turn into criminals and murderers.

I don't know how I've managed to hold the rest together and kept them from killing each other. None of the officers can find cartridges for their weapons. Captain Harding says there will be no shooting aboard his ship. Apparently stabbing and mutilation are allowed, even encouraged. I already know what I will report when we return, but I am intelligent enough to wonder how many will, indeed, return. The radio shack is held by an armed Gunther, who has watched over us on those occasions when Harding has engaged a driver and guides to take him into the Old City. It seems he is negotiating with someone, for long sessions of harangue coming from his cabin have been heard by everyone. Sullivan and Bentz have become the only two I trust, my eyes and ears, while at least one—Idalgo, an asshole of a slimy Spaniard who'd play his mother against his grandmother for a cut of any profits—seems to keep the captain informed of our actions.

This day takes Harding to the Old City—someone has said to the Cathedral, the Basilica Bom Jesu, where the dark-haired Sullivan tells me the remains of Saint Francis Xavier are kept, mummified in some sort of crypt.

"What the hell are you talking about?" I say, unbelieving.

"Ye think me daft, eh?" Sullivan shakes his head. "It's the God's own truth. Francis Xavier came here a missionary in 15-somethin' and was made some sort of local hero among the heathen, see? Then he gets sainted and whatnot, and his place of death is like a shrine."

"Where did you learn all this?"

"I had me some book learnin', you know! Okay, and I overheard Gunther talkin' to the Spaniard during last night's watch. They dint see me, lucky me, or maybe you'd be layin me out in the cold room."

"But what does all this have to do with Harding?"

"I don't know, and fuck if I care," says Sullivan, "but I think it ain't no coincidence his captainship is out yakkin' it up with some o' those lowlifes who're takin' him to the very cathedral where them bones are kept. Ya see?"

"No," I have to admit, "It can't be any coincidence."

"Watch your back, Core," he says. "You're our only chance outta this hellhole. Now let me go get rid of dinner— the faster the better!" He waddles away, holding his stomach.

By the end of the day, a Greek sailor is reported missing—a friend says he resolved to sneak ashore and find food and water despite our orders. Anything he carried will have made him a target for ambush. I add his name to the list and bide my time, but we never see him again.

***

In the last few weeks, Sullivan, Bentz, and I had begun to keep a closer eye on the dealings of our captain and his henchmen (for that was how we thought of them). Harding would shut himself up in his cabin for days; seemingly, venturing out only to stand watch briefly over the loading, which now had reached a halfway point. Of the crew, only Gunther and Idalgo would ever be seen entering his quarters, and then they would stay inside for hours. Occasionally, I thought I heard a faint chanting or singing, but it could just as easily have come from the porters who still lined the harbor front and pier when not in line.

One day, the locals who often piloted Harding to the Old City marched aboard with a woman. I watched as they dragged her up the gangplank, past the weighed-down porters and across the deck to the companionway that would lead them to the bridge and the captain's quarters. I was close enough to see her face, though half-veiled, her lovely eyes wide with fear. The veil fell away as she struggled, and I saw her lush, purple-stained lips and her straight, white teeth, a mouth and features as fetching as any woman I have ever seen in any of my travels, and I stepped up to intervene, but then Gunther was above me at the railing, a German handgun held loosely in his paw clanking on the metal of the rail, and my fear made me step back, to my undying shame. The woman disappeared into the captain's quarters with the rest of them, and we saw no one until the next day. We told ourselves we heard no screaming, no sounds of flesh upon flesh, and fist upon bone, or blade upon skin, or blood upon deck. We told ourselves we had not heard these things, and we saw no woman leave, though the haughty locals did take the captain to the cathedral again that following day, from which he did not return until late and then his return was accompanied not only by the locals, but also a group of near-naked porters who struggled with a long crate in the darkness. They maneuvered the crate into the captain's quarters, somehow, and I let the thoughts run unfettered through my imagination.

It was six weeks, forty-two endless days of searing heat and nights of damp, humid cold that cut through to the bone, since we had sighted the jungle and far-off hills of Goa and dropped anchor in Panaji's split, shallow harbor, and I knew that the men were at the end of their tether. A spate of less serious fights had occurred in the last few days, over a ladle-full of water or a bowlful of rice, but they'd ended in draws, the men too weakened by hunger and thirst to fight to the death, or even beyond a first landed fist. But where could you cool off men when the heat reached one hundred fifteen degrees Fahrenheit regularly, until the night dropped the mercury down to a frigid forty? We looked like castaways by then, as we had all taken to wearing ragged clothes, the fabric falling apart with the acid of our sweat and grease, and the lack of washing all catching up to us.

The hold appeared three-quarters full, if anyone was keeping track.

The days which led up to our desperate attempt to wrest command of the ship from Harding and his henchmen are blurs of barely-suppressed horror at the actions of the man who had been placed over us and who had become some sort of modern-day version of Bligh even though we had done nothing to deserve such punishment.

Harding's murder of an Egyptian sailor, caught stealing water from the galley in the middle of the cold Goan night, was perhaps the trigger, though we had seen and ignored many other triggering events. Though a smirking Harding swore to us from his perch above our heads that he had only lectured the dirty Arab, at which point the sailor had jumped him, wrested his sidearm from its holster, and blown his own brains out all over the captain's quarters, we felt a sort of emptiness in the pit of our stomachs. I know that Sullivan and Bentz, my trusted lieutenants, acknowledged feeling the same—an emptiness born of desperate fear and hatred.

For we knew that the Egyptian was too weak to wrestle a giant such as Harding for a weapon, and we were certain that had he managed such a feat, the 9mm slug would have splattered Harding's brain onto the deck. Any one of us would have done the same.

"Core, you gotta take command," Sullivan whispered later, as we reclined under the makeshift tent I'd stretched from a lifeboat davit to the rail. Almost everyone had given up their cabins or crew's quarters during the day, when the sun baked the inside of the ship like a Tandoori oven. During the day, the deck had become a sea of tarpaulins and stretched blankets, as men swung from homemade hammocks and tried not to think of their misery even as the chants of the porters threatened to overwhelm their brains with the constant reminder of where we were.

"Do you hear me, lad?" Sullivan was older than me by only a few years, but he'd taken to calling me "lad" as if he was an old man. Come to think of it, he looked older. We all did.

"I hear you. Bentz says the same thing. But if we fail, Harding's going to have us all tried for mutiny. Those he and Gunther don't gun down. Or maybe he'll kill us himself."

"Yeah, maybe he'll kill us anyway." Sullivan punched my arm. "So we ain't got much to lose. This kinda life ain't so much like livin', it's more like floatin' in limbo. Or a coffin."

The anchorage had indeed become a living tomb, and we the walking dead who lived there. I had waking dreams of the open sea, a fresh breeze blowing through my porthole, fresh cool water to drink, beer for the hottest time of the day, and then warm coffee for the cold of the night. All we had to do was abandon the rest of the ore and steam north a day or two to Bombay, where all we needed would be at our fingertips. Where the authorities would arrest Harding and his goons and liberate us, and the Corporation would fly in another captain who would take us home and end our stay in hell.

I didn't know how the decision had been made, but it had. Bombay—I would set a course for Bombay and our salvation.

I nodded, and Sullivan waited to see if I would change my mind. But he knew I wouldn't, and he braved the blistering sun to spread the word that the end was in sight, if we stuck together.

***

A third of our remaining crew would have nothing to do with it, claiming it would only make things worse. They retreated to the waterproof compartments belowdecks, fully willing to broil inside their bodies until the deed was done, successful or not, so they might be spared by Harding, whom they considered the winner even before our attempt.

The rest crowded into the companionway and massed, waiting for one of us to step forward and bang on the captain's door. I knew that would be me, Corelli, the second officer. I waited for courage to flow into my veins and move my limbs, but that was when the door opened and Harding stepped out with the Mauser in his fist and Gunther with his Schmeisser behind us, and Idalgo with his lady's gun at his master's elbow, and I made my speech with conviction and fear of imminent death.

The wave of odors, which escaped the captain's quarters and washed over us in that close companionway will remain etched in my olfactory memory until my last moment—a stench of death, decay, spices, sweat and urine, and something darker, mustier, and somehow more repellent than all the others put together.

"Sir, we have been in this port forty-nine days. The loading will take at least three more weeks to finish at this pace. We are down to a cup of water per man per day. The local water is contaminated, or so we are told. Our alcohol rations are running low, as is our food supply. The men have been warned to avoid leaving the ship due to the cholera epidemic. We have dead men in the cold room, and we now number nearly a dozen cases of dysentery in the infirmary. I speak only facts, sir, and I must insist that you cut short our stay and allow us to head for a friendly port where we can recover from the disaster that has been this voyage since we first set out. With all due respect, sir, we implore your humanity."

The lamps twitched as if tugged on a single chain pull.

The pressure in my head built until the pain seemed almost too much to bear. I looked at Sullivan, and at Bentz, and their grimacing faces confirmed what I felt. A keening wail seemed to slice through our eardrums and I saw that blood was indeed leaking from the ears of some of the men. I saw that we were no longer a group of well-intentioned seekers of justice, but a mob of ragged scarecrows in the grasp of something larger— something more complex than anything we had ever imagined in our puny lives.

And through it all, Captain Harding's eyes, surveying the landscape of my soul.

Through the open cabin door I glimpsed the long crate, open now and propped onto the captain's desk, positioned so the body within stared at me through mummified eye-sockets that were screwed shut but somehow still managed to bore into my eyes with an intensity that nearly loosened my bowels where I stood. It was Saint Francis Xavier himself, of that I have no doubt any more, though at the time I was hesitant to admit to myself what I had seen. Harding had somehow procured the sainted remains for his own uses, of which we would never have the opportunity to learn. I scarcely had the chance to register the sight, or turn toward Bentz and Sullivan and the others, or call out, or shout a warning, or indeed even cower in the face of the fear I felt. I scarcely had the chance because just then the connection was broken as Idalgo, the spineless Spaniard henchman stepped slightly aside, coming between me and the saint's horrible gaze, and the words Captain Harding spoke were slow and deliberate, delivered in some sort of chant which lulled my mind and dulled my senses—I am more convinced of this every day now—and spoke to my soul and to the souls of the others and drew from us a promise, or a vow, or some sort of assent, and made us all complicit in the actions that he had taken and those he was about to take.

And then Harding's other hand, the one he'd hidden behind his back, flashed out and in his grip was a strangely rippled blade (a *kris*, I have since learned), its long bejeweled hilt and crossguard reflecting the blinking, strobing companionway lights even after its point had found and penetrated the belly of Idalgo, whose surprised look before the pain came proved that he'd been unaware of this part of the plan, yes, and then he dropped the empty revolver. Only then did I realize that I had seen subconsciously the empty cylinder chambers—that Idalgo had always been a part of the plan, just not the part he thought.

The Spaniard dropped the revolver into the gore pooling at his feet and looked up at his master, who still held the knife deeply embedded in his organs. Harding then jerked the blade upward, sawing into Idalgo's living torso and making him twitch like a life-size marionette until he'd been split open from belly to sternum like the corpse he already was, even if his brain had not yet registered the fact.

We—foiled mutineers—stood in the strobing lights,

the smell of blood and feces mingling with the other, more pervasive stench from the captain's cabin, and suddenly our purpose seemed as dim as a light far away down a railway tunnel. We had no purpose except to obey our captain. When he and Gunther passed around the flagon filled with Idalgo's hot, coppery blood and watched as we partook, Bentz, Sullivan, I, and the others, bodies shivering as if suffering from the ague, we were then united under the weight of our complicity—the sacrifice of one for the lives of many, perhaps.

I accept now that I will never know, only suspect.

The memory is a funny thing, for it took nearly forty years for some of these images to resolve into a whole I could almost understand, and by then it was too late.

It is too late.

You see, after the hasty inquest established that seven crewmen had died of disease due to the primitive conditions of our port of call and not negligence of the officers, I was able to track Voss Harding eventually—to a new name and face, and the CEO's office of a three-letter company you would surely recognize, where he ruled with a legendary iron fist and made billions. At least until last month, when he suddenly disappeared.

I remained a long-distance friend of Sullivan and Bentz, my compatriots in our failed mutiny, who helped me finally take the *S.S. Caritas* back home laden with silver and other, more esoteric treasure. Their memory, too, was flawed, but we agreed that something had happened to us at the hands of Captain Voss Harding. Occasionally we even tried to talk about it. At least until a month ago, when Bentz disappeared. And two weeks ago, when Sullivan went missing.

I have since seen photographs of the mummy of Saint Francis Xavier, and its features strangely resemble those of the treacherous Idalgo.

Perhaps payment is now due for whatever he—we— purchased that day, long ago, in the split harbor of Panaji, Goa.

I fear the collector is on his way.

BENEATH THE SURFACE

Stuart Keane

"I always did love this beach."

Felicity caught the inflection, the almost romantic notion, in her husband's voice. She smiled at the back of his head as he ambled in front, taking in the gorgeous scenery before him. To the left, a gentle wave lapped the soggy sand.

Felicity smiled. "Is that why you proposed to me here?"

Simon turned. "Yeah...that and I've never seen a syringe or a lump of shit on the sand."

She gasped. "You animal."

"You know I am," he smiled. "C'mon, let's go for a stroll."

Felicity glanced up at the sky. "It's getting dark, though."

"Kissing on a beach, under the stars, just moonlight and our unrequited love. Surely that gets me husband points, does it not?"

"Maybe." Felicity took her husband's hand, stroking the back of it, feeling the downy hair there, and strolled beside him. "Maybe it'll get you more than that." She winked and led him further along the spotless, sandy dunes.

Simon followed his wife of two years, smiling, not a care in the world.

The air was sea-fresh and just the right temperature, warm, but not humid. He normally refrained from public displays of affection, but he'd scoped out the beach, and no one was around. Dune Beach didn't have a reputation for its original name but it was famous for its privacy, its intimate seclusion. Many a time, Simon had relaxed on the beach, undisturbed for hours. The dunes rose and dipped in a way that gave everyone, in theory, their own private patch of sand.

As Felicity skipped ahead, he gazed up at the sky. The darkness of dusk was starting to ebb into the blue of daylight. *Maybe we should come back*, he thought.

Felicity rose and disappeared behind a dune, startling Simon for a moment when he realised she wasn't there. His eyes narrowed before the strain on his legs informed him that the sand below his feet was rising slightly. As he rose, he smiled, hunching over mischievously, wanting to surprise his wife when he appeared. "Where are you?"

Simon stepped over the dune and stumbled slightly, his white trainers disappearing into the soft sand. As he moved down, he noticed his wife in the distance, her back to him. She'd stopped off to the left, standing before Ida's Ice stand. Checking his watch, he wondered if the shop was still open. *I could murder a 69*, he thought.

As he neared, the situation became clear.

Three young men were standing before Felicity, their faces twisted with youthful menace and abandon. The leader—therefore the one closest to his wife—was smiling, his yellow teeth lacking a serious brush and floss. His black hair slicked to the side of his head, through grease and dirt rather than product, exposing a pimply complexion, and his torn jean jacket, along with the tight, faded denim on his legs, was too small. His two companions were hanging back, admiring Felicity with their hormone fueled, virginal eyes. The one to the left had his tongue out, the flesh pierced with a fat blob of silver, which clicked on his teeth as he slid it in and out. The third, with a shaved head and biro-like tattoos on his forearms, stood silently, his face comparable to the complexion of a pizza.

It took three seconds for Simon to gauge the situation, and one thing told him all he needed to know: The look on Felicity's face was one of pure terror.

That's when he noticed the menacing switchblade, previously hidden behind his wife. Then, he noticed other things—the swastikas interlaced throughout the tattoos, the dried blood on their clothing, and the knives sheathed on their hips.

He stepped up, breathing in calmly. "Can I help you, gentlemen?"

"This ain't none of your business, cunt. Get fuckin' lost."

The language took Simon aback. Nevertheless, he stepped forward again. "My wife and I were going for a walk, so please excuse us."

The leader of the gang smiled, and then laughed. It sounded like barbed wire tearing into a chicken. "You move, and I'll slash your whore's pretty face."

"Now...there's no need for violence," Simon uttered, terror seizing him. His eyes flicked from Yellow Teeth to Baldie to Tongue Stud, all in one motion. Beyond them, the marina was empty, void of any human life. The boardwalk, it's faded, creaking boards and dated amusements, no longer attracted a huge crowd. The sea lapped innocently at the pier as several white gulls stood on a beaten, sunken rooftop. A caw broke the air now and then. Simon had read that the owner of the pier no longer opened for profit; he did it for the nostalgic value and fond memories. Which was just as well, really.

However, it didn't help their situation. No one walked by, no one stopped to look.

No one was there to help.

Simon's eyes landed on Yellow Teeth once more. He said nothing.

"Violence? Violence is the least of your worries, cunt. Me mate here, well, let's just say he don't have a way with the ladies." His stuck a thumb out, aiming at Baldie." He's been hankerin' to bust his nut, for ages now. You see, no one wants to fuck him, the cheerleaders at school are too high and mighty and even the fat chicks have better things to do. Their vibrators or cucumbers probably. Man, I wouldn't be surprised if they got off on a fuckin' Twinkie."

Baldie chuckled, revelling in the attention. Felicity took a half step backwards, her hand curling behind her husband. She laid her palm on the small of his spine and tapped several times with her fingers. Simon noticed. She was trying to tell him something, rendering Yellow Teeth's incessant ramblings a second priority.

Yellow Teeth waved the switchblade around, spinning it like a sparkler on November 5th. "Baldie wants to lose his virginity. We owe it to him; his sexual appetite makes him sloppy, sporadic. You ever tried robbing a convenience store when there's free porno magazines to be had? He don't care about the fuckin' money, all he wants is to hide in the broom cupboard and unload on a pair of titties, using fuckin' Fairy Liquid as lube. Sexual urges, I tell ya, are a fuckin' liability, and I can't have a liability on my side, it's unpredictable." He sneered, the jaundiced teeth poking towards them. "That's where your lovely wife comes in."

Felicity continued her tapping calmly, despite the situation. Simon knew what she was saying. He nodded. He had to distract them.

"Why don't you get a prostitute?" Simon said, apologizing to his wife through a sideways glance. He took a step forward, Felicity slid behind him, safe from harm. "Surely you can find someone to fu…have sex with your friend?"

"You're kiddin', right? And risk catching a disease?"

Simon stifled a laugh.

On first appearance, a disease might do the inferior gene pool on display a favour, he thought. He composed himself. "Yes, but you get a choice, a selection. Why settle for one when you can choose from a whole basket?"

Tongue Stud laughed. "Listen to this cunt. He thinks he can talk us out of this."

Baldie nodded. "I already made ma choice." His lecherous eyes looked Felicity up and down. She shivered. "Do I make you nervous, hon? Trust me, you'll be shivering when I spunk me load in you. You should see the socks I've ruined in my time."

Simon swallowed, breathed deeply. Felicity had stopped tapping.

Yellow Teeth. Tongue Stud. Baldie.

Months back, following their lovemaking, Simon and Felicity had laid in bed, not a care in the world. They had all the time they needed—a two-week honeymoon in Barbados. That day, it was raining; the tropical climate unleashed its torrential anger on the beautiful country and rendered a walk on the beach, a drive through the zigzag country roads and breakfast on the balcony, a no-go.

So, they'd talked and talked, like happily married couples do. Felicity began tapping on her husband's fuzzy chest, stroking her fingertips across his defined contours. Both relaxed, blissfully happily. In that moment, or three hours as it fast became, she'd created a code, a language specific to them, one that was easy to identify. It would come in useful during snooze fest dinner parties, awkward family gatherings and, once, at a funeral. A few taps on the table, wine glass or chair, and everything was set.

Yellow Teeth. Tongue Stud. Baldie.

Only Yellow Teeth had a weapon.

Simon knocked it from his grasp, an awkward palm slap from the side, one that slipped the weapon from its grip. The blade twirled and thudded into the sand. "Run," he shouted, the youths momentarily off-guard.

Felicity jumped towards Baldie, swiping him in the balls with an outstretched, toned leg, pushing off his bulky frame and into a sprint. He dropped to the sand in a puff of golden dust. The path clear, Simon followed, leaping over the fallen youth. Yellow Teeth spun on the spot, confused. Tongue Stud simply watched in awe, not believing the events that were quickly unfolding before him.

The first few metres of sand snagged at their speed, but eventually they landed on the boardwalk, their feet clonking on the wood beneath. Felicity took the lead, dipping and sliding past litterbins, benches and several abandoned hot dog stands. Simon followed her, mimicking her movements with an added, muscular abandon. He looked over his shoulders and noticed the gang hadn't moved. Baldie was still on the ground, clasping his groin. Tongue Stud was seeing to his friend, helping him. Yellow Teeth simply stared, hatred screwing his face into an ugly grimace.

"Left here," Felicity beckoned. She darted left, past a neglected candyfloss stand. Simon nearly collided with it, moving off to the right. He leapt across a crazy golf course, missing the holes and structures by inches, and rejoined his wife. "Where are we going?"

"Not sure. I've never been here before." She angled right, ignoring the empty aquarium, and reached a long straight that ended at a huge, nine-foot metal gate.

A closed gate.

"Shit," she gasped, bending on her knees, the adrenalin now kicking in. "Is it locked?"

"Only one way to find out." Simon ran towards the gate and knew, his belly sinking prematurely, that they were trapped. A foot away, he saw the huge padlock, one that laced two chains together, both as thick as his wrist. "Shit," he said.

Felicity appeared beside him. "What do we do?"

"Why lock it? The beach lets anyone walk onto the boardwalk. Fucking pointless!"

"Simon, we need to *do* something. They'll be right behind us."

Simon said nothing. He glanced around, seeking an escape. He looked up, the thought of climbing immediately diminished by the menacing barbed wire atop the gate.

"*Simon…*"

"Quick, in here."

Simon ushered Felicity into an abandoned booth. The faded, peeling door fluttered on the breeze, so he pulled it open, shoved his wife inside and closed it behind him. They both hit the deck, ducking out of sight.

Seconds later, footsteps drummed on the boardwalk.

Simon placed a finger to his lips. He slowly latched the door closed. It wobbled between his fingertips, the fixings loose, unsteady and unsafe. It would have to do.

If they kick it, we're done for. He nodded, accepting defeat as a screw fell between the cracks below. He turned and ushered his wife forward, deeper into the booth.

Felicity nodded and turned, moving silently on her hands and knees. The booth stank of old cooking oil and fried potato. Felicity noticed a sprayed stack of menus on the ground, some crumpled, some twisted and some soaked through. Across from her sat two deep fat fryers, both cold, both coated in a sheen of dust. The floor, red tiles uneasily bonded with white gum, was cool to the touch and slick, as if it hadnt been mopped in some time. Felicity imagined old trainers squeaking on the surface during business hours.

"Where are youuuuu?" Yellow Teeth beckoned.

Simon crawled past her, past the fryers and to the end of the booth, keeping low, not announcing his presence through the grimy, shuttered windows. He found another open door. Felicity watched him. He frowned, reacted to something, and then beckoned. Felicity scooted over to him and looked through the door.

A set of rough concrete steps angled downwards, into a vast darkness. The air was crisp and cool; it caressed their sweaty faces with chilly, invisible fingers. Footsteps became louder on the boardwalk and shadows flickered through the windows. The youths approached the gate. The couple heard the chains rattle as they tried the padlock. A muted voice sounded throughout the booth. "Where the fuck did they go?"

Simon glanced at Felicity and nodded.

Silently, he went first, stepping into the stairwell. He shivered as the cold air curled around him. Felicity followed suit, sliding her mobile phone from her pocket. She lit the screen up, illuminating the steps before them. Gently, she closed the door behind them.

"Careful, Si. It's dark, don't slip."

"Here, give me that." He took the phone from his wife and held it out before him. He held it waist high, aiming at the steps below, steps that could potentially send him falling to his death.

Slowly, but surely, he descended the stairwell.

After three minutes, they reached the bottom. His face,

glistening with sweat and hued crimson in the cheeks, flickered with a relieved smile as his feet touched a flat, reliable surface. He placed his hands on his thighs, which twitched with muscle spasm. He'd concentrated precisely on the steps, not knowing when they would stop. They trembled beneath his slick palms. Felicity, her hair now tied in a bun, stepped onto the floor behind him.

"Fuck me," he gasped.

"Not now, it's hardly the time," she said coyly.

Despite the situation, he laughed. "How many steps was that?"

"I lost count after sixty."

"You were *counting*?"

"Colour me curious. How often do you see a set of concrete steps delving deep below a boardwalk?"

"Fair point." Simon held the phone up and noticed a flickering rectangle off to the left. He walked towards it, reaching back for Felicity to ensure she followed. She gripped his forearm between her cold fingers.

They emerged into a huge rectangle of a room. Crude lighting was built into the concrete ceiling, the lights—bare yellow bulbs in sockets—were placed equally apart, one every couple of feet. The only lights active were the ones above them. The rectangle shot off into the distance, the darkness swallowing the walls and floor. Simon spun on the spot, looking for some clue to their whereabouts. He handed the phone back to Felicity.

"Now what?"

"On the floor," Felicity muttered. "Coloured lines."

Simon saw them; printed precisely and neat onto the slick surface. One red, one yellow, one blue and one striped, like a wasp or a hazard sign. He recognised them immediately. "They're directional guidelines. Yellow for one room, red for another. Warehouses use them all the time."

"Great. What do we do now?"

Simon spun, staring into the darkness, seeking a shape or telltale sign. After a moment, he found one. He ambled into the corner, left of the door they'd come through.

He found a dusty desk, metal, with no chair. Nothing sat atop it but a blue book, bound with metal, rusted spirals and with the word ATLANTIS crudely drawn on the front in faded black biro. Simon was about to reach for it when Felicity started probing the walls with her fingertips. "Look, there's the code. Right there."

Her fingers traced several blocks of tiny writing. Simon made out thin lines, one for each colour. Felicity read them aloud. "Yellow for workers, red for management, blue for visitors and striped for emergency. Weird."

"What is this place?"

"I don't know. It took about three minutes to get down the stairs. It's fair to say we're pretty deep underground. Maybe it's a former air raid shelter or something."

"Beneath a boardwalk? Have you ever heard of such a thing?"

Felicity's blue eyes, dark in the low light, flittered around the room, taking it in, lingering a little on the dark, uneven shadows. "No. You never know, though."

Simon nodded. "It can't be a store room. Health and safety would have a field day with those stairs. It doesn't make sense either since it's so far away. I mean, three minutes or so just to go downstairs and grab a bag of potatoes. It's a pointless exercise."

Felicity pointed upwards. "Power is still on. Means it must still be in use," she uttered.

"Probably linked to a permanent generator is all," he responded. Simon looked back at the book. "Fuck it." He opened it up, the rusted hoops squealing against the sudden movement. The cover slapped the desk. The title page, jaundiced by age, also had the word ATLANTIS printed on it. Simon turned another page.

Felicity walked back towards the door, her eyes scanning the room. All of the walls and floor were concrete, merged together and built together, as if enforcing the room; one dilapidated with age and history. Air raid shelters, in the U.K.

anyway, were brick structures on the exterior. The tunnels were then fashioned from the ground itself. Felicity was no expert, but she knew the ground, dirt and clay and mud, wasn't the most reliable building material, hence the concrete. She stroked her goose-fleshed arms, wishing she'd brought a coat.

Mind you, she thought, *the beautiful sunny beach and a hidden underground lair are two different things entirely.*

Lair.

She shivered at the word.

"Felicity, take a look at this."

She turned and walked over. Simon flickered another page. "This place is called...wait for it...Atlantis."

"We know that. It's written on the cover."

Simon nodded, saying nothing, his eyes scanning from side to side.

Felicity sighed. "Okay. So what is it?"

"From what I can tell, it's an underwater facility."

"Well, yes, we're under the...wait a minute, underwater?"

"Yep. Well, more specifically, it's built underground, on the precipice of the water itself."

"I don't get it. Why build it under a boardwalk?"

"It's been here since the forties, after the second World War. It came first, the boardwalk second. They needed to keep it accessible though, government protocol or something."

"Sounds weird."

"That's not the best part though," he continued, reading the book. "Apparently, the government built it as a safeguard, a backup. An emergency facility for the human race, providing them a safe haven in the event of a disaster."

"I doubt it would be any use during an earthquake," said Felicity, flippantly. "What a dumb idea."

"Well, it was in the forties. A lot has changed since then. Anyway, it says the facility is a huge circle of concrete, interconnected by two glass tubes, one either side. The second part of the facility is on a small island out in the ocean."

"So, if the world floods, they're okay. If water is becomes a problem and dries up...well, it's useless. Then there's the earthquake problem."

"Indeed," he responded. "I doubt they planned for such disasters. However, if we follow the yellow lines, it takes us to the main entrance on land."

"Let's go then."

A sudden crash echoed through the facility. Simon ran to the door and glanced at the stairwell. A faint beam of light pierced the darkness. Familiar, muted voices bounced off the concrete stairs.

"Shit," he said. He stepped back into the rectangular room and located the yellow line. "Right, let's go."

Felicity stared at him. "Why the rush?"

"We're being followed."

***

What is that?

That infernal racket.

Silence is my friend; silence accompanies me on my daily ritual, my daily routine.

Which means...

Noise. Racket.

That means I'm no longer alone down here.

Interesting.

***

"Where the fuck are they?"

Baldie kicked the locked gate in frustration, wincing as he did so. The chains rattled, echoing throughout the empty boardwalk. He rubbed his groin through his dirty, ripped jeans, groaning. "Fucking fucks!"

Tongue Stud glanced around, watching the dusty windows and faded, chipped amusement stands. A torn flap of plastic, wobbling from a sunken tent roof, whipped on the air. "They didn't come through 'ere."

Yellow Teeth nodded. "No, they didn't." His eyes surveyed the gate, the sturdy monolith like construction. Slowly, his blue eyes travelled across the fence down to the withered, beaten boards and along the nearest amusement stands. Chip's

Chips. *Hilarious*, he thought. *And they wonder why it went out of business.* He breathed out gently, thinking.

"When I get hold of that broad…my lord, the things I'm going to do to her." Baldie rubbed his injured crotch again. "Well, if my dick is still fuckin' working." He kicked the gate again, the noise louder this time. A low creak averted his gaze.

Yellow Teeth and Tongue Stud spun on the spot, trying to locate the sudden noise. The door from Chip's Chips narrowly opened, revealing a dark interior and a possible escape. Yellow Teeth grinned. "Gentlemen…after you."

They didn't need telling twice. Tongue Stud went first, ripping the door back, the rusted hinges yelping in unused protest. The locking mechanism clanked to the boardwalk, the wood that formerly secured it puffing into termite-ridden splinters. The door didn't return, simply staying open until all three men had entered the booth.

Baldie ambled into the corner, bumping into a set of double fryers. Tongue Stud was in front, opening cupboards and looking beneath the counters. Trays and containers clattered as he shoved them aside, searching for the impossible inside the small alcoves. Yellow Teeth shook his head. "What the fuck are you doing?"

"Looking. You never know where they'll be hiding."

"I reckon they'd have a mare trying to fit in those fuckin' holes. Get out, you fuckin' retard." He kicked his companion, moving past him. "Look, there's a door here." He yanked it open, the chilled air greeting him silently. He sniffed, shook his head and looked down. Within seconds, his companions joined him,

The dark stairwell, descending into pitch black, welcomed them.

None of them spoke.

For a full minute, silence filled the musty, dirty booth. Seagulls flew by, their calls filling the salt-tainted, silent air. Six eyes canvased the steps, each one individually then as a set, the walls surrounding it, the chill of the sinister unknown fragrant on the air.

Yellow Teeth nodded.

Seeing this, Baldie shook his head. "Fuck that."

"I ain't going in there," countered Tongue Stud.

"We are," Yellow Teeth said with confidence, one-hundred percent certainty.

"Why?"

Their leader sniffed the air. "Because that succulent piece of pussy is down there. I can smell her. We go down there and they don't come back out. No one will find the bodies; look at how dark it is."

Tongue Stud and Baldie glanced at one another, the former grimacing, the latter rubbing his swollen testicles, both nodding, defeated. "Let's go," they said in unison.

Yellow Teeth sneered. "When I get hold of that cunt, I'm going to fuck her, then wring her neck, not necessarily in that order."

***

They must have found the entrance.

Protocol 8 always predicted they would, humans by nature are an inquisitive...scratch that, a nosy, prying bunch, a species that exists on the unknown, rumour and other people's business. They've found the opening.

Better late than never.

Only took them two years, two years longer than expected. They did say the human race is dumber now, more so than the previous twenty years. The data pack confirmed this.

I've been down here for ten years now. It's about time.

Good job I'm prepared, good job I'm ready.

I've trained for ten years for...this.

Time to go to work.

***

"Wow, it's beautiful."

Felicity was staring straight up, her eyes mesmerized by the unbelievable sight before her. Simon followed suit, his mouth open, agape in wonderment. His wife turned to him. "I can't believe this is here, have you ever seen something like this?"

Simon didn't respond, but he hadn't, not in his wildest dreams.

Seconds earlier, they'd emerged in a tube, a room rounded at the sides. The corrugated steel floor was level, but the walls were circular in design, like a miniature tunnel. As always, the yellow line dictated their course. After a few more steps, a dull thud halted their walk. The appearance of glaring, powerful lights, which filled the room with immense whiteness, sent them scurrying for cover. Initially blinded, Felicity and Simon shielded their eyes with their arms, crouching down, exclaiming in fright. After a second, the lights began to dim and the couple was able to remove their arms from their faces.

What they saw was astounding.

They stood in a vast glass tube, the panes curling above them like the roof of a transparent tunnel, ribbed and strengthened with metal railings. Their feet were rooted to the spot on corrugated steel, but the rest of the tube was a glorified window. Gallons of seawater surrounded them, for as far as the eye could see. Shoals of fish swam by in patient silence, not a care in the world. Other marine life went about their business as normal, ignoring the new visitors to their home. The blue was calming, infinite and stunningly beautiful.

In the murkier depths of the water, a slope of land arched downwards and disappeared, the contours and definition speckled with black, spiked sea urchins. A tall tower, constructed from an unknown metal and embedded in a rough rock, stood high and wide, spraying bright light down onto them. Several crabs skittered over the frame, making a home for themselves.

After a moment, Felicity looked at her husband. "This is beautiful."

Simon nodded, amazed and perplexed at the same time. "I…I never knew this sort of thing existed."

"Well, government protocols exist for a reason," she mocked. "Are we on the seabed?"

Simon bit his lip. "I don't think so. Over there, next to the urchins? It goes deeper; see where the water becomes blackish in colour? We're probably just above a rocky outcropping or something. We're deep, but not that deep."

"So who built the lights? And the tunnel?"

"Governments have money and secrets. A lot, apparently. You know this...well, if you didn't, you do *now*."

"Amazing." Felicity walked to the window and placed her outstretched hand on the glass. A lobster floated by, going about its normal business. Felicity's eyes were wide, amused, amazed.

"We gotta go, hon."

"Alright..." Felicity turned around and ambled over to her husband. "Wish I'd bought my camera. Wait a minute..." She pulled her phone from her pocket and swiped the screen. "Just quickly..."

"No, Felicity. *No!*"

"Why? What are the chances of us seeing something so beautiful again?"

"If this *is* a government facility, you could be breaking all kinds of laws. Photos are a no-no. They kept this place hidden for a reason."

"So, they won't know." She positioned herself for a photo.

"And what if we run into one of them? We're headed to their HQ, remember?"

Felicity nodded, realising her husband was right. "Fine."

"Thank you. Now, let's go, before they catch us."

The couple moved on, Felicity's eyes remained on the deep sea above them until they entered another doorway.

A strange figure watched them go.

***

I knew this day would come.

It was inevitable, predictable, just like a simple riddle or the one-hundred pound question on those easy quiz shows. Everyone knows the answer. Humans are a simple race, always pandering for attention in the wake of ignorance and stupidity. They think they are superior. After all, Earth belongs to them.

Wrong. Humans aren't superior.

I am.

There's two of them here now. One is pretty, like that blonde woman in the white dress who walks over the steam grate. Or the woman with an exposed buttock on that tennis poster. The other is like me, only less developed and intelligent. This will be his downfall.

I knew that, one day, this moment would come.

But why did it have to?

Why did they have to come into my silence, into my abode?

Why did they have to intrude?

That's easy—they're after the oil.

***

"What is this place?"

Tongue Stud stepped into the dark hallway and gasped, sweat dripping from every pore. Baldie followed him, his hands on his hips, lungs pumping for oxygen. Only Yellow Teeth seemed unaffected by the downwards ordeal. His sinister eyes scoped the hallway, looking for clues to their targets whereabouts.

"Boss?"

"What?"

"What is this place?"

Yellow Teeth didn't answer. His eyes scanned and perused every corner, every shadow. He saw several doorways, all silent, all similar. His gaze fell to the floor and found the coloured lines. A smile etched his lips, tugged on his cheekbones. Following the striped line, he ambled over to one of the open doorways and stepped through it.

On the other side stood a large metal door, similar of a bank vault. In its centre stood a huge wheel. Yellow Teeth reached out and clutched it, tugged it with one hand. It didn't budge. Looking down, he saw the striped line disappear beneath it.

He smiled and returned to his companions.

"Right, good news. We're not alone down here, they are here somewhere. Look at the floor, see those lines?"

Both men nodded, Baldie slower than Tongue Stud.

"They lead somewhere in this…whatever it is. There are four lines and the fourth one, the striped one, ends at a door just over there. They didn't go that way. Which leaves yellow, red and blue."

Baldie nodded. Tongue Stud clicked his tongue against his teeth. Neither seemed to know what Yellow Teeth was suggesting. He sighed. "Pick a colour, morons."

Baldie nodded. "Red."

"Blue," chirped Tongue Stud.

"Which leaves me yellow. Right, we split up and we find them. This place can't be that big so, when we find them, we call out, okay?"

"Can't we use our phones?"

Yellow Teeth slapped him on the head. "We're probably miles under the ground, you daft cunt. There won't be any signal. No, we *call* out and make a big fuckin' ruckus. The echoes down here will probably scare them shitless. It'll work in our favour. Got it?"

Both men nodded.

"Right…"

"…I don't wanna, boss," Baldie squeaked.

Yellow Teeth sighed, the air hissing between his teeth. "Why not?"

"We don't know what's down here, do we? Anything could be lurking in these…through those doors."

"Like what? A yeti? Dracula? The fucking boogeyman?"

"Maybe."

"You really were dropped on your head as a fuckin' sprog, weren't you? No, scratch that, your mother played football with you and punted you around your dingy, one bedroom trailer. How fuckin' stupid can you be?"

"I see the movies."

"You see shit, you dumb cunt. Now, follow your line and shout if you see anything. *Go!*"

Both men trudged off, without another word, their footsteps fading as they walked through their respective doorways. Yellow Teeth sneered, licking his gums, the thin coating of plague tickling his dry tongue.

"Not long now," he laughed. "Not long now."

***

Not long now.

The one with the bad dental hygiene is right.

Not long to go now.

I've observed and watched from the shadows. I know every inch of Atlantis, every nook and every cranny. It is my home. Mine to defend, mine to uphold.

I know every alcove and every hiding place.

Only moments ago, when that pretty one walked into the tube, I could have reached out and clutched her leg.

Or stroked it.

Or grazed her supple flesh with a stubby fingertip.

Her skin looks like bronze. It smells of cherries.

I love cherries. I wonder if she tastes the same.

But, it seems they are following her. Maybe they want her cherry skin for themselves. What do we call them? A whore? A hussy? The female who tempts the male? Harlot, that's it.

Temptation is a sin. No, it's a sin to mishandle temptation, get it right.

I can't allow that to happen.

Shouldn't be difficult. They don't seem too intelligent; they sought guidance from their superior.

Superior.

What is it with humans and that word?

It infuriates me. I'm superior, not them.

And they are about to find out why.

***

"C'mon, Bryan, you can do this."

Baldie gulped, the sound of his own name sending a shiver down his spine. He began to open his mouth again and stopped, a grin exposing his teeth. He pushed open a wooden door wracked with rot and damp. It squeaked on its hinges, the edges of the door curled from age.

First sign of madness.

What? Talking to yourself?

Yeah.

Not if it's in your head.

It's the same thing.

No, it ain't.

Baldie emerged in a square room, one void of any furniture or decor. The cold, grey floor was spotless, shining in the light from the vast glass partition that covered the furthest wall. The remaining walls matched the floor, their colour exact, purposefully designed that way.

As he stepped nearer, he realised the glass partition was a window. Beyond, he could see the ocean. A bright blue glare filled the room as he edged nearer, his breath halted unintentionally, amazement coursing through his surprised brain.

"Wow…"

Baldie placed a hand to the glass. His eyes flicked back and forth, up and down, sideways in a slow, observing motion as he took in the amazing view. Small shoals of fish, miles or metres away, he wasn't sure which, swam by, going about their normal marine life without a care in the world.

Could fish even care?

I heard they had a six-second memory span.

Like Dory in that movie…

That's goldfish.

Is not.

Who cares? You gotta find the woman and her husband.

Baldie rubbed his sore crotch, the painful memory still strong. He closed his eyes and saw the beautiful woman leaping towards him, her foot striking him in the balls, her sole crushing his semi-erect penis and his testicles together. A lightning bolt of pain crippled him, sent him sprawling to the sand as his lunch decided to evacuate his stomach. He remembered his breath catching, his misery rolling down his cheeks, the vomit choking him until he opened his mouth and purged. He remembered Dave helping him up and Duncan just staring, watching their prey go.

Duncan. The guy could do with a visit to the dentist.

You know what? Fuck him. He didn't care that I nearly had my dick stamped into a pulp. Let him find them on his own. Fuck him.

I was fine until she kicked me. Stored her image in the wankbank for a later date.

But no, he had to push it.

Had to pull a fucking knife.

Baldie spat a thick, phlegmy wad of sputum on the glass and flipped the ocean the bird, chopping his elbow to useless effect. "Fuck you, Duncan."

He watched the green slime roll down the glass, leaving a white smear in its wake. He lowered his offensive gesture, uncurled his fist and turned around, aiming to head back to the entrance. "I'm out of here."

It wouldn't take long, although he didn't cherish the climb back to the boardwalk.

"Hello."

Baldie stopped in his tracks, his eyes rising from the floor. Narrowing them, he wasn't sure what he was looking at, some kind of shadow in the darkness, standing before the exit. A hulking figure, an absolute monster. The door disappeared behind it.

Yet, that voice…

"Hello," it repeated.

"Hi," Baldie responded, taking a solitary step back. "Can I help you?"

"I very much hope so, Bryan."

Baldie's breath caught, and he was about to respond when logic trickled across his brain. He felt his heart thump a little harder, a little faster. He felt his bowels loosen a tad.

How does he know my name?

You said it aloud, not five minutes ago.

Oh, yes.

Nice try, meathead.

The shadow stepped forward and seemed to grow three

feet in height. "I see your brain working feverishly behind those lost eyes. Behind those inexperienced orbs, I see an abandoned, hopeless future. I see the signals, all over you. The clothes, the hairstyle, or lack thereof, and the boots. The haphazard stains of a youth in revolt. You couldn't be more cliché if you tried."

Baldie licked his lips and fingered the sheath on his belt. "Who are you?"

"No, the question is…who are you?"

"I don't have time for this, fucker."

"Oh yes, I forgot. You're angry at…Duncan is it? Who's he? Your friend? Your abusive father? Your lover?"

"You better shut your mouth, cunt."

"I would. But, you see, Atlantis is my home. And you're trespassing."

The figure walked forward, his frame emerging in the blue hue cast by the silent ocean beyond the glass. His feet appeared, then his legs and his body, before his head finally emerged in the light.

Baldie felt his legs buckle in absolute terror. He pissed his pants, the hot urine spraying down his trembling legs. His bowels completely loosened and filled his underwear, the weight and foul stench staggering him backwards. His boots slipped from beneath him and he landed on his rump with a dull squelch, the excrement forced outwards by his sudden weight falling on it. He felt his heart hammer on his ribcage, attempting to escape.

He felt his eyes burn and tear at the horrific sight before him.

He didn't feel the blade at first, only saw the swift motion below his eye line as the blade entered his chin, pierced through his sweaty, supple flesh and scraped against the back of his teeth with an agonising screech. As the sharp tip probed his brain and rendered his body deceased, his eyes closed, the life ebbing from him slowly.

His eyes saw the blue, the silent peacefulness of the ocean beyond.

The man stepped into his view. He could see the thing smiling, its tongue licking the inside of its mouth, an action visible through the multiple ragged holes in its mutilated cheeks. The tongue poked through one of the holes, slipping aside the stringy flesh, drooling saliva down the mottled surface of his pale, gaunt flesh.

As his eyes closed, he heard one word.

"Trespasser."

***

Simon stepped through a deserted, battered doorframe. After a moment, he saw the door, discarded, shattered and broken on the tiles below, tossed into the corner in ragged pieces. Felicity walked to his side and caressed his back. "Someone didn't like that door much."

"Someone strong."

"Huh?"

"Strength. You ever see the movies where a guy tries to shoulder a door down and struggles? That didn't happen here."

Felicity said nothing. She swallowed gently, her eyes flicking left to right. "I don't like this; the yellow line is going on for quite a bit."

"Yeah, but they said the HQ connects to another island. Last I checked islands don't linger within swimming distance of the shore."

Felicity nodded. She stepped over the broken door, avoiding the larger shards of wood for fear of puncturing a shoe, and turned a corner. Before her was a rusty ladder. Ducking to the right, she emerged in a large alcove.

Her eyes widened. Her forearm instinctively raised to her face. "Erm…Simon…"

"Yeah," Simon said as he stepped into the room. A stagnant smell assaulted his nostrils and he recoiled, nearly banging his head on the ladder. "Jesus Christ, what the fu—"

He didn't finish his sentence as his eyes fell on the sight before him. Felicity screamed and turned around, vomiting heavily on the floor below. She hid behind Simon, using him as a barrier to prevent her seeing the horror.

Simon walked forward, mesmirised by the mess before him.

The room was a bedroom of sorts. The similar looking grey walls glistened with mildew and condensation. In the corner sat a pair of iron bunk beds, the top bed holding a flattened, beaten mattress. The cotton was dark with age and dirt, the white lining now yellowed with stank. A pathetic blanket hung at its foot, two pillows on top of the bundle.

Simon coughed, the smell choking him.

To the left of the bunkbeds was a dead body, a female with no head, identifiable by her slender legs and mutilated breasts. The fleshy mounds had huge bite marks in them, the soft flesh ragged with torn chunks of muscle and skin. A nipple hung off, waving on the humid air, purely attached by bloody gristle. Her legs spread wide, as if she was doing the splits in the air, her back pushed against a blood-soaked leather chair. The flesh on the inside of the thighs shone black in the light, ravaged by gangrene and mould. Specks of yellow and orange pitted the dead flesh. The buzz of flies filled the room, enhancing the acrid stench.

Surrounding the body were multiple spatters of blood.

Simon closed his eyes, willing himself to remain calm.

That's when they heard the scream.

***

Well, that escalated quickly.

He didn't see me coming, yet, he stayed alive the longest… so far, I've only killed two of them, so it's early days. He's in the lead…at the moment.

I don't like his odds though.

Predictable too. He ran. They all run. Or try to.

He didn't see it coming.

My tripwire certainly gave him something to think about. Trip is probably the wrong word; I placed it at head height. Simple physics. A moving weight—I believe he was about one-hundred and twenty kilograms—against a razor-sharp wire equals a grisly, brutal decapitation.

The sound of his toppling head smashing my old coffee table was majestic.

The blood went everywhere. I forgot how beautiful it is when it sprays and arcs in the blue light of the ocean. It's been a while. No worry, I have ample time and ample victims to play with.

His tongue was very chewy, a little sour—I think he was a smoker—not to mention the metal in it clacked against my teeth. Soon spat that out. I left most of the stringy bit in his head when I tore it out, so overall, it wasn't bad.

The head.

Yes, that's why the other one screamed.

Something about a big naked brute strolling along with a severed head in his hand. Didn't help that the head belonged to his friend. Anyway, his scream rattled the facility. I reckon the other two heard that.

I'm chasing him now, intentionally staying back, and toying with him. I think he followed the lead of the first one and shit himself. I have that effect on people.

Ah, he's heading to my quarters, to my abode.

He's in for a surprise.

Wait, what's that smell? Wait a minute…

We're not alone.

***

"Simon!"

Felicity leapt from the floor as Yellow Teeth walked into the alcove. She slipped on the bloody floor; her legs spread-eagled until she regained her balance, and ambled to her husband. He turned his back to the corpse, his focus on the intruder, the person who'd threatened them not two hours before.

Yellow Teeth looked terrified. His face was dripping with hot sweat, his hair slicked to his shining forehead, and his hands flapped randomly, padding his empty pockets and knife sheath, before fingering his jeans for something.

Simon stared at their tormentor, confused. He said nothing.

A noise pricked his ears. It sounded like long, cumbersome footsteps, dull booms of patient feet on a metal surface. Simon looked at Yellow Teeth, his insane, petrified stare that focused on the entrance to this slaughterhouse, and it clicked.

He lowered his head, leaning into Felicity, her fragrant hair brushing his cheek. His eyes didn't leave the thug before them, who was still jittery, his very being shaking like a cold kid on a December morning.

"Flick…honey, listen to me. I need you to hide."

Felicity twisted her head, her lips brushing his, his warm breath comforting her a little. "Why?"

"Just do it, okay? Trust me."

"I'm not leaving you, not after all…"

"*Flick*, we don't have time. Do it. Over there, get under the bed. Please."

Felicity saw the uncertainty, the hidden fear in her husband's eyes. They stared at her intently, willing her to do his bidding. She hesitated again and gave in. Flick. He only called her that when he was serious. He'd used it at the funeral and when paying his taxes. He'd used it once during sex when she'd leant back too far and nearly cracked one of his vertebrae.

Flick.

How much trouble were they in?

She knew her husband had no way of knowing. He was protecting her, hiding her.

She nodded and kissed him hurriedly. She walked off and dropped into a roll. Within seconds, she was under the bed, laying on her front, breasts and hands pushed against the grimy floor, staring sideways. She didn't look down, she didn't dare.

Simon breathed in. His eyes settled on Yellow Teeth, who still hadn't removed his eyes from the door. Simon closed his eyes, breathed out and focused. "Hey, you."

Yellow Teeth turned to him, his eyes darting wildly. He no longer looked imposing or terrifying. Simon looked him up and down. His legs were trembling. His jeans were stained dark brown in large splotches. Lumpy smears were visible on the top of his boots. That's when the smell hit Simon, masked by the rot and slaughter that already invaded the room. Seconds later, a large shape bloomed in Simon's peripheral vision.

Yellow Teeth buckled and screamed, taking Simon by surprise. He backed up, beside the dead woman and stood still. He leaned against the wall, bracing himself.

His eyes couldn't believe the sight before him.

A hulk of a man waddled into the room. Simon estimated he was about seven foot tall and at least three foot wide. He was naked bar a pair of flapping shorts, torn at the thigh. Every inch of his body rippled with shredded muscle. His definition was reminiscent of a body builder, minus the oil and replaced with a sheen of sweat. His feet were bare, his arms soaked in crimson. He carried a severed head in his left hand, one Simon recognised as Tongue Stud. He felt a little remorse, despite the situation.

Simon almost gasped when he saw the creature's face. He held a hand to his mouth.

His severely burnt visage was ripped and torn, his skin had burnt away to leave holes and gaping voids in his skin. From here, Simon could see his teeth through the red raw flesh, could see his tongue as it rolled along them. His hair was long gone, nothing but a stray, blonde tuft atop his mangled head. His face muscles were tight and luminescent in the light, creating the image of a waxwork model. He had no lips and no eyebrows, no eyelids or earlobes.

The thing stepped forward. Yellow Teeth stood stock still, his legs shaking. Simon heard the thug follow through; the trembling sound of a fart filled the room as he voided his bowels again. The thing stopped and looked at his foe.

He dropped the severed head onto a table beside him with a rattling clonk and raised his arms. He held them out, wide, as if pretending to be an airplane.

Then, he clapped.

Simon yelped as Yellow Teeth's head exploded between the beast's large, veiny palms. Blood, brain, and viscera sprayed outwards, a cacophony of squelching filled the room, splattering the walls and floor with gore and gristle. When the thing removed his hands, Yellow Teeth dropped to his knees, his skull squashed in, the top and back opened like a cracked coconut. Slivers of brain oozed from the fractures and dropped to the floor as the corpse crumpled in a bloody heap.

The beast turned towards Simon. Its eyes, void of life and emotion, sized him up, establishing a threat. The deep blue in them reminded Simon of the beautiful ocean that surrounded them. It took a step towards him. For the first time, Simon noticed a green hue engrained in his flesh.

"What's your name?"

Simon jumped at the sound of his own voice. The beast stopped, its head tilting slightly, surprised at the question. Simon closed his eyes for a second, resisting the urge to look at Felicity. *Could she see him? Was she watching this?*

Simon took a slow step forward, hands out, showing he was unarmed. He remembered the sheath on Yellow Teeth's belt and wondered if that was the reason for his death. He addressed the beast again.

"What's your name?"

"Poseidon." The voice was feminine, high-pitched, like a young child's.

"Okay. What's your real name, Poseidon?"

"That is my real name. I live in Atlantis, this is my domain."

"I know you were probably told that. What was your name before you came to Atlantis."

"I didn't have one."

"Yes, you did. You had a home, a family, a life."

Poseidon said nothing. His eyes twinkled in the light, seemed to bulge without the eyelids and skin to protect them. *Was it...he...he thinking?*

Its eyes flicked to the right, Simon's left, and stared at the mutilated corpse. Simon swatted away a fly as he gave the rotting body a wide berth. He noticed the look, one of longing, one of despair, buried beneath unknown tragedy and heartbreak.

"How long have you been down here?" Simon asked, taking a gamble.

The creature didn't respond straight away, its eyes glued to the corpse. After a moment, he averted his gaze and looked at Simon. "Ten years."

"That's a long time." Simon moved his body, kept level with the being, ensuring it didn't glance down and see Felicity. He placed a hand on his back, in full sight of his wife. "You were stationed here?"

"Atlantis, yes. Poseidon, yes. I was part of a ten-man crew who came down here, to do research and study the seabed, to study nature's true calling."

Simon nodded. "And what is that?"

The creature narrowed its eyes. Simon marveled at how the orbs shrunk but the torn muscle stayed as it was, didn't restrict. He wondered how long it had been since Poseidon last had a conversation.

He continued. "After a year, we found…something. An oil, unlike any other I'd ever seen, deep beneath the seabed. It was blue, like the sea, easily lost in the gallons of water that we take for granted every day. I wouldn't even call it an oil, except for the smoothness of the liquid. Once it's on your skin, you can't get it off…which is why so many people died."

Simon gulped, starting to regret his line of questioning.

"They all died, one by one, slowly, in a random pattern. The first succumbed to the pressure; the bends turned him insane. I saw him bash his brains in on one of the strengthened panes of glass. He kept going, head butting the glass; long after his cerebral material had turned to absolute mush. At the end, all I heard was the sound of empty, cracked skull scraping on the glass. It took me a day to clean the pink spongy tissue from the rec room. That's when I realised something was wrong."

Simon nodded. He was about to speak when Poseidon took a giant step forward.

"Have you ever seen a man pluck his eyeballs from his own head? Or a woman, who was six months pregnant, abort her unborn child with a pool cue. I mean, really shove it up there. It ripped her internal organs. I found her body slumped in the bathroom, head cracked on the sink, blood spraying everywhere. Some killed themselves, driven insane by… something. They said it was the oil and I believed them."

Simon swiped his forehead, wiping away the sweat. He started tapping on his back with his right hand, hoping his wife could decipher the code. "Where…where is the oil now?"

Poseidon shook his head. "No, I can't tell you that. I swore I would protect it, keep it hidden from harm. I won't allow the human race to have it, to bring humanity to its knees. These guys were trying to take it." The man pointed to Yellow Teeth, and the mutilated head of Tongue Stud. "I wouldn't let them. And I won't let you."

Simon held up his left hand, his right still on the small of his back. "I'm not here for the oil, I'm…I'm here because those guys chased me down here." He swallowed. "You saved my life."

Poseidon shook his head, laughing. "You don't fool me. You see me and think I'm a freak. Others did, when I started… morphing, changing. People gave me a wide berth, but I heard the sniggers, the whispers, I caught the sideways glances. No one helped me when my skin started to flake, then drop off in large chunks. No one will ever feel the agony I experienced when my muscles expanded and stretched, tearing and forming before her very eyes." He pointed to the corpse behind Simon. "No one tried to stop me when I dunked my face in petrol and set it alight. No one!"

"So, you weren't here alone?"

"No, I had a bunkmate. Her."

"So where is everyone? Did they all die?" Simon asked, knowing the answer.

"Yes, some had what I had, but not to such an extent. One lucky bastard died immediately, his heart exploded. His body started to form and mutate long after his last breath. It was a weird and horrific moment, watching his twitching corpse slide and wiggle along the ground, bones cracking, muscles tearing."

"How did you cope?" Simon edged towards Felicity. He knew they had to escape, no matter what. Staying was not an option. He tapped it out on his back, telling her to get ready.

"We returned to our basic instincts. We fucked like animals, fighting the pain and sadness that was enveloping Atlantis. Before long, everyone was dead, except us. We cleaned the bodies up, disposed of them. After a while, she died too, my mutation became too strong. I broke her back and suffocated her without realizing. After several minutes, I realised she was no longer moving. I finished inside her before I climbed off, scared to withhold such urges under the power of the oil."

A wave of nausea made Simon lick his lips, gasp for air in the humid room.

"It's all about the oil," Poseidon finished.

"So, you're the only person here?" Simon tensed his legs, ready to run.

We can outrun it; we know the way back. He killed the thugs, which gets them out of our hair. We can make it.

"Now, it's just me. Me and the oil."

"I'm sorry about your wife," Simon said. *Time to distract him enough so Felicity can run.*

"I never said it was my wife."

Simon stopped, his eyes locking onto Poseidon, a tremor or horror trickling through his body. "What, she was your girlfriend?"

"My sister."

Simon felt his stomach rotate, his lunch started to bubble down below, the words he'd heard came back to him slowly. *Fucked. Animals. Broke her back. Finished inside her.* "What…?"

"The oil tells you what to do, not the other way around. There are no rules, no boundaries on the seabed, no laws of life. No restrictions, no taboos. There is man, woman, and the oil. Primitive, like in the olden days. My sister knew this, I could tell by her screaming, the resistance, and her refusal to give in to her sexual urges. The oil affects everyone differently."

Simon heard Felicity climb up from beneath the bed and turned, his equilibrium stunned by the revelation. Felicity gripped her husband, her eyes watching Poseidon. Simon turned to her, the taste of vomit burning his throat. "Run…go."

But it didn't happen.

Poseidon swiped out. Felicity flew back into the bed, toppled over it and crumpled to a heap on the floor. Simon turned to the monster, his eyes blurred, his legs trembling.

"That's the thing with the oil…get too close and it renders even the most intelligent useless."

Simon felt his eyes close and blackness enveloped him.

***

It's been an eventful week. People tried to take the oil, and failed. Protocol 8 dictated that, one day, this moment would come. It did. They failed. I expected a bigger fight from the human race, a bigger threat from the rulers of Earth.

Seems they didn't prepare for the oil.

The oil is the all-consuming being.

Right now, I'm sharpening my blade. Kerry, bless her, is no longer of use. I can only consume so much gangrenous flesh. Now, I have fresh meat, enough to last me a few weeks.

I watch as…what does the man call her? Flick? Yes, I watch as Flick struggles, tied to the pool table. I'm quite getting used to its new coppery colour. Green never suited it.

The man struggles, but he is weak, near the end of his tether. I feed the female first, after all, I can get much more use out of her. The man is useless, surplus to requirements. He'll soon be joining Kerry on the treacherous seabed.

Yes, the woman has much more use.

Much more.

ONCE TOLLED THE LUTINE BELL

Jack Rollins

"Yer a damned cold, hard man, Jack Snow," said the silver-haired Scotsman, Matthew Dent.

"Dent, now ye know as well as I do that business is business."

"Now you sound like your father. You're becoming him through and through."

Snow cast his old mentor an angry glance, his narrow jaw clenched, and head cocked at an angle, almost suggested curiosity. His mouth betrayed his mind with the question, "Now what on earth do ye mean by that, ye old conniving bastard?"

Dent chuckled. "It means yer a throwback to the auld man after all."

"And do ye mean tae suggest that this is a bad thing, Dent?"

Dent pursed his lips and turned to gaze out of the window of the luxuriously appointed offices of Snow and Sons, at the scuffed masts and battered chimney of the aged *Red Scout*, noting the ragtag band of men scurrying about her, making ready for sea. "Yer father was a successful man, Jack. But he wasnae a very happy man."

"I'm not sure I care for your line of conversation, Dent."

"If ye dinna care for the men oan that ship, then I dinna expect ye tae care for the ramblings of old friends. But ramble I will. I've lived long enough tae earn the right tae ramble awhile. It always aggrieved your dear mother that she couldnae lift the spirits of old Jock Snow. I want you tae think about that, Jack. Think of how your mother was, and I want you to think to your own household, in future, a family, if ye should see fit." Dent turned to face his young master once more. "You see, what she found out the hard way was that it is impossible to lift the heart of a man, when that organ is so weighted with regret."

Snow stood and took position at the window, staring down at the doomed vessel. "You sound like a man tempted to offer his resignation."

Dent sighed and patted the younger man's bony shoulder. "I'm with you til I drop, lad. Not because I want to, but because I see in you my destiny."

"Which is?"

"With what I know, Jack, my resignation letter might as well be a suicide note."

Snow squeezed his mentor's fingers with a firm pressure meant only to reassure, not to threaten. "I have seen what I have to become to make way in this world, Dent. If stand idly by, then I get to bear witness to this company, the legacy of my father and his father, waste away. The Burton Company has pecked and nibbled away at us for decades. I can't let that old bitch take it all away from me now." His fingers danced across the lip of a hat-sized, ash-filled brazier stood on a steel pedestal to the left of the window.

"This superstitious nonsense will do you no good, either, Jack," Dent sighed, noting Snow's preoccupation with the brazier. "What good it does to burn money while you say you are so in need of it, is anyone's guess."

As Snow observed the busy London and St Katherine Docks, he considered the *Red Scout* standing convincingly fast as ominous tendrils of fog probed her starboard side. Laden with the poorest quality coal he could purchase, to then run with the shabbiest sails in his fleet. The battered steamer, and the crew of drunks he had assembled to man her, made for a damned pitiful sight by comparison to the vision of next berth, where the *Red Stallion* made ready, a sturdy crew cutting about her with rapid, precise movements.

He turned to his selection of whiskies, trying desperately to stifle the gulp he could feel swelling within his throat. He had to conceal this show of concern from Dent.

"Something on your mind, Jack?" Dent was wise enough to turn his gaze back to the bustling docks, rather than maintain his watch over Snow. He knew the younger man would unleash that savage tongue of his, should he realize that his gulp had not gone unnoticed.

Snow did not respond. Not with words, anyway. The heavy bottle of fine Basker's single malt thumped against the back of Dent's skull, felling the man with one blow. Dent's legs gave way, and his forehead struck the glass pane before him.

A crack arced across the blood-smeared glass, and Dent settled in a heap on the floor. Dark blood soon matted the grey waves of hair that met his crisp white shirt collar and leaked from his broken nose.

Snow strode to the office doors, snatching them open. The red-faced Dutchman, Gosseling and one of his foul-smelling ship thugs stood ready. "Take this traitor aboard and make away within the hour. Nobody, *nobody* is to approach this man until you are ten miles out, do ye hear?"

"Aye, sir!"

"And when ye reach Calcutta, ye are tae drop him there with only the clothes oan his back!"

The doors closed once more, and Snow opened his strongbox. He selected a wedge of twenty valuable pieces of paper—debts he was yet to collect—debts which any of his advisors would instruct him to call in immediately, or sell on to a factor to free up the cash. Instead, he strode to the brazier, stuffed the documents into the aperture and picked at the shilling-sized scab on his left palm. He scratched the raw skin beneath the scab, exciting blood from the wound. A few drops was all he needed and before long, thick dark crimson droplets splattered heavily on the notes. Snow struck a match and coaxed the flame to catch the corner of one of the bills. Within seconds, the paper curled and blackened as the confined fire devoured it.

Snow bowed his head, muttering incantations under his breath, with his eyes shut tight. Beneath, on the docks, Dent's polished shoes scraped across the wooden planks of the gangway and up onto the deck of the *Red Scout*.

***

The *Red Scout* lurched over the back of another crushing wave, and Gosseling cursed his orders, cursed that bastard Jack Snow and cursed the treacherous Portuguese coast. He wiped briny spray from his thick eyebrows with the sleeve of his greatcoat and stalked amidships of the beleaguered steamer in his charge. Around him, the crew worked to shut and seal with tarpaulin every hatch and opening they could, fearful that this terrible gale could only get worse before their situation could improve at all.

"Dacre!" he yelled, eyeing the sails as the wild wind threatened to tear them from the ship, masts and all.

"Aye, sir!"

"Where is my steam? Do these men intend to power this ship under the heat of but a single candle?"

"Sir, with God as my judge, the men spend so much coal I fear we won't make it but ten more miles! It gives off no heat, sir! They would be better suited with a handful of candles, I would swear to it!"

"Reef these sails, damn you!" Gosseling bellowed, then his eyes caught sight of the great grey swell rising before the ship. "Brace!" Gosseling roared in horror as the churning sea reared up before the *Scout*, tipping the bow skyward. Men staggered even more drunkenly than their usual disorderly gait as they fought against the violent lurch of the boards beneath them.

The wave broke, pouring gallons of frothy brine over the deck. The bowsprit dipped low as the *Red Scout* surged forth, tipping down at ever such a steep angle that for a moment the captain feared they would sail in a straight line downward, ever downward, fathom by fearful fathom, right to the bottom of the sea.

Wood groaned against the irresistible force of the sea as the beautiful Cherokee girl figurehead vanished beneath the waves, and the bowsprit cracked as the *Scout* fought to right herself once more, scooping up another treacherous wash of rushing water to flow across the deck.

"Man overboard!" came the cry.

"Dacre, take the name!" Gosseling bellowed as a clutch of crewmen leaned over the port side bulwarks, throwing ropes to their doomed fellow, screaming as the furious waves smashed his head against the waterline, before pressing him into the crushing deep.

That the *Red Scout* had turned a few degrees was almost imperceptible, but even years of sloth and drink could not dampen Gosseling's instincts that much—least of all his survival instinct. The captain turned to face the bridge, where the pilot, a weather-beaten fellow Dutchman name Van Semple swayed and clutched the helm as though his life depended upon it. Unfortunately in doing so, he had allowed the ship to veer starboard ever so slightly, revealing more of the port side to the elements.

"Van Semple, you fool! Turn this bitch three degrees to port!" Gosseling had mistaken the shift for an intentional move. He feared the pilot was about to order them men to attempt a starboard tack, to work upwind without the benefit of the engines. He knew with such powerful waves the ship could be forced over and capsize, and that they had to sail dead ahead to cleave through the wild sea.

Van Semple responded with a booming, "Aye, Sorr!" But it was too late.

Before the ship could correct its course, another almighty wave carried her aloft, not breaking until she had risen forty feet. "Jesus Christ!" Gosseling bellowed, grasping the starboard bulwark and hanging on with both arms locked in place.

The damaged bowsprit finally gave way, tearing loose as the wave broke over the bow, carrying the timber rod backwards where it lodged against the forecastle, splintering planks of that structure, prevented from flying further back across the deck by the sheer tension of the rigging. The *Scout* lurched to port with a sudden, jerking violence that cast another three crewmen into the deep.

Gosseling gritted his teeth in anticipation of the *righting moment*, as Van Semple battled to carry the ship a few degrees to port. He shouted with exertion, and the captain tried to haul himself along the deck, against the downward momentum of the ship as it finally tipped over the back of the wave, trying desperately to get to the pilot to assist him to return the ship to a safe course.

The rigging squealed and snapped at the front of the ship. A capstan broke loose, freeing the fore mast boom, allowing it to swing wildly in the gale. The capstan whipped across the width of the deck. Gosseling yelled a warning, but it was too late. Dacre took the full force of the bulky iron node in his chest, sending him cartwheeling across the ship to land in a bloody heap against the port bulwark.

"Davis! You're with me!" Gosseling called, beckoning the most capable hand he could see, and the two pushed into the shelter of the cabin, beating a course straight to the engine room where the stokers and greasers swore and damned the poor coal Snow had provided them with. One of the engineers took a long swig from a bottle of cheap gin he had picked up in London.

Gosseling snatched the bottle away and hurled it into the open jaws of the starving firebox. "Drink will do no good, lads! If we can't get some power into this bitch, we'll all be on the bottom, now I need your wits about you!"

"Wits? I've wit aplenty, but unfortunately wits are as combustible as this fucking coal, *Sorr!*"

Gosseling should have been shouting to be heard under the normal conditions of a steamer's engine room, but the engines were so underpowered, and the pistons driven so slowly that the conversation was held at an almost civilized volume. The captain's ears pricked up as a sound met his ears, one as unwelcome as the lack of sound in the engine room. The sound of laughter. Hysterical, mad laughter.

***

Dent lay curled up in a shadowy corner to the stern of the cargo hold, tied to a metal ring fixed in the deck, usually reserved for tying crates down. It was usually an effective way of keeping the ship's goods in place, but ropes and chains groaned against their burdens as nature's frenzy tested the *Red Scout* to the very limits of her design.

Dent's laughter came in fits and starts and he cowered, averting his eyes, as Gosseling's bullseye lantern cast light across his face.

"You appear to find humour in the strangest of situations, my friend," Gosseling growled, steadying himself against a crate.

The hold had begun to carry water, and Davis called the crew to man the pumps. This command brought about the greatest response from the men, either because they knew this meant they could all be about to drown, or because it meant they could work as far from the battered deck as possible.

"Snow has murdered us all. We are to be chalked up along with the goods and chattels lost on this ship, I am afraid."

"He would never do that, liar!" Gosseling roared.

"You and all the drunken wee miscreants aboard signed a contract to take this ship to hell! Any minute now the hull will begin to fracture; he paid well to have this ship sabotaged."

"Impossible!"

"Gosseling, you've lost your touch, man! You are every bit of you the rum-soaked idiot Snow took you for. Ye set sail and didnae check your ship properly. You were too busy taking your pay for dragging my arse aboard. Well, my friend, here we go, down to the fucking bottom together! Lloyds have Snow well insured for the loss, and as soon as that Lutine bell tolls, he'll be at those underwriters, and a handsome wee profit will be made from our souls!"

"You are a liar and a traitor, Dent!"

"You hesitated, Gosseling. You hear those bilge pumps doing their work and all that clanking is like the cogs in your fucking thick head turning over. If ye dinna believe me, check these boxes. What is it supposed to be, barley, wool, whisky and soap or some such?"

Gosseling firmed his jaw, not wishing to confirm Dent's assumption, but his eyes averted the old Scotsman's gaze. He could no longer pretend. "Davis! Open these crates. I want to see what our Mr. Snow has arranged for us to carry."

"That's my boy!" Dent encouraged. "Do as he says, Davis. And then ye'll see. Ye'll see that this is a ship bound for Hell!"

As Davis pried open the first box, Dent fell back into his maniacal laughter. Worthless rags fell loose from the opening, and Davis reached in deeper, drawing out a clutch of paper. "*Sorr! Sorr!* It's money and… I think it's paintings…and chairs!"

"It's fucking what?" Dent howled, delirious in these, his final moments. "Listen to me, Gosseling. Snow is a desperate man. He has appealed to a force darker than you or I could believe possible. He has struck a bargain, sacrificing his personal wealth, and it is we who are to be forfeit."

"The Devil? I need no ghost stories here, old man!"

"No' the Devil, but you're close. 'Tis Mammon, the demon of greed! Now, when I heard about this, I thought old Jack had gone mad under the pressure of the Burtons making ready to take his company off him, but your old pilot up there, he's done nothing to get you out of this fucking tempest has he?"

"The storm came upon us from nowhere!" Gosseling snapped.

"Then a deal indeed was struck. You and your men best be on good terms with God, is all I can say!"

Gosseling ran full pace against the tilting ship, bursting out onto the deck in time to see the fore topgallant mast plummet towards him, harpooning the redundant chimney. Eyes narrowed against the lashing rain, the captain scanned his ship, assessing the despair of his wounded, bleeding crew, the shredded sails, tortured rigging and collapsing masts.

Metal and wood screamed off the port side, and Gosseling dared to peer into the deep, black sea in time to bear witness to the coppered hull splitting apart, opening a vast rent into which hundreds upon hundreds of gallons of water rushed.

The captain tore at his hair, screaming defiance to God, who even in his limitless power could not save them now. Producing a dagger from his belt, Gosseling wept bitter, angry tears as the *Red Scout* dipped down, the sea seeming to suck away from her, impossibly shallow, and at a terrifying, sharp angle. Before him grew the killing wave, the final stroke. He knew that the ship could never right before the surging tower of water claimed them.

"Snow, you bastard! You are not the only man under the sun who knows the dark old ways! I pledge my soul to vengeance! I pledge the souls of these poor doomed bastards before me! I shall have my revenge on thee!" The captain yelled to any crewman who could hear him above the roaring sea, and the panicked cries of those who knew they had met the end, "Hear me, men! All hands, if ye would visit vengeance upon the whoreson who sent us to die, take any lanyard, chain and scrap of rigging ye can find and lash yourself to this damned vessel!"

Davis heard the maddened captain scream even against the deafening rumble of the impending swell of death and watched as the men scrambled to fasten themselves to the ship in vain hopes of surviving the cataclysmic wave approaching. He bore witness to the captain's suicide, the plunging of the dagger deep into his own heart. Gosseling turned to him, teeth grinding together in agony, chipping and snapping apart under his bite, his eyes bulging in utter insanity as he twisted the dagger, chewing through the cardiac muscle, opening the wound into a gaping, crimson maw. The captain withdrew the dagger once more, drawing with it a fountain of hot blood and gristle, only to plunge the dagger in deeper, this time with such force that the tip of the blade tore through the back of his dirty greatcoat.

Davis fell to his knees as the sky before him became the

sea.

***

Jack Snow raised the bottle of Basker's to his lips after his left sock was in place. He did so again after the right sock, his shirt, his tie, his trousers and every item of clothing he applied to his person. By the time he strode past his concerned servants and out to the waiting liveried brougham, he was a man halfway to drunkenness even as his untouched breakfast of soft-boiled eggs still steamed in the dining room.

Snow had detected the whispers of shocked conversation over the days spent tearing oil paintings from the walls, freeing them of their frames and hurling all into the mighty bonfire he had set in the ornamental garden. His loyal manservant Ackley had confronted him in horror as Snow tore down the priceless *Pond* collection and committed to the flames what he had not placed in crates and sent to the docks.

Chanting and dancing around the fire had instilled in his staff the belief that he had completely taken leave of his senses. They saw him burn a fortune in antiques and heirlooms, but could not understand, could never even learn that this was not the random act of a madman, but the mad strategy of a man committed to restoring glory to his family's name. Restoring the glory, and retaining it forever.

The coach bumped and bounded along the route to the Royal Exchange. Dribbles of whisky stained his once-pristine white shirt and soaked into the lapels of his black jacket. He stared out of the coach at clutches of ragged flower and match sellers, the glint of a shilling catching his eye every now and then as a transaction took place in mere seconds.

The coach slowed to a crawl, joining the crush of traders and businessmen eager to learn of their fortunes, and to create new ones, at the Exchange. Snow's hands trembled at the realization he was so close to learning the fate of his dynasty's fortune.

He gazed through the coach windows at those perfectly framed portraits of trade. So straightforward, so beautiful in their simplicity. Give me tuppence and I shall give you this *thing*. The purity of that fundamental idea of trade was long lost to him. Thinking of the dark master he now served, he could only think that the lifeblood of that creature had flowed at one time solely on one man's happiness to trade, and another man's desire to have *more*.

He allowed himself a wry chuckle as he thought that Mammon could have no better wife than the widow Burton. Every thought in that woman's mind would serve to keep the master alive for a thousand more years.

The coach drew to a halt and the footman opened the door. Snow decided, in something resembling pride, to leave the whisky behind and stepped out into the bustling crowds of the City. A card table showdown thrill rushed through him as he glanced once at the statue of the Duke of Wellington. That grand statue, forged from the canons of his defeated enemies, just as his own throne was to be built of the bones of the *Red Scout's* crew.

The crew, and Dent, of course. Dent, who would have been there with him on any normal day. Dent, whose wise counsel always seemed to stave off the fear of tangling with these savage creatures who mounted the Royal Exchange steps alongside him.

He had barely set foot in the foyer of this vast center of commerce when he broke step, only for a second. *She* was already waiting for him.

"My dear, dear Mr. Snow," the widow Burton gushed, hobbling across the checkered floor to meet him face to face. "But I have simply been *dying* to see you this day." She extended a gloved hand, which Snow received, kissing the black velvet at her knuckles.

"Oh, if only that were true, Mrs. Burton, I should have been sure to wait a wee while longer."

Burton was attended by two young men, both dressed alike in greatcoats, buttoned tight across broad, muscular chests and shoulders, each man sporting a top hat, their faces framed with neatly trimmed mutton-chops. They looked like twins. One of them stepped forward with his fist clenched. "My Lady, would you have me cast this man into the street?"

"Down, boy," the widow growled in a playful tone, with a flirtatious glint in her eye, which excited in Snow a faint sense of nausea. "Mr. Snow here is our friend. I have travelled here with the sole purpose of conversing with him."

"Well, that is rather kind of you, Mrs. Burton, but I must be moving along," Snow insisted, stepping aside with a mind to circumnavigate the group.

"It was lovely to see you, young Mr. Snow. I look forward to meeting with you later as we discuss monies outstanding on *Red Stallion*."

The insinuation was clear, but Snow feigned ignorance. "I believe you are mistaken, my good lady. You see, the ship you mentioned was constructed by Russell and Aspinall's in Baltimore. It is to them that I owe the belated funds."

"Ah, but I thought that with your business so far indebted, perhaps I should grant you a boon, and so I bought the debt from them to save you having to send that money on its exhausting trip all the way to Baltimore. True, Russell and Aspinall were happy to wait and accrue interest at first, but when my American agents delivered telegrams from your other erstwhile creditors, they were only too keen to take my offer of sixty percent. Does it not make more sense for the consolidation of all of your debts? To have all of your debts held, in fact, by a friend?"

"Were it only that I had a friend in our line of business, Mrs. Burton."

The widow clutched at his hand once more, squeezing with a pressure totally at odds with her fragile, aged form. Closing in for the kill seemed to wipe years away from her, filling her with new vitality. "Oh but you do, Jack Snow. You do have a friend. And like all friends, I will guide you back into honour by ensuring that you repay every single penny owed on *Red Stallion* by the end of this day."

"It is a risky business, owning ones ships outright. A lot of capital is shed in the early days as well you might know from your dear departed husband...or, did I not read somewhere that he was a pirate and a thief? Well, who knows, eh? One mustn't believe everything one reads. I bid you good day."

The widow snatched back her hand as though avoiding a venomous snakebite. She muttered curses under her breath. That arrogant bastard had dared to cast aspersions at the memory of her beloved Henry. Even more than before, she relished the moment when she would bring about the end of Snow and Sons.

Notes and calls passed back and forth on the trading floor, and Snow felt the thrill of the action. He could see the lifeblood of Empire coursing about him. He could feel the pull of Mammon's influence. Wealth and gain justified the loss of any lives. So it had always been. So it always shall. In that sense, he could almost admire the ruthlessness of the widow, and the whispered tales of her long-dead husband.

Snow could not help but notice the widow watching him across the trading floor, flanked by her foreboding guards. She sipped at a delicate china teacup and whenever their eyes met, a sly malevolent energy seemed to radiate from her.

One thing was absolutely clear to him: the news she awaited was exactly the same as he. But not with the same motivation.

The resounding chime of the mighty Lutine Bell brought the trading floor to a standstill. The traders held their breath, waiting for the second chime which would indicate the news received was of a late ship now found to be safe. The second chime did not come. It was bad news, and that news spread like a wave throughout the room, filtering its way to Snow.

The widow clapped her hands and tugged at the sleeves of her henchmen, pointing at Snow as he learned that the *Red Scout* had not arrived to replenish coal reserves at Tripoli as expected. The ship had not been seen by others who had left London shortly after her.

The underwriters scrambled to make their deals, conspiring to make business to offset the anticipated loss of a mighty cargo.

Mrs. Burton could not contain her amusement, but found, to her chagrin, that Snow maintained an impassive look. Through narrowed eyes, she began to wonder why the man, whose last lifeline appeared to have sunk into the briny sea, seemed not to care. She decided that her young rival was in shock. She raised her cup in salutation, mocking her fallen foe.

When he heard murmurs of *Red Stallion* passing around the floor ten minutes later, he braced himself for a victorious salutation of his own.

The Lutine Bell chimed once more. Snow looked around, wondering which poor bastard was about to receive bad news.

Again the announcement passed around the room and reached his ears. *Red Stallion*, it seemed, had not collected her coal either. Snow clamped a handkerchief over his lips to catch the acidic whisky and bile mix that scorched his throat and filled his mouth.

Mrs. Burton had the reaction she wanted. Her laughter rose above the hubbub of commerce and tore into his soul.

***

Smoke billowed from the chimney of *Red Stallion*, as good quality Newcastle coal brought life to the vast condenser and pistons driving the screw paddle at her rear, driving her onward, ever onward. Her precious cargo, 200 tons of soap, wool, candles, books, glass and china thundered ever closer to Calcutta.

The *Stallion's* captain, Charles Hollingworth stood to receive a hefty payment from Jack Snow for his secrecy on this mission, carrying a cargo over-insured and supposed to be carried on the doomed *Red Scout*. Every ton of opium collected in Calcutta upon the sale of the aforementioned goods would travel to Lintin on the *Stallion*, there to trade for silver. That silver was destined for Hong Kong where 200 tons of the new tea crop would be loaded and raced back to London. Not a shilling received in London would reach the accounts of Snow and Sons, as none of the trades or cargo would be borne in the company name. All transactions and monies stood for Jack

Snow personally. Jack Snow, and of course, those who had assisted him in this daring bit of maritime fraud.

"*Sorr*! You should see this, *Sorr*!" came the call from the poop deck. Hollingworth strode across the deck to join a gathering of men staring overboard into the deep. "Do you see it, *Sorr*?"

"See what, exactly? I see only the glare from the sun, you fools."

"That's not the sun, *Sorr*. That's fire."

Hollingworth wanted to berate the man for his folly, but the more he stared into the deep blue-green of the water, the more he realized the shimmering white-orange glow *did* look like fire.

As they plowed across the sea, the glow seemed to follow them, as though something deep below kept pace and tracked them.

"Keep watch on this phenomenon, men. But keep it to yourselves." The captain turned to his First Mate and ordered him to send word to the engine room: "Full steam ahead!"

Hollingworth checked his pocketwatch, noting that half an hour had elapsed since the phenomenon was made known to him. He returned to the ship's aft, where a silent vigil was held. The men appeared almost hypnotized.

"What do you think it is, *Sorr*?"

"If I knew I'd have fucking told you by now, boy!" he barked. It was then that he noticed the activity of the water. Even in the wake of the racing propeller, the sea seemed to be unusually disturbed. Not only had the orange glow of the deep kept pace with them, but it had grown larger. Larger, or closer. Squinting, Hollingworth tried to determine if the vapour he could see rising from the turbulence of the propeller was simply the mist of churned water, or steam.

"Do you see it, *Sorr*?"

"Be specific, man!"

"Do you see how the sea boils?"

In that moment a muffled horn sounded. Hollingworth looked about the *Stallion*, expecting to see a distant ship, but he saw nothing. The horn sounded again, closer this time, but still no ship could be seen.

The raging orange glow exploded from the churning surface of the water, and a chimney reached towards them, spewing thick, black fumes. The ghastly, screaming horn blast that emerged with the chimney sent a chill down the captain's spine.

"'Tis the Devil!" came the cry, and in that moment, all was panic, and the chimney was followed by a bowsprit constructed of an array of bones. The figurehead appeared next, in the form of a screaming skull whose arms swung back and forth, seaweed clinging to each vertebrae of the spine.

The demon ship's mighty prow exploded from the sea, reaching almost to the deck of the *Stallion*, before reaching the tipping point, where it slammed down, shattering the waves.

It was then Hollingworth noted the name of the ship, cut deep and proud either side of the figurehead. "That's no devil ship. It's the *Red Scout!*"

Hollingworth stood frozen in slack-jawed incredulity at the sight of the ship's crew. Bloated with seawater, and gnawed upon by the denizens of the sea, the roaring crew waved cutlasses and brandished rifles, threatening his crew.

Flames grasped for the sky from the opening of the cavernous chimney as the ship, now fully revealed, bore down upon the *Stallion*.

Although he knew it was impossible for the gunpowder to be dry, shots roared out from the firearms of these ragtag raiders. A man Hollingworth vaguely recognized as the ship's captain, Gosseling, stepped to the fore of the throng, placing a tattered boot above the bony bowsprit, his chest a slick, cavernous wound and with eyes that glowed as ferociously as the chimney's flames this creature met his gaze and bellowed, "Prepare to be boarded!"

The *Stallion* lurched as the *Scout,* at some point beneath the Plimsoll line, made contact with the screw propeller. Metal screamed as the mechanism was forced to a grinding halt. The propeller tore away as ropes and hooks flew up onto the

Stallion's deck. In moments, the bilious sailors of the *Scout* began to clamber along the tethers.

Hollingworth called his crew to arms, but too late, as he turned back to face the enemy as Gosseling's gnarled hands clasped his head. "Your weapons serve you no good, lad! Not against the dead!"

***

Jack Snow watched the approaching coaches and wagons, knowing fully well what lay in store for him that afternoon. *Red Stallion* had gone unseen for days. The news had spread far and wide of the imminent downfall of Snow and Sons. Stockholders harassed the servants at his home and banged on the doors of the warehouse at the London and St Katherine Docks,

At his feet lay the black brazier in which he had burned so much of his money in worship of Mammon. It seemed, as the debt collectors closed in, that his prayers had gone unheard and a plan that at first seemed foolproof had disintegrated into the same ashes as the fortune of his family.

That sixty men were sent to their deaths, knowingly by Snow, barely registered with him. That sixty more, it seemed, died in his service on the second ship, again, mattered not to him. His only thought was that all he owned was either gone, or about to be taken away. He had bet all on a single coin toss, and lost.

The staccato drumming of horse-hooves, and the rumble of trundling wheels ceased, and he dared to look out of his window once more. As he expected, *she* was there, the widow Burton, a glad spectator in attendance of the death of his business.

The insurance for the loss of *Red Scout* could cover the money outstanding on *Red Stallion*, but Burton had called in all of his outstanding debts. His gamble had been on that new tea crop returning in *Stallion's* hold, in his own name. He could have raised credit against that and kept the old bitch at bay for a time. Now the insurers were certain that *Stallion* was lost, if he were to reveal that he had knowingly over-insured *Scout,* and underinsured *Stallion,* then he would not only lose his company, but he would lose his liberty for the fraud.

He had no choice, and as the collectors broke the warehouse doors in, accompanied by bailiffs and police constables whose job it was to see that the acquisition of the property of Snow and Sons was carried out in line with the law, Jack Snow knew that there was no escape. His fate was sealed.

In a trance, he signed over the warehouse, stock and chattels. He took one last swallow of whisky, fastened his coat and trod the stairs with leaden steps, down into the warehouse and out onto the cobbled dock.

"It is simply devastating to see a fellow giant of maritime trade laid low," goaded Mrs. Burton from her coach.

Snow set his jaw, eyeing the wrinkled, pudgy, white face with sheer hatred. Unable to speak a word, he simply spat on the Burton livery upon the carriage door, to the disgust of those gathered.

"Your father would be ashamed," Mrs. Burton snarled. "Speaking of your father, when I finally take your home from you, when all of our business is settled, there is the matter of the Snow family mausoleum. I believe it to be on the grounds of your home. You must put your mind to it now, young Jack, where those bones shall go when I have my men exhume them."

Jack stared into the swirling greenish-brown Thames water, fancying that to die gulping down such a filthy liquid would be almost the perfect end to this foul ordeal.

Burton's coach made away, and before long, Snow was alone. No more a master, but a simple observer of the shipping trade, watching the ships come to port, watching them slip away into the growing twilight. His shoulders sagged as he wandered the docks, without aim, without purpose. He had no money on his person to buy even a small beer or fare for a ride to his home. It was then that he made out alarmed whistles, bell chimes, and horn blasts to the East, all along the Thames.

The ever-present Thames fog shrouded the ships by the

time they reached the end of the dock, and so any ship arriving would be within the berths before he would see them. So it was that Snow *heard* the approaching vessel long before he saw it. A mournful horn blast filled his heart with dread, and a steam engine surging ever closer, with thunderous pistons hammering so loud that he thought the crew of this ship must be deaf.

An orange glow swelled within the gloaming and within moments, the fog seemed to part as though cowering aside.

Snow's eyes remained fixed on what he knew to be flames, and the ship's chimney came into view first, through the dissipating head of the fog. The maddening hammer of the pistons grew louder and louder with each moment and although he wanted to run, a mad curiosity compelled him to stay. He covered his ears, certain that his eardrums would explode any second.

Dockworkers and sailors stood agape, bearing witness to the spectacle as a wide-mouthed skull presented its chilling image at the head of this hellish steamer. Another blast of that horn, that chilling, dying animal howl, made Snow tremble, as suddenly the hammering ceased, the flames died down, and the hulking steamer glided into port right before him.

His eyes confirmed what his rational mind could not believe. He saw the name of the ship and fell to his knees. Hollow eyes and cavernous mouths loomed over him from the bulwarks as the gangway clattered into place only feet away from him. The spectral crew spoke no words, they merely hissed through cracked and blackened teeth.

Footsteps on the gangway made Snow's heart tighten. Only when the footsteps approached him on land did he dare to look. He opened his eyes to see Hollingworth glaring at him.

"Jack Snow, you are a disgrace and a murderer!" Hollingworth announced.

"Hollingworth! I thought ye were dead!"

"Well now, Jack, it appears I know a thing or two about death more than you do!"

Snow recognized the voice immediately, as Gosseling's ghastly, cadaverous form lurched into view.

"I sank your *Stallion,* and with it your fortune, Snow. But I'm no murdering bastard like you! Every man on board the *Stallion* is here, safe and sound. My men and I may have made for a shabby looking crew to your eyes, but we have some honour, even beyond death!"

Hands caked in salt grabbed Snow's coat, pulling it down over his shoulders and bracing his upper arms. Jack cried out, gagging on the foul death-smell of his captors as they hauled him up the gangway and onto the gently rolling *Red Scout.*

"A friend wishes to greet you," Gosseling snarled, gripping Snow's hair, dragging him across the deck to the prow.

"Please! Not Dent. Tell me it's not Dent! Don't let me see him like this!"

"Like this? What, like us? No, I'm afraid your old friend was not part of the crew, so be became part of the ship! In fact it is his hatred for you that fuels the fires in that engine to such extremes as the depths of the sea could never extinguish the flames!"

Bone ground against bone as the skeletal figurehead juddered into life. The skeleton's spine creaked and groaned as the skull came around and arms reached out. Finally, Snow's legs buckled as the figurehead's spine snapped away from the fused bones of the bowsprit, freeing its reach.

Gosseling's men thrust Snow forward, towards the embrace of Dent's waiting bones. Snow screamed, pleaded, promising anything, promising the world, if only they would let him live.

Dent wrapped his arms around his former ward, turning him, drawing him close as his ribcage creaked open, accepting Snow's upper torso, so that the businessman's head rested against the bones of Dent's neck. The ribs closed as Dent tightened his embrace. Snow's screams renewed when Dent's ribs closed in around him, puncturing his flesh, biting into his chest deep enough to hold him, but not deep enough to penetrate his organs.

"You said you were no murderer, and yet here you come to slay me!" Snow wailed.

Gosseling chuckled as Dent crept back beneath the bowsprit with Jack Snow held fast. "Who spoke of slaying you, Snow?"

Beneath the decks, the engine room thrummed with life once more, the pistons hammering a slow, steady tattoo, rising in volume and speed with each repetition. The ship stole away from the dock, turning about to point East once more.

The crew of the *Stallion* gazed on in awe, as their erstwhile paymaster screamed and cursed, thrashing his head about, kicking wildly at the head of the ship now slipping away to the river proper.

"As I said, Jack, I spoke nothing of your murder," Gosseling called down to Snow from his position at the ship's prow. "But we have decided to change the route we're bound to take, now that our colleagues from the *Stallion* have been returned safe and sound. I must confess that on this particular journey, it does make travel more comfortable when one has no need to breathe!"

And upon Gosseling's final word, the *Red Scout's* engine roared, the horn screamed and the pistons hammered out their deafening beat. The ship slid deeper and deeper into the frigid, foul water of the Thames, filling Snow's nose, filling his mouth, smothering his screams. And his greed.

SHE BECKONS

D.G. Sutter

There's always a moment of pause when you go under. You wonder—as the oxygen slowly leaves your brain and lungs, pressure mounts your skull—when you submerge, if you'll ever return. As with any part of life, there are incredible amounts of uncertainty. In the murky depths, all internal signs of life are obsolete. You feel at once featherweight, free to float on to Heaven, to the ethereal limits of human perception.

Down, down, where the old wolfish creeps, where blue dogs clamor for prey, the danger is ever-present and nearly palpable. The skintight suit of neoprene is enough to keep one warm and dry, but beyond comfort, does nothing to prevent the onslaught of creatures that could brand anyone other than a New England swimmer, a coward. Vincenzo's father had taught him from an early age to love the sea and fear its welcoming spirit; for once you gave in—wholly—to her, there was no reason to ever let you go.

Some days, he could stay out on that open water from morning 'til sunset, dependent on the weather, and when there was a salvage job, even longer. Vincenzo was at ease on the sea. He felt like himself, rocking with the dips and bobs of the ocean. As he dug for steamers out past Salt Island, down below the surface, Vincenzo wished for more hours of daylight. After palming one of the clams, he rose towards the thinning light above, near to his vessel.

Vincenzo slung his molluscan till over the side of the dory, followed by his diving tank, and climbed aboard. His old bones were making it harder, each time, to steadily mount the small boat. He'd scavenged plenty of food for dinner, including two blackbacks on spears and a handful of mussels. Denise would sure be excited. It'd been a while since the last flounder and steamer excursion. He usually went for other whitefish.

The suit peeled off like old skin. All day he'd been wrapped up, sweating in the late-June sun. He left his shirt spread out, drying on the other bench, and started rowing to his truck on the Long Beach side of the cape. As he pushed on, his empty beer bottles rattled in the bottom of the boat. Nearly four o'clock and the old, salty dog was drink free for hours. That wouldn't do. The pressure of your buzz wearing off was almost equivalent to 40 meters deep.

The anxious thoughts made the elongated muscles sewn with old sailor tattoos pulse faster. Within minutes, he was dragging the dory by the headline hawser, forcing it onto the trailer to be towed behind the rusted red Ford pickup. The ignition jammed, as it always did, and Vince cursed the wheels on which the truck rolled. For all he cared, they could blow out on the side of 95.

When finally he made the hulk initiate, he was ready to walk home. The only thing holding him back was the heat that was beginning to turn him asthmatic. When the humidity let on, it could sure bring some distress to your lungs, his chest tight and muscles working overtime. Times like these made him wish his son was home to pull that boat ashore; he was getting too old for the shit.

The truck kicked up sand, and Vince fashioned himself towards the home up on the hill. It didn't take him but for five minutes to get there—where the houses were packed tight as sardines, along roads narrower than pin bones—and Denise was waiting for his arrival, sitting on the Adirondack chair, crossed arms and legs.

***

Time never crept so slow as when Vincenzo stayed out late. Every drop of rain or creak of a board made her jump right to her feet. So, her friends said, have a drink—we're fisherman's wives. From time to time, it helped, yet when the night pedaled into view, the sun vanishing past the breakwater, the stark reality of never again seeing the old man crashed down like the waves of the cold and unforgiving North Atlantic.

Denise gazed out, past bows steaming hard, husbands come home, and wondered why she hassled him not for making her worry night upon night. For most, Nor'easters brought with them fretting and displeasure, but for her comfort in knowing Vince would stay home, warm and safe by the fireplace. Today, she would tell him how she felt. She would lay down the law—retirement and settling out west, away from the ocean. Vince loved the water. Denise, on the other hand, had enough. Her entire family, her friends, and co-workers were obsessed with fishing and the industry. Frankly, she was spent. She wanted something other than creating a fifth generation.

Vince finally came home nearing dark. He made seafood—as almost every night—and they talked about their days. She told him of how the ladies asked about him at knitting club, to which he replied that he "didn't care about any of those ole biddies". It frustrated her to no end that Vincenzo was so disinterested. His mind was always far and away; they could never converse in depth. In anger, she dropped the retirement bomb.

His fork hit the wall. He slapped the table, said "out of the question—absolutely not—ridiculous." Denise feared he would one day strike her in his drunken rants. She needed to escape the situation.

"Excuse me," she said with a frog in the throat, meekly stepping upstairs and dressing in layers.

It was swiftly darkening, but Denise needed a moment of pause, longed for fresh air, separation from *him*. She snuck out the back door, through the kitchen, and past Vince's mess. The mesh on the screen door let in all the cold wind and also let out the snap of a fresh can of beer and Vince's stomping footfalls. He was always heavy-footed when mad.

The curved roads were all lined with parked cars. Families were home watching primetime; here she was trying to escape, cold and alone. A golden retriever popped out of a driveway, barking at the air. Denise started and staggered. She nearly went head over heels from the recycling bin at her feet. His bark was a toned down foghorn.

She passed the church and the cheese shop, and walked a few more minutes until the wide boulevard gave way to ocean and a glimpse of Ten Pound Island. Denise took a seat on one of the green metal benches and watched as pedestrians with dogs and children walked the stretch of sidewalk. Down the road the drawbridge rose, letting some other husband, son, father out into harm's way. It was easy to see the attraction to sea. There was solitude; there was, at times, peacefulness; and there was, of course, a sense of adventure, adrenaline-fueled antics.

The wind was kicking up a gale. It sure felt like oncoming harsh winter. The other townies walking about seemed unaffected—bare hands, short sleeve shirts—but Denise felt altogether a cold-blooded being, not like these tough blue-collared men. She didn't know how they do it on the regular.

Along the railing, there came a body with a familiar face attached. Denise knew his gait, recognized the casual slump of his shoulders. Sammy was one of her and Vince's high school pals, one with whom she'd been in a short tryst. He was a kind boy who'd grown into a kinder man, serving on school committees and working as a volunteer at the Stage Fort farmer's market. Denise was never one to speak first, so she waited on him to notice her.

His round, greying head turned in her direction and Sammy Moriarty raised his eyebrow. "Denise? How ya been?"

A small smile ran onto her lips. The absence of sound through her throat made the words creep and crack. "Go... good. Same-ole, same-ole."

"How about Vince? That old salty dog. He still divin and fishin?"

Denise nodded. "You know it. That won't ever stop. What about you? How's the vet biz?"

"Always a sick pet. Somethin' with fleas. You know people around here love their dogs."

Sam took a seat by her side; his knees cracked on the way. They were close enough that their legs could brush at any moment. Denise almost wanted to give it a shot, see his reaction.

"Do you remember when we drove up to Canada—that weekend?" Denise said. "That was the best weekend of my life."

Sammy's head turned to look at Denise, who was staring out past the breakwater, the half-mile stretch of rocks that blocked the ravenous waves, in reverie. He looked in the same direction, then down at the sidewalk.

"Oh, yeah, I remember."

Denise sighed. "Vince only took me off the island—you know, more than a few miles—a handful of times, when we were younger. It's almost..."

She stopped talking, remembering it wasn't in her head, but out loud. "Sorry."

"No, please. Ya know. I don't have many friends. It's good to converse...with adults. The few guys I do talk to are still knuckleheads, think they're sixteen."

Wasn't that exactly what she'd been reminiscing on—teenage years? Denise slowly shifted her knees together. "Thanks for listenin to my rant."

"Eh, it's nothing." Sam pressed the points of his elbows into his knees, and let his hands hang between his legs. "Truth is...I ain't been a vet for a few months." It was his turn to sigh. "Joanne left me. I started staying home from work—depressed—and, well, lost my practice."

Sammy ran a hand through his hair.

"I'm so sorry, Sam." She put a hand on his shoulder and gave it a quick, consoling, rub.

He laughed softly. "My turn to rant."

Denise noticed his battered sneakers. His jeans were torn. "Are you doing okay now?"

"Being homeless ain't easy...or all it's cracked up to be." He tried for a smile, but it was a pathetic attempt.

"My God, Sammy, do you need some money, to get back

on your feet?"

He swatted the air. "No. I just need a new start. Something to put the life back into me. I feel deflated."

They sat in silence for a moment. Both had been in relationships so long and come into disappointment. It almost made Denise envy those old couples with the gleam in their eye, walking hand-in-hand. Sometimes, it was enough to make her sick.

Her stomach grumbled, but not from being green with jealousy. Between all the drama, Denise hadn't the time to finish dinner. Maybe she'd grab a boardwalk pizza from Poseidon's on the way home. She turned on the bench to see if the shop was open.

Sam was squinting. She then followed his stare past the rusted green railing that lined the shallow beach. "What?"

"I don't know."

Beyond the breakwater, a massive shadow jutted out of the water. "Past the Dog Bar?" she asked.

"Yeah, you see it too?"

"Not a schooner. It's a strange shape."

Sammy walked to the railing. "You got a couple quarters—for the viewing machine?"

The space between words seemed unintentional, forced. He didn't want to seem needy, reliant.

"Yeah, I think so."

Denise dug into her coin purse, past a few ones, twenties, a hundred—which she took out—and pulled out the two coins, putting them into his palm.

"Take this, too—"

"I can't," Sam said, shaking his head.

"*Yes*," she returned firmly. "Get a nice meal."

"C'mon now..."

"You will."

Sam smirked, genuine this time. "Still the same 'Nise."

He deposited the coin and the gears started to turn with the timer. The metal viewer spun until he seemed focused. "Damn. I don't know what the hell. Have a look."

Denise hadn't used the things in years. Usually, the tourists had control. The waves were huge, maybe fifteen-twenty footers. Amid the crashing, was a definitive body, no ship. It could have been a whale, save for the tail that swung like a bullwhip. In the breaking sun, she wondered if anyone else had come gazed upon the visage. Then, before she could say a word or give Sam another chance at the viewer, the body submerged once more.

***

"Mr. Moriarty," the girl at the counter said, "your prescription's ready."

Sam took the bag of lithium and signed off on the paper. "Thanks for being so quick."

The girl smiled; she was always pleasant. "We try our best."

"Oh, I know ya do, gals. Have a great day."

Sam slipped the pills in his back pocket and headed for the shelter down on East Main. The grocery store was busy as all hell, most definitely for the weekend of Fiesta. When Sam owned a home, he tended to stay indoors during the majority of the Italian festival, where the greasers walk the streets shouting and the boneheads started trouble downtown. It had changed from a celebration to a citywide party, with carnival rides and events, rather than something of religious and communal values. He used to bring the kids down there, but these days wouldn't dream of doing so.

He walked Prospect all the way to Flanagan's, where there was a long line for fuel. Waiting to cross, something hit Sammy in the back of the head. A plastic bottle of Poland Spring with a half an inch of water rolled away from his feet.

Sam's fists clenched. He turned to face the antagonist. Dave Orton was hanging out the window of his truck cackling, one beefy forearm suntanned to a cocoa brown.

"How ya been, pal?"

Sam shook his head. "Seen better days."

He walked over the broken curbing and shook hands with Dave.

"Busy?" Big Dave said.

"Not particularly."

"Hop in, we'll steam out and grab some dinner. On my way to Rocky Neck now."

The attendant slapped the truck's rear end, letting the driver know the tank was full. Dave sparked the engine.

"Well, whadd'ya say?" A cheesy grin covered Dave's face as he patted the 30 rack of Budweiser heavy in the center seat.

Sam didn't like going out at night. It was nearly pitch black. However, he knew a nice couple of drinks might do him well, seeing as he couldn't afford any at the current moment.

"I don't know, Dave, we ain't exactly kids anymore."

"That's exactly why we need to live, Sammy. Come on, hop in!"

Sam licked his lips and swallowed, made his way around to the passenger's side and climbed aboard. The cars behind them honked and honked, waiting for their turn to pollute the atmosphere.

***

Dave steamed out hard past Ten Pound Island, past Niles, where a twenty footer hunted for Stripers. At the breakwater, a few teenagers tossed out for flounder and rock cod. He was looking for Haddock or Pollock, something for a late night fish and chips.

"Got a bunch of brews in one of the rear holds, full of ice."

Sam eased back there, unsure in his older age of sea legs. Dave bounced the boat over the waves with grace, years of practice. The sound of a bottle cap unleashing carbon dioxide barely overcame the diesel engine. The smell of burning fuel was comforting to Dave, but he knew to those landlubbers it could nauseate.

He anchored past the groaner, a huge red buoy in the middle of the ocean that made the sound for which it'd been named, whereby a gurry ship dumped the leftover racks, guts, and fins from the fish auction. Dogs and squid tended to rule the late afternoon and evening. Come night, the local were practically jumping on deck, when the propellers tended to abate.

"I got a few sabikis down there. Made 'em myself."

Sam took one of the PVC covered poles, rigged with seven hooks each, for catching local Mackerel and Herring, baitfish.

"Nice craftsmanship," Sam said. "Haven't used one of these in ages."

"Hopefully, we'll come upon something big enough to take home."

Sam huffed and lifted his pole in and out of the water, jigging. "I ain't got a home, Dave."

"Whadd'ya mean?" Big Dave spit out through a fire-red cigarette.

"Joanne kicked me to the curb."

Sam looked as though he didn't want to go too in depth. Dave didn't press. "Where you stayin?"

Another sigh from Sam. "East Main."

"The shelter?"

"Mmm-hmm."

"Shit," Dave said, putting a grease-matted hand on Sam's shoulder. "That won't do. You're staying in my extra room."

"I just—"

"Nothing," Dave said, "That's what it is."

"Okay."

Dave reeled in his line, tossing five mackerel into the bait bucket, enough for the moment. Sam also contributed to the pot with three or more locals.

"Mind raisin' the anchor?" Dave said.

Sam pulled the rope above deck and rigged it to the starboard cinch. Dave steamed out another half-mile past the groaner, deep enough water for some decent sized fish. He watched the sonar for drop-offs and red spots, indicating that rocky floor where Haddock and Pollock might hide and, once more, threw the steel anchor overboard.

"They're rigged for groundfish," Dave said to Sam, who'd

cracked another beer.

Dave cast out over what looked to be a school of fish. He placed the end of the pole in the mounting and followed Sam with having a brew.

"Your vet business doing all right?" Dave said, trying to advance the conversation away from the brooding Sam.

"Naw. Gone as well."

"I need a lumper down at the dock."

"How much?"

Dave tilted his head to the right, weighing his option. "Usually I pay ten. I known you a good click, though. Most I could go is thirteen. It's tough work—grunt work."

"I'll do it. Don't have much going for me. Some stability would be nice."

"You start Monday, five thirty. You got Mucks?"

"No."

"I got a few spares. Your feet might get wet in 'em. Holes in the soles."

Dave went to work cutting up the mackerel. He filled a chum pot with pieces and threw it aft, then baited his hook with a tail. Sam hooked an eighteen-inch haddock minutes later; Dave cast out ten or so times with no result.

"Thought you were rusty," Dave said, getting frustrated twenty minutes later.

"Guess I still got it."

Dave clicked on his bait runner and sat down. He needed a new Captain's chair. The thing felt ready to break off its post.

Sam tossed out another line. "You remember Denise?" he said.

Dave put his arms over his head. "Oh yeah, sweet woman. Sharon knits with her down at the club."

"I saw her today. She seemed down on the times, too. We got to talkin' on the Boulevard."

"Yeah, well, that blowhard Vince is her problem. She's always so happy, until he shows up. He's a jerk...always was."

There was a click, click, clicking from Dave's pole. Something was hooked. He jumped to his feet and gave it some slack, then reeled a bit.

"Something big!" Dave said, "Maybe a slammer-dog!"

He reeled and reeled, but his line went out by the yard; the bearings spun out.

"Shit," he said, grabbing for his pocketknife to cut the line free.

The pole flew out of his hand, with it his shoulder felt pulled out of socket.

"Damn it!"

Sam put his pole down. "You all right, Davey?"

"Yeah, lost my best pole, but I'm good. Damn thing nearly took my arm off."

A wave rocked the boat. The ship dipped and rose. Another wave broke the calm from the opposite direction. Sea water spilled onto the deck.

Sam gripped the topsides. "Shit, what's that?"

"Hold tight, might be a whale or shark near."

Ten yards off, a massive tale breached, and then submerged. Sam pointed it out to Dave. "Over there!"

By the time Dave caught sight, it was nearly gone. It was big enough to be a blue. Yet another wave crested into the uprights, and Dave lost his footing. One foot slid over the wet deck; his groin pulled and back slammed into the wall.

"It's a feisty one," Dave said, laughing, crawling to his chair and taking a seat.

***

Sam didn't want to sound like a pussy, but he wanted the comfort of land. Dave was set on catching something. It led Sam to cower in the cabin, constantly scoping out the horizon.

"Remember I told you about meeting Denise earlier..." Sam said.

"Sure," Dave responded, casting out one of his other Bass poles.

"We seen this huge fish. It weren't a whale's tail, though, not forked. I think that's what's under us."

The radar flashed a gigantic red spot.

Dave chuckled. "Serpent of Gloucester? They figured out those stories were whales with herring nets stuck on their tails."

"It didn't look like those drawings either—not a long skinny body, but something wide."

"A boat, Sam, a low boat."

He let the line out and reeled in, slowly. Dave walked around the bow, standing on the very tip, seeming almost to avoid the conversation and float above the ocean, weightless.

Sam followed close behind. "You don't have to believe me."

"Good I don't."

Sam put his hands inside of his jean pockets, wondering what he was doing out there. He no longer fished. His entire life had been based around saving animals, not killing them. It felt time to go home. They were two different people in their older age.

As if sensing Sam's uncertainties, Dave said "Grab a pole, Sam, you're making me nervous."

Sam took a seat. "I think I'll just hang out."

"Aww, come on, Sammy," Dave said over one shoulder, "we probably won't ever do this again."

So, Dave had drawn a line between them. He knew this wouldn't go longer than a 'hey, how are you', on the street. Their friendship wasn't meant to last.

The bait runner on Dave's reel started clicking.

"Got a hit!"

He raised the pole, letting it bend, gave it a small turn, then let the fish drag.

"A big one."

Sam stood up.

Dave's back leg was bent, holding his weight. He reeled slowly, fighting, letting the line hold tension. Then, the tautness released and Sam could hear the reel spinning out. Dave reeled faster.

"Swimming toward the boat," Dave said.

The line snapped, audibly, and Dave's back leg gave out.

He tumbled onto his ass, catching himself on the windshield, his back inches from the water.

"Close call," Dave said.

Sam put a hand out to help.

"I got it," Dave said, crawling to stand from his crouch.

Past Dave's body, the phosphorescent danced in neon green in the water. Through them came a set of jagged teeth, over which sat two spherical eyes.

"Shit!" Sam shouted, grabbing for Dave's forearm.

The mouth snagged the cotton of Dave's secondhand shirt, pulling him into the water.

"The hell—"

Dave went under. He surfaced a moment later, bubbling, like a buoy. Swiping the water from his eyes, he clawed for the hull like a wet cat.

"Help me out here!"

Sam grabbed the chubby man under the armpit and hauled. Both Dave's palms pushed him, straining over the gunnels, slipping on the wet metal. The boat dipped towards Dave, and Sam knew it wasn't from his weight, but the surfacing fish.

Dave's scream cut the night air. His hands released and he vanished amongst the phosphorescent.

***

"The hell was that?" Austin said.

His friend, Nelson, switched on the fishing lamp. "What was what?"

"I thought I heard a yell."

In the distance, he heard it again—definitely someone yelling in pain, a man. "Right there. Listen."

Nelson cocked his neck. "Shit, you're right, we better check it out."

He hit the engine and steamed determinedly southwest, toward the direction of which they thought the sound had originated, using the squid lamps to guide them along, and a few marine lights Nelson had affixed to the bulkhead. A shadow of a small boat breathed into the glare of Nelson's light onslaught. Nelson leaned forward at the helm, baseball cap pointed straight ahead.

"Grab the life ring, Austin."

Austin swung aft and untied the foam circle from one of the cinches, uncoiling the rope, ready to toss it in. As they drew closer, he recognized Big Dave Orton's vessel—his father's good friend. A man was on top of the bow, looking into the water.

"Ahoy," Nelson said, "everything okay?"

"My friend's been attacked," the man said. It wasn't Dave Orton's gruff voice. "He fell overboard and something took his leg...then under he went."

"Holy shit," Nelson said. "You call the Coast Guard?"

"I ain't a ship farer. I don't know how to do that sorta thing."

"I got it," Nelson said.

Austin grabbed one of the squid lights submerged it in the black ocean. The waves rocked the plane of fluorescent blue like a flag in the wind. There were no squid, which they'd been hunting, only darkness. It was the non-fiery underworld. Dave was most likely never to return. Too many friends and family had gone that way.

A patch of large bubbles floated by, a glimpse of rough brown skin. Austin backed off, raising the light from the water. "Something's down there."

"Hit it with a gaffe," Nelson said, returning to Austin's side.

Austin dug into the side compartment and pulled out the metal hook attached to the wooden pole. The rust-tinged tip of the hook sank into the brown skin, and the animal swam downward. Austin's knee knocked the wall and he flipped over the sides, losing the gaffe enroute to his big splash. He panicked momentarily, swimming upwards. His head burst through the surface, and he swiped the water from his eyes with one hand. Before he could grab for the hull, his foot was caught in something sharp as a fox trap, and he never again breathed in that sweet Massachusetts air.

Nelson leapt from the vessel towards Dave Orton's ship "Fishy Business", landing short as the monster breached. He watched as pieces of his prized boat shot through the air, and the bulk of it went along with the creature.

The guy on the other ship pulled on his arm covered in red slime, until both were safely aboard.

"Look out," Nelson said, taking the helm.

"What about them—"

"The hell with it at this point."

The engine choked to life on its last legs and took them south-southwest, slapping off encroaching waves. Nelson continually glanced over his shoulder. It was following them, gaining.

When it had smashed his boat to smithereens, Nelson caught a good glimpse of it; wide mouth, pinnacle sharp teeth, rough scales like those of a dragon, small fins for feet at its rear. The thing looked like an enormous monkfish. The only part visible was the long antennae dangling above the surface, highlighted by the red lamp of Dave Orton's lights as it chased them down like a dog.

"Punch it," the guy name Sam said.

Nelson yelled over the boat's exertion. "This hulk doesn't have anything else."

Inch by inch, the antennae came closer, hunting them with nowhere to go. After a few minutes, Eastern Point Lighthouse came into view, rotating its bright red light. They were nearly to the breakwater. He cut the wheel starboard and the boat cased waves and sliced riptides, bounding towards safety.

He glanced back. The dangle was aft, close enough to touch. The bow cut right at the last possible minute and the monster sailed past. Nelson counted his blessings, but held his breath. The harbor was long, and the thing was practically on top of them.

Nelson slammed it back into gear. They shot into the breakwater, broke a rogue wave and caught air. The bow pointed straight down as another string of white foam followed in its wake. Ocean water filled the deck and doused the men. Both scrambled for the stern, Nelson for a bucket to start bailing, but too late. The monster was circling.

***

When Vincenzo stumbled out of bed, his legs were dull and numb, barely able to carry him forth. Now, sitting on the state pier, unraveling the rope that harnessed his boat to the stanchion, he felt much better. There's something beautiful that fresh air and a 32-ounce Gatorade can do to a hangover.

Early morning, Denise had woken him with news from the police scanner. Dave Orton's boat had sunk in the harbor and three men were missing. Vincenzo was asked to dive down to Orton's boat, look for answers and, possibly, bodies. He steamed down the channel slowly. Dead men can wait.

The chances of finding anyone alive were slim to none. If anyone made it out, most likely they were already at Pratty's, drinking away the memory. A few Coast Guard ships were around Ten Pound Island. A man lay on the beach, unconscious. Not far away, the stern of a ship was jutting out of the water.

Vince hauled along portside and dropped anchor. He geared up, made sure his air supply was firmly covered, and then fell back into murky waters. The water was thick with oil run-off and red slime. He always thought it a terrible area to fish with all the pollution, though people always cast off the breakwater.

On the harbor floor were bunched nets, smashed bait boxes, lost tackle. The bow of "Fishy Business" was planted in the mud. The cabin was empty. A few fishing poles remained in the mounts. The only signs of life were a few scup and a small school of herring picking at the sides of the boat.

Vincenzo swam through the opening of the boat with ease, fluid in water, with grace more than he had on land. His breath was taken away, as always, by the ebbs and flow of the tides. The murkiness only added to the mysticism of the ocean, causing an unexplainable feeling of both dread and wonder. Beneath your feet were seaweeds that held what only God knew, and to either side certain death or a fresh meal.

The majority of the ship's body seemed intact, leading Vincenzo to believe something mechanical had led to the vessel's downfall. In order to further diagnose he'd need to yank the hulk out and tow it to the salvage yard. It didn't work every time, but in such shallow water, there was a good shot.

He moved along the bulkhead, ready to ascend, when a cable caught his eye, washing left and right in the surf. Vince reached out and the cable rose, attached to a massive head. It was *her*.

The beast Vince had named Glenda swirled about, rubbing against him in a motherly manner. Beneath the rubber mask, Vince smiled. Ten times out of twelve, she was there. They dove together, fished together. Any given day she could call him to sea, and as long as she lived, the ocean would never claim him. If only Denise knew, she'd be green with envy.

Vince pat her on the head, felt the rough skin glide under the tips of his fingers. Nobody would ever, could ever, understand. Glenda was his life.

CAPE HADEL

Brad P. Christy

The storm raged on as the crew of the Research Vessel Cape Hadel braced themselves for another massive swell that nearly capsized the seventy-foot boat.

A gust of wind ripped the cabin door out of Hal Banks' hands and banged it against the port side wall. He could barely see through the rain and dark. Shoes slipping on the deck, he shouldered the door shut and held the hood of his raincoat tightly. His glasses were fogged over, but he could see the research team leader near the bow.

"This is insane!" he screamed hoping she would hear him, only to be drowned out by the roar of the Atlantic.

Ocean water kicked up over the hull. He spit the saltwater off his lips and shimmied his way along the deck. Hal's stomach rose up into his throat as the bow of the Cape Hadel suddenly pointed up to the night's sky. Eyes wide, His hand slipped from the guardrail, and he fell hard against the deck.

Saltwater washed down his shirt as he scrambled to his belly.

Hal didn't know how long he lay shivering, only how many waves had crashed against the hull. Fifteen. He had been held frozen in place for fifteen waves. Hal rubbed the water from his glasses and crawled to the bow.

"Catherine!" he yelled, hoisting himself up to his knees.

Catherine Singer looked ghost-like in her white raincoat and pants. "I'm a little busy, Hal!"

"We have to go back!" he shouted at her, trying to keep his balance and his dinner down.

She dropped to a knee and pointed over his shoulder. "Go help Sven secure that VHF antenna!"

Hal looked back and forth between the struggling crewmember on the observation deck and Catherine, who continued to point and held her look of annoyed resolve.

"What? No! We have to get back to land!" he said, spitting saltwater.

"And which way is that, Hal?" Catherine yelled, her hair plastered to her pale cheek.

He swallowed hard. The only directions he was sure of were up and down, and sometimes even that was debatable. He shook his head, letting water run off his nose.

"Listen," she said, grabbing his shoulders and looking into his eyes. "I wasn't kidding! If we lose that antenna, we won't be able to call for help!"

Hal ground his teeth. "Damn it, Catherine!"

"Go!" she yelled into his ear and helped him to his feet.

The Cape Hadel rose and fell without notice as the ocean ebbed and flowed, making Hal's hands ache as he kept a death grip on the guardrail on his way to the back of the boat. Wind blew the hood off his head.

With his ears no longer insulated by plastic, Hal could hear high-pitched creaking and whistles cutting through the storm. He looked overboard. Something, many somethings, were racing alongside the boat, bounding in flashes from wave to wave just out of sight. Hal wiped his face and tried to get a better look. In the poor light, chaos, and through foggy glasses, they almost looked human.

The Cape Hadel floated over a swell and slammed back down. A wave splashed over Hal's head, making him duck down to avoid being swept away. A flash of lightning in the distance revealed much larger, angrier waves ahead. Hal gripped the guardrail tighter as the distant light dissipated.

"Up here!" yelled Sven, in his heavy Scandinavian accent.

Hal's face was frozen from what he had seen as he turned to acknowledge Sven.

"Move your ass!" yelled Sven, grappling with the fifty-foot antenna.

Hal didn't think, he just slowly and deliberately moved to the ladder. Each step was made with the greatest of care as the wind and rain picked up, whipping his coat and hood around him. Visibility was nil, not that he had his eyes open.

"Here!" yelled Sven through the roar of the wind and crashing waves.

Hal took the rope and wrapped it around his wrist so it wouldn't slip away.

"No, no, no!" yelled Sven, taking the rope from him and tethering it to one of the cleats bolted to the observation deck. "Better it takes that than your arm," he laughed and patted Hal on the cheek.

Hal shook his head in nervous agreement. "How can you be this calm?"

"Eh?" said Sven, cupping his hand behind his ear.

"I said, how are you so calm!" said Hal.

Sven smiled. "The ocean is like a woman! You must love her even when she is not so kind!" He laughed madly and howled at the sky, water pouring off his blond, dreadlocked beard.

Hal laughed, too, despite himself. For the first time since the rain started, the thought of the boat sinking wasn't at the forefront of his mind. He blew out a cloud of frozen air. "Sven?"

Sven stopped howling. "What is it, my friend?"

Hal pointed to the water. "I saw something!"

"Yes, big waves!" said Sven.

"No, listen!" said Hal, closing his eyes and holding still so that he could hear the whistles and clicks. "What is that?"

Sven closed his eyes to listen. The smile faded from his face, and he looked over the edge.

"What is it?" said Hal, no longer feeling at ease.

Sven forced a smile. "It is nothing! It is only dolphin!"

"Dolphins?" said Hal. "I don't think so! I've seen lots of dolphins!" He pointed down at the water. "They don't look like any dolphin I've ever seen!"

Sven grabbed Hal's hand that pointed at the water. "Do not point!" He screamed in Hal's face. "It is only dolphin!"

Hal tried to back away. "Okay, okay."

Sven turned away in a huff, muttering in Swedish.

"Sven," said Hal. "I'm sorry if I…" he started to say, but was cut off by a sudden jolt. The entire boat jerked backwards as if it had reached the end of a towline at full speed, sending Hal and Sven tumbling towards the bow. Hal's back bent awkwardly around the guardrail, knocking the wind out of him and sent bolts of pain through his limbs. Sven rolled and slid by, but managed to hold onto Hal's leg before being tossed overboard. Hal ground his teeth and rain bouncing off his face as he grabbed the back of Sven's jacket.

The bow began to slowly rise as the stern dipped into the icy waters. Hal held what little breath he could manage to gulp into his lungs. The boat was steadily being pulled into the ocean depths.

A deep crack shook every inch of the seventy-foot research vessel. The bow dropped and splashed down, making everything on board bounce, to include Hal and Sven, who clung to each other and the guardrail. The Cape Hadel was freed to be tossed about the waves once again.

"We must get off the roof!" yelled Sven.

Hal shook his head in agreement, but his back and legs were numb, making it was hard for him to navigate the slippery observation deck. He grabbed Sven's shoulder, "I think you and the ocean are in an abusive relationship!" For a long second Sven stared blankly, then let out a boisterous laugh. Hal smiled, leaned against the guardrail, and closed his eyes.

"You found your humor! Good!" Sven said and howled at the sky, a howl that abruptly stopped.

The rain that hit Hals cheek and lips was warm, tasting coppery and familiar. He looked up and around. He was alone on the deck. He wiped his face and looked at the red stain that was being washed away.

"Sven?" Hal screamed and spun in circles, looking over the edge. "Sven!" He crawled quickly to the bow. "Catherine!"

he yelled, but she was nowhere to be seen. He turned to go back to the ladder. He had to tell someone the crewman was likely overboard.

Hal flinched and turned around as another flash of lightning lit up the night's sky. For the briefest of moments, the lightning trailed behind a one hundred-foot wave rolling their way. Though paralyzed by the sight of the wave, he could clearly see the silhouette of an enormous tentacle, spanning nearly the length of the wave, curling inside it. There were also dozens of smaller creatures in the wave, the ones he had seen swimming around the boat he reckoned, racing up it toward the tentacle.

"Dear God," Hal mouthed, unable to actually speak. The light receded back into darkness. His eyes were locked on where the monstrous image once was.

The rope Sven had tied down broke. The antenna whipped up and caught Hal on the side of his head. Unconscious, his prone body slid off the observation deck and nearly overboard, but instead landed on the main deck. The antenna snapped from its base and sailed into the night.

***

"Hal," said Catherine inches from his face. She gently smacked his cheeks to rouse him.

The sun behind her stabbed at the migraine headache through his eyelids. He groaned and tried to block it out with his hand, but a sharp pain in his shoulder made him hesitate. His whole body felt battered, like he'd been run over by a street sweeper. He squeezed his eyes shut and rolled to the side to vomit.

"He's fine," announced Catherine. She rubbed his back and looked away, not breathing through her nose. "You couldn't have done that over the side, could ya," she said between her teeth. She couldn't look directly at him, but handed over a canteen of water. "Here. Drink this."

Hal graciously took the water, washed out his mouth, and splashed it in his face. He rubbed his neck and tried to sit up.

"Sven. We were on the observation deck." His throat burned.

"Yeah," said Catherine. "Figure he's probably in the same place as our VHF antenna." She pulled Hal's glasses out of her pocket and handed them to him. One of the lenses was shattered and the frame was taped together.

"Thanks," he said and tried to get to his feet.

The ocean was calm and still. There wasn't a breeze to be felt.

"Easy," she said and waved to a couple of research assistants, Joe Bixby and Tom Cohen, to help.

The vessel's Captain, Peter Leven, stood on the observation deck, looking down at Hal. None of them had ever seen him smile, but the scowl on his face now seemed more unpleasant than usual. Hal chalked it up to him losing one of his crewmen, and possibly a friend, in the storm. He sympathetically nodded to the old man, who held the remaining rope still tethered to the cleat and squinted down at Hal.

The cabin's interior was a wreck. Food, papers, and personal items lay strewn across the floor. Anything that was not tied down during the storm was now pushed to the side to make a walking lane. Fumes from all-purpose cleaners stung his eyes, but it wasn't enough to mask the stink of his seasick and unwashed colleagues in the poorly ventilated cabin.

Joe cleared the couch while Tom lowered Hal down as easy as he could. Out the window, Hal could see Captain Leven having an intense yet hushed conversation with Edvin, the remaining crewman, and Sven's younger brother. Hal could tell they were intentionally trying to not look his way. Edvin threw up his hands and stormed off.

"Clara?" said Catherine. "Anything yet?"

Clara Brighton, research assistant and tech manager, popped off her headphones and mussed her purple hair back into its intentionally-messy position. "Still nothing on the radio, Doctor Singer."

Catherine pinched the bridge of her nose and squeezed her eyes shut. "I could have told you that."

"Then you need to be more specific with your questions,"

said Clara. Joe and Tom hid their smirks. "But it looks like our beacon is kaputski, too."

"Awesome. Does anyone have any ideas about figuring out where we are?" said Catherine, resting against the wall.

"Maybe the captain can tell by the stars?" said Joe.

Catherine sighed, "It's 8:00 am, Joe."

Pain shot through Hal's shoulder and hip as he sat up. "If it still works, we could have Clara check the sounder. We can get an idea as to where are by looking at the ocean floor."

"Way ahead of ya, chumley," said Clara, clicking away at the terminal. "And, surprisingly, we are good. Wait."

Catherine pushed away from the wall. "Wait for what."

"Must be a glitch. I'm going to reboot," said Clara, frowning.

"What's the glitch?" said Hal. "How close are we to the Continental Slope?"

"According to this? Not far." said Clara.

"Clara," said Catherine. "What is our current depth?"

Clara twisted the headphone cord between her fingers and mumbled, "4,700 meters."

"What?" yelled Tom, running his fingers through his hair. "That's almost the Abyssal Plain."

"We're not equipped to be out this far," Joe said weakly, staring into nothing.

Catherine folded her arms over her chest and took a deep breath through her nose.

"Clara, please reboot the system and check again," said Hal.

"Dude," said Clara. "This is the weirdest topography I've ever seen."

Hal grimaced as he leaned closer to the monitor. "Just looks like a hill with some draws coming off of it."

She spun around in the chair and gawked at him. "Yeah!" she said. "Eight long draws. You know, like an octopus? I am so claiming this little hill as my discovery. Hello oceanic society, meet Brighton's Kraken."

"That's great, but don't you think we have bigger concerns

right now?" said Hal.

"Clara, just take down the coordinates and make a note," said Catherine impatiently. She sighed. "We still have a job to do. Are we at least able to get a read on the Great Whites we tagged?"

"Actually," said Clara, "That's one of the few things that still works."

"Great Whites?" said Joe, wiping his eyes. "Screw the job! How is it possible, even in a storm, to get 400 miles off course?"

"You don't!" said Captain Leven loudly in his slight Scandinavian accent. There was no telling how long he had been standing in the doorway, and it was obvious he wasn't wearing his hearing aid anymore. He took a step inside the cabin and scratched the grey scruff on his neck. "Maybe if the engines were on full and we were heading due east, but like I told you before, doctor, we have no engines and we aren't pointing east."

"Enough," said Catherine.

"We were dragged here," said Captain Leven.

"I said that's enough!" shouted Catherine. "All I need from you right now, captain, is to know how you're going to get us going again. Do you understand me?"

Captain Leven nodded, "Aye, doctor." He turned to leave, but not before looking every member of the research team in the eye before he ducked out of the cabin.

Joe rocked back and forth, shaking his head, "Dragged by what?"

"Joe!" said Catherine, regaining her composure. "Joe, I need you to get a grip. Yes, we are experiencing some setbacks, but you need to see the upside."

"Upside?" said Joe with a nervous laugh.

"Yes, upside," said Catherine. All eyes were on her. "From what I can tell, this is unexplored terrain. We may have already made one discovery."

"Brighton's Kraken," interjected Clara.

Catherine ignored her. "And I'm sure there is plenty more

out there to occupy ourselves with until the boat is repaired or we can make contact with the mainland. It's our obligation as scientists to keep pushing forward. So calm down or I will calm you down." There was a haunting coldness in her voice.

Hal cleared his throat to break the awkward silence. A few minutes ago, the idea of moving out into deeper waters would have sounded like lunacy to him, but she was right: fortune favors the brave. "She has a point. Panicking won't accomplish anything. We should keep going."

Joe and Tom shook their heads in reluctant agreement.

"Clara, where're the sharks at?" said Catherine.

"Chillin at Brighton's Kraken," said Clara.

"Pardon?" said Catherine, walking over to the monitor. The blip on the screen showed at least three of the five tagged sharks clustered directly below their feet. "I thought you said the tags were working."

"Clara," said Hal. "Reboot the system, please."

"Rodger-dodger," said Clara, powering down their radar. She winced and balled over, throwing her headphones against the wall. A high-pitched squeal pierced through the headphones loud enough that everyone covered their ears until the machine turned off a few seconds later. "What the hell was that?" said Clara, massaging her ringing ears.

"It sounded like some sort of whale song on steroids," said Tom, wiggling a finger in his ear.

More of the same moaning whistles could be heard outside. Tom held up his hands to silence everyone in the room. Another whistle and clicking seemed to pass by the boat. Tom rushed to the door and looked over the edge.

Hal's heart sped up, and his mouth went dry. He heard those same noises shortly before Sven died. "Stop!" he yelled at Joe, who was walking to the door to see what Tom was looking for.

The boat rose and fell as the ocean swelled underneath them. Everyone held onto something bolted down. Another swell, a larger one, rocked the boat. Pens, maps and bottles of water rolled off the tables and desk. The Cape Hadel was starting to spin.

Hal got to his feet and stumbled to the door.

Catherine blocked the door. "Where are you going?"

"I need to get Tom before he falls overboard," he said, feeling it was as much as he could rationally explain. Outside, the seas were getting choppy, and the clouds zipped by as the boat spun faster. "Stay here," he told her.

Hal fell out the door and hung onto the guardrail. Focusing his eyes on the deck helped keep his stomach from acting up. "Tom!"

Tom was on his knees with his forehead resting on the guardrail.

Whistles and clicking echoed around the boat. Dolphin noises again, Hal told himself as he crawled to Tom. Saltwater sprayed upward all around. Every step closer to Tom reminded Hal of his bruised hip and pounding head injury.

Hal couldn't tell if it was drool or just water running off Tom's chin. His face was white and his pink eyes were wide open. He was slack jawed and mumbling. Hal shook him until he looked at him.

"They're not real," said Tom. Tears ran from his puffy, quivering eyes.

"What?" Hal started to say as a hand, its skin was slick and grey-blue like that of a dolphin's, reached over the guardrail and palmed Tom's face. Its talon-like fingernails dug into his neck. His screams were muffled by the thick webbing between its long fingers. A pair of oversized blue eyes crested the guardrail and stared at Hal. The creature made creaking, clicking noises as Hal scrambled backward, eyes locked with the creature. A second hand reached over, grabbed Tom's coat, and pulled him overboard. Blood sprinkled the gunwale. The boat spun faster.

"Tom!" yelled Hal, pulling himself up to look for his friend. Waves splashed around the hull. Bile pushed its way up from his stomach and his head swooned. They were caught in a whirlpool, and there were at least three larger whirlpools occurring around them.

The creatures jumped and skipped along the waves, distorted humanoids with fins where legs should be. Hal slumped to the deck and pulled his knees to his chest until the Cape Hadel eventually came to a halt.

When he opened his eyes, Captain Leven was standing over him. "You can't seem to stay out of trouble, Mr. Banks," said Captain Leven.

"Hal!" said Catherine, dropping to his side. "Where's Tom?"

Shaking, Hal pointed to the red spatter on the bow.

"Oh my God," she said.

"Doctor Singer, we need to talk!" said Captain Leven.

"Now is not the time," she said, and shouldered Hal with Joe's help.

The cabin was in greater disarray than before. Hal was dumped back on the couch. Somebody definitely threw up again.

Captain Leven and Edvin stepped into the cabin behind Catherine. "They were murdered!" Captain Leven bellowed.

"Preposterous." said Catherine. "Nobody on this boat was murdered."

He leaned in to hear her better, which made Catherine give him the stink eye.

He smirked at her. "I would tend to agree with you, Doctor, if it weren't for this rope." He held up the frayed piece of rope that had held down the VHF antenna. "Do you see this? This rope did not break by itself. It was cut. Tell me, Mr. Banks, what happened to poor Sven? Did the antenna truly knock him overboard? And what of Mr. Cohen? I doubt he bumped his head while we spun around like a top."

Hal took a sip of water. "I'm not sure." He licked his lips. "I think that maybe Sven fell off before the rope broke."

Captain Leven walked up to him. "Did you kill my crewman and your colleague, Mr. Banks?"

Edvin locked eyes with him. Hal looked away and around the room for help.

"Don't worry, Mr. Banks," said Captain Leven. "You

could no more kill a man than you could reel in Leviathan by yourself."

Hal laughed and slunk down into the couch.

"But something cut this rope," said Captain Leven. "Tell me, Mr. Banks, what did you see in those waters just now? I wager it was the same last night."

"Hal, you don't have to answer that," said Catherine.

"No, it's alright," said Hal. "I saw dolphins."

Edvin chuckled and echoed, "Dolphins."

Captain Leven shushed him and looked back at Hal. "They weren't dolphins, were they, Mr. Banks?" said captain Leven.

"I don't know," said Hal.

"They were Merfolk, weren't they?" said the captain, scratching his chin.

Catherine scoffed. "Really? We're going to blame Mermaids? Captain, I didn't hire you to tell old fisherman tales and we sure as hell aren't going to waste our time singing Under the Sea!"

Clara giggled, drawing all eyes on her. "What?" she said. "It was funny. Unda da sea," she sang briefly before sitting quietly.

Captain Leven looked around the room. "This is no joking matter. Merfolk are not what you think, and you, Mr. Banks, are lucky to be alive. Merfolk are omens. Vicious creatures; harbingers of death and despair."

"So, we're being hunted by Mermaids?" asked Joe, visibly shaking.

"Don't be stupid, boy!" said the captain. "No, we are not being hunted. Sven and Tom were convenient."

"Convenient?" asked Joe.

Captain Leven looked at Joe as if a stench was rolling off him. "Sea creatures have to eat, too."

Joe leaned against the wall and stared at nothing again, "Well, that's disappointing."

The terminal beeped as it came back on, making Clara jump. "And speaking of disappointments other than Disney lying to us, it looks like I totally forgot to jot down the coordinates to my claim-to-fame before we drifted off."

"That's not funny, Clara," said Hal. "But are you saying that we're lost again?"

"Sorry, and yes," said Clara. "Sadly, we are no longer at Brighton's Kraken."

"What about the Great Whites?" asked Catherine.

"For the love of God, Catherine," said Hal. "Two people are dead."

Catherine folded her arms over her chest. "I know. And I don't feel like coming back out here on another expedition if I don't have to. Do you?"

"I have them on radar," interrupted Clara. "They're, uh, right next to us."

Catherine was the first out the door, pushing past Captain Leven, who barely acknowledged her. Clara and Joe fought to be next as Hal managed to get to his feet.

Captain Leven stopped him. Hal was captivated by the look in the old man's eyes and his trembling bottom lip. "I know what you saw," said the captain and let Hal by.

Hal finally broke eye contact when Clara screamed. The water was painted red. The tattered carcasses of four Great White Sharks bobbed in the waves. Some were torn into segments, others were barely recognizable as sharks. All looked as if they had been chewed upon by something vastly more imposing than themselves.

"What could do that to a shark?" said Joe meekly.

"A shark? Try four sharks," said Clara. "I think there's four," she continued with a nauseous burp.

"Land!" yelled Edvin from the bow. He ran back to the researchers with a beaming smile. "There is an island not too far from here."

"Oh thank God," said Joe.

Clara hopped up and down, clapping her hands.

Captain Leven stared at the island and removed his stocking cap, holding it to his chest.

"Edvin," said Hal. "Do you think everyone can fit in the life boat for one trip?"

Clara and Joe led the way to the bow to see the island with Edvin and Hal following close behind. The trip could be dangerous, thought Hal, but at least they wouldn't be out in the open water to be eaten by sea monsters.

A tremendous thud against the hull rocked the Cape Hadel, tipping it sideways. Everyone held on the guardrail or one another.

With everyone fixated on the island, Captain Leven caught a fistful of Catherine's hair and threw her into the cabin by her scalp. He slammed the door behind him and locked it.

It was her screams that caught Hal's attention. He tried the latch but it wouldn't budge. "Catherine!" he yelled and pounded on the door with his fist. She screamed again and it sounded like something crashed to the floor. Despite the searing pain, Hal braced himself and kicked the door open.

Captain Leven had Catherine pinned down, and a filet knife held to her throat. Blood trickled from her nose and there was a gash below her eye. "Stand back, Mr. Banks!" ordered the captain. "She must pay for what she's done to us!"

Hal held up his arms. "Easy now. How would killing anyone make things better?"

Captain Leven let out a desperate laugh. "You know nothing of the sea, boy. She's no more a woman than that is an island out there!"

"Hal, please," sobbed Catherine.

Others were standing in the doorway behind Hal, who kept them at bay. "Captain, let's think this through."

"Aye," said the captain. "Let's do. Was it not her pretty words of fame and fortune that convinced us all to board this vessel? Was it not her pretty words that convinced us beyond our good judgement to venture too close to that storm? And even now she is trying to lure us into continuing onward to our deaths. I had my suspicions after losing my hearing aid during the storm and could no longer hear her song, but the Merfolk made me a believer. She's a Siren, and you are all under her spell."

"Hal," said Catherine, her voice shaking.

"A Siren?" said Hal, trying not to upset the captain. "Like singing bird-women who sit on rocky coasts, drawing sailors to their death?"

"Aye," said the captain.

"Listen. Once we get our bearings and find out what did that to those sharks we'll all just go our merry ways. But we need to get to the island," said Hal, inching closer to him.

"Do not think of me as a fool, Mr. Banks. You've seen the Merfolk. Now separate truth from legend," said Captain Leven. Spittle hung from his lip. "She must die!"

The vessel swayed and bobbed, then shook to a halt as if they had landed on a sandbar in the open ocean. Everyone stood still, holding their breath.

"Must have drifted closer to the island," said Clara.

The ocean bubbled and splashed around the boat. An enormous tentacle shot out of the deep and wrapped around Edvin, yanking him into the air. The crewman kicked and screamed until the life was squeezed out of him and he was plunged beneath the waves.

Another tentacle crashed through the hull and guardrail, snatching Clara from Joe's arms. "Clara!" he yelled, but she was gone.

Hal turned back to Catherine. She was smiling up at Captain Leven, who still held the knife to her throat. "Too little, too late, old man," she said and inhumanly screeched like a bird of prey. Hal slapped his hands over his ears.

Captain Leven pushed down, turned her screeching into gurgles as he cut through her esophagus with a single, powerful slice.

The hull groaned and splintered under their feet, spraying ocean water and fiberglass up into the cabin. A tentacle ripped up and thrashed around the room, smashing Captain Leven against the ceiling. Catherine's body sank from sight into the frothing water.

Hal staggered backward out the door. The cabin windows exploded as the tentacle slapped against the inside wall, sending Joe overboard in a rain of glass. The bow of the Cape Hadel submerged, pulled down by the massive tentacles wrapped around it. The island rose up from the depths.

The eyes of the Kraken crested the waves. Hal stood petrified, an insignificant man in the presence of a god. The freezing waters of the Atlantic flooded in around him as the Cape Hadel was claimed by the terrible deep.

SEASTRUCK

John Everson

Be careful what you look for…it might find you first.

The hair rose on the back of his neck, and Andy suddenly had that creepy feeling that he was being watched. He did a slow 360-degree turn, staring down the empty, rock-strewn beach, and up the winding path of dozens of crooked stone steps that had led him down from the tiny French village to here. There was nobody around… and no place for anyone to be hiding. The sea moved and moaned ahead of him as a gull screeched somewhere just off shore, long and plaintive. Then again. The bird sounded anxious, but there was no reply. Although the sun still hung strong at the edge of the horizon, the place was grey, foreboding and lonely.

It was a familiar feeling for Andy. He'd been feeling that way since the night he left Cassie lying lifeless beneath the waves near an empty beach in California.

But that was years ago, and he was far from there. *And that hadn't been his fault!* He told himself that same thing every time he thought of her, but it didn't make a difference.

He felt as if he stood at the edge of the world. There was something different about this place; he had walked the beaches north of San Francisco a thousand times, and while it had always felt isolated…he'd never felt this remote.

But he had flown halfway around the world to be here because…well…this was where the map had led him.

He pulled the photocopy of the ancient parchment out of his pants pocket and unfolded it. The edges were so creased the thing was in danger of falling into four separate pieces. Evidence of his attention; he'd stared at it a lot. In his apartment. On the plane across the ocean. In the cab on the way to his hotel.

The map had been very specific. It plotted coordinates using old school sailor methods that, with a little work, Andy had been able to match up with Google maps. The Internet was a wonderful thing. And the old rum-runner captain who'd stuffed that map into a bottle and kept it corked and stowed in his cabin trunk had probably seen a very similar scene when he'd been on this beach a hundred years ago to what Andy was seeing now. The tiny village at the top of the stone steps most likely had fewer people living in it now than then. When he had passed through it to find the steps to the sea, he had barely seen a soul... most of the buildings seem to have fallen into disrepair.

Andy walked down the beach and traversed the arc of a long rocky finger that jutted out into the ocean. While, in the scheme of things, this was a small inlet, it still took him 10 minutes to reach the tip of the finger once he'd rounded the corner.

When he did, Andy stopped, and stared out at the ocean. The waves were moving slow, and steady. According to the old map, the reason he was here was just beneath his feet. But the white crash of saltwater on the rocks three feet away didn't lend confidence to that. It felt as if this bank was a solid wall of stone and sand leading steadily down to the ocean floor.

Andy set down his backpack, kicked off his sandals and stripped off his shirt.

He wasn't going to wait another minute to find out if the map he had studied—literally for years now—was true.

This was the moment of truth.

As he set his shirt, sandals, and pack in a pile, Andy again had the feeling that he was being watched. But when he looked up the hill towards the dying village...he saw nothing but browning grass...and old rocks.

Andy turned and dove into the ocean.

The water was cold...enervating...and quickly dark.

Andy swam down into the surf, struggling to keep from

being slammed against the wall or pulled out to sea. The old pirate's map had basically said the thing he was looking for... was here. At the apex of the apex.

He slipped through the waves and a pang of uncertainty overtook him. More than uncertainty...pure, depressive panic.

He had been fingering and dreaming of the treasure at the end of this rainbow for years. All based simply on just a map that he'd found in an old wreck at the bottom of the ocean. A jot from a rum-runner stuffed in a bottle. Who was to say that it hadn't been false from the start? And if not...who was to say anything was left of the treasure stowed at the red X a hundred years ago?

A hard slosh of waves pushed him forward, and then sucked him back from the edge of the rocks...

And then Andy saw it.

The dark hole in the rock that said...there was no rock there. It was *too* black.

He struggled to keep his aim and kicked to move forward. His head slipped through the gap, and he grinned.

The map had not lied. There was a buried passage here, a cave-like opening, meters beneath the waves. Andy kicked to push through. He had a flashlight clipped to his belt for just this reason. The undertow threatened to drag him back, but he pushed forward, grabbing at the slick rocky edge of the wall with his hands. His fingers scraped and slipped.

And then, Andy got a push from the current as the water slid back. It allowed him just a small grip on the rocky edge, but it was enough. He pulled himself through.

The world grew strangely silent. Not that he could hear in the water before he'd entered the divide but...still...things seemed to get even quieter. The rush of the waves behind him was gone...he was hanging in a wall of dark water. It was like floating in limbo; he wasn't moving forward or back. He swept his hands out and pushed ahead.

Andy's head moved past the lip of the entry, and just beyond, he saw the slope of the ground moving up and away. He already felt his breath getting thin and he kicked to launch himself towards what he hoped was an internal opening where there would be a pocket of air above the waterline…otherwise, he had to double back quickly.

Something brushed against his back…something soft and cool. Andy shivered. Probably a fish…or seaweed. His head broke the top of the water, and he inhaled sharply, gasping for air. His eyes couldn't see anything at first, but he could breathe. The air smelled fishy and stale…but there was air. The cavern vented to somewhere.

But he couldn't see any light indicating where.

Andy swam until his knees cracked the silt. And then, he stopped swimming and climbed up on the sloping shore. When he crawled up into the darkness, he took a breath, and closed his eyes. Something brushed against his back again, and Andy jumped. He looked around sharply…but his eyes couldn't make out anything in the blackness. He reached down and felt for the flashlight he'd stashed in his belt on a loop. Found it and flicked it on.

As the room flashed painfully into view, a white explosion on his pupils, he could have sworn he saw a gray form slip off to his right.

Andy flashed the light back and forth, exposing a deep cavern of hanging stuff (seaweed?) and distant walls. He didn't see anything that might have brushed against him.

Again, at the edge of the cavern…something almost grey…not quite white…something like a flash.

It was gone.

In its wake, Andy spied the wood of ancient chests. Seven of them, lodged against the back rock wall of the deep underground cave.

This was the place. He had really found the end of the rainbow. The X on a pirate's treasure map. How unlikely— and amazing—was that?

Andy crawled over to one— the ceiling was too low to stand—and after setting the flashlight on the ground, put both hands on the edges of the wooden trunk.

Ever since he had found the map while diving off the

shore near Gull's Point in the wreck of an old rumrunner, Andy had wondered if its description was real...or if it remained still undiscovered.

And now...

He knew the map was true. There were chests from ages ago, still sitting here, in a hidden cave near a tiny shoreline town. But what did the chests actually contain?

He pushed against the lid to try to find out.

The wood creaked, and he strained to break the seal of decades of salt and warping and decay. Andy swore as his hands slipped up the side of the wood, and a sharp pain jabbed his palm. Splinter. He held his hand in the middle of the light and could see the dark spot in the skin of his hand. He grimaced as he pried it out with two fingernails.

"Damn it," he murmured again. The hand stung.

The light of the flash lying on the ground next to the chest was faint, but he could see the lid clear enough to know that it hadn't budged. Andy picked up a rock lying nearby and took aim. He slammed the rock against the corner of the chest. His shoulder stung with the impact; the chest was solid. He put his hands on the corners and shoved upward again, and this time, there was a sharp squeal as the lid lifted; the rock had loosened the seal.

Andy grinned as the heavy top rose. But as his eyes rose with the old wood, he saw that there were two legs on the other side of the chest. And attached to those was the pale V of a female crotch, the fish-white pucker of a bellybutton, and, above that, a pair of small but clearly feminine breasts, tipped by dark, coin-sized nipples. And above that...a face that made Andy gasp.

She was beautiful.

Her eyes were a piercing sea-green; her mouth small, lips a cupid's bow of bees-stung pink. Her nose rose thin and proud; her cheekbones high. Ringlets of glossy black hair swooped across her cheeks and down her shoulders.

Andy fell back from the chest to land on his butt. His heart was pounding a hundred beats a minute from shock at seeing her…and from excitement at seeing her.

But who was she?

Before he could ask, she cocked her head, opened her mouth and let out a high ululating scream. Andy put his hands to his ears as the sound pierced his head; there was a pain in the back of his eyes, but then it faded, and instead of pain, he suddenly yearned for the sound. It wasn't a scream at all, he realized. It was a song. A high-pitched trembling note of sadness that began to change as she moved. His hands dropped from his ears, and he stared at the beautiful naked woman in front of him. She stepped around the chest to stand over him, as he still sat clumsily on the damp stone. Her mouth remained open now in a perfect O, as she sang in a weird operatic soprano. The notes shivered and shifted, sounding both exotic and ancient, moving down a scale as their effect moved down his spine. He could feel his body relaxing, his groin warming. She pushed against his chest with two hands and somehow suddenly she was straddling him, her mouth inches from his own as she ran gentle fingers across his cheeks and neck. Her nails were long and dangerous. Her eyes looked into his, and he felt pinned, a butterfly on a board.

She sang a strange, entrancing melody that had no words.

He could do nothing but listen.

Andy looked into her eyes and saw the flecks of brown and amber that shifted as her pupils grew wider. He was drawn into her gaze, and as she sang, he saw nothing but green… her eyes were inches from his; somehow, she had laid him down and he couldn't remember his head touching the stone, but he didn't really care. Her lips were centimeters from his own, and her breath blew across his mouth as she still sang to him, a sensual, ululating melody that played him like a harp; each note touched a nerve of pleasure; his body moved of its own accord now, he had no will, his waist shifting with her song. He thought he saw her lips curl upwards in a smile, but that couldn't have been right because her mouth was open, and her song did not stop, she never took a breath, she just kept singing, and her eyes kept staring and…

Andy was naked and engulfed by a strange naked woman in a foreign cavern and that thought came and went as quickly as his own orgasm; he wanted to ask her for her name but then everything was black.

***

The sky here was full of stars. So many stars you could drown in their light. Endless constellations of faint and brilliant light. A myriad milky way of endless eloquent glamour, glimmer, grandeur...

Andy realized that he was lying on a beach and mentally babbling.

He sat up with a start.

Why was he lying on a beach in the middle of the night staring at the stars?

And...he realized with the heavy movement of his erection as he shifted...why was he naked?

It came back to him with a flash, the swim to the hidden cavern, the trunks of treasure, the naked woman who had never said a word to him yet somehow had stripped and taken him.

Holy shit.

But how had he ended up back here? And where were—? He stopped asking the question as he turned and saw the dark outline of his swimsuit crumpled next to his waist. Andy shook his head and yanked one leg hole over his foot. It was almost painful to pull the waistband over his manhood...which remained throbbingly, painfully erect.

"What the fuck happened tonight," he whispered, as he began to walk, a little unsteadily, back up the beach towards the faint lights of the town above.

***

Rollin-de-Callais was a dead town. When Andy woke up the next morning, and walked through the empty lobby of his hotel, he realized that while there were a lot of buildings, nobody really lived here. There had been an old stone sign, upon entering the town. And a long row of buildings, classic, long-standing stone structures that had clearly been constructed long before Andy's great-great-grandparents had been conceived. The buildings were hundreds of years old, and there was a hotel and nearby bar...but really, when you began walking around...it was quickly evident that there were very few structures that were actually occupied. Most had glass that was not only spiderwebbed with cracks, but frosted brown with the age of disuse.

Andy left his hotel and walked a few blocks, noting that all of the facades seemed well-aged. More than "well." Cracked stone. Dirty, spider-webbed windows. Closed doors. The place was a museum of dust and age. As he walked down one block, Andy wondered if anyone had been there in months. Maybe years.

It was depressing.

Eventually, he found a block where there was a fruit market, another hotel, and a café that was serving breakfast. He found a table and sat down, ordering a coffee and some eggs from a dour-looking old waitress who may or may not have spoken English. He honestly wasn't sure if they'd communicated or not when she nodded and walked away from the table.

But she did come back with a steaming cup of something black...so he had hopes for his plate.

It had scrambled eggs, a biscuit...and a brown, dried out thing that could perhaps be called bacon. He chewed it and determined that no bacon had ever tasted so poorly. It was burnt and crusty.

He drank his tiny bitter cup of coffee and stared at the pictures on the brick walls. Black and white stills of people who he did not recognize, and brands of food (or beer) that he had never tasted.

There was only one other patron at the place, at a table in the corner near a window. Andy stole the occasional glance in her direction, but she did not appear to share his curiosity. He worked on his breakfast in silence, and then, when the sullen waitress took his credit card for the bill, he finished his last bitter, salty bites of food, and then left the depressing restaurant to walk around the rest of the seaport town.

Andy wandered the next few blocks, where the town still seemed to have some life. A small news and sundries stand seemed to still be open, along with another small restaurant. There was a tiny grocery (which appeared to pull in no patrons at 9 a.m. in the morning), and a fish market, where an old Chinese man was still stocking the tray with fresh caught. It was early…and eerily still.

But the quiet was not the sleepiness of a town just before waking up. It was the silence of an abandoned place. The silence of loss.

Andy passed the tiny fish market and a small café, and then walked another three blocks past shuttered buildings before finding a corner with another open door; a small tavern called *The Gentil* which advertised "rooms available" on a small placard sign above the tall wooden doors. He looked down the street that ran along the edge of the cliff that led down to the ocean…and didn't see any other buildings that appeared occupied. Everything appeared grey and eaten by the salt and wind. The wood facades showed wide dark cracks; the windows were boarded and broken.

He looked over the edge of the cliff to the ocean, which surged grey and green against the shore below. It looked like a long fall down. The wind gusted against his chest, and he rocked with the force for a second before stepping back. If he fell, he suspected nobody would find him before the birds or crabs picked his bones completely clean below.

There was nobody really around here to find him. Andy turned away from the ocean and walked back toward *The Gentil* behind him. He was curious about the place. It was like a last outpost before the wastelands. And when he walked inside…it was a different world. The air smelled warm, full of smoke and onion. The bar was long; heavy dark wood stretched down one wall and angled 90 degrees to jut against the other. Two golden taps stretched up from the center of the bar, and behind it, the wall was covered in mirrors and glass shelves; Andy could make out a long collection of bottles of scotch—McCallan and Old Pulteney 21 years—on the second shelf, most of them dusty with age.

"How kin I help ya?" an old man's voice came from the back of the room. Andy walked deeper into the room and saw the man finally, far to the right, sitting on low wooden chair just behind the edge of the bar. The man was portly and old; his head was nearly bald, but there were long tufts of white at his ears, and a strap from his glasses that hung behind his ears.

"Just looking around," Andy said.

"Where ya from?"

"San Francisco," he answered. "Just got in last night."

The old man nodded. And raised a thick-tufted eyebrow. "And what in the serpent's name would make ya come to these parts from there?"

Andy shrugged. "A death wish?"

The old man stifled a grin and nodded.

"Might have some truth to your mouth there."

Andy walked across the creaking planks to rest an elbow on the bar. "What happened to everyone here?" He said. "It looks like the whole town closed up shop and walked away."

"They didn't walk away," the man said. "They swam."

"Did the fishing dry up here?"

The man shook his head. "The fish are just fine. It's about the other things that swim in those waters."

"What do you mean?"

The old man shrugged. "The ocean giveth, and the ocean taketh away. Some of us leave…and some of us have stayed."

Andy stepped closer to the man. "How long have you lived here?"

"All me life," the man said. "It's where I was born. But that don't make it a place that's safe. That don't make it a place where people can survive and thrive. Take a look outside and you'll see what I mean there."

"That's my point," Andy said.

The man put a hand on the edge of the bar and pulled himself upright, with a grunt and a moan.

"I will tell you this," he said. "The faster you get out of

this town, the longer you'll see the sunset."

With that, the man turned his back, and hobbled to a doorway behind the desk. He disappeared through it and never looked back, leaving Andy in an empty lobby.

"Well," he said aloud. "I guess it's a good thing I don't need a room here. He should be in sales."

Andy looked around the old room and shrugged. Then he pushed open the door and stepped back out on to the street.

He'd learned nothing. Apparently, he had been dismissed.

Andy shrugged, and walked back to his own hotel as he considered. He was here to swim to the pirate's hidden chests. He wasn't going to accomplish that by diving into the waters that other people told him to.

He walked back through the mostly mothballed town and decided to change clothes and head back to the cave he had been in yesterday. When he walked into the lobby of his small hotel, he heard a couple speaking vehemently in French in the sitting room…and an old man demanding something at the front desk in German. To him, it felt as if the town had decided that the tourist was gone, and the real people had taken over again. And the real people didn't speak English.

He walked past them all and walked up the creaky back stairs to change and get the things he needed from his room. After the previous night, he thought what he really needed was a pepper spray that worked underwater. A woman had stopped him from getting what he'd come for yesterday, and while the flashes of memory he had of the event made him feel both warm with excitement and queasy with guilt, he didn't need her to get in his way again. This had been an expensive journey…and he needed to walk away with something to show for it.

Andy walked down the creaky back wooden stairs with a backpack on his shoulder that he hoped to fill with some shiny things from an old abandoned pirate's chest. But first, he had to swim there again…and after yesterday, it was not looking like he could bet on being there alone.

Andy stripped down to his trunks on the beach, and

dropped his clothes next to the grey and listing lifeguard station that remained (and appeared to have been long relegated to abandoned status). He pulled the straps of the backpack onto his bare shoulders and walked down the cool sand and into the breaking waves.

He hoped that in the middle of the day that he wouldn't run into whatever force he had yesterday. With a deep breath and a leap, he was head down into the shadow of the waves.

***

The dark spot in the wall underwater was easy to find after yesterday…it came up quickly as he swam along the rocky finger in the water, and Andy pulled himself up and through it. When he stepped onto the dry area above the water level, Andy's heart began to beat double time. What if the woman who'd found him yesterday was still here?

The best thing he could do would be to work fast.

Andy flipped on the waterproofed flashlight that he'd packed and looked around the cavern. He quickly found the chests he'd seen the day before. He shone the light all around the underwater cavern, but other than grey walls, there was nothing to be seen. It was silent here, and dark.

Andy held the backpack open next to one of the chests, and began to move the gold chains and coins from the treasure chest into his own holder. The pirate's chest didn't need these things any more. It wouldn't care if he divested them. He worked fast. But tried in vain to do it quietly. With every clink of metal on coin, Andy shivered. And looked around. He saw nothing moving in the shadows, but he felt as if a hundred eyes were watching him. He was a beacon in the middle of the dark.

The backpack filled slowly, and Andy lifted it several times to make sure it hadn't grown too heavy. It would be just his luck to strap it on his back, end up sinking to the bottom of the ocean, and drowning because he couldn't carry it and couldn't get it off his shoulders.

He hefted it when it was about three-quarters full and decided that that was the limit. Then he swung it onto his back and stood. Holding the flashlight out in front of him, Andy started walking deeper into the cavern. He knew the safest course of action would be to dive back down the hole that he came in through…but he was curious. Where did this cavern lead…was there anything else to see?

The floor was grey and glossy when he shown the flash across it. The walls around him looked the same and grew narrower the farther he walked from the entrance. Andy stepped carefully across the damp surface, and after just a few yards, the room narrowed to a small corridor. He held the flash ahead of him and looked at the space beyond. The corridor narrowed, but on the other side, he could see that it opened out again into a wide space. And in that space…there were things that should not have been there. Things that would not normally being in a cave that was only accessible from a doorway beneath the mark of low tide.

The flash moved across a latticework of wooden walls, and something that looked, from a distance, like rumpled blankets. Andy took a breath. He knew now that the woman who'd pressed him to the ground (now, there was a euphemism) wasn't just someone else who had happened on the cave at the same time he had. People *lived* down here.

A chill went down his back when he realized that the booty in his backpack was not just lost goods. If people lived down here, then the chests were not abandoned. And that made him a thief, not a scavenger.

Andy stepped back from the corridor and moved the flash back from chest-high to focus on the floor. He was not putting the stuff back. He'd waited years and flown halfway around the world to find it. So he could not be found here.

Something slapped, wetly, on the floor somewhere nearby. He didn't wait to see what it was. Andy ran to the small open pool that led back out to the ocean. He jumped in feet-first, and as his head slipped below the surface, he thought he saw something move in the cavern he'd left behind. It could have been the shifting shadows, but to him it looked like the shifting curls of a woman's hair.

Whatever it was, it vanished a second later as his face slid beneath the steadily churning saltwater.

He panicked at first, as the water sucked him and the backpack down; he didn't float in the waves, he sank…like a stone.

He imagined arms parting the water behind him, following him down into the blue. The thought propelled him to action; he kicked hard, cupped his hands, and swiped them to his side. A moment later, Andy stopped sinking, and instead began moving slowly away from the rock ledge and towards the shore. Every feathery touch of seaweed fronds on his feet made his heart jitter.

But he walked out of the surf unchallenged. One large heavy backpack dripped water slowly but steadily down his back as he began the walk back up the sand and stairs to return to the town above. Or what was left of it.

Every few steps, he turned his head and looked behind. But all he saw was the empty, untenanted sand of a lonely beach. No angry seawomen were chasing him down. He was alone on an empty beach.

Andy left it behind as fast as humanly possible.

The dining room of the inn was all but empty that evening, and Andy ate a bowl of soup and homemade bread alone in the back corner of the room. A fireplace blazed on one wall, throwing flickers of uncertain light against the wall of trophies. Large glossy-scaled sharks and other large fish were mounted across the room. Their eyes seemed to stare and watch the room with the shifting of the light. A shiver ran down Andy's spine as the open eyes of the four-foot long, blue-gilled monster nearest to him seemed to swivel and stare straight at him.

He looked away, refusing to hold eye contact with the dead. Instead he downed the last remnants of the bland but filling stew of beef, potato and leeks in a brown gravy, and then emptied the flagon of lager the waitress had offered.

Waitress was probably a misnomer—she was likely the owner or wife of the owner, he thought. She had checked him in yesterday and was the sole person moving in and out of the kitchen. For all he knew she had cooked this dinner as well.

An older couple sat in the other corner of the room talking in whispers. Every now and then, he caught one of them staring directly at him. They quickly looked away when he met their gaze. Between them and the fish…and the guilt of having a backpack full of treasure sitting unguarded upstairs, Andy decided not to stay for another lager. He put two foreign bills into the holder and pocketed a receipt. Then he pushed back his chair and went upstairs.

There was nothing to do here but turn out the lights and go to sleep—the room had no television and was just a long and narrow space carved into the attic. The ceiling slanted down nearly to the floor on the side where his bed was shoved up against it, a tiny window broke the darkness of the night just to the other side of his headboard.

Sleep came quickly in the tiny room. But it was a troubled sleep.

Andy dreamed of that night so long ago; sex on the beach with Cassie, rough sex. And the darkness that spread out across the sand beneath her head when he realized too late what he'd accidentally done. She had brought him out to that empty stretch of beach to help her cast a sex magic spell…and her implements of magic or voodoo or whatever you wanted to call them—candles and stones and a book of spells—he'd left buried in the sand as he'd walked her body to the edge of the California precipice and dumped it into the black waves. It was a memory he'd dreamed and relived a thousand times, only this time, as her limp body splashed into the ocean below, he suddenly felt himself pulled along. He was yanked off the cliff and sailed down the rocky bank behind her, splashing into the whitecaps just behind her feet. He could taste the salt on his lips and the burn in his eyes as he opened them to see her floating just below, a naked white cruciform, arms spread-eagle, hands reaching out, it seemed, to touch the bottom of the sea.

Reaching out to touch skeletal fingers outstretched from

the ocean floor.

***

Andy woke with a jolt, his heart pounding.

His forehead felt wet, and cold.

He had come halfway across the world but he would never escape the horror of that terrible, deadly night. The guilt weighed on him like an anchor. And right now that anchor was making him feel suffocated. He wiped the water off his face; it covered his hand and he wiped it clean on the bed. Too much. He couldn't have sweated so much. Crazy. He wiped it again and felt how damp his hair was. Andy sat up, threw the covers off and stepped out of bed.

He stepped across the room to reach the lamp on a small table just beyond the window. His right foot stepped in something cold.

Something wet?

The light clicked on, and he looked at the narrow passage that led from the bed to the hallway door just 12 or 15 feet away.

There were footprints in his room.

Wet footprints on the old wooden planks. They led to… and away…from his bed.

"What the fuck," Andy breathed.

He sat down on the bed for a moment, gaping at the evidence. Someone had been staring at him sleeping. The footprints near the bed didn't even look like prints…they were small pools, the water there had dripped and spread, while someone stood there, staring. The prints nearest the door had nearly evaporated.

Who had watched him sleep?

He knew without question.

The woman from the cave. Probably here for his gold. Her gold. His heart leapt, and he jumped up and went to the backpack, still wet from the ocean. He'd set it on a towel in the corner. But his panic was unfounded. It remained undisturbed.

Andy pulled on a shirt and some jeans, and stepped out

of his room to the hallway. The faint, drying prints continued out there, and led down the stairs to the open room of the main floor. They were harder to see now, but he followed them almost to the front door before they disappeared.

"Something you need?" a gruff voice said from behind.

Andy jumped, but it was only the innkeeper woman. She stood like a tank in the center of the room, her hair in a net, her nightgown covered in a thick blue robe.

"Someone was in my room.

"What do you mean?"

He pointed at the faint smudges of wetness that led up the stairs. There were footprints in my room," he said. "Wet footprints that come all the way down here."

The old woman's eyes widened. "*Sirena*," she hissed. "What have you done?"

"What do you mean?" he asked.

"How dare you lead them to this house? In the morning, you will be gone."

"But…"

"In the meantime, lock your door," she said. And with that, she disappeared back down a dark hall behind the innkeeper's reception desk.

He looked once more at the steps that led to the front entry of the inn, and saw something glimmering in the light from the one orange lamp that remained lit on a table near the front window. Andy walked over to see what it was, and knew before he reached it that the woman had left it for him to find. He picked it off the floor and pocketed it after turning the wet coin over and over in his hand. A piece of the treasure.

Andy opened the door and stepped out of the inn onto the stone steps. Before the door closed behind him, he caught the glimmer of another coin, just a few steps from the door. He bent over and picked it up with a frown. Was this what he thought it was?

The harsh light of the moon grew stronger as he stood there, contemplating. A cloud slipped to the horizon, and he could see now almost as clearly as in daylight. The grass sparkled with early dew, and the walkway was too damp to see any individual footsteps. But he did see another coin just a few steps away. He picked it up, and continued to play the game, walking along the path. He had a feeling he knew where she was trying to lead him. When he reached the steps down to the beach, he hesitated.

But then he heard a voice from below. A beautiful, unnerving, nakedly sensual voice. A woman had begun to sing. High and tremulous notes that seemed comprised not so much of lyrics, as emotions. With every lilt of melody, his heart seemed to pump harder, and his legs moved forward almost of their own accord. Absently he shifted his pants and realized that he had an erection.

Andy put one hand on the rail to start down the stairs to the beach, following the voice. But then something smacked him against the leg.

"Ouch!" he cried out. Another one hit him in the chest.

"What the hell?"

The pain broke his attention from the song for a second, and then he saw the innkeeper standing just a few feet away, gesticulating wildly to him. She'd thrown rocks!

"What the hell?" he said.

"Get back to your bed now or you will never sleep on land again," she yelled, then turned and ran back to the inn.

Andy realized that his legs had completely answered the call of the song, and for the moment, the old woman had broken the spell. A violet tremor overtook his legs; for a few moments, he had completely lost control. Andy turned and staggered after the innkeeper. He felt sick…and drawn to the song that continued to echo from the beach below. He covered his ears and screamed, refusing to allow his mind to hear the beautiful melody. He vaulted up the steps to the inn, pushed his way through the door and then slammed it shut, holding both palms against the wood as if he was holding back a force pressing on the other side trying to get in.

When he finally turned around, the innkeeper stood near the front desk, holding a crucifix aimed in his direction. "What did you *do*?" she hissed. "Why have the *Sirena* come to my house?"

She shook her head. "Don't tell me, they will want my soul as much as yours. They have taken too many here already. I should throw you out into the night right this moment. But I am not so cruel. At the dawn..."

She let the phrase dangle, and shook her head at him, as if he were a son who'd proven a huge disappointment to her. And then she disappeared, presumably back to her bedroom.

Andy didn't sleep well. His dreams were plagued with a woman who smiled at him and sang—a beautiful, horrible, entrancing song. When the sun began to lighten the old orange and yellow threaded comforter on his bed, he rose and packed up his few belongings, slung the backpack over his shoulder, and walked out into the hall.

There was a faint murmur of talk coming from the great room below, and he leaned over the rail to look down. The innkeeper was pouring a small cup of coffee (he hated the coffee cups here, they were *all* small!) for two older men who sat in dark coats. Seamen, by the look of them, ready for any weather, though it was supposed to be a nice day today.

As Andy began to descend the stairs, the chatter stopped. He had the unnerving sensation of three sets of eyes following his feet on the steps. When he reached the bottom, one of the older men cleared his throat, and whispered something to the other. The innkeeper walked to the desk and waited for him.

Andy walked over and pulled out his billfold to pay for the two nights he had stayed. She told him the amount, with no preamble or apology for kicking him out, and a moment later, he was signing a receipt.

As he pocketed his copy, and began to walk towards the front door, one of the men called out to him.

"She'll never stop, you know. She'll follow you wherever you go."

Andy looked at the man. He looked like the sort who'd been on a fishing boat since he was seven years old. Now he was probably 50 or 60, his hair a tangle of grey waves and his eyebrows just tufts of salt and pepper fuzz.

"I live on the other side of the world," Andy said. "I don't think she'll swim across the ocean."

"Don't be so sure," came the response.

Andy shrugged and stepped out of the door.

As the door closed behind him, and he took a deep breath of the salty mist of morning, Andy realized that he didn't have a plan. He should probably have called for a cab from the inn… but he hadn't really intended to be leaving town immediately.

Andy walked away from the inn on the lonely road into the center of town. There were precious few businesses that still were *in* business here, as he'd already noted, but none of them were open now. It was too early. He wandered for a bit, and then made his way to the road that bordered the descent to the beach. The water looked grey and cold this morning, the sky still overcast as the sun burned sullenly orange on the horizon.

Was there really such a thing as a siren? He wondered. He hadn't truly believed in the sex magic that Cassie had tried to craft with him as her "donor" a decade ago, and he didn't really believe superstitions about sexy, toothy women who lured men to their deaths on the rocks of the shore. But he *had* met a strange, silent woman in an underground cave who'd left him confused, breathless, and wondering if it had all been a hallucination.

And he had been drawn like a puppet to the sounds of a woman's voice just a few hours ago. Was that proof of a siren? Or proof that he was still suffering from jet lag? He had to admit the events of the night before had left him spooked. The wet footprints next to his bed even more than the intoxicating lure of the song that had caught him in its hook. Andy walked down the broken steps that led in a winding path down the hillside to the beach. The scent of the sea was strong as he stepped over froth-covered brown fronds of broken seaweed until he stood on hard packed sand, still wet from the last large wave.

He looked out along the promontory that extended into

the grey-blue expanse of water. Did Sirens live there, tucked out-of-sight below the waterline? Or, more likely, a band of gypsy squatters?

The beach gave no answers.

Part of him longed to swim back out there with his backpack and unload the treasure to return it to where he'd found it. Then he could at least alleviate himself of that guilt. If the gold belonged to that woman, who was he to fly across the world, walk into her home, and steal it from her?

On the other hand...

Andy shook his head. He would not give up what he'd come so far to find. Tonight he'd sleep miles from here, and tomorrow he'd be in a plane flying halfway around the world. The gold was now his. Simple as that.

He turned away from the endless horizon to walk back up the stairs and out of this forsaken town.

And found that he was no longer alone.

A woman stood on the first step leading up, blocking his way.

A woman with long, kinked black hair, and startling eyes.

A familiar, naked woman.

Andy averted his eyes in embarrassment for a moment, but then looked back at her once more. He was not spying; she blocked his way.

It was the woman who had seduced him in the underwater cave. He would not fall for that again. Andy began to walk toward her. She remained stationary, a perfect carving of flesh and beauty. A signpost between the strange world of the sea, and the human world above. A toll keeper? He had a feeling he knew what she wanted. It was in his backpack.

Andy drew closer, and as he did he felt his heart pump faster. She was beautiful. And dangerous. There was something about her stance that told him she was no frail flower. She may have been naked, but she was not helpless.

"Hi," he said, when he was just a few steps away. "I was just leaving."

She shook her head at that, very slowly. And then opened

her mouth to let loose a piercing cry. No, not a cry, a song. That initial note drew his attention, and then turned into a quivering, baleful note that shifted and dove, changing emotions and pitches without notice. Andy felt his bones weighed by sadness and then buoyed by joy. Erotic longing, and then desperation. He realized as she stepped towards him, still singing, that he could not move.

Literally could not move. His legs were locked, his fingers frozen.

She slipped her arms around his shoulders, and he felt the hard points of her nipples press against his t-shirt as she drew him close, all the while, still singing. The sky behind her grew faint and his vision blurred. All he could focus on were her eyes...sea-green and hungry, staring deeply into his own as her voice drew him into her.

Then her lips met his, and the sound shifted inside him. Andy felt his feet moving, cold slipping up his calves. Part of him wanted to scream, as the chill of water reached his waist, but her eyes held his, and the vibration of her song filled his mouth. Then her face pushed his beneath the water, and Andy tried to scream. She only stroked his back and drew him with her through the waves. He closed his eyes to block the salt and found that he couldn't reopen them. And why would he want to? He was held safe in her arms, drew breath from her song, moved forward on her kicks.

***

Andy lay in a bed of moss. He didn't know how long he'd been there, and couldn't tell whether it was night or day; there were no windows here, though there was a faint light. The walls held what looked like faint flames; patches of phosphorescent green and orange glowed atop golden torch holders. Sea lights.

Something warm and soft covered him; a blanket of some kind, though not made of cotton. It felt thin as paper, but held in his heat. And a good thing, he realized, as he shifted to roll on his side and realized his clothes were gone.

A rustling nearby. Cool thighs slid into the small bed

beside his own.

The woman from the beach. She rolled atop him. In the faint light, her cat-green eyes seemed to glow with their own energy. Her heavy lips parted, and with a thin pink tongue, she traced the edges of his lips. He felt himself respond beneath her, and she spread her legs to meet him, shifting slowly, sinuously across his hips until his eyes widened, and her breath hitched. She lowered her sex and her lips onto his simultaneously, drawing him into her from both ends. Andy's eyes almost rolled back in his head as the pleasure of her washed over him, animal pure and amazing. His tongue wrestled with hers, and then he jumped when he caught his tongue on what felt like a hook. She opened her mouth and he withdrew his tongue, just barely catching a glimpse of the teeth within. They looked too numerous…and shark sharp.

It clicked in his brain then that she truly was not human. Not exactly. But that didn't stop his hips from moving faster to meet her own, or his cry of release when he couldn't hold back any more and he let go, encouraged by the sharp bleats of her own orgasm. His head rolled back then, and he struggled to catch his breath. His mouth held the faint taste of iron, from his own blood, and his waist felt nearly numb.

Her long nails trailed across his forehead and down his chest, slowly, exploring him without a word. And then, she pressed a kiss to his lips and slid away.

Andy felt sated and strange…and slipped easily back into sleep.

The next time he woke, she brought him food: fresh slabs of fish and green fronds of something he knew grew from the ocean floor. He was tempted to refuse it, but his stomach growled, and she pushed a cube of the white meat to his lips, nodding her head. He accepted it finally, and saliva burst throughout his mouth with the first taste. It was rich and creamy and wonderful.

He didn't need her encouragement to finish the rest.

When he was finished, she led him out of the bed to walk around the shadowy expanse of her home. The phosphorescent torches lit their way, as they stepped through a small path between two large boulders and into a larger space, which clearly was where she spent most of her "home" time. And clearly, she didn't do it alone. Seated at a long driftwood table were three other women. All of them lithe and attractive. Andy was acutely aware of his nakedness now. But the women were as bare as the siren who'd led him to them.

They spoke to each other in a language he could not fathom; it was high-pitched and fast, and one of them, a pale blond-haired girl with ice blue eyes, looked directly at him at one point and laughed. The girl nodded quickly, and laughed again.

"Do you speak any English?" he asked, and the women only looked back and forth at each other blankly. Then they continued to jabber amongst themselves. At one point, one of them walked across the room to an old chest, and opened it to rummage around within. She pulled something out, and then walked across the room to present it to him.

He took it and marveled at the ancient leather. The front cover read simply, *The Bible.*

He didn't believe in *The Bible* anymore than he believed in Sirens, he thought. And then raised an eyebrow at himself given the change in his situation. Perhaps he would have to reconsider *The Bible*.

He shook his head and pushed it back across the table. The woman frowned, and then went back to the chest. She pulled out two more books and dropped them on the table in front of him. They were of different vintages, one with a black cover, one of red leather.

The Bible, they both read.

"So that's the way it's going to be, huh?"

He leafed through one for awhile, before settling back in his chair to stare up at the dark ceiling of the cave. He didn't know what was expected here, or how long he was to stay, but he was not going to memorize the "good book" as he waited to find out.

Someone had gotten up from across the table.

The blue-eyed girl. She was the tiniest of them all, a thin waif with almost a boyish chest, her small nipples only raised slightly from the plain of her tummy. But she was gorgeous, he thought. Her skin was pale and covered in a faint down, and her smile contagious.

She was smiling at him now.

She drew him to his feet with one slender hand and led him down a different hall then he had entered this room by. They ducked beneath a low ceiling and then they were in a tiny little side cave. It was decorated in pink—pink tapestries and flowers and beads. When she pushed him towards the small cot against the wall he saw it was draped in pink sheets that clearly were not woven underwater...these had been taken from the mainland. While his captor lived naturally, this Siren was clearly entranced by human things.

And apparently he was one of the things she was taken with, he thought, as she pressed him to the bed and straddled him without any foreplay.

She drew his hands up to cup her nascent breasts, and once again, he was ready for a woman's need in a heartbeat. She wasted no time in making use of him, and grinned a sharp-toothed smile when he broke that tight boundary and slid inside her with a wet jab. Her jaw yawned back, and then she slammed her chest down against his own, and rolled, drawing him to his side and then pushing him to take her from the top, missionary. Her fingernails dug into his back like tickling knives, and he gasped and thrust faster, urged on by her wild desire. It should have been over fast, but she milked him for what seemed like an hour, shifting and turning and scratching him until they both screamed together, her eyes and mouth wide and sexily inhuman.

When they were done, she draped herself over him. Without saying a word, she went to sleep with her head on his chest.

The next time he woke, there were bodies on *either* side of him. Neither appeared to be the women from before. But when the one with long straight black hair saw he was awake, she put her finger to her lips and hissed "Shhhhhh," before slipping that same finger between his legs to prod and tease him awake once more. He didn't think he could possibly go again so soon, but this girl teased well, and…bit; his chest was bleeding in three different places when she finally finished grinding herself to happiness.

But she fucked him silently, and when she was done, and he was empty, she put her finger to her lips again, and slipped back out of bed to disappear back out of the hall.

Andy waited a few minutes, but the other girl next to him didn't stir. Slowly, he slid a foot out of the low mattress and tiptoed out of the room. He thought he was going in the direction of the main room, but instead he found himself at a set of stairs carved into the stone. Shrugging, he decided to explore, and walked down. The walls provided enough illumination to see a few feet in front of him, but it was the smell that ultimately reached him before the source.

He rounded a corner and found himself in a cave of death.

A literal boneyard.

The air stank of rot and dank fish and decay. Stacked against all the walls were piles of bones. Leg bones, rib cages, hands. Stacked like a tower in the center of it all were a hundred human skulls, all of the eyeholes aimed at the doorway. As if they were watching.

"Oh hell," Andy whispered. Lying near the doorway were four bodies that were clearly waiting to be disassembled to join the rest. While most of the bones had been picked clean, there was still some yellow fat and red gristle hanging from the joints, and the legs and arms were all still connected to the core. That was what the smell was, he realized. Not-so-old remains.

Andy backed away from the room, his heart pounding.

He had a horrible suspicion that if he didn't find a way out of here, that his recent pleasure would quickly be turning to pain.

"No fuckin' way," he said, and stole back along the corridor, listening carefully to make sure he didn't stumble on one of the Sirens. This was their lair, and he had no idea *where* he really was...but he knew one thing—he was not going to be caught. That said, he probably didn't have much time until someone realized he was missing.

The open room with the driftwood table was still empty when he finally found it, and he stole across the center, back to the hallway where his captor had originally led him in here from. He passed the place where he'd first awoken in her bed, and moved fast down a corridor that he hoped led back to the outer room where he'd originally found the gold. He couldn't afford to be cornered now.

The corridor opened out on a familiar space. Andy smiled. Home stretch. He'd found it easily.

The chests were just across the room. And so were his backpack and clothes. He ran to them, and pulled his cold, soggy jeans over his legs with difficulty. His shirt was still soggy too; it made him shiver, but he got it on. And then, he picked up the backpack. He could leave it...but to hell with that. After all of this? No. He had earned his reward.

He slung it over his shoulder and moved to the small pool in the corner where the ocean exit was. Andy put one foot in the water and grinned. From here to the beach before they woke. He could do it.

That's when the song hit him.

A quartet of painful harmony. The most beautiful thing he had ever heard. He turned slightly and saw them, four naked Sirens, all signing in unison, a song that echoed in his mind with inhuman screams and angelic sighs. A song that brought his cock to erection, and his eyes to a leaden droop. A song that made him feel like puking and gorging at the same time. A song that brought every emotion he had ever had back at once, a fury of dreams and nightmares.

His captor, she of the curled black hair, strode forward ahead of the others, and gripped him by both arms. She continued to sing, but shook her head at him in disgust. Then she lifted the backpack from him and tossed it easily back to the chests. With one palm, she slapped him across the face.

Between that and the force of the song, Andy fell. The melody rose louder and angrier until he felt his ears grow hot with pounding blood. He was sure his brain was leaking out onto the floor, but he couldn't move a muscle.... He could only lie there and tremble as they took out their anger on him in song.

When the pain in his eyes grew to be more than he could bear, he let go. The waters of unconsciousness washed the sound away.

***

Andy woke naked once more.

The bed was soft, softer than any bed he'd ever slept in.

Not only hadn't they killed him, but they'd made him even more comfortable than before. So...that was something. But what did they *want* from him? Why had she brought him here and why wouldn't they let him leave? Surely they weren't just going to play musical beds with him until he finally got a bad case of erectile dysfunction?

He opened his eyes and stretched.... There *were* worse ways to be held prisoner, he thought. And then realized he couldn't move his arms. Or his legs. *Shit.*

He craned his head and confirmed that he'd been tied, spread-eagled, to the bed.

And it wasn't really a bed, but a thick mattress of something downy soft on the floor. As he looked across the room, he could see two small toddlers hunched over something in the corner. He looked around and saw that the ceiling was very low here, and mobiles made of the white bones of fish heads and colorful seashells twirled and spun. He was in a nursery.

Something tickled his foot, and he twitched, trying to push whatever it was away.

There was a faint noise. A baby's cry.

Something soft and wet covered his big toe. The wetness was followed by a sound. A coo. Tiny hands on his thigh. Grasping fingers, tickling near his belly, reaching lower to his groin. Touching something that shouldn't be touched, not by a baby. And then, he felt something wet suck down on him there too. Testing. Tasting.

No, he panicked. *Wrong. No.*

He shook, trying to dislodge the babies, but instead, he only attracted the attention of the two toddlers across the room. They both turned from the toy they'd been playing with, and squealed in delight when they saw what was going on in the bed. They stumbled towards him, and he could see now what they had been playing with.

Bones hung from the low ceiling. It looked like a ribcage.

The wet suckle on his toe turned from mildly pleasurable to a sudden bolt of white-hot pain, as the baby's tiny shark teeth bit down. "Ouch!" he cried, and at the same moment, the wet gnawing on his cock turned from teasing to teething. He writhed against the binds, trying to shake the babies away, but it only had the opposite effect. More teeth bit down on his thigh and his belly. On one of his nipples. And then, the teeth began not just to bite, but to bite and pull.

And rip.

"Stop," he cried out.

"Shhhhhhh," a voice said nearby.

The woman with the black hair.

She crawled into the bed next to him and patted the head of the babe latched onto his chest. He felt blood running down his ribs.

She kissed him and shook her head. A cascade of curled black hair fell over him. It trailed down his chest as she shifted. She gently disengaged and moved the child that had bitten him where it counts the most. She bent lower and took the child's place. Her tongue traced the tooth marks; he could feel the sting of the tiny wounds as her tongue moved across him, soothing him.

Despite the pain of all the bites, he responded yet again to her provocation. But before he got fully hard, he felt a horrible, sharp stab. His middle went cold, and then the pain came in a nauseous wave. The Siren raised her head from his middle, the remains of his manhood bleeding between her lips.

She chewed him with razor teeth as he watched, and then swallowed before she bent down to kiss his lips. The blood from his lost cock dripped down her chin to pool on his throat, which had finally begun to scream. She put her fingers on his lips, encouraging him to close them.

Then she slipped off the bed and moved away, out of his sight as he wailed and swore. He could feel the blood pumping out in a steady heart rhythm between his legs and he cried in desperation, "No, no…please no…" over and over.

The babies didn't care. Some of them screamed right along with him as if it were a game…tiny howls that made his spine jerk and his arms twitch uncontrollably. Whenever one of them made a sound, it was as if invisible nails drove into his nerves. Untrained Siren talent.

One by one, all of the babies in the room climbed onto the bed, drawn by first blood. There were seven of them. The oldest looked to be about four. She hovered over his face for a moment, studying him. She had the curly black hair and wide sea-green eyes of his captor.

At first, the children simply pinched and poked and prodded him, like a human toy. They laughed and gurgled and squealed as they explored his captive body.

Then a piercing heat burst from his left shoulder as the oldest one bit down. He felt—and heard—his flesh separate from bone.

Presently, the sounds of play stilled, as the younger children followed the lead of their older sister. Playtime was over.

The Sirens all began to feed.

ALONE ON THE WAVES

Eric S. Brown

"Contact!" Petty Officer Jenkins reported. "CBDR and fast. Upwards of 40 knots!"

It took Steve a moment to realize that Jenkins was yelling at him. He still wasn't used to being the "acting captain" of the USS Night Walker. When he did, he jumped from his seat with a start. "Military?"

"No transponder, Sir," Robertson shrugged. "Could be anybody or…"

There were only the three of them on the bridge and they were all playing multiple roles. The rest of the USS Night Walker's crew was dead. Their own survival was nothing short of a miracle.

When the Kaiju rose from the waves, the great beasts hadn't been alone. With them, they carried the K5 virus into the world of man. Between the war with the Kaiju and the virus, humanity, for all its technology and power, had lasted less than a month. Civilization crumbled as the K5 virus ripped through its heavily populated areas like wildfire before spreading to the more rural regions of the world. At best, one in a hundred exposed was immune to the virus. Another ten or so of that same hundred died from it. The remainder survived but not in a state that could be considered anything remotely human. They were "changed" into creatures dubbed Kaiju Spawn. Their eyes burnt yellow as their skin became scales. The nails of their fingers grew into claws. Teeth were pushed from their mouths as new razor-like ones grew through bleeding gums to take their place. The rate of transformation varied wildly from person to person but was always fast, never taking more than a few hours. Those most susceptible to the virus changed within a matter of minutes. All traces of human intellect were stripped away from those that changed leaving only an overpowering desire to feed. And feed they did on any left alive who weren't like them. The crew of the *USS Night Walker* had been no exception. Those who hadn't turned fought desperately to maintain control of the ship. In the end, they had won but with only six survivors left. One of those died later from his wounds, another took his own life, and the last to die had been the sole surviving, fully qualified engineer, leaving only Robertson, Jenkins, and Steve, himself, to clean up the ship and keep her functional.

"Hail them," Steve ordered. He outranked both Robertson and Jenkins, but he knew he wasn't cut out for command. Neither of them wanted the job either though so he was stuck with it for the time being.

"Already have been sir," Robertson answered. "No reply on any frequency I've tried so far."

The *USS Night Walker* had power to all its systems. No issue there. However, three men could not run and operate a United States Frigate that was built for a crew of over three hundred trained personnel. They were doing their best however and it was all they could do. Their days were spent on maintenance with one of them always staying on the bridge to monitor both the comm. station and the Night Walker's radar/sonar array.

"Should I activate the CIWS, Sir?" Jenkins asked.

"Robertson?" Steve asked.

"Still no reply," Robertson answered.

"We're running out of time here, Steve," Jenkins said, breaking protocol. "The contact will be on us in less than three minutes."

"If it's a Kaiju, the CIWS isn't going to do more than tick it off," Steve pointed out. "And that's the last thing we want."

"Steve," Jenkins pleaded.

"Think!" Steve snapped at him. "If it's a Kaiju, it might

shake us around a bit but it isn't likely to waste its time tearing apart a dead ship!"

"It could tear us apart during that shaking," Robertson added.

"Could is better than will," Steve argued. "We hit it with the CIWS, and a Kaiju WILL tear us apart."

"Might not be a Kaiju at all," Robertson rocked back in his chair, turning his head to look at Steve. "And if it's someone finally coming to check on us, it would be best not to blow them out of the water. For all we know, their vessel might be having systems issues. That would certainly explain the lack of a transponder, and them not replying to our hails."

"Agreed," Steve nodded. "Everybody gear up. We're going out to meet whoever, or whatever, the contact is."

Steve stood with Robertson and Jenkins watching the small, speed yacht that had come alongside the *USS Jima*. All of them wore full combat gear borrowed from the Jima's now dead Marine contingent. Steve and Jenkins carried P-90s while Robertson held an automatic shotgun ready. Each of the three men also carried sidearms holstered on their hips, and Robertson was even packing a grenade.

"Well, that sure ain't a Kaiju," Robertson laughed, staring at the yacht.

"It isn't military either," Jenkins said. "Pirates?"

"We are a pretty big and nice looking target to anyone left alive on the waves," Steve admitted. "We got food, water, fuel, and weapons onboard."

"Can't be more than a few dozen people on a ship like that one," Robertson commented. "If it's pirates, they've picked the wrong bloody ship to mess with. Oorah!"

"You are not a marine, man," Jenkins sighed. "Accept it already."

"Binoculars," Steve extended a hand towards Jenkins who passed a pair to him.

Steve raised them to his eyes and zeroed in on the yacht. There was no sign of its crew on its main deck or anywhere for that matter. Somebody had to have been at the yacht's helm though to pilot it up to the Jima and bring her alongside.

Then Steve saw them. He jerked the binoculars down, took a breath, and raised them again. The reason no one aboard the yacht had tossed over lines to Jima was that the crew hadn't needed them. The crew had left the yacht and was now in the water, swimming towards her.

"What is it?" Robertson demanded.

"It's Kaiju Spawn," Steve answered, the fear he was feeling abundantly clear in his voice.

"You're freaking kidding!" Jenkins ragged. "Spawn can't helm ships!"

"Apparently they can now," Steve flung the binoculars aside to take hold of the P-90 that dangled from him by its shoulder strap. "I counted seven of the things in the water, and two already climbing up the portside hull to the main deck."

"Frag it, frag it, frag it," Jenkins was mumbling.

"We got no choice but to engage them," Robertson said. "Hiding and hoping they go away isn't an option."

"I know," Steve frowned. "Best we do it and get it over with, one way or another."

The three men raced towards the Jima's main deck. By the time they arrived, the first two Kaiju Spawn were over the side of the ship and stood facing them. The creatures flashed gleaming rows of teeth at them as they snarled and raged at the humans who had stumbled into their path.

"Take them out!" Robertson screamed as he opened up with his automatic shotgun. His first shot gutted the closest of the Kaiju Spawn. The creature went sprawling onto the deck with chords of its intestines leaking from its ruptured abdomen.

Steve followed Robertson's example, hosing the Kaiju Spawn who were just climbing over the deck's railing with a stream of automatic fire. Several of the monsters howled in pain as the rounds bit into them but only one lost its hold and toppled back off the ship into the waves below.

The other of the two Kaiju Spawn that had already been fully aboard the ship charged Jenkins. Jenkins met it with a burst from his P-90. Bullets tore at the scales of it right arm and shoulders, sending chunks of meat flying into the air but didn't so much as slow the thing down. It plowed into Jenkins, knocking him from his feet.

"Jenkins!" Steve screamed, sweeping his P-90 around towards the spot where the man and monster wrestled, but didn't dare try to take a shot at the Kaiju Spawn. Odds were he'd hit Jenkins too if he did.

Kaiju Spawn were far stronger than humans. A single swipe of the thing's claws left Jenkins throat a mess of tattered flesh, and his body twitching, as he bled out on the deck underneath the monster.

Robertson's shotgun thundered. The head of the Kaiju Spawn sitting atop Jenkins' corpse disintegrated in an explosion of blood, bone fragments, and brain matter.

"Your sector!" Robertson barked. "Focus on your sector!"

Steve snapped out of the shock that had locked him down for a moment and spun to see that all of the other Kaiju Spawn were on the *Night Walker's* main deck with them now. The creatures were so freaking fast. Cursing, Steve jerked his P-90 up and held the weapon's trigger tight. The lead Kaiju Spawn racing at him was caught full on. It lurched about, staggering backwards as the P-90's rounds ripped its torso to shreds. The Kaiju Spawn finally flopped onto the deck and lay dead as the P-90 clicked empty. Steve ejected its spent magazine and fumbled in his attempt to ram a fresh one into the weapon. Frustrated and desperate, he swung the P-90 around in his hands and used it as club. Its stock broke apart as he smashed it into the face of the next Kaiju Spawn to lunge at him. The once human thing's nose caved inward from the blow. Steve hammered the Kaiju Spawn with what remained of the P-90 again before it could recover, catching the monster off balance. The second blow took it down though it was far from out. He could hear Robertson still blazing away with his shotgun even as he yanked his sidearm free of the holster on his hip. Another Kaiju Spawn was almost on him as he shoved the barrel of his Glock into the thing's face at point blank range and pulled the pistol's trigger.

The Kaiju Spawn whose nose he had broken was already on its feet again. With an angry roar, it leapt at him, knocking his Glock from his hands. Steve looked into its burning, yellow eyes and saw death staring back at him. The Kaiju Spawn tackled him. The two of them thudded onto the deck, a mass of flailing limbs. The monster's claws slashed across his chest, leaving bloody trails of torn flesh in their wake as Steve fought to get out from under it. Steve drew the combat knife tucked in the top of his boot and plunged its blade into the side of the Kaiju Spawn's neck, twisting the blade rapidly back and forth. The monster half squealed, half gargled, choking, as blackish blood poured out of its open mouth. Steve released his hold on the knife, dodging another swipe of the Kaiju Spawn's claws as the thing used its other hand to try to pull the blade buried in its neck free. With all his strength, Steve reached up, slamming his fist against the Kaiju Spawn's hand that gripped the knife's hilt, driving the blade deeper still into the creature's neck. The monster went limp as it died and collapsed on him. Steve rolled its corpse off, scrambling to get up and away from it.

A quick look around the deck told him the battle was over. All of the Kaiju Spawn were dead. Their bodies scattered about, pools of the blackish goo that passed for their blood growing around them. Robertson's body rested on the deck only a few yards away from where Steve stood. One of the Kaiju Spawn, with a gaping exit wound in its back, lay on top of him.

Steve ran to Jenkins's corpse and snagged the dead man's P-90, hurriedly checking its magazine. His rational mind knew that all of the Kaiju Spawn were dead, but his nerves hadn't caught up with it yet. Besides, having a weapon was better than not having in a world where things like Kaiju Spawn existed.

What to do now was the question Steve was faced with. He was alone and that scared the crap out of him. The Night Walker had all the supplies he could ask for and then some aboard it but he didn't honestly know if he could stand to remain on the ship by himself.

Steve walked to the edge of the Night Walker's main

deck and saw that the yacht the Kaiju Spawn had somehow managed to use to board her was drifting away. It was proof the monsters were learning, evolving in their own fashion. Sooner or later, more of them would find the Night Walker and when they did, everything would be over. That was a concern for tomorrow. Right now, he had bodies to dump overboard... and a dire need to get so drunk that he couldn't see straight anymore.

BAND OF SOULS

C.M. Saunders

The light from the full moon shone brightly, slicing through the midnight blackness, and reflecting mirror-like off the gently rippling surface of the sea. Although chilly, it was a beautiful night. The kind of night that never failed to make the old man fully appreciate the surreal, enigmatic, and somehow mysterious beauty of the sea.

He stood on the deck of the tiny fishing boat, leaning against the rusty guardrail, and looking across at the twinkling lights of a nearby coastal village. Lighting a cigarette, the man watched as the gray smoke was carried away effortlessly on the salty breeze. He liked being alone on his boat. Fishing was just an excuse, for he very rarely tried to catch anything, he simply enjoyed the solitude. He never strayed too far from the coastline however; he was no sailor. Just far enough to get away from it all.

Placing the cigarette between cracked lips, he shuddered as a light, but icy cold northern breeze blew through him. Without warning, his battered and weary train of thought abruptly stopped, turned, and started chugging slowly back down the familiar and well-worn set of tracks stretching into his dim and murky past. The past he would never allow himself to forget.

The old man had been born into a poor family, had scraped and struggled his way through a lifetime of adversity, and was soon going to die poor. Though not as poor as some, he was quick to remind himself. At least he had a roof over his head and a plentiful supply of food in the cupboard. He should be grateful. It was an unfair, and sometimes cruel world, he mused. Where the rich prospered the poor kept on getting poorer. A resigned sigh escaped him as he surveyed the dazzling array of stars overhead, comparing it to the false neon glow of the nearby village.

He was well into the winter of his life now, the final chapter. He looked upon life as a tenuous ordeal, a little like climbing a huge mountain, overcoming numerous obstacles and pitfalls along the way, then looking down from the summit and seeing a lifetime of hardship and labor with nothing to show except the view.

Inevitably, his thoughts turned to children and his own childhood. As a small boy he had been like a ball of snow: Innocent, pure and uncorrupted. But as he progressed through childhood and into the reaches of adulthood, it seemed as if he had been molded and manipulated by countless pairs of hands, violated and corrupted until nothing much remained of the oh-so-delicate snowball. He had been shaped and squeezed dry by all those around him and then discarded, his purpose fulfilled. Here he stood at the pinnacle of life, feeling wasted, cheated and used.

He was powerless to prevent them as a wealth of nostalgic memories flooded his head, pushing at the weakened boundaries of his tired mind. He was burdened with many regrets, but one in particular haunted him like no other. Children. Or rather, the lack of them. He was an unhappy, bitter old man, but above all, he was lonely. So lonely that sometimes, when sleep eluded him, he lay alone in the empty darkness and thought about dying. During the nights when the arthritis was especially bad, and he lay crumpled under the sheets writhing in agony as white-hot splinters of pain seared through every joint in his frail body, he would even welcome it. Death was looking more and more like a means of escape rather than something to run from, and that worried him. It worried him a lot.

The man's fragile frame was racked by a deep, retching cough. An unhealthy cough. He gagged and spat over the railing, and after a moment's thought, pitched the half-smoked cigarette in after it. Only then did he notice a faint knocking against the side of the boat. A brittle, yet rhythmic tapping, keeping time with the waves that gently lapped around the tiny vessel. Curiosity forced him to peer overboard into the cold, dark water surrounding him. In the silver moonlight, he could easily distinguish a small object bobbing up and down with the current and gently bumping against the side of the boat.

The movement of the object was almost hypnotic and as he watched, transfixed, the old man's thoughts turned to pollution. It was funny how his mind worked nowadays. Not so much as a TRAIN of thought as a mad fairground ride of incoherent thoughts and notions, veering sharply this way and that, steaming through one subject into another. The old man had given up trying to control it and was resigned to being little more than a passenger on some wild, demented ride.

He had to struggle just to focus on anything, let alone concentrate. Pollution? Where did that come from?

The sight of the flotsam probably. Just one more insignificant piece of litter to add to the eternal cesspool of the sea, which had been poisoned so badly, so completely, that it now resembled a gigantic festering toilet. Generations of ignorance were to blame, and it was now far too late to start preaching the gospel about pollution. The tipping point had come, and now it was too late for change. People had known the dangers, known the risks, for decades, but persisted to systematically destroy the environment, our life-support system. This piece of floating debris was just one of many millions such despicable items that filled every sea and ocean in the world.

Or was it? Another new idea, until now silently lurking in the ever-expanding shadows of his mind, thrust itself forward for its moment in the limelight. This item wasn't just rubbish. It was unique, special. He didn't know how he knew. He had stopped asking 'why' a long time ago, and now he just went with the flow.

He wanted it, whatever it was. He wanted it so badly that before he could reason with himself, he was down on his hands and knees, stretching out one withered arm as the rest of his body howled in protest. Frustratingly, the object bobbed just beyond his reach.

The old man leaned further, balancing precariously on the smooth wooden deck and clinging to the safety rail with his other hand. He could slip at any moment, lose his grip, or the old metal rail could simply give out, but the old man didn't care. From this new vantage point, he could identify the strange object, though at first he chose not to believe it. It was a bottle, of all things. Not the modern, plastic kind, but the old-fashioned, heavy glass variety.

Even as he considered the possible implications of his find, he smiled triumphantly to himself as his gnarled fingers closed around the cold, clammy neck of the bottle. Gingerly, he got back on his feet.

Why? Why did he just risk slipping or losing his balance and falling overboard into a certain watery grave for the sake of a discarded bottle? A piece of rubbish. Standing motionless with a puzzled frown on his face, the old man searched through his muddled and confused mind for a plausible answer but found none. All he knew was that the bottle was somehow special, valuable perhaps. It seemed to call him, *implore* him to rescue it from the watery depths.

His suspicions were compounded when he finally looked down at the bottle he held. There was something in it. Something small and white. It looked like a folded piece of paper, a message perhaps?

He could barely contain his excitement. A message in a bottle! It was the kind of thing books were written about. Images of one-eyed pirates and long lost buried treasure surged through his head, fueling his growing excitement. Then his mental roller coaster took another of its unscheduled little detours, and thoughts of a different nature began to surface. Young school children sealing their names and addresses in bottles and, spurred on by thoughtless, uncaring teachers, launching them into the already litter-infested North Sea with the half-baked notion of contacting people in Oslo or some other faraway place in the name of a school project.

Whatever the case, the rational side of his mind chipped in, there's only one way to find out.

As gray mist began to settle outside, he carefully carried his find into the cramped, dimly lit cabin to study it more closely. It certainly was an old glass bottle, not the common cheap plastic variety. Maybe an antique. A sturdy cork had been rammed into the neck, which had then been dipped in hot wax. Somebody, somewhere, had obviously gone to a lot of trouble to preserve the contents of the bottle and keep it away from the ravaging sea.

This fact spoke volumes to the cynical old man. It couldn't simply be a children's prank, or even a school project, kids were far too lazy these days to go to such lengths, much preferring to spend endless hours watching television, allowing their young and impressionable minds to turn into useless fleshy masses. There had been no such thing as television when he was a boy, and as a result, he always seemed to be doing something worthwhile with his time, always active. Without doubt, television was one of the pitfalls of modern life. A shameless device, which rotted the brain and devoured huge chunks of the most precious commodity of all…time.

He stood the bottle on the small, but sturdy, oak table in the cabin, and pulled up the rickety old kitchen chair on which he sometimes sat to ease the flaring pain in his joints and aching back. Leaning forward, he clasped his gnarled hands together between his knees and rubbed them together vigorously in order to restore some feeling. The bottle stood to attention on the table as he squinted at it warily. Judging by the style and overall appearance, it was obviously very old, but strangely unmarked by its time spent floating amid the murky depths. It was slightly scuffed and scratched, but otherwise in perfect condition.

Picking the bottle up again, he tried twisting the cork to break the seal. It didn't move. Undaunted, he twisted the cork again, harder this time, bolts of pain shot through his arthritic fingers, but he carried on regardless, eager to uncover the secret of the bottle. He twisted and strained until his face was a deep purple and veins stood out on his forehead, but eventually the combination of sickening pain, shortness of breath, and sheer exertion forced him to stop.

Moments later, as he sat in the decrepit wooden chair still gasping for breath and nursing the bottle protectively in his arms, the strangest feeling overwhelmed him. The bottle belonged in the water. He should throw it back immediately or face severe consequences. The notion was so strong that it banished all seeds of doubt from his mind. This was something way over his head. Something he could never hope to understand. He should not be involved. He instinctively knew that whatever he had stumbled across was far more sinister than a simple school project.

It was more than his troubled mind was able to comprehend. His out-of-control mental roller coaster ducked, dived, and took another unexpected turn, leaving him confused and disorientated. Half-remembered images from old horror movies flickered inside his head along with fragmented memories of eerie ghost stories read as a teenager during the Second World War as the bombs crashed and the fires of destruction burned through the night.

GET RID OF IT!

This interfering voice was so strong, so commanding. A low, primal voice urging him to forget the whole idea and just return the damned thing from whence it came before it was too late. There was something strange and faintly absurd about the whole situation, finding the fabled message in a bottle for Christ's sake. It was so unlikely and so unreal, it simply did not happen. Not in real life anyway.

Which was all the more reason to open it. What possible harm could it do? It was only an old glass bottle with a scrap of paper inside. He had to know what secrets the bottle was hiding from him. Besides, even if it was dangerous in some obscure way, he would rather regret something that he had done than something he wished he had. Throwing the bottle back for somebody else to claim was out of the question.

The old mantra *curiosity killed the cat* suddenly appeared

from nowhere in the rancid stew of the man's brain with such power and clarity that he actually spoke the words out loud then looked around, startled by the sound of his own voice. The phrase now held a dark, chilling undertone, and he found himself wondering about the origins of such a disturbing yet popular saying.

His heart was beating fast, and he was still trying to catch his breath following the exertions of the last few minutes. His heart beat faster still when he realized that inexplicably, he held in his right hand the comically oversized wooden mallet, which he kept on the boat for odd jobs.

Despite the biting chill in the night air, the old man's face and torso were covered in a greasy film of sweat. Now his heart positively *hammered* away inside his chest cavity, making his head ache, and his hands shake. Momentarily, he actually feared a heart attack. This could be the end right here, alone on his pathetic little boat clutching a mallet and an old bottle. For some reason, the thought struck him as funny, and for the first time in weeks, he chuckled softly. The overriding emotion, however, was one of luckless despair. If he died now, he would never know. The bottle would have won.

The chuckling stopped when he realized what the mallet was intended for. While he had been preoccupied with playing psychological power games with himself, embroiled in what seemed at the time a fair and democratic fight for supremacy, he had obviously failed to even consider what was probably the voice of reason. His mind had already been made up, though he hadn't even noticed in all the excitement. Apparently, he had decided to smash the bottle some considerable time ago, then spent more time locating the mallet, which could have been anywhere. The ensuing private argument had been nothing more than a smoke screen to distract him from the business at hand.

As his mind had already been made up, thereby avoiding any tricky decision making, the old man decided to go with it. He lifted the mallet high above his head, held his breath, then brought the heavy instrument crashing down. The bottle was an easy target even for a man of his age and stature. It disintegrated under the considerable force of the blow with a loud "pop", showering fragments of twinkling glass onto the wooden floorboards around his feet.

Most of the remains of the bottle lay scattered on the unsteady table before him, and sure enough, amidst the sparkling debris lay a folded piece of yellowed paper. The message. Now, at last, he was going to discover whatever dark secret the bottle had been keeping. Mindful of the sharp splinters of glass the man gleefully snatched up the message, tongue protruding rudely from the corner of his mouth in a childlike gesture of triumph.

It wasn't paper exactly, more like some kind of thick parchment. As he eagerly unfolded it, the man thought of ways in which the message could change his empty life for the better. It had to be money, *had* to be. At the very least, he could perhaps sell the thing to a museum or something. Maybe he could even repair the smashed bottle, or find a suitable replacement in a junk shop somewhere. Money was the route to happiness in this day and age, love was a dated cliché that had nothing to do with it. He had been in love once though, a long time ago, but dear Alice had died and left him alone in this cruel, heartless world. A world, which he couldn't fully understand and could play no real part in. At best, he was an unwilling spectator, doomed to watch from the shadows as other people lived their lives. He no longer had any family or close friends to speak of, and the only people who ever visited were those who had to in the course of their work—social workers, home help.

But all that was soon going to change. From this day on, nothing would be the same. He was convinced of it. He could hardly contain his excitement when he thought about the plethora of opportunity that would surely be heading his way.

Reading the message proved to be the hardest task of all because the almost unintelligible spidery scrawl had faded considerably with age. Even so, the old man was captivated.

To the Finder,

I have to be quick, they are coming for me now. I cannot go without first telling my story, the truth must be known so whoever you are, spread the word - Death is not the end, somehow we go on. Though I am not sure whether this is a blessing or a curse. I shall explain: Myself and my good friend Jonathan Campbell left Southampton dock on the day of November 10th, 1879, aboard the good vessel Christina. The night on which we left, there was a terrible storm that took everyone by surprise, and by the time it cleared most of our instruments were damaged beyond repair and worse, we were hopelessly lost. We had supplies for only a few days, and so all we could do was pray to be rescued.

Before I continue, please tell me dear reader, are you superstitious? Do you believe that the dead can come back? I never did until tonight. There is a legend around these parts, which tells of a group of restless spirits who roam the oceans and seas in search of folk who are ready to die. The spirits are known as the Band of Souls, and are truly real. I know for I have seen their faces in the mist that surrounds me. They know of the wicked thing I did, God help me. They know that I murdered Jonathan while he slept and stole his food and water. When it was all gone, I tried eating his flesh to sustain me but I could not, even though I was so hungry.

I must hurry as they are waiting for me. I will seal this account in a bottle and fling it out of the window if they will let me. I trust God to deliver it to a deserving quarry.

Remember, death is not the end. Maybe it is but a gateway to a better place, though I think not. Perhaps it depends on how you choose to live your life. If so, then I am damned and deserve to burn in hell for all eternity. I am not fit to live among men any longer. Goodbye and good luck, dear reader.

Yours faithfully,
Henry Blake

The old man had been sitting at the table for over an hour, reading the letter over and over again. His entire body aching and stiff, all except for his legs, which were numb through lack of use. His doctor maintained that loss of feeling was common amongst senior citizens, poor circulation did it, but it was doubtful whether that was the correct diagnosis. The doctors garbled broken English and quirky air of indifference was infuriating, it was painfully obvious that he couldn't care less whether the old man lived or died.

At first, he had not believed the letter. It had to be some kind of elaborate hoax. It looked authentic enough but the years had made him wary and skeptical, he no longer took anything at face value. The entire episode was too surreal and far-fetched to say the least, and some aspects seemed to have been too contrived. Could the bottle really have been floating around aimlessly for all these years? And all that scare-monger nonsense about ghosts, life after death and lost souls. The old man didn't even believe in God. It had to be a joke.

He refused to believe, until he caught sight of a face peering in through the cabin window at him. He was alarmed at first, and who wouldn't be? He panicked. A detached sense of disbelief washing over him in waves while at the same time terror and revulsion consumed him.

He had hurried to the tiny cabin porthole, hoping against hope that his eyes had been deceiving him, that it was merely a trick of the light or something equally as mundane. Trembling with fear, he pressed his own contorted face against the thick glass. The sight that met his anxious gaze caused him to gasp harshly. He felt weak and nauseous, the shock threatening to overwhelm him. Outside, a thick mist had settled, coming from nowhere it seemed. In the swirling mist were dozens of disembodied human faces. Not heads exactly, just faces. They floated and danced in the air, bathed in ethereal light in much the same way as angels probably were.

Could they be angels?

As he watched, dumbstruck, they seemed to take turns in coming up to the glass as if to introduce themselves. Some of the faces leered at him offensively, some appeared to be laughing, some were frozen in masks of horror, and others simply stared blankly.

The old man thought he must be asleep and dreaming. He kept expecting to be woken up by the shrill cry of his alarm clock or the crunch of his boat floundering on rocks. These faces in the mist couldn't be real, yet there they were.

The comings and goings made the old man uneasy at first, he felt like the star attraction at a circus or a zoo. Then he started noticing how peaceful they looked, how gracefully they moved. In its own way, each pale face was the image of serene beauty. Suddenly, he was no longer afraid. The faces weren't exactly menacing, and didn't appear malevolent or malicious in any way. They looked happy enough. Or perhaps *content* would be a more fitting word.

In fact, after watching the strange but fascinating display for some time, the faces, and the uncomplicated world they seemed to inhabit seemed positively appealing. A timeless world without feeling, totally devoid of emotion of any kind. No pain, anger, frustration, fear or guilt (though it was slowly becoming obvious that the faces possessed some kind of playful intelligence).

Only one thing bothered him, and that thing had been weighing on his shoulders more than ever tonight, like an immovable lead weight pushing down on him. His wife's death. It had not been a result of natural causes, and had not been an accident either. He had murdered her. Sneaked up behind her one morning while she had been slowly making her way down the stairs and shoved her. Hard. So hard that he had almost tumbled down after her. Mercifully, she had died instantly. Poor, loyal, dependable Alice. He had no way of knowing that he would miss her so much until it was too late.

He tried telling himself it had been a mercy killing, that dear Alice was too old to enjoy her life anymore. But that was a lie. When the end came she had clung to life like one of the limpets on the bottom of his boat and he had been forced to bang her head on the wooden floor until she finally succumbed. Only then, did it occur to him that you leave this life the way you come in…kicking and screaming.

He had done it for the money. The insurance money. And her meager savings, of course. How stupid and amateurish he had been, he might have known that things wouldn't go according to plan, they seldom did. Life was like an un-plotted minefield. He should have done his homework. The damned insurance company refused to pay out pending an inquiry, and the bank followed suit, freezing their joint accounts. The money grabbing bastards.

The inquiry concluded that Alice's death had occurred *under suspicious circumstances,* and therefore the insurance company wasn't obliged to pay out. Miraculously, he was not considered a police suspect. They had interviewed him. Twice. And taken endless statements. But he was a good actor when he needed to be, and they seemed satisfied with his story. They said they were considering the possibility that an intruder had been responsible.

A single line from the letter kept repeating itself in his head, over and over again. *"Perhaps it depends on how you choose to live your life".*

Did the faces know about Alice? He thought maybe some of them did, he could see it in their cold, fish-like eyes. How much did they know, and where did it leave him? He could see no expression on their placid features. No harmful intent, no anger, nothing. Looking into their eyes was like staring deep into an infinitely black sky. It brought on a swimmy, faraway feeling, as if everything was just a tedious, insignificant game and not real at all.

How bad can it be? Could death and whatever follows really be worse than living life itself? Recently, the old man had been persecuted by grief and guilt. Each morning when he awoke from his light, troubled sleep, it was there. There was no escaping it. He had even considered ending it by his own hand a few times, but lacked the nerve. He couldn't go on like that. And here he was presented with a chance to go quietly and peacefully, without shame. An opportunity to make his peace with this world and the next.

For once, his out-of-control mental roller coaster slowed

to a shuddering halt. The two imaginary voices that had struck up the earlier argument concerning the fate of the bottle seemed to grow weary of ravaging his overused mind, and they too fell silent. There was nothing left to say. For probably the first time in his long wretched life, the old man was sure of something. Absolutely positive, beyond any lingering doubts.

The faces seemed to be growing restless now, impatient. Their activity had increased tenfold; they no longer hung in the air but zoomed through it, almost frantically, without rhyme nor reason. They ducked, dived, and occasionally passed through one another. Their image of serenity had gone to be replaced by one of anxious longing. They were getting tired of waiting. Just like he was.

On trembling, aching legs, the old man made the short journey from the table to the cabin door. With one last painful pang of regret echoing around his empty heart he unlatched the door, swung it outwards, and embraced the faces with open arms.

AFTERWARD: Extract From Local News Report

"... A search is underway for George Griffith, aged 76, after his fishing boat was found abandoned off the Welsh coast near Porthcawl early this morning. Griffith, who has a history of psychiatric problems, was wanted for further questioning by police investigating the murder of his late wife, Alice Griffith, who was found dead at their home ten days ago. More details to follow..."

A THOUSAND THICK AND TERRIBLE THINGS

David Mickolas

Let me tell you why I was afraid of the ocean.

Maybe afraid isn't the right word. I was afraid of all the normal stuff as a little boy—the dark, strangers, getting lost. But the ocean, I was terrified.

The first day I saw them I was maybe six. I remember the clouds were low and almost green on the bottom. Like it was ready to pour. It didn't matter though, Brigantine Beach was packed.

"Just…come on," my dad would say, frustrated, dragging me toward the waves. "I'm not wasting my time trying to get you to go in," he'd tell me, clamping down on my hand and pulling me along like a reluctant ragdoll.

I pointed to the foamy green water. "There's, there's things in there.…"

He laughed. "Of course there are. Lots a stuff in there, boy. The big things with teeth though, they're far out there, so don't worry about them." He chuckled, thinking he was scaring me.

But I wasn't afraid of fish, of crabs, or even sharks. This was something different.

I could see them. Close. Thick, wriggling, semi-transparent worm-like things that swam just under the surface, waiting to attach themselves to my father's legs once he waded in. All down the shoreline, hundreds. Maybe more.

"So, let's go." My father pulled me toward the waves, and I erupted in a wail that could be heard the length of the beach. He turned his head away and let go of my hand, cursing as he held his ear, and my little feet padded across the sand to the safety of my Transformers towel.

He walked up a minute later. I played with my Hot Wheels cars in the sand hoping that he wouldn't say anything. Of course, he did. He knelt down beside my towel, and I had to put my hand to my eyes to see him against the sun. He talked through clenched teeth.

"You ever pull a goddamn stunt like that again and I'll whoop your ass in front of every goddamn person on this beach." His angry silhouette pointed a finger at me.

"What is it, Donny?" My mom was too far away to hear. She leaned forward in her beach chair and held her hat to her head as the wind tried to take it away.

"Nothin'. Just talking to Will. Go back to your book." He turned, spraying sand on me, and went back to the edge of the surf.

He hadn't seen what I had. No one had. And everyone was out there, having fun, unaware, not realizing that a thousand thick and terrible things swam around them. Just looking for the right moment to latch on and suck.

***

I always dreaded those annual trips to the shore. I kept my distance from my dad during our vacations and I was constantly on edge, thinking that at any moment he would scoop me up and run over the sand with me screaming in his arms until he threw me into the surf and the snakes would curl around me and take me away forever.

***

And then one summer, I saw it happen. A couple of teenagers were throwing a tennis ball far out where the waves weren't breaking yet. I don't know what caused me to look, but I saw it nonetheless, a huge tendril, as thick as my father's thigh, shot upward out of the water and back down on one of the teens, pushing him under and holding him there.

His friend was right next to him. But he hadn't seen what I had. No one had. What looked to be ten to twelve feet of plump, writhing tentacle remained invisible to everyone, including the friend, who was being sprayed with its twisting and coiling. If anyone had seen those things when they entered the water, they would have run the other way.

I scrambled back on my towel, looking and pointing and saying something under my breath, while a hot ball of dread filled my stomach.

The boy's friend was laughing and looking around to see where his buddy went, expecting him to pop up next to him somewhere. But he eventually stopped laughing, gave up waiting and went back in.

Ten minutes later, his dead friend was washed up by the waves, rolling over and over until the ocean deposited him at the edge of the foamy surf, limp and blue.

That's when the screaming started.

I never went back to the ocean again until my mom was dying.

***

The exterior of Ocean Breeze Retirement Home was bleak and washed white by the salt air and constant wind from the sea. The gulls liked to circle it, caught in the updrafts from the horseshoe shape of the two-story gothic structure, maybe waiting to see the patients as they were wheeled out from time to time on sunnier days. Today wasn't one of them.

Brigantine Station lighthouse was lit, though it was three in the afternoon. Its bright shaft cut through the fog and created brief, unnatural shadows of the building against the dunes that surrounded it.

I wheeled my mother outside, and though the skies were dark with low hanging clouds, getting away from the stuffiness and smell from the interior was a relief, even if it was a little chilly. She had a knitted shawl around her shoulders that she pulled tight.

"See Mom, not so bad." She didn't respond. She rarely did anymore.

The surf crashed just below us, beyond the cliff that the home sat on. It echoed up to us, mixed with the sounds of the circling gulls, and created a loneliness that is hard to explain. I wondered if my mother felt the same.

"Why did you take me outside?" she asked, slightly turning her head back to me as I wheeled her along the sand blown path.

"Just to get some fresh air Mom. That's all. We'll go back in a bit."

"I'm not your mother." I inhaled slightly. Here we go. I hated this part.

"I'm William, Mom, your son. You have two sons. Brian isn't here, but he visits, too."

She laughed in her wheelchair. "I don't have any sons." When she stopped chuckling she said, "Let me look at you."

I wheeled her to a bench, and the wind blew her hair over her face. I turned her to me, locking the wheels, and sat on the cold wood. Her long bony fingers brushed the hair from her eyes and after a short moment of looking at me, her face changed. "Yes," she said. "Yes."

She looked at me for a long time, maybe a minute. I let her look. I let her come back. And then, with the smile still on her face she said, "Don't go in the water, Will." My blood froze inside of my stomach.

"What?" I asked. Her eyes began to lose focus. She looked through me now, out to the ocean.

"Don't go into the water. Tell your brother. Don't go in there. I've seen them. "Now her finger pointed at my face but I knew she wasn't pointing at me. She was pointing out there, to the grey sea beyond the cliff. Her hair covered her face now. "It reached out and grabbed a surfer last month. I saw. From my room. I saw, Will. October second. At three-thirty in the afternoon. Miss Ayanna didn't believe me but it did. I told her."

Her brittle black hair spun wildly.

"Like snakes," she said, "like long, watery snakes…"

I grabbed her hand and slowly returned it to her lap. "Mom. How long? How long have you been able to see them?"

"See what?" she said behind the mess of her hair. "What have you done with the remote? I can't change the channel without the remote, you know that!"

***

I sat in a pizza shop on the deserted boardwalk, the only thing open besides one small souvenir shop that sold t-shirts and magnets and seashells and whatever type of paperback you wanted, as long as it was from the 1980s and had a faded cover. Nursing a weak coffee, I stared out to the cold beach below.

They were still there, the worms. I watched them float lazily in the surf, half-transparent, their long forms stretching far into the surf until they disappeared in the darkness. Were they all attached to something? A monstrous mountain of black fish flesh that sat submerged in the dark depths, letting its millions of tendrils seek out and find, graze and taste, clamp and take?

So she saw now, too. I wasn't crazy. Or, maybe I just was as crazy as my mother.

Mom got dealt a bad hand. Both the Alzheimer's and the cancer were taking her. But the cancer was faster. Eating away at her intestines. Just as these things did, but from the inside out. Which was worse? I didn't know anymore.

"I'm just ready Will, that's all," she told me from her bed the week before. "It's all so tiring. And it hurts, so bad sometimes. Not even the medicine helps. I know everyone here tries to take the pain away, but they can't, not really. Because when it doesn't hurt, I'm not here. I'm in a different place where you're not, just like when I can't remember. I don't like feeling like that, I'd almost rather have the pain. And I know you'll miss me, but when you leave there are nights when I just cry in my bed and I can't take it Will and no one understands that, and I am just so ready, that's all."

The hospice doctors had told me another week, but they wouldn't be surprised if it was that night.

"Do you want me to help you?"

"Yes, please. Help me."

She disappeared after that, when she thought I was a cab

driver, come to pick her up.

Because of the state my mother was in, I had unrestricted access to her during her final time. This was the best care facility her money could buy in this area, and she chose well. I helped her withdrawal from the trust fund her grandfather had left her, so many years ago. We were always somewhat well off, but it was always mom's wish to live comfortably. Not beyond the means that my father and she provided, but comfortably. Once she was gone, the money would go where she wished. But I'd give it all to get my mother back.

My cell phone buzzed on the table. I flipped it over. A New Hampshire area code. Though I never typed in his name above the number, I knew immediately who it was.

I reluctantly picked it up. "Hey."

"Hi there, Will, it's your dad."

"I know."

"I, ah, I heard about your mom. I mean, of course I did, right? Yeah. It's not like I don't keep in touch with her or the home or anything. Didn't want you to think that I didn't. But yeah."

"Okay."

"I, ah, I just wanted to let you know I'm coming down there, maybe in a few days or so, a few days, so yeah the lawyer said it might be a good idea just to see where things stand, you know, with the dispersion of funds, things like that, all that legal… stuff. Right? What a pain in the ass. Plus, I'll see your mom."

"Right." I stirred my coffee and watched the little white pieces of bad cream break apart and turn in circles.

"Right. So yeah. So how is the old girl doing? Any change? Does she need to sign anything or, you know, answer questions?"

I didn't answer him, but just stared out at the drifting appendages.

"You know, for legal purposes? Just wondering. I guess the lawyers will tie all that stuff up. No need to worry about it now. Right?"

"Mm..."

"Alright, well good. Just wanted to touch base, check on your mom. I'll be in touch I guess, when I get there. Great catching up, Will. Let's hope this whole thing is over with soon."

I hung up. I really didn't want to hear any more.

***

Walking past the twenty-foot columns that led into the convalescent home was like a weight falling onto my shoulders. I hated stepping through those doors. But this time when I did, it wasn't as quiet a scene as usual. A nurse ran by pushing a cart past the reception desk and down into the hallway in which my mother resided. Another nurse followed, carrying what looked like a tackle box. I walked down the hall following them, worried about which room they were headed toward. It looked like they were gathered around my mom's room.

But as I approached, I realized that the nurses and one doctor were focused on the room next door. Mr. Folsom. Apparently, he had no DNR like most of the residents here.

The cart was left at an odd angle outside of the room, bottles and instruments strewn all over the top. Almost without thinking, I grabbed a small brown bottle of Nevatal, fumbling for it as it skipped around the metal surface. I finally gripped it tight and slipped it into my jacket.

"Sir," an older nurse said as she tried to squeeze past me, "please, give us some room."

"Of course." I pretended to peer inside at the activity in Mr. Folsom's room before I stepped into my mother's.

***

My dad called three days later. He was staying at the Sea Shell Motel on Atlantic, right across the street from the ocean. He said we should catch up. Grab a cup of coffee. He'd make me a special one of his "pirate coffees" I remembered from being a kid, which was two parts rum, one part Chock Full O' Nuts. I declined, but said I'd be over later that night.

***

Shift change was at 10pm, and when I entered Ocean Breeze at quarter after, pushing the code into the steel box at the side of the sliding door, it was quiet and still. The nurses met at their station in the opposite wing to go over charts and events from the day.

No one saw me enter. Of course, if later the county insisted, they could always review the tapes and see when I had entered and left, but for now, I was counting on remaining invisible. I made my way to my mother's room.

***

There was a pair of wheelchairs parked under a cabana next to the side of the building. Each had large wide wheels to navigate through the sand, and a teal webbing seat, which the sand could easily fall through. A trail at the edge of the parking lot led to a ramp down to the beach, about fifty yards away.

There wasn't much talking coming from the chair, mumbling mostly. So faint that with the sounds of the surf slapping the shore, I could hear little more than a word or two lost to the wind.

The lighthouse beam swept over the shoreline and I saw them, billowing in the waves and peeking out of the water. Sensing. Reaching.

More mumbling from the chair.

It was difficult to push through the sand, even with the large tires. But once I was on the wet level shoreline, it became much easier. The tires hissed now as I pushed. By a sliver of moon, I could see the white caps and bubbling foam as it tried to reach the chair, but nothing else. I pushed forward toward the ocean.

The light swung around again and for just a flash I saw the thick green translucent worm things rise out of the crashing waves, excited. Expecting.

Close enough. I locked the brake on the side of the chair and leaned down to my father's ear.

"End of the line, you son of a bitch."

Either the Nevatal was wearing off, or in this moment at the end of his life he could see the pale arms begin to reach for him. He tried to turn around to see me, but he slumped in the chair, one side of his mouth pulled down involuntarily. He tried to speak.

"Will...what're you doing?" I could barely hear him over the sounds of the crashing surf. A dark wave spilled beyond the chair and bubbles and foam sparkled and popped against the tires. I backed up.

Another flash of light. A pea-green tendril reaching toward the chair. Smaller ones around it, eager. A mouth within a mouth at the end of the largest one. My father struggling to get out.

And then, he howled. I think he saw them.

I heard a wet slap, then a high screech. It was so inhuman, I didn't know if it was my father or those things. But when the light swung around again I could see his mouth open, the tendons and veins in his neck standing out in the harsh light as he was pulled. The sound escaping him was pain and fright and misery. All the things he caused his family over all these years.

"Will!" he screamed into the blackness. I sank to my knees in the sand.

There was only 9 ccs of Nevatal left in the bottle I had stolen. I needed to use at least 6 for my mother. To be safe, I had made it 8. Which left 1cc to mix in my father's pirate coffee. Not enough to put him to sleep. Just enough to keep him awake.

"WILL!"

The lighthouse revealed a dozen more arms, shooting out of the water like arrows. They latched onto his arms and legs, pulling him out of the chair as it fell, waves crashing over his rolling body. He clawed at the ground. And as he was dragged through the soft sand and rough surf, he pleaded with me, hands outstretched, his voice becoming higher and more ragged. His fingers dug in, leaving a trail as he was dragged further out to sea.

I had kept a record all these years. Of the thousands of terrible things my father had done. To me. My mother. My brother. So many others.

I heard bones breaking. The next sweep of light revealed the tangle of worm things separating dad's foot from his ankle.

Mom had gone quietly. That was what she had wanted—what all of us had wanted. And my father? This is what I had wanted.

A broad, pale tentacle wrapped around the top of his head as he screamed into the dark, blinding him from seeing me crying on the shoreline. His neck was stretched unnaturally backward, farther and farther, until it was snapped in one short tug. His scream died with him.

I killed my mother because I loved her. I killed my father because I hated him.

And now, it was my turn.

I crawled to the empty chair, slowly sat up in it, and waited.

MAELSTROM

Doug Rinaldi

Night grew fast over the Atlantic Ocean.

Above, the clouds floated dark and menacing. They stretched from one end of the world to the other, engulfing the great vastness of deep blue sky and swallowing the moon. Waves smashed against the side of the ship, spitting sea-spray high into the air, wetting its wooden deck. A chilled wind blew in from the west signaling the onset of the storm. Bobbing unsurely on the frigid Atlantic, the lonely vessel played a game of chance with the throes of nature. Lost from its course, it drifted without direction, riding the current of the mighty deep.

The sky opened and the heavens released its load. Violent daggers of rain pummeled the ship, drenching the deck and soaking the massive sails that swung neglected from each mast. The wind blew with such force that the rain fell in horizontal sheets, and the waves tossed the ship about the choppy surface.

The darkened sky raged as it spit forth an angry groan. Thunder and lightning cracked the earth open and rent the nether above. In a vicious flash another ship appeared, but only for a moment. An eerie afterimage cast like a ghostly apparition, quickly fading back into darkness.

Swell after swell, the ocean pulsed with an erratic heartbeat. Torrential cloudbursts soaked everything in the storm's imminent path of ruin. Fierce waves crashed onto the deck while the bow of the ship sunk dangerously close to the water's surface.

The angry sky ripped open again with a deafening clap of

thunder as it ruptured the atmosphere. The thick masts shook, bending critically close to snapping. Sails billowed as they filled with wind, propelling the craft in directions other than those intended.

As if by magic, the other ship reappeared. This time the storm had brought her closer, its bare masts swaying in the melee. Lightning flashed again, igniting the sky in a bluish frenzy for what seemed an eternity.

Struggling against the formidable Mother Nature, the incoming craft steered, sluggishly at best, toward the debilitated craft as light dissolved back to gloom. The two ships, however, now had clear sight of each other, their silhouettes painted against the darkened backdrop. The staggering power of the tempest seemed as if God, Himself, had unleashed His wrath with nothing but scorn.

Miraculously, the two ships remained afloat amid the seething chaos. In closing the gap, the only things holding the two behemoths of wood and steel together were master artisanship and prayer. Nevertheless, those barely proved to be enough as the heavens continued to weep in anguish and groan in despair.

***

All calmed after the storm's passing. Wispy white clouds decorated the bright blue sky. Still and reflective as polished marble, the ocean stretched beyond the reach of naked vision. Mile upon mile, water kissed the horizon, never once granting a glimmer of hope for the sight of land...it offered only the mirror-like reflection of the sky above.

Silence and solitude had fallen over the seascape like a shroud. The two ships, now side by side, floated on the steady surface. Cleansing rays of sunlight shimmered like diamonds off the minute ripples of the sea's current, bathing everything in their warmth. The apparently derelict ship remained lifeless and quiet, its torn and tattered sails nothing more than useless rags now hanging rain-soaked from its wooden masts.

With great mastery, the helmsman guided the *Galileo* into

place mere feet away from its silent and mysterious neighbor before dropping anchor and tethering to it with a heavy rope. At the quarterdeck, the deckhands placed wooden planks across the expanse between the two crafts.

In a single step, a lone man, face raw from windblown salt, crossed the breach. His white shirt clung to his sea-strengthened body and perspiration dampened his brow as he firmly planted both feet on the deck of the apparent deserted ship.

Once onboard, a sudden and overwhelming stench overcame the man. It took all he had not to wretch. He covered his mouth to stop from gagging, attempting to block out the vile odor that accosted his senses. After several seconds had passed, and steadied by a brief reprieve afforded him on the current of a gentle ocean breeze, the *Galileo*'s captain called out to any soul listening.

Only silence returned his salutation.

He peered up at the sky, noticing several gulls circling overhead with their white wings black against the blinding background of the sunlit clouds. Along with the stench, a sense of death hung in the air.

He walked with caution to the center of the main deck near the hatch that led down into the cargo deck of the ship. He called out again and his voice thundered against the quiet of the sea. Despite the warmth of the day, a chill tickled his spine. The burden of his rain-soaked clothes saturated his skin through and through. He wrapped his arms around himself, trying to rub some warmth back into his dampened limbs.

Silence whispered on the air with an arid cry. He forced himself to open the hatch. Dread danced in the void nerves left in his stomach as he reached for the rusted ring. The weathered door groaned with the decades of being at sea, as he lifted it from its frame.

Below, the ship's cargo deck was abysmal before the sun's shimmering radiance infiltrated the darkness and chased the shadows away. He descended from the deck deeper into the belly of the wooden beast. As his foot made final purchase with the floor of the steerage deck, he found a wet stickiness to the ladder's rungs. Fighting for focus, his eyes adjusted to the sepulchral gloom just beyond the ladder's base. Obsidian blackness lurked even further in the corners.

Just on the outskirts of his vision, something moved in the murkiness as if in reply to his growing unease. He wiped the stickiness from his hands, unknowingly staining his white shirt a sickly shade of red, while, as each moment crept by, the stench of death grew stronger.

A flash stung his eyes as someone somewhere in the darkness lit a lantern. Its blaze cast a fuzzy glow throughout the dampened chamber, throwing grotesque shadows on each of the slanted walls. In that exact moment repulsion bled into his vision.

The constant sound of chattering teeth and desperate moans now filled the otherwise silent space. In the darkened corner of the ship's cargo hold, huddled and frightened, a group of roughly thirty souls—men, women, and children—sat shivering. They clung to one another, each face sharing the same tearful downcast eyes. Not once did they dare glance up at the man who had just boarded their ship.

White powdered wigs, the Captain noticed in the little light that he had to see, adorned some of their heads; the dankness and humidity caused them to droop and cover some of their faces. Others, it seemed, had pulled the periwig off a while ago. The rest just left it there sitting there atop their sweating crowns, as if too tired to care about such things anymore. The Captain surmised with ever-growing dread that they were Englishmen, presumably upper class by the powdered faces of the women and ruffled and once opulent accoutrements they all wore. He thought, staring into their faces, that this must have been a passenger ship sailing either to America or back to England.

Unable to divert his eyes from the unnerving scene, the Captain scanned the damp chamber. Their withdrawn eyes revealed volumes of some pain and sorrow they must have lived through, but gave no revelation to all his unanswered questions.

"Dear, God. Please help us," the old woman with the lantern spoke, her voice brittle from disuse. Powdery makeup that she once worn proudly had vanished, save for some residue smeared across her aged face. The ripped ruffled collar of her Mantua hung lazily from the rest of the material.

Shock took hold when the wide-eyed and confused Captain fully noticed their bloodstained mouths and chins, the dry crimson life framing their grim frowns. He covered his mouth, trying desperately to subdue the rise of bile that boiled inside his gut.

His eyes welled with tears from the taste of vomit brimming at the back of his throat. All at once the stench of his surroundings hit him like a boot to the stomach. He spun around and gasped. Before him, bodies strewn about in varying degrees and all askew littered the wooden floor of the cargo hold as if a master puppeteer had discarded his favorite collection of marionettes.

Corpse upon corpse, an estimated twenty or so had been torn open in a grotesque still-frame. Some were still partially clothed while others were prone and naked. They had left the bodies congealing in a sticky lake of bloodied water that pooled at the Captain's feet as tiny ripples spread out across the corpse-ridden planks.

***

"Bloody hell!" Captain Harkcombe cried as he erupted from below deck. He crossed with great haste back over the gap between the two vessels. Back on his ship, his sacred ground, he felt awash with safety—even if only for a brief moment—from the horror he just witnessed.

He hunched over with his hands braced on his knees, gasping for breath. All hands were on deck, and all eyes were on him. His crew, the crew of the galleon, the *Galileo* of Her Majesty's Royal Navy, stood before him. Color had drained from his salt-chapped face leaving him a pasty white.

"What is the matter, Captain?" Williams, the Quartermaster,

asked as the rest of his men stood at a nervous but respectful attention.

"Those people…" stammered Harkcombe, "…all the blood…white faces covered in blood…bodies…" Unable to regulate his breathing, he passed out.

"Fetch the Captain some water. Now!" Williams barked as he darted over to the felled Harkcombe, dreading the worst. The Captain's eyes lazily rolled open. On his knees beside him, Williams took hold of his shoulders and shook him and Harkcombe's mouth released a moan as his eyes fought hard to focus.

"I'm fine…I think…" Harkcombe mumbled, slow to rise to his elbows. He looked up at his Quartermaster as he took a sip of water. "Thank you, Williams."

"I knew I should have gone with you, Captain. Please. What happened!" begged Williams. A light breeze blew off the Atlantic tossing his hair into his face.

"You had us worried to death, Sir," offered a nearby midshipman.

"Men," began Harkcombe, "If indeed my eyes haven't deceived me altogether, I believe Hell itself has opened up in the hull of that ship."

***

Even as daylight filtered in through the portholes above and cast a hazy beam of light down into the deck below, darkness ran rampant in the farther reaches of the hold.

It had been days since the passengers aboard the *White Laurel* had seen light—real light—light from a yellow sun, riding so high and bright in the cloudless sky, light that would pierce their eyes and warm their skin. However, having been too frightened to venture above decks, they passed the time weeping and praying for forgiveness. All hopes of returning to their affluent life full of status and good cheer shredded, disappearing the instant they succumbed to a haunting primal need.

So choosing the taciturn comfort of shadow over the

glaring adjudication of light, they remained below decks nestled together in the company of vermin, eschewed by the light, one with the dark, and, most important, alone with their sins. Together, they bore a transgression of incoherent necessity beyond their control—and that had become their undoing. It all had happened too quickly for their minds to comprehend the full implication of what they had done, but in each of their minds they remembered every agonizing second of the ordeal.

Discovered by a stranger, they might as well have been found dead. To them, this was their grave, the bloated belly of this battered ship. Inside the hull of this floating tomb, formerly known to all as the *H.M.S. White Laurel*, ghouls collected in the shadows awaiting their fate.

Instead, underfoot, rats scampered about, hoping to share in the feast, drawn out from hiding by the scent of blood permeating the stale atmosphere. Unlike the rats though, the miserable mass was beyond accustomed to the unrelenting reek of death—those that hadn't taken their own life, of course, and succumbed to the cruel fate of the sea.

At first, it sickened them after realizing what the urge had driven them to. Yet, now, the stench was just as much a part of them as any other feature of their bodies, clinging to them, unwilling to loosen its grasp. Their blood-soaked clothes stuck to their sulking forms, dampening their bones. Just as they thought salvation had come for them, in the form of a man, to take them away, they knew not his intentions.

They prayed. Even those who did not supplicate learned and accepted the need to cleanse the soul. From their first step into spiraling insanity, to their ultimate discovery, they knew that nothing could be done now except to pray to a god that would have no alternative but to damn them. They knew nothing could save them now from the course lunacy had charted. No god, in Heaven or Hell, would hear their cries— for the cries of ghouls were as still and silent as the clandestine sea surrounding them.

***

"Captain! Sullivan!" Williams shouted as he burst through the hatch like a lunatic. His face, along with the faces of the men that were with him, was ashen—the color of oatmeal. His eyes had become strangely different, cracked mirrors into his freshly tormented soul.

Captain Harkcombe recovered from his fainting spell and was now on his feet moving about, running from the quarterdeck and down a stepladder. There he watched the four men, including his Quartermaster, stumble over each other, fighting to be first to cross back over the wooden plank that led back to the deck of the *Galileo*—back to safe ground.

Williams, Johnson, Connelly, and Hearn had all ventured below deck of the *White Laurel* to investigate Captain Harkcombe's claim of indescribable pandemonium. What they had found proved too much for them to bear.

They had zeroed in on the hatch that led below deck, the foul stink becoming nearly intolerable. The awful darkness, beyond the reaches of the light that shone down from the open hatch, had been thick and foreboding—they almost dared not enter.

With the lantern lit, the pale yellow flame had chased the dark away, but, in return, cast bizarre shadows and dancing apparitions that played with the men's eyes. However, nothing could mistake what they had seen; the blood that somehow splattered and smeared onto the walls, running slick from the wooden frame, pooling onto the floor. Some of the filthy passengers below looked as if they had been rolling around in the crimson mess, sopping it up like gravy.

Compassion and disgust intermingled, entwined within the hearts of the crewmen. It was a thin, yet defined line that had been erased the instant they turned around and caught glimpse of the grisly display behind them—the same display Captain Harkcombe had seen moments earlier.

The horrid sights, the bloody tangle of limbs and gore, hurried the men faster from the ship, however, not before stomachs discharged their vomitous burden adding to the human sewage at their feet. The need to get away, escape with their souls intact, forbade them from thinking with any sort of rationale. Instinct had carried them in their flight to safety, not one of them at all certain as to how to reconcile the landscape from which they had just fled.

They reeked of bile and death. The sour smell mingled with the yellowish glaze and blood mixture that had splashed over them when Connelly and Johnson took an ill-fated fall. "Captain...it is the most vile...thing I have ever seen," Williams stammered between breaths. A tear welled up in the strong man's eye.

"It is the Devil himself," blurted Hearn. "It is most surely his evil work."

"I agree, Captain," offered Connelly.

"What should we do, Captain?" asked Williams before absently wiping his soiled sleeve across his mouth.

Harkcombe stood silent, glancing over at the ship. No one must ever know what secrets it held. In the afternoon light, the figurehead on the prow of the ship held some of its original luster despite the battering it had received during the previous night's storm. From where he stood, he could still make out the gold embossed letters of the ship's name, the gold-leaf filigree work that surrounded it, and the hand carved eagle placard mounted beneath.

Nothing of the ship's outward appearance spoke anything of what it held within its walls. However, Harkcombe knew better. He knew, from his own experience as seen through his own eyes, that somehow, hell had found its way here, and the unholy enemy had taken up residency in the bowels of that beaten ship.

"Williams. Men," the Captain began, his voice pronounced and serious, carrying over the low din of the sea. His gaze fell upon his crewmembers as if to infuse within them his own fear- renewed strength. "We must do what the Lord would want of us. We must burn the evil out of her. We must burn the *White Laurel* into the sea."

***

After what seemed an eternity, daylight stung their eyes. Overhead, the sun ablaze in its high afternoon glory, shined like a spotlight to accentuate their guilt. They had been below deck rabid with fear and near madness for days. Their squinting eyes were opaque and shifty, hooded with suspicion and vulnerable to the glaring sunlight.

Harkcombe had ordered the crew to clean the passengers of the *White Laurel* the best they could. The frigid sting of the salt water was like a slap to their collective face, completely dousing them. With each dump of the bucket, the thick red stains rinsed off their bodies, the tainted water seeping between the wooden planks into the deck below.

"Captain, they are as clean as they are going to get," reported Sullivan, the ship's Lieutenant. "What shall we do next?"

"This catastrophe has already become the bane of my existence," Harkcombe sighed. "Gather them together," he began. "Take some men and begin bringing them to the ship."

Sullivan, stunned by the orders, paused for a moment. He stared the Captain dead in the eyes. "Then what?"

"Put them below," Harkcombe blurted. "Take whatever necessities we may need out of the cargo hold and pantries. Only the essentials. Then put them there."

Puzzled, Sullivan answered, "Aye, Captain. Right away, Sir."

Sullivan turned to walk away. However, the Captain had one more order he wished his Lieutenant to fulfill. "Give them some food to eat and fresh water to drink. There should be extra loaves of bread we could afford to part with?"

"But, Captain," Sullivan started, his voice lowered so not to be overheard. "That is our food, Sir. What if we run out?"

"We won't run out," Harkcombe rebutted, "We are only a few days from the Massachusetts colonies and we do have reserve rations in case of an emergency."

Sullivan's face flushed unable to comprehend his Captain's orders as he treaded the line between the two of them, closing in on insubordination.

Seeing Sullivan's expression turn sour, Harkcombe raised his voice. "That is an order, Lieutenant."

"Captain, they are bloody cannibals. They murdered their crew and then some...and ate their flesh on top of that, for God's sake. Who knows what other sick deeds they performed on those innocent people? Even if their virtuousness was tarnished, no man deserves a fate such as that and you want to let them live? Moreover, feed them on top of it all? It's bad enough that their foul carcasses are about to be standing on our decks, but you want to keep them only meters from where we sleep?"

"Do you not have any shred of compassion, Sullivan?" Harkcombe questioned. His eyes glassed over with emotion. "Yes, what they had done is without a doubt unforgivable in the eyes of man. And yes, perhaps it is dangerous to have them aboard this ship since we are unaware of the whole truth of the thing, but are we to be as wicked in our deeds as they? We do not know all the answers. We do not know why they did what they did nor do we know the whole story, the utter truth.

"So, do as I say, please and by whatever means possible we will get through this terrible ordeal. We will survive and it will be by the good graces of our Lord."

The mix of emotions gnawed at Harkcombe's conscience—disgust and loyalty, hatred and fright. He turned away from Sullivan, fighting back a swell of emotions that threatened to rain from his pale and somber eyes. He had to remain strong and vigilant now, showing no more sentiment or perceived weakness.

"I apologize, Captain. Please forgive my disrespect." Sullivan turned and walked away, back to the *Galileo*.

***

Light began to fade.

The sun hung low in the western sky hidden behind clouds during its slow descent. In a careful and controlled manner, the able seamen led the passengers below deck into the cargo hold of the *Galileo*. The crew had collected and placed all useful supplies in another location—they left everything else alone.

In a sudden flash, brought on in part by lantern oil lacing the *White Laurel*'s wooden deck and a soft easterly wind, they set the vessel aflame. Ignited by the crew, through God's will, flames sputtered high into the air. It snatched the oxygen from the wind to fuel its burning fury. In the swiftly coming twilight, the blaze stood out against the violet horizon as fiery tongues consumed their sacrifice. Watching from the starboard side of their ship, the crew stood transfixed on the spectacle.

The *Galileo* slowly drifted from the inferno. Even at their increased distance, the heat of the fire still warmed their brooding faces. The crew beheld the burning pyre with detached awe as orange firelight danced in their eyes. This event brought them no joy or feeling of accomplishment. With only half the job done, they realized torching the *White Laurel* was the easy part.

From deep within the ship, the fire raged. It engulfed everything in its hungry path, feeding with flaming dedication. Wood crackled and popped. Sparks jumped high into the air, casting little streaks behind them until vanishing in the night air. Smoke billowed up from the bowels of the craft, rolling out of every opening.

A deafening crack resounded in the calmness. The weakened deck collapsed upon itself almost folding the ship in half. Flames erupted as the masts snapped and plummeted into the waiting ocean. Right before the crew's eyes, the *White Laurel* crumbled and burned into nothingness and the smell of burning flesh wafted across the water.

Blazing fragments floated on the ocean's smooth surface, bobbing helplessly to their demise. They watched on as fire consecrated the ashen bodies of the dead to the depths below while hoping the souls of their brothers of the sea climbed from their desecrated husks for the final incline into the everlasting.

Captain Harkcombe and his crew, with knots of anxiety crushing their insides, continued to watch the burning horizon. They bowed their heads and held a prayer in their hearts, begging for forgiveness.

Before Harkcombe realized it, daybreak had arrived. Having been standing there looking out the porthole all night, he had witnessed dawn. His tired eyes burned from exhaustion; his feet hurt from carrying his burden for hours on end. With so much more to do before they arrived in America, he knew there was no time now for rest; his mind would not let him do so.

The *Galileo* and its crew were still over a day's journey from land. He opened the door onto the stern castle and the early morning sun scorched his eyes as it hung low in the east. Most of his crew remained on the main deck for the night. Fear and revulsion held them from sleeping in their bunks. Some men still slept, while others sat wide-eyed and wary. Could he blame them? He put a huge burden on their shoulders. Yet, almost to their new home, Harkcombe knew that this would be the last time most, if not all, of his men would ever sail with him again.

Yet, they continued on this course, following this path of lunacy. He wanted more than anything to just apologize to his men, to tell them that they made him proud, but the angry stares kept him silent and the looks of contempt clawed at his spirit. Somewhere along the way, he had failed his men.

As he looked out at the cloudless horizon, a cool morning breeze lifted off the Atlantic. The predicament he now found himself in made the distance left to travel seem arduous—near impossible. Without a doubt, he was scared, scared of what had happened, scared for his crew, scared of what might come to be in the end.

***

First mistake had been letting those monsters onboard, Sullivan thought. Without a doubt, that opinion held strong. Still in awe and astounded by the sheer foolhardiness of Captain Harkcombe's orders, the foundation of his loyalty to the man had shifted. Leading this crew, captaining this ship, should be his responsibility to hold now. He knew, as did some of the other men, as well, that Harkcombe was no longer fit to be in charge and that something had to be done.

Second mistake had been raising the sails while a strong breeze blew sufficiently enough to carry the Galileo a little faster. However, when the crew had finished tying the sails into place, the call from the crow's nest came down.

"Storm clouds, dead ahead!"

The looming gray clouds appeared from nowhere; the swirling mist danced above the horizon. Thunder rumbled in the distance as the clouds threatened to capture the floating sun. Soon the storm would cloak everything in dusky gloom. Harkcombe climbed up to the poop deck, barking out commands to the boatswain and making sure Master Reynolds, the navigator, was on point. With their orders, the crew rushed to lower the sails and tie them down into place in preparation for the approaching storm.

A tremendous vein of lightning ripped across the sky. Rain fell from the breach in massive droplets. Instantly, the tempest soaked everything. More thunder interrupted the constant drumming of rain hitting the wooden deck as the sky whirled a dark purple. Wind whipped up in a fury and the ocean's salt stung the crew's skin.

***

The rain fell like silver needles piercing the amorphous skin of the sea. Clouds collected in the sky that had lowered itself like a misty canopy over the Atlantic. Frigid wind blew through the frothy crests of the waves as they rose high into the air crashing down upon themselves with mighty slaps. The ocean roiled and the thunder, monotonous in its constant rumbling, rumbled over the howling wind.

The mighty gales bellowed in their fury almost forming coherent words. Lightning streaked across the sky, energized bluish tentacles of light licking the wounded clouds. The wind's deep wails of laughter crashed down on everything while over the sea, the murky sky drooped, hanging low from its weight. Its grayness overshadowed both vessels as the veil of clouds circulated, disrupting the already ever-changing shape of the sky. The storm produced illusions, portrayed abnormal images while the darkened heavens swirled.

In the great awning of the storm, shapes formed in the clouds—indistinct visages with eyes deep and sullen. Shifting faces adorned the sky like a great bas-relief carved in granite, dulled by the grayness, only illuminated by the violent flashes of lightning. And it was from these faces, graced with vague outlines of horns and gapping maws, the wind's mirth seemed to emanate.

***

Sullivan's insides twisted with his anger as he listened to Harkcombe shouting orders. He could now see through his captain's mask of competence and knew he was leading the crew to certain death.

And the windborne whispering concurred.

Sullivan stopped everything. He had had enough of the absurdity and refused to take it anymore. He pulled a knife from his boot and stared at the blade; it glowed from a streak of lightning that lit up the sky. He left his post—his duty—and made his way across the deck toward his captain. Last mistake—following Harkcombe's orders.

Now, he had no more room for mistakes. It had come to this. Delirium swam in Sullivan's eyes, but he never felt so in control in his life. Intent on shifting the balance of power forever, he felt the life in him renewed along with a need that wouldn't subside. Turning back was never an option. Above, the thunderous laughter grew louder.

Harkcombe stood at the helm of the *Galileo*, clutching the wooden rail, his knuckles white with purpose. The racket of the weeping clouds canceled out every other sound. He could barely hear his own shouted orders as he blinked the rain from his eyes. "Hold your positions, men. Let's see if we can wait her out," he hollered to anyone in earshot. Yet, no sooner did the words leave his lips did he know beyond doubt that he put them on a course of failure.

The last storm paled in comparison. The strength of the waves lifted the mighty galleon out of the water. Sea froth spit onto the deck as the sea tossed the ship about so relentlessly that Harkcombe felt as if she would break apart at any moment, signaling the final voyage of the *Galileo* and its crew.

The world ignited in a blinding glow blinding Harkcombe. In another thunderous instant, Harkcombe saw a different brilliance dance before his eyes. Searing pain shocked his body and he went numb. He gracelessly spun around only to catch a glimpse of Sullivan and the incoherent rage gleaming in his eye.

"I hate you, sir. I have always hated you," the Lieutenant shouted over the deafening storm. His voice trailed off, combining with the universal clamor.

Harkcombe's lips moved to speak, but they formed no words. Instead, he fell to his knees, gripping the side where Sullivan sunk his knife deep into his abdomen. Fighting for his sight not to fail despite deathly slowly claiming him, Harkcombe still managed to witness Sullivan lift the soiled knife to his lips and lick it clean of the blood clinging to it. He studied his Lieutenant's emotionless face as the edges of his vision blurred. He could find no traces of sanity left, only the swirling pools of radiant madness where the man's eyes once were. Understanding eluded him in his final moments; his struggle to fathom why Sullivan had done this, why none of his men offered him help—fought to save their Captain— evaporated.

Sullivan had relieved the Captain of the *Galileo* of his duties. The voices whispering on the wind had spurred him on, the unseen laughter compelling him to action. His cold, uncaring eyes appraised Harkcombe's dying body. If not for Harkcombe, this nightmare would never have happened. Harkcombe, unknowingly the catalyst of this fate, the gatekeeper for what ached to be unleashed, brought this nightmare upon them and upon himself. Yet, without the Captain, Sullivan could have never felt this powerful, this in control—this hungry.

Giving in to the urge, the necessity to close his eyes, Harkcombe could no longer stomach looking at Sullivan's face, into his wrathful gaze. The pain faded from the wound that was stealing his life. No more could he feel the cold rain pelting him or hear the pounding thunder echoing from the heavens—or even Sullivan's maniacal laughter. As he sat slouched over and dying on the soaked wooden deck of his ship, he only heard the creeping murmurs that seemed to rise from the icy wind—blaming him, condemning him—and he only saw the brightness of imminent death.

***

The air tingled.

Everything became blurry in the crew's eyes. Their movements felt sluggish despite the rapidity of their motions. In a dreamlike progression, time seemed to have slowed. The thunder became an interminable din, a constant grumbling from the above sky. Pellets of rain fell in slow motion, floating down like tears from the clouds and leaving cascading trails of mist behind them.

Confusion held the *Galileo*'s crew in its vice as they watched everything slowly come undone. Williams placed his hand out, palm up. Drops of rain fell softly into its center, one by one collecting into a small puddle. Lightning flashed for what felt like minutes at a time as it lit the sky in one uniform glow. Shadows caressed the unnatural faces in the clouds.

Despite trudging through the cresting waves, the *Galileo* felt at a standstill. Each man looked to the heavens for an answer that did not—would not—come. Lethargy thickened the air. The stagnant odorless atmosphere tickled their nostrils with invisible static fingers.

A violent shout of laughter broke the crew from their bewilderment, tearing them away from the mesmerizing language of the storm. On the quarterdeck, Sullivan kneeled in front of Captain Harkcombe's body, his arm moving back and forth—a blur of bronze flesh. Williams and the others ran to Harkcombe's aid, but they were too late. Down the deck and between the wooden boards flowed their Captain's water-downed blood.

The crew stood mortified watching Sullivan repeatedly plunge his blade into Harkcombe's dead body, laughing and wailing like a banshee. Stab after stab, Sullivan probed the knife's blade deeper and deeper into the corpse. Each movement swift, each thrust splayed out in graphic detail, the blur of motion contradicting the sluggishness of the world around them. They watched in cinematic illusion the Captain's skin stretch and rip as the blade pierced through, frame by frame almost in time with the intermittent lightning flashes.

Sullivan, blood stained and insane, threw the knife over his shoulder without care.

The crew felt rooted in place, petrified with fear. Swirls of chaotic pandemonium ran amuck, encircling their bodies. Yet, the instant Sullivan ripped into Harkcombe's flesh with his bare hands they felt the need, shared the yearning. In that moment, they finally understood the consuming insanity, the volumes of depravity that had claimed so many before them. Voices in the air, tickling their ears, compelled each man to succumb to their primordial instincts. They were useless to resist as the urges reacted faster than rational thought.

In fluid deceleration, the crew tore into each other, striving harder to be the next to get at Harkcombe's corpse. Monstrous hails of laughter ripped from above. The wind snickered with pleasure. Blood's coppery scent permeated the air, intensifying the lunacy. As they piled onto each other, they ripped, tore, bit, and clawed. The violence, not enough the satiate the inner craving that led to some bestial bloodlust, strove them to battle harder. Rain continued its slow descent and, in sweeping expanses of time, lightning set the sky alight.

Below, the passengers of the *White Laurel* heard the commotion and the screams of pain and hunger. They were not strangers to the slow motion sensation of time crawling; they knew it well for it had once claimed them—and they, too, had once understood. For when the great storm had imposed its infinite burden, it stole from them every shred of innocence.

However, now, the voices on the wind, the laughter from the clouds, sounded foreign to them, as if a script rewritten for the next cast. God had left them to die—an eye for an eye. No escape, no reprieve would be granted, no quick painless death. They silently wished to hear the voices again, to feel the longing so the weight of the slaughter would dull the pain of attrition.

Instead, they prayed for forgiveness.

Forgiveness from God evaded them, yet they forgave each other. Praying would do no good, yet they mumbled the words to Heaven nonetheless. Cleansing their souls, purging the guilt from their own minds had them prepared to succumb to the eventual.

On the deck above, the madness quieted. Some shouts and screams did persist, drawn out falsettos and grunts echoing, for this was only the beginning. Outside the door that locked them into their fate, someone lifted and threw the wooden bolt. With a heavy clank that shook through their bones, the bolt smashed against the floor. The door creaked open and lantern light flooded in, pulsating with each flicker of the flame. Beyond the light, the passengers could not see any faces but could sense the swarming hysteria, the unquenchable ravenousness.

One of the deck hands pushed the big wooden door all the way open. Williams, covered in crimson, walked into the room with a lantern in hand, followed by Sullivan. Behind them, others, equally grisly with their ruby stained grins and clothes, entered the hold. Each group stared the other down. Death had finally come to take them with unmistakable certainty.

"We are sorry," Williams muttered, breaking the silence. "Please forgive us." Despite those words, the twisted bloody smile never left his face; the dementia never left his eyes. At his heels, each man held the same fury and need in his eyes, just as the passengers' once had.

A violent crash shut the door tight on the cargo hold and on their lives as the whispering murmurs of the wind and rain continued to slice through the air like knives—only to eventually dissipate and return to tranquility.

The Abenaki elder stood on the precipice of the high cliff—watching.

"S*alki kinlôn*," he mumbled as a treacherous breeze blasted off the ocean and up the jagged rock face, tossing his long, braided hair. He looked out over the churning sea in terrified awe. In the distance, his angered gods molded the clouds, spinning them into a mass of destructive power. As the super cell enveloped the sky, its forceful winds wreaked havoc on the lone vessel caught in its center.

He heard the laughing and faint chatter of his gods as they unleashed their fury. His worry grew; it was happening again. What his tribe had done this time to incur the wrath of the heavens he didn't know. Yet something disturbed or displeased his gods.

The storm raged closer and his group of hunters saw it, too. They called out to their elder, but the howl of the wind drowned out their voices. If they didn't do something to appease the gods, the approaching tempest would trap them on this island with no way back to the mainland. Out there on the desolate rock, miles from their village, they would most certainly die, if the storm didn't claim their lives first.

Turmoil filled the sky. A wall of horizontal rain slammed into the elder and he held fast to a tree. The gale rocketed up the cliff knocking him off balance, yet he remained steadfast, his sullen eyes never wavering from the sight. He whispered prayers but the scowling faces in the clouds laughed and mocked him. Below, the ocean swelled with crashing waves against the rocky outcroppings at the base of the island, rattling the foundation of the landmass.

In an instant, the storm engulfed the whole island. On the far side, the squall's breath lifted the hunters' canoes right off the beach, dropping them against the rocky shoreline where they exploded into deadly wooden shrapnel now flying through the air at perilous velocity. Those hunters that didn't cling to a tree or a rock—or anything secured to the ground—were snatched by the calamity and sucked up into the air only to plunge to their death on the hard ground below or be whisked off into the churning engine of the sea.

The elder squinted against the razor blades of rain that sliced at his earth-strengthened form. He hooked his arm and leg around the trunk of the flailing tree so the frigid gusts wouldn't sweep him away as well. In the center of the massive storm, he spotted the helpless ship once again as the wind and waves ravaged it. He thought he heard screaming coming from within the belly of the craft even over the wail of the wind and mighty claps of his gods' overwhelming resentment.

One of his tribesmen lost hold of the tree he struggled to hold fast to; the whirlwind seized him and bounced him mercilessly across the hard ground before launching him over the side of the sea cliff. The elder reached out for his fellow tribesman, but failed to make the catch in time. The poor man's shriek echoed all the way down the rock wall into oblivion.

Again, the elder looked up to the sky, his eyes pleading for mercy. He heard shouts of dissent behind him, rising over the din—another prayer gone unheard or ignored. His remaining tribesmen bellowed rage in their native tongue as the storm's fury now coursed within their veins. The elder clenched his eyes tight against the pelting rain and debris, hoping that it would end quickly while below, the battered shell of the *HMS Galileo*, cradled within the grasp of a tidal wave, slammed into the rocks, exploding into nothingness.

HALLOWED POINT

Andrew Bell

July 17th. Just one week to go.

The house wasn't the same after my older brother, David, died. Mum and dad had practically stopped communicating altogether, drifting from separate beds to virtual alienation. And as we drifted through the rooms like ghosts, moving the furniture occasionally so we could sit and view the world from different angles, we failed to notice the seasons wither and turn full circle. Late at night I'd stand at the top of the landing, listening, straining to capture some deviation in the silence. But between the sound of the old floorboards settling, and the hum of the wind widening the gaps in the old slate roof, each day blended seamlessly into one.

Dad had taken to keeping his distance from me and mum for as long as possible. He'd telephone, text saying he'd be home late—that someone had called in sick and he had to cover. Soon mum stopped answering the phone at 4PM. And into her habits, her intricate stitch-work and soap operas, she'd disappear; to the point where, if she stood in the sun, she wouldn't cast a shadow. The walls quickly filled with her small tapestries. Some of them were a riot of colour, like rainbows, captured behind glass. Dragons and sea creatures, landscapes bursting with colour. And others were too dark and lifeless. Crumbling churches and images of broken crosses and crying children. It was her way of escape, and I could deal with that. It had been a year of therapy, doctor's appointments, counselling sessions…nothing seemed to work. But this seemed cathartic. We both knew Dad would have some excuse for not being here. All those hours, I thought. All the money he must be bringing home from Frozenworld Foods. Yet he still drove the same Ford, wore the same jeans and shoes, and occasionally dragged an old paintbrush along the weathered hull of our small fishing boat. She didn't have a name. Sometimes I think she didn't even deserve one. No. He was avoiding us. But mostly, he was avoiding me.

You see, David drowned. And I don't think my Dad ever forgave me.

I'm ten years old now. A year older than the little kid that could have saved his sixteen year old brother when he got cramp; a year older than the boy that should have died—

Stop it! It wasn't your fault he couldn't make it back to the boat. He was drunk for God's sake! IT WAS NOT YOUR FAULT!

***

Saturday had finally come around, and I awoke that morning to warm bright cubes of sunlight emblazoned on my bedroom wall. Soft, kind voices from the old radio in the kitchen, accompanied the mouth-watering aroma of fried bacon; passing me on the stairs like lovers.

"Did we win the lottery last night?" I said, about to sit at the table.

"No time for that, sunshine," said Dad, licking his greasy fingertips, stuffing the freshly made sandwiches into a small plastic bag. "We're going for a little walk."

"Is mum coming along?"

"Nope. Just you and me."

"Where?"

He didn't answer.

I felt a block of ice settle deep in my stomach, and as it melted, it replaced my blood.

***

I didn't want to walk along Seaton Beach. An icy breeze raked the top of the sand, waking dust devils, rocking the car gently. But after sitting quietly, eating the cooling bacon sandwiches, listening to my dad's jaw crack and squeak, being outside in the fresh air, so close to the creeping ocean, didn't seem so bad.

The sun had died it seemed from the moment we left the car. So did my hope.

"Cannot believe it's been almost a year," said Dad, looking down at his bare feet as they sank deeply in the wet sand. He jerked slightly, moving quickly to keep from slipping. His words drifted between blue curls of cigarette smoke, the butt dangling at the corner of his mouth.

"I know—"

"Remember when David tried to kiss his girlfriend in the dunes over there?" he said, chuckling silently, nodding toward the large patch of sand and weeds over by the Gas works, a hundred metres or so to our right. It could have been a hundred miles away for all I cared. In fact I wish it were.

I nodded, but I looked down at my own feet instead.

"He got a proper slap in the face for his trouble!"

"Dad, I—"

"He just didn't have the knack, is all. Takes after your mum," he said, shaking his head. A broad smile, lacking warmth, was etched on his face, locked in a memory it seemed.

"I tried to save him."

If he heard my words, then he was a master of concealment. The smile remained.

"I really tried."

I expected a heavy but gentle hand to grab my shoulder, the love of a father battling with his pain, embracing me, telling me not to say—even *think* such things. I expected strong words, a reprimand even. But that moment by the water's edge, buffeted by the increasing strength of the icy wind, I heard the crash and hiss of the water as it dashed against the old piers that scarred the Seaton Carew skyline to our left. I shouldn't have even been able to hear it. But Dad's silent reply helped.

"I had a weird dream last night," he said finally, looking out at the sea as it moved like mercury beneath the canopy of silver, bruised clouds. A large seagull lacerated the water with a wing, something dangling from its beak, before shooting up into the air. "Remember when we'd go out in the boat, just us—you, me, and your brother—drink beer and talk about football, even girls?"

"Dad, I don't feel like hanging around here," I said, folding my arms to generate a little warmth. "It's getting colder—"

"Why don't we take the boat out?"

"What…now?"

"Next weekend would be good," he replied, nodding his head slowly, narrowing his eyes as if to make out an object bobbing about on the horizon. "Just you. Your mum. And me."

I turned to say something, but he had already started making his way up the beach, his stride now strong and steady as he headed for the car.

***

We ate our supper in silence, as always, and I couldn't wait to finish my plate and dart off to the attic. It had been David's bedroom. Mum had been reluctant to let me have it. But eventually she gave in, waving my insistence away as if it had been a pesky insect. As for my dad, well, I don't think he even knew I had moved my stuff in there.

A large window overlooked the vast expanse of the North Sea. And on long cloudless nights such as these, the moon hung motionless—as light as air—above the galaxy black water. A couple of times I wanted to be nosey, but I kept my curiosity to myself. I didn't want to look through David's old telescope, didn't even want to peek at what caught my brother's interest before he died. I mean, what if I accidentally moved it?

But tonight I *did* take a look. And I almost jumped out of my skin with fright.

Despite the late hour—

God, why couldn't you have covered the moon with clouds? Why did you let me see it?

I saw maybe the last place David had surveyed the night before he died. Hell, it could have been the last thing he saw an hour before…

I tried to brush off what I had seen through the scope.

An hour later, I watched my hands shake, trying to brush my teeth, seeing my pale, tired face stare back at me in the mirror. And no matter how much sea air I had had that day, it took me a long time to drift off to sleep. The scope had been, had been pointing at the place—the *exact* place—David's body had been washed up on the shore.

***

I couldn't sleep that night. When I closed my eyes, Dad's piercing brown eyes appeared in my head, unblinking, knowing. My stomach rumbled, and no matter how many times I licked my lips, I couldn't get the sickly taste of under-cooked bacon and tomato ketchup from my mouth. So I climbed out of bed and made my way downstairs to the kitchen for a drink of milk. Portraits followed my every move. Old family photographs of me, David, Mum and Dad. People said we looked the same, like four peas in a pod. Despite having brown eyes, I couldn't work out the similarities—

Just keep your head down and move, for crying out loud, Jake! The kitchen is just a few feet away. But the faces watched me.

On my return to the stairs, carrying a tall glass, I heard the sudden grunt and whistle from Dad's snoring corpse in the lounge. I could just make out the hiss of the TV Station and see the white brightness flicker about the door frame. I had a mind to go in the room and turn the damned thing off. But all I wanted to do was get back to bed as soon as—

Pain the likes of which I hadn't felt in all my life suddenly lanced through my right foot! White lightning separated the darkness as I struggled to place the glass of milk down and cradle my foot without spilling the liquid everywhere. Finally, I sat heavily on the bottom step and rubbed my tender toes, searching in the darkness for the bloody object I'd kicked. It was poking out from what appeared to be Dad's work rucksack. It was a thick hard backed book. I couldn't quite make out its title, and the last thing I needed was Dad waking up to the hallway light burning away. So I took it back to bed with me, climbed beneath the duvet with my torch, and looked at the cover.

For a boy of ten, with an eternity ahead of him, provided he played his cards right, I wasn't sure my heart could take another jolt. The torch fell on the book, and as I quickly grabbed it once more, my eyes never leaving the ghastly image on the cover, I heard my heart pounding and saw the pulsating burns on my retinae. I have no idea what the words meant but I knew it wasn't English.

Illumination omittuntur prohibetur ab operibus et fabulis
–Dr. Harold Lynn

I didn't care about the strange words, they meant nothing to me. It was the image embossed in, what appeared to be, its leather cover that drew my attention. I gently traced a trembling fingertip around the raised illustration, wondering if it would burst like a blood blister. But the creature depicted didn't move or break apart like ash.

The ocean had always held many wonders for me and David. In fact, the whole town thrived on its generosity. It would tease us sometimes, leaving us guessing as to whether or not we would actually eat during the winter, for Frozenworld Foods had depended upon its haul for many years. But now, looking at the creature, with its three rows of spear-like teeth, the wide jaws biting down on what appeared to be a small ship, its eyes as wide and bright as full moons, the water was the last thing I ever wanted to see. I wanted to throw the book across the room, but I needed to browse through the dry, rough paper inside, eager to know why Dad had been so interested in it. If a gun was pointed at my head I still couldn't recall him ever reading a *magazine* let alone a book.

The pages crackled as I turned them, showing me strange yet beautifully sketched shapes. Of stars and circles; stars within squares. Moon shaped things beside what could only be faceless human beings. Sharp, pointed steaks piercing the human, his or her face caught in a rictus of sheer agony; the moon creature, its arched back, gazing upwards, mouth open wide...*laughing?*

Laughing.

I turned the page, and then another, finally coming across a narrow passage of words. They resembled the language on the book's cover. I didn't know what they meant; I only knew that they were important to my dad. The corner of the page was folded. I couldn't help but feel a chill rush over my skin as goose bumps shifted the hairs along the nape of my neck. It was fair to say that sleep gave me a wide berth that night.

***

I left the house bright and early that Sunday morning, knowing that the town library was open to the public for three hours. So I had from nine o'clock till noon to try and make sense of the whole mess my life had become. I considered using the home computer, but if Dad were to find out I'd been snooping on him, there'd most certainly be bloody war. No. The day on the boat was approaching, and I couldn't help but feel my every nerve twitch with dread.

I had scribbled the strange title of the book on a piece of paper, and as I typed it into the browser, I took a deep breath before pressing ENTER.

***

The following day, instead of going to school, I made off to the local park, and sat on the swing. I needed to think, to do something. I couldn't concentrate no matter how much I tried. I had known about the book for four days, and each passing hour, I came closer to telling mum what was going on in Dad's twisted mind; his intentions. But every time I bucked up the courage, looking over at my Dad while he bit down into his chicken leg, his eyes never leaving mine, I looked down at my own food; aimlessly pushing it around with a fork.

And so the days passed.

"It's Saturday tomorrow," said Dad, scooping up a fillet of fish from the plate before him. Drool hung from his chin, and I wanted nothing more than to punch it from his jaw.

"It most certainly is," mum replied, her voice little more than a whisper. "Are we still going out on the boat?"

"Well," said Dad, "It's only right. After all, it *is* the anniversary—"

"I'm going for a lie down."

"Emma, we cannot live in the past," said Dad, trying to keep his voice at an even keel. "The fresh air would do us good..."

We watched mum suddenly stand up, almost knocking over her half full glass of red wine as she left the table. And like the ghost she had become she drifted silently up the stairs. We didn't even hear the door close behind her.

"So," he said finally, sipping from his glass of wine, "Tomorrow we go fishing."

I had lost my appetite.

***

Despite the calmness of the sea, and the sun-dappled waves as they climbed up the black ribs of the skeleton pier, it was the sound of silence that turned my stomach. It seemed almost *too* perfect, as though Dad planned this whole trip down to the letter. The thought that today marked the anniversary of my brother's death did little to unclench the tight fist in my belly. What made icy fingers trace patterns down my back was the way Dad looked out to sea. His pale, stony face looked haggard and etched with a hundred lines; his eyes, steely, unblinking.

We were heading for the spot where David died.

I wanted to grab Mum's hand and jump overboard, to tell her we weren't here to bloody fish!

"Cast out, matey," said Dad, nodding at the fishing rod in my hands. "Fish won't jump in the boat by themselves, I tell you." He feigned a smile as though he were in pain. I noticed the slight tick at the corner of his mouth. So I cast out.

Mum had packed a box of sandwiches, a bottle of Cola, and some beer and wine for them. My mouth kept drying up like tinder, and sipping from the cold drink helped me keep an eye on my Dad too, stealing glances at his hands as I tilted the bottle. I didn't like the way his knuckles remained white, the skin stretched to breaking point as he squeezed the rod.

"It's certainly a beautiful day," said Mum, sipping at her wine. She had tied her hair in a plat, and I noticed a trace of lipstick on her mouth. "Hard to believe that it was a year ago today," she said, staring out at the hazy horizon.

I noticed Dad looking at his wristwatch and then at me. There was no hint of a smile on his face; I knew what he was thinking. In ten minutes, it would mark the *precise* moment David died, exactly one year to the moment that I failed him—failed *all* of us! I had been but inches away from his outstretched arm, his shaking fingers, his wide eyes—

That's when I noticed the object tucked behind the fishing equipment.

No! No! No! That's it!

I threw the rod aside and stood up, swaying slightly.

"Mum, I want to go home," I said, pins and needles creeping across my neck and jaw, lips quivering. My hands shook like the fish we used to catch and throw in the boat, just before Dad impaled them to the decking with his knife. "I want to go home. I don't feel so good."

"What? Don't be silly, sweetie. We just got here."

"Mum, please! I—"

"What's wrong, son?" asked Dad, sipping from his beer can. He stared out at the point near the quay where-

"You know *exactly* what I'm fucking talking about, Dad!"

"HEY! DON"T *EVER* USE LANGUAGE LIKE THAT INFRONT OF YOUR MUM!"

"It's okay, Bert," said Mum, waving away my words like smoke. "It's a tough day for all of us."

But Dad had already put down his rod. Now he was standing, the sun at his back—a silhouette—watching me. When he moved, I took my chance and bolted for the object tucked beside the fishing box.

"Here!" I shrieked, holding up the book, pointing it at the silhouette as if to ward off whatever cruel intentions it had in mind. But I already knew. *I already knew what the bastard had in store for us!*

Dad frowned, tilting his head to one side like an inquisitive Labrador, a crooked smile on his lips.

"Give me that, thing," she said.

"Look Mum, look at it," I said, thrusting the book in her open hands. "We need to get back home."

Mum whispered something. I couldn't hear her voice, but she was reading from the book.

"A beer and half a glass of wine, and this party has already gone crazy," said Dad, shaking his head. "Maybe we *should* head back. Emma, what're you saying?"

Mum whispered, but not from the book; from the heart. The tome was face down on the sodden decking now. That's when I noticed the small rectangular object sticking to the cover. I bent down and peeled it from the book. I shook my head in disbelief, glancing at my Dad.

"What is it, son? Here, give it…"

"It's a bookmark."

But not just any kind, this was made from a loving, pain stricken heart. The small strip of cloth was covered in hand stitched flowers and tiny aeroplanes. And scrawled across it were the words: DAVID, MY LOVE, MY LIFE

"Rituals of illumination. Forbidden works and other legends by Dr. Harold Lynn," said Mum, smiling crookedly.

The razor sharp knives were thrust at our throats, piercing Dad's bobbing Adam's apple. He winced but the blade remained, sunlight shimmering through the thin sheen of blood.

I wasn't bleeding, but I already felt wounded, seeing the hatred burning in Mum's eyes. As she stepped forward we were helpless to comply, our feet sliding a little.

"Emma, just give me the knives."

"Shut your *fucking* mouth, or I'll cut you from ear to ear!"

"Mum, please…"

"And you can shut up, too! You little bastard. Couldn't even save your brother. So close, so bloody close."

"I tried, Mum!" The tears blurred my vision now. "But he was drinking, and I couldn't help him!"

"DRINKING! And where were you, Bert?" she screamed, pushing the knife further into his throat. A geyser of blood sprayed across Mum's face, but she didn't even blink, not one flinch. "Were you too fucking drunk to save your son? Sleeping it off while David drowned?"

"*Conforta arma sanguine tuo carnibus vestisti me, adunare, et obstupuerit...animas conspiciunt.*" (Fortify thy armour with thine own blood, knit flesh, unite sinew...souls entwined. To the depths I send you).

"What the hell are you saying?" Dad croaked, blood coursing down his chest.

But I knew what she was saying, even though I didn't understand the language. It was the words from the book.

We stepped back once more, Mum's voice was getting louder as she uttered the verse.

"*Deducunt ad te mitto, clamores simul horrendous ad voces a susurrus, sicut iacuit cum iacuit cutis, quod est vinculum, cibos de ore profundo!*" (The voices from whispers to screams, as layer after layer the skin that binds feeds the mouths of the deep!)

I saw movement at the corner of my eye. The still water was frothing, bubbling as though a volcano had quietly erupted beneath the sea bed. Steam rose, pasting my clothes to my body like a second skin. My heart skipped a beat as something moved passed the boat, something large and scaly. It peered over the ledge; its pale red eyes, blinking. And as it watched, even for a fraction of a second, it looked at us with murderous, heinous intent. I watched its jaw drop, like one of those large reptiles dislocating its bones to accommodate a large pig.

Another creature peered over its shoulder. And another. They seemed similar in shape and, although facially abhorrent, youthful. Like children they clamoured over the edge of the small railing, only to slip and slide back into the water.

I tried to turn my head, as a wall slowly appeared behind me. Its shadow cooled my skin, blocking out the sun. But I knew it wasn't a wall. We had reached the place David died. It was the end for Dad and me, I just knew it.

Whatever stood behind us breathed a fetid stench, so foul I almost threw up. It was waiting for us.

Mum spat her final words, pushing the blades, urging us backward, our feet teetering on the ledge.

She kept moving.

"Tollitur creaturas creare unum, alterum in semine. Revertere ad one—" (Forfeit the creatures, one to create, the other of the seed. Return the one—)

That's when our whole world became nothing less than an explosion of colour and screams. I managed to pull myself away from the knife edge as Mum slipped on the decking. They both fell in a tangle of arms and legs overboard. I think Dad was already dead in the water before the enormous amphibian like creature tore him apart, his blood didn't spray. He just stared up at the bright blue sky, eyes unblinking, the crack of a smile on his mouth; accepting his fate. But Mum screamed, determined to escape the ravenous, talon like claws of the other three beasts. She tried to head for the place David died. I could see her pulling in that very direction. But when her arms broke away from her shoulders, the sound of tearing flesh like ripping leather, I looked away. I fell to the deck. The color went black—the screams turned silent, and—

***

You read such stories about the comatose, and how they can hear what's going on around them as they slept. It's true, of course. And my three long weeks in the hospital were no different. I remember hearing the doctors and nurses shuffling by; their shoes squeaking on the highly polished floors. The tang of pine disinfectant will surely haunt me until the day I die. Voices passed the room, and I felt the breeze across my brow as they diminished into silence.

At night I was vulnerable, afraid of the sound of the door slowly opening, bringing with it the most God-awful stench! My heart hammering wildly as the footsteps slowly approached my bed. And there it would stand, watching me; breathing in slowly, exhaling even slower. I screamed inside. To be awake, to run from my bed and hide! Anywhere! Anywhere but here in the dark! But then it would turn about, its footfalls diminishing, along with the rotten stench it brought with it.

Then I heard him.

"Hello, young Jake."

It was an old voice, coffee and cigarettes, making me want to turn away, but I couldn't. And as a nurse or someone else shuffled by the room, he went quiet, talking about procedure and even the weather, until...

"My name is Doctor Lynn. Harold Lynn. And you've been under my wing for a few weeks."

I knew that name. *I knew it!* But, I couldn't remember where from.

The door creaked loudly, a breeze flowing through the room as whoever stood there let it close. Then the footsteps made agonizingly slowly to the bed. The stench of the thing turned my stomach.

"Ah, a visitor," said the Doctor.

Silence replied.

"It worked, my boy. It worked. If your mum could see you now..."

***

The night I woke up I knew it had been beside me, sitting in the chair. I was disorientated at first, barely able to lift a finger or even blink. But as I turned, whatever had been sitting beside me vanished, suddenly appearing at the door. It had its back to me. I tried to call out, to scream, but I had lost the use of my tongue; almost forgotten how to breathe.

But then, I realized that I didn't need to speak, for I didn't need to know who the visitor was.

It turned around at the threshold, silhouetted in the brightly-lit hallway.

That smile.

Those eyes.

WANDERER

Shane Lindemoen

Evidence item C-33 CN# 24-001387
From the Personal Journal of Victor E. Rhodey [original transcript]
Master: not for distribution, under penalty of law.
December 1, 2028

There was a painting above the desk in my father's study of a man standing on a rocky shoreline, staring into the crashing sea. It was called *Wanderer*, or *Wanderer in the Sea*. I can't remember. He had it all my life.

One day I asked him what it meant, and he told me that it was about the unknown. The man, he said, represented every man. And the sea represented every sea. Every frontier we set our eyes upon in the hopes of learning more about where we fit in this world.

I didn't understand. I'm still not sure I understand now, as a man. But my father looked at me, and he could see me failing to put things together, and he told me to look at the horizon. I said that there wasn't one. He asked me to look closer. I said that I could see dark rocks and waves and a man. He told me that I also see the blades of squall cutting up out of the water. I see the vast gray sky above them, the stars hidden behind the sky, and the milky bands of galaxy beyond those. I see even farther, to the very edge of our universe. He said, as a spiritual being—as something with the agency to know what it is, where it's been, and where it's going—I see more of the painting than meets the eye.

So can the man standing on those rocks. He can picture

what's below the choppy waves. He can imagine the immense shadows that circle each other at the bottom of the world. Prehistoric shadows that live under conditions unchanged by time. Environments that have remained the same since the birth of our planet.

The man, he told me, is looking at all of that. Up into the endless sky, and down into the deep dark murk. Because far enough in both directions, there is only darkness.

And darkness, he said, hides everything except who we really are.

[End of excerpt]

***

From the Headline of The New York Times, online edition, July 7:

MAN RESCUED AFTER BEING SUBMERGED IN THE OCEAN
FOR NINE DAYS
THREE RESEARCHERS STILL MISSING
By Roderick Herstien

(A photo of a cylindrical three-man deep sea submersible is shown at the top of this article, and it's dented badly on one side. You can see that the hatch has been ripped open, and beyond the airlock, there is only the gaping maw of darkness. Streams of water can be seen coming from the vehicle as it hangs like a carcass from the thick chains of an industrial crane, pouring out of the dark unseen compartment onto the wooden dock slats below. A shadow of water spreads across the warped wood beneath it, and beyond the submersible, beyond the crane and the chains and the boat is the sea. It curls in the backdrop of liquid fractals and ripples like the vast aeonic darkness of space. Like the accused lusting over the broken remains of his victim.)

At 1:30 pm, Sunday, *The Deepsea Meridian* emerged

from the depths of the Western Pacific. Nine days prior, it was sent on an expedition to one of the deepest known points on Earth. It was to descend to what's called the Challenger Deep – the deepest part of the Mariana Trench – and launch a smaller remote submersible for the purpose of surveying a newly discovered crevice named the Meridian Line, which could have dropped the Mariana Trench's current recorded depth of 36,000 feet to somewhere around 50,000. After the *Meridian's* surface crew lost contact with the submersible at 12:30 PM on June 25—nine days before its resurfacing—there was little hope that they would find any survivors inside the cramped crew chamber. When the *Deepsea Meridian* surface crew and the Philippine coast guard finally opened the pressure hatch, a single researcher emerged. And he was alive.

[End of excerpt]

***

Evidence item A CN# 24-001387
Victor Rhodey Video Interview #13 [original video recording, pre transcription]
Master: not for distribution, under penalty of law.
August 8, 2023

Begin playback:

(A man sits in an armless lacquered chair at a wooden table of pressed particle board. He's thin and gaunt: the bones of his clean-shaven face encircle deep shadowy eyes. It's hard to tell his age. He could be in his late twenties, or early forties. He looks as though he could be someone recovering from a devastating drug addiction: his joints are knobbed and swollen from his ordeal, and his skin is pale blue and veiny. He's calm, but guarded and insecure, reaching one arm across his body to grasp his own bicep. He compulsively flicks his reddened eyes at the door just out of frame and mindlessly picks at a medical tag around his wrist. There's another man with him, an older

man sitting on the opposite side of the table. The other man is tall and big with a balding head and thick-framed glasses, wearing a white button-up and a lavender necktie. This man is holding a thick manila folder bursting with paperwork.)

"Nine days isn't that big a deal," Rhodey says, lost in thought. He turns his head and stares into the wall, chewing his lip. "People have been lost for months at sea, in worse conditions than ours. And they made it through fine."

"That's true," Edgerton says. "But nobody's ever been lost like that."

He thinks about that, looking seriously into his hands. "What about coal miners?"

Edgerton smiles, readjusting his glasses. "I guess they'd qualify, wouldn't they."

Rhodey ignores him, and then glances down at his hands again. "Part of me feels like I'm still out there," he laughs nervously. "I know that's stupid, but. . . I feel like I never really came back—" his smile falls a bit, his eyes going distant and afraid, "—have I come back?"

"Yes you did," Edgerton says. "You're right here. Sitting here, talking with me."

"I know, it's just…it's a *feeling*. Like a dream that never really goes away."

"I understand," he nods, leaning back into his chair. "How are you sleeping?"

"Uh…" Rhodey takes a deep breath, thinks and tries to answer, but he can't. He looks away and fiddles with his medical tag.

Edgerton frowns, unsure how to take that, and changes gears. "What do you think happened differently in your case?"

"The whole thing is," Rhodey hesitates, rolling his eyes up toward the ceiling, searching for the right place to start. "I mean it's, it's like it happened to somebody else…" He trails off, trying to find the right words.

"Can you try for me?"

"Things were going really well at first," Rhodey sighs

deeply and shakes his head, closing his eyes. "And then it just...blurs out."

"At what point does it get blurry?"

"I'd say," he thought about it for a moment, studying his bracelet. "When the last of the light disappeared. When the darkness took us completely."

Edgerton nods, frowning deeply, trying not to push him too hard.

"Can I ask you a question?" Rhodey says.

"Sure." He readjusts his glasses, apprehensive, but open.

"What's the longest period of time you'd spent alone?" he asked, leaning forward. "I mean really alone, isolated for an extended time."

Edgerton sucks air through his teeth and tilts his head up at the ceiling, thinking about it. "A day or two, I guess." he shrugged, "Something like that."

"So you're asking me to describe things that you can't possibly understand," he said, nodding at the folder. "Things I've already failed to say a millions times before, to a million different people."

"I know," Edgerton nods, opening the folder a few pages deep, crossing his arms. "Listen, I want you to know that I'm not here to hem and haw over mistakes. I'm not here to play coulda-woulda-shoulda. Things happened. I understand that. They happened, and you can't take 'em back, and you can't change it—"

"And I have to live with that."

"Yes," Edgerton says. "Yes you do. But you have to also understand that my job is to find the facts. I gather, collate, and organize. Not so that I can understand *what* happened, but so that I can understand *why* it happened."

"What do you want from me?"

"Perspective," he says, shrugging his shoulders.

In this moment of the video, Rhodey shakes his head, annoyed, and looks away.

"I want to be able to stand back," Edgerton grasps the air with his hands. "And see the big picture."

"The big picture. . ."

"Yeah," He shrugs again, liking the sound of that, so he says it again, "Yeah, that's it. You got it."

Rhodey sighs heavily into his hands and then leans forward, resting his forehead onto the table, staring at the floor. "I want this to be over, Mister Edgerton. I want it to end."

Edgerton shakes his head sadly and sits back into his chair. "I wish it were up to me. God knows I do, son. But it isn't. It's up to *you,* Rhodey. *You* decide when this ends."

End playback.

***

From the headline of the LA Times, June 27 2023:

MISSING DEEPSEA SCIENCE EXPEDITION TRIGGERS MULTI-NATIONAL SEARCH
By Bernard San

(A photograph can be seen at the top of the article showing the three researchers who were aboard the Deepsea Meridian when it disappeared. All were academic looking men, wearing the same kind of relaxed clothing, dressed for the chilly sea breeze: jeans and khakis and polo shirts tucked in, each wearing a red vest over a navy blue fleece jacket with a nametag above the left breast. They stand on the main deck before launch in the sun, smiling in front of the pristine submersible glinting in the light. Of the three men pictured, only one would ever be seen alive again.)

Water rescue is searching for a deep sea submarine that has lost contact with its mission control after diving thousands of feet below the ocean's surface, near what is widely accepted as the deepest part of the planet. Authorities say Douglass Sayvor, Treat Goodman, and Victor Rhodey—all oceanographers, biologists, and professors at the University of California—

have been lost below the sea for twenty-two consecutive hours without radio contact. Operations are currently underway to search the seabed around the submersible's planned point of contact, but the authorities know it's a long shot.

"There is a drop off," said Abigail Ruth, director of the Scripps Center of Oceanography. "The deepest drop off we've ever recorded. And before we lost contact, these men were heading straight for it."

When asked how long researchers were expected to survive, the director replied, "Three men have enough onboard oxygen to last sixty hours, but there are a lot of variables to think about. The only thing that's certain is they did successfully reach the sea floor, and they were beginning their approach toward the Meridian Line. That's all we know at this time."

[End of excerpt]

***

Evidence item Z-13 CN# 24-001387
Transcribed Audio Log, Deepsea Meridian
11:53:44 hrs, June 25, 2023
Static, a man's voice (later identified as research diver Treat Goodman)

"Surface, this is Deepsea Meridian. We are on the bottom. Depth is thirty five thousand, six hundred and fifty feet, and everything looks good. Over."

More static, transmission break—

"I repeat, Surface. We have touchdown."

Static, transmission cutting in and out, a woman's voice (later identified as surface controller Abigail Ruth)

"Copy, Meridian. How's it look?"

Static—

"Desolate."

Static, breathing, canned voices in the background—

"But undeniably beautiful."

"Copy that, Meridian. Take lots of video for us."

Static, transmission breaks, the sound of people cheering

over com—

"Roger that. Surface, be advised, we are starting our transit toward the south chasm, over."

"Copy that, 36,000 feet, we have you headed toward the Meridian Line. Co2 is good, vitals are good, A-Comms are good, good to go, whenever you're ready."

[End File]

***

From the headline of Rolling Stone Magazine, June 25, 2032:

RIDDLES OF THE ABYSS AND THE ENDLESS FALL
OF THE DEEPSEA MERIDIAN
By Damon Scribner

(*A photograph of the dented crew chamber of the submersible Deepsea Meridian, taken from outside of the hatch, looking in. Most of it is dark, but there is enough light to see that the floor and the walls, the plate glass viewport are all awash in dark red granulated blood, and when you look closer, you can see hundreds of smeared handprints in the visceral muck.*)

It wasn't the first time anything like this had happened.

Another diver disappeared before, in a submersible like the Deepsea Meridian. But unlike the crew of the Meridian, he was alone in the vast darkness. Not nearly as long, though–fifty three hours, compared to Victor Rhodey's two hundred and sixteen–but long enough to know that he'd never again set foot on another submarine for the rest of his life.

"You've never known any darkness like the darkness of the ocean," Francis Hoop says, the man who'd been lost in the Solomon Sea's New Brighton Trench after his lander-weights malfunctioned and left him adrift at 18,000 feet between Papua New Guinea and the Solomon Islands. "And in those last hours, when the floodlights had gone out, when the air started coming out of my mouth in thick clouds of ice," he lights a cigarette and takes a deep, deep drag. His eyes go distant for a moment, and his jaw pulsates like an exposed artery. "You learn pretty quickly just how deep that darkness can penetrate. It stabs right down into the muscle, right through the bone, into the marrow." He leans forward and pushes his index finger into the skin of his forearm, as if to show me how vulnerable it is. "You find out just what kind of man you really are."

He opens the wheel of a revolver and dumps the bullets onto the thin card-table in his empty kitchen, many of them clattering onto the floor. Hoop is fifty-two years old, thin and swarthy, and his muscles below the flannel cutoff at the shoulder twist like knotted rope.

More than twenty years ago—eleven years before the disappearance of the Deepsea Meridian—Hoop had been on dozens of dives into some of the deepest places on Earth. Now he lives in an apartment in Cleveland, "As far away from the ocean as humanly fucking possible."

He picks up a bullet off the table and stares at me with wide eyes.

"You know what this is?" he asks.

"Yes," I say back. I'd come here to try and understand what Victor Rhodey might have gone through. Many of the files on the incident have been locked away by the Philippine government in diplomatic limbo, out of media reach for the better part of a decade. But I needed to know.

Hoop, however, explains that no matter how badly I try to understand the truth of what happened down there, I simply can't. "You have to experience it for yourself," he says. "That's the only way."

"I have part of a picture," I tell him. "From the notes gleaned over the years. From testimonies given by the people who were involved."

"But not the only testimony that matters," he says. "Not from the person who was there."

"That's kinda why I came to you—"

"Maybe what you know isn't what really happened," he says, coring into me with his eyes. "You wanna know what it's like down there?"

He drops the bullet into a chamber, spins the wheel, and then slaps it shut.

"Do you really want to know?" He asks, and then presses the gun to his own temple.

My guts go warm, and beads of sweat form on my chilled skin.

"Not like this," I rasp. "I don't want to do it like this."

"I know you don't," he says, screwing the muzzle deeper into his head. "Nobody does."

He pulls the trigger...nothing happens. Before I can stop him, he quickly pulls the trigger three more times. Four total. There are only five chambers in that gun.

I panic, reaching for his arm, and he pushes away from the table and stands.

"Stop it!" I demand.

He looks at me with intensity, like a Samurai preparing himself for death. And he pulls the trigger again.

And nothing happens. A crude smile parts his leathered skin, and he keeps pulling the trigger. Still alive.

"I can do this forever," he says, pulling the trigger over and over again. "I can do this a hundred times. A thousand. And nothing'll ever happen. Why? Because you don't have all the facts. You are forming your idea of reality on something that isn't true. Despite all the facts you think you have, you are wrong."

Just like the Deepsea Meridian, he tells me. Just like the second and third-hand testimonies, I've been pouring through. They're all convenient answers for an inconvenient moment. An attempt to make sense of something that we just don't understand.

[End of excerpt]

***

Evidence item U-33 CN# 24-001387
Victor Rhodey Video Interview #62 [original video recording,
pre transcription]
Master: not for distribution, under penalty of law.
August 20, 2023

Begin playback:

"We made good time," Rhodey says, cutting the silence. "For the first few minutes, it was actually, pretty beautiful." He tilts his head and smiles sadly, closing his eyes. "The dim light faded with each passing second, blending with hues of blueish green and violet, as far as you could see, a dense formlessness that enveloped everything in this awesome uniformity...and then the light slipped away, until there was nothing but us and the quiet words of God."

Edgerton sits as still as a river stone, lost in the other man's images.

"Our human eyes have forgotten what it's like to see in the ocean," he continues. "Because nature hadn't selected us that way," Rhodey stopped and took a deep breath, his eyes still closed. "We'd see things, but there was no sense of scale. It takes your brain a while to realize whether or not it's looking at a speck of plankton, or some leviathan navigating the darkness far, far away. And after hours of marveling at the enormity of it all, dropping like a stone toward the center of the Earth, the sea floor emerged from below and rose up in the cones of our light like the shoulder of Atlas...and as the Meridian kissed the bottom, giant plumes of fine ancient sediment erupted like ghostly clouds around us."

"And then you made your way toward the chasm," Edgerton says, pulling himself back from the dream.

"We stayed on the bottom for a long time," Rhodey says, opening his eyes, and the ghost of a smile melts back into the grim lines of his face. "It was like another planet. Completely sterilized of life. When we made our way toward the crevice, following the seafloor until the white dusty sediment cut to blackness like a wound at the Meridian Line, we launched the probe. It hovered far from the precipice, and we lowered it into the darkness."

"And what did you see?"

"Nothing," Rhodey shakes his head, opening his hands, "The blackness was so thick it sheered the drone's light a foot or two away from the camera. It was absolutely seamless. Pristine. Almost like we had been frozen in a glacier of volcanic glass."

Edgerton slowly lowers himself into the opposite chair and waits for the thinner man to continue.

"It's hard for me to describe what happened next," Rhodey says, looking away. "I can't remember if we had been pushed over the edge by something, or if the Earth just… just opened and swallowed us. I remember hearing a loud crack, and I thought something had imploded in the battery cache…"

Rhodey is becoming visibly stressed. He reaches up and presses hard into his temples with his palms, and we notice for the first time that he's shaking badly, trembling under the stark light of the room, trying very hard not to lose control.

"Rhodey," Edgerton says, very slow and very clear. "What did you see?"

"I saw," he breathes, feeling everything slipping through his fingers, remembering something salient and deep and terrifying. "I don't know *what* I saw…"

"Tell me," Edgerton says with intensity, edging forward on his seat. "Tell me what you saw."

At this point in the video, Rhodey is shaking his head from side to side, clamping his mouth shut, the skin on his forehead going white from the pressure of his hands. Edgerton seems to come to his senses and realizes what's about to happen, and he holds his arms out like he's afraid that the smaller man might detonate.

"Okay, okay, okay let's back up a bit—" Edgerton soothes, rising again to his feet, stepping around the table to put a gentle hand on Rhodey's shoulder. Edgerton rubs his arm, trying to coax him out of whatever personal hell he'd fallen into. "—

you're okay, Rhodey. It's all right, come back now—"

"We fell," Rhodey hisses suddenly, tears brimming in his eyes. There's panic there, building on the edges of his vision—a deep terror and trauma corroding the sanity like acid. "We just kept falling."

Edgerton wraps his arm around the smaller man's trembling shoulders, who collapses into a freshet of choking sobs. Rhodey comes to pieces under the contact, and he claws into the bigger man's embrace, pressing his face deep into his shirt, as if he were trying to hide from something malicious and terrible. Shocked, Edgerton opens his arms, afraid to touch him. The thin broken man screams suddenly—a high-pitched wail of terror—and sobs like a lost child alone in the darkness of night, and the bigger man just stands there not knowing what to do, frowning behind his thick framed glasses and clenching his jaw like gunfire.

End playback.

***

From the headline of Rolling Stone Magazine, June 25, 2032:

RIDDLES OF THE ABYSS, AND THE ENDLESS
FALL OF
THE DEEPSEA MERIDIAN
By Damon Scribner

"When they do eventually find you," Hoop says, "They won't let you open your eyes for hours."

It's 7:15 am. Cartoons flicker quietly in the living room. Toast burns on the counter near the stove, but all of the smoke detectors have long since died, and Hoop stands at a window in the virgin daylight spilling in, staring out into the half-lit dawn wearing nothing but a pair of boxers and some flip-flops.

"I mean, you've just survived this major spiritual odyssey, and the only thing you want to do is lay eyes upon the face of another human being," he turns, staring hard into me.

"Because this isn't the first time somebody's rescued you," he nods, looking back out at the new dawn. "Oh yeah, you've been there already a thousand times in your dreams. Rescued. And just as you open your lungs to drink in the fresh sea air, you find yourself back in the pilot chamber. Back in the dark, where you'd screamed yourself hoarse a long, long time ago."

The sun breaks the horizon somewhere far to the left, crawling up Hoop's knuckles that rest on the screenless sill.

"That last hour was the hardest," he said. "I kept expecting to wake back up in the capsule. I kept thinking I'd realize my eyes had been open the whole time, staring into the unblinking gaze of nothingness, and that I'd completely lost my mind and imagined the whole thing."

Even when you're sleeping, he told me, trace amounts of light still get through the thin skin of your lids. This is why your eyes have a tendency to roll up into your head during REM. Your brain seeks the darkest parts of the cavity so it can recalibrate itself as efficiently as possible. You're not aware of the light, because it's a relative lightness darker than what you're used to, but it's there. And in the deep alien realm below the crushing-line of the Solomon Sea, 27,000 feet down, there's no light whatsoever. It's the complete lack of light, darker than space. Darker than the grave.

"When I imagine the darkness of a black hole, I think of the ocean," Hoop explains, taking a drag on his newly lit Marlboro. "And when they find you, they scream to keep your eyes closed, because they've atrophied so badly," He raises his chin up and out of his cracked window. "After days of floating through that pitch nothingness, even the soft sunlight that bleeds through an overcast sky can melt your retinas right out of your skull. And then it's lights out for good."

He pulls back for a moment, thinking about something deeper and more personal than anything he wants to share.

"They take this thick black piece of fabric," he continues, pulling back out of a memory. "And wrap it around your eyes about four times." He demonstrates this by pantomiming around his own head. "Hours later, after several bags of saline have been pumped into your veins, they finally peel it off. The only light you can stand is the soft flame of a candle. And after enduring what you'd endured, that tiny flickering light looks like nuclear explosions on the sun."

[End of excerpt.]

***

Evidence item R-88 CN# 24-001387
Transcripted Audio Log, Deepsea Meridian
12:10:44 hrs, June 25, 2023

(Paper-clipped to the top of a stack of Transcripted audio logs is a photograph of a team of men wearing hard hats and gloves working frantically to pull open the hatch of the Deepsea Meridian. They're lifting a naked man out of the crew capsule, whose limbs appear dead and lifeless, as if he were unconscious. The dangerously thin man is blindfolded, and there is a thick paintbrush swipe of dark coagulated blood smeared across his gaping mouth, which is full of unidentifiable chunks of muck. When you look closer, you see that his hands and arms are coated with a brownish black grime up to the midline of his forearms.)

The following transcript was recovered from the Meridian's black box. You hear the voices of the crew of the Deepsea Meridian, but it's hard to tell who is speaking over the confusion. Because there's no record of this recording, it is assumed that the crew had lost surface Comms moments before transmission.

— "Surface, Deep Sea Meridian, do you copy, over?"
— We got no voice Comms
—Depth gauge is not changing
—Just lost thrusters
—Not good, not good
—Thrusters not responding
—We got a problem
—Reading several failures here, anybody got a depth?

—We can't stop without thrusters

—This is not good

—Clocks stopped, depth gauges stopped, everything's stopped.

—Speed is three knots

—Come on guys, think, sort it out

—Three and a half knots

—Surface, Deepsea Meridian, we have fallen into the chasm, and we are aborting our descent, over

—Dropping weights

—Four and a half knots

—Weights not dropping. I repeat, weights are not dropping

—What?!

—Trying again

—That's a negative

—Oh god.

The tortured whale song of contracting metal can be heard in the background, and then there's a loud crack

—Dropping weights

—Weights are not responding, over. Surface, do you copy? Our weights are not responding. We cannot abort descent, over

Screams erupt from the transmission, followed by a single pop of static and a long stream of dead air. These were the last words of the Meridian crew.

End file.

***

Evidence item T-1 CN# 24-001387
Deepsea Meridian, crew capsule [original video recording, pre transcription]
Master: not for distribution, under penalty of law.
July 5, 2023

Begin playback:

A man is crouching before an opened hatch with a shocked

look on his face, stealing nervous glances from the person manning the camera. A light drizzle mists his damp hair, and a sea wind flattens his navy windbreaker against his chest. The sky is overcast, but it's warm, and the Deepsea Meridian looms over his shoulder like a hollowed monument.

"This is July fifth, twenty twenty-three," he closes his mouth and swallows, delaying the moment, gathering his thoughts. "Uh... location is the Port of Manila, and we're going to move into to the actual crew capsule..."

The man pushes back onto his knees so the camera can edge forward.

"Watch your head," the man says out of frame.

The camera light flicks on and blinds the image for a moment until the lens readjusts to the darkness. The camera blades forward unsteadily, shaking the image, but then it settles, and slowly pans the inside of the capsule, illuminating an awesome sight.

"As you can see," The man says in a daze. "This...this is..."

And his voice fails him. There isn't another word spoken for the rest of the recording. As the camera pans and tilts slowly around the cabin, we see filth and gut-ripping viscera caked all over the inside, and it's hard to tell exactly what you're looking at. There's some kind of meat paste coating the walls: blood and hair and bubbles of what could be remnants of skin and internal organs. But no bones. No bodies. Nothing to identify any single human being that went down into the deepness ten days before this recording. Just brackish coagulated layers of blood and excrement, coating every square centimeter of the capsule's interior, smeared by a thousand glistening handprints.

End Playback

***

From the headline of Rolling Stone Magazine, June 25, 2032:

RIDDLES OF THE ABYSS, AND THE ENDLESS

FALL
OF THE DEEPSEA MERIDIAN
By Damon Scribner

"When the lights finally went out," Hoop says, plugging a thumb drive into his laptop. "I had this detached feeling of acceptance, and it didn't take me long to come to terms with what was going to happen next."

Gauges, lights, and thrusters all started malfunctioning, he told me, at around 17,500 feet. He dropped another thousand before forcing himself to abort the descent, a depth only a handful of humans on the planet can ever say they've reached.

"I hit the weight release," he leans back into his chair. "And nothing. No drop. And I couldn't stop falling." He shrugs, "So I dumped all my shot to slow myself down, and calmly informed the surface of my situation. A moment came when I could finally feel one of the weight-salvos detach and fall away. The other didn't. I found out later they got snagged on the release mechanism."

He stares into the screen for a long time, from a thousand yards away, rolling something invisible between his thumb and index finger, perhaps remembering the dead *snick* of the weight-release switch flicking back and forth over and over again.

"I was stuck," he says finally, shaking his head. "Trapped between the weight of the submersible pulling me down, and the pressure of the ocean pushing me back up."

His eyes focused, and he opened a folder labeled *MERIDIAN*. A thousand photos, documents, and videos poured out onto his desktop.

"For two days," he continued, lighting a cigarette. "The ocean pulled me between 18 and 16,000 feet. They said I drifted seventeen miles before a US seawolf-class submarine picked me up on sonar completely by accident. The only reason I'm here today is because of that submarine, and the fact that we had another deep sea submersible on standby to tow me to the surface."

That's exactly what happened to the Meridian. Except when their weights failed, they got stuck about 30,000 feet deeper than where Hoop ended up. He leaned forward and clicked a video file that opened to a dim circle of light afloat within an indistinguishable blackness. It was footage from one of the two cameras attached to the Deepsea Meridian's boom.

"They were out there for nine days...*nine fucking days*, stuck at 43,000 feet." He sucked air through his teeth and shook his head. "I was out there for a little over two, and I can't even imagine what that was like."

Hoop presses play, but the image on his desktop remains static and unchanged but for the flicker of shadows that pass behind the airlock's tiny viewport. Which meant somebody was alive in there. Somebody was moving.

"That deep? Nobody's coming for you." He aims his hand at the computer screen like a gun, and pretends to pull the trigger. "The only chance Rhodey had of ever seeing the light of day again, was if he himself found a way."

I followed his eyes toward the screen, and deep prehistoric strings pulled in my gut—instincts written into me by thousands of years of my ancestors watching the shadows for the telltale eye-shine of a predator. On the playback, something seethed up out of the darkness. Some obscure mass pulsating and unfolding like the meaty petals of a desert flower, gravitating toward the smothered light of the Deepsea Meridian, which looked so small and so fragile.

"He was alone, and there was nobody coming to save him," Hoop breathed smoke, and froze the image, leaning deeper into his chair. "And he knew it."

[End of excerpt]

***

Evidence item U-33 CN# 24-001387
Victor Rhodey Video Interview #62 [original video recording, pre transcription]
Master: not for distribution, under penalty of law.
August 20, 2023

Begin playback:

"There was something in the chasm," Rhodey says helplessly. "Some…something none of us had ever seen before."

Edgerton leans into him, searching his face. "What did you see?"

"A man," Rhodey whispers, staring up into the florescent light. "A man, like you and me, but…but different. Pale… almost…almost clear enough that I could see right into him, see down into his guts."

The video file pixelates for a moment as Edgerton stares at him, transfixed and completely taken off guard.

"He was terrified," Rhodey says suddenly, searching Edgerton's face. Tears gather beneath his lashes. "And I knew…I just knew by looking at him that he'd do anything to see the surface again. Anything."

"A man," Edgerton echoes quietly. He pushes himself away from Rhodey, sliding himself back against the opposite wall, and tries to make sense of it all. He removes his glasses and stares at the other man pressed into the corner with his knees pulled up to his chest. "A man in the ocean. At 43,000 feet…"

"A pale man," Rhodey wipes his red rimmed eyes, and shakes his head. "A terrified man, who would do *everything in his power* to survive."

End Playback.

***

Evidence item A-12 CN# 24-001387
Breaking News Report of the Deepsea Meridian Resurface
[original video recording, pre- transcription]
Master: not for distribution, under penalty of law.
July 4, 2023

Begin playback:

A woman in her sixties approaches a podium stationed outside somewhere near the sea, and the wind blows the collar of her light blue shirt beneath the cusp of her thick wool jacket. Men and women surround her in the margin of the frame, and we can hear the endless clicking and clacking of cameras snapping photographs in the background. She's attractive for her age, even puffy from hours of latent tears and anxiety. Only her mouth betrays her classic beauty: it is grim and confused and sad, unsure of the words.

"Today, at 12:30 this afternoon, the submersible Deepsea Meridian resurfaced in Western Pacific Ocean after being lost for nine days. It surfaced intact, 124 miles off the coast of Guam. I and the Scripps Center for Oceanography extend our deepest gratitude to the rescue workers of the Philippine coast guard, who have worked tirelessly these past days in partnership with the United States Navy to find our lost sons, and bring them home. It is with great sadness that we announce the passing of two researchers, Douglass Sayvor, and Treat Goodman, who were beloved husbands and fathers and teachers. Victor Rhodey is in critical condition, but he is alive, he is speaking, and he is doing well. We'll have more information in the coming days, but for now, we ask that you have the grace to let the families and friends of the people we've lost today mourn. Thank you and God bless."

Without another word, the woman steps away from the podium and takes the offered arms of a man and a woman who lead her out of frame. The crowd behind the camera erupts in a chorus of hurried voices and the clicking of even more cameras, like the scuttle of crab migrating over a killing-ground of smooth stone.

End Playback.

***

From the headline of Rolling Stone Magazine, June 25, 2032:

RIDDLES OF THE ABYSS, AND THE ENDLESS FALL
OF
THE DEEPSEA MERIDIAN
By Damon Scribner

It's a wide shot of the Meridian hatch. The submersible floats by the stark cones of floodlight that extend away from the hull, angled down toward the undifferentiated bottomlessness beneath it. All around is darkness. Pitch darkness, like an ocean of tar. The Meridian is hanging in the balance at 43,000 feet, drifting far away from the rescue workers searching the waters miles above. There is no life down there. Nothing on this planet—that we know of—can survive the crushing pressures of those depths. So when a blur of pale light unfolds from the darkness and glides up toward the floodlights—the very fringes of it kissing the margins of the frame—just out of view—I find that I can't breathe.

"When the Deepsea Meridian came up out of the water," Hoop intones. "We didn't know what we would find in there. We prepared ourselves for three dead bodies that had long since succumbed to hypoxia. And when they lifted it up overhead with the crane, and I was just staring up at this thing—dragging my eyes along the crack that spanned the length of it—you know, all that I had gone through in New Britain came back in a wave of panic. Suddenly, I wasn't sure if I was the guy standing on the deck waiting for the Meridian to be lowered, or if I was one of the terrified people stuck inside the capsule. All I knew was that I had to get whoever was alive out of there. Because… if you take what I went through and multiply it by eternity, and bring it all the way to the edge of forever, you'd still have only the vaguest conception of what Rhodey went through."

I stare at the image, studying the small curl of something at the bottom of the frame, and Hoop scrubs the playback, moving deeper into the timeline, speeding the shadows inside the capsule into a flurry of activity.

"And when I opened the hatch and looked down into the

crew capsule," he breathed, shaking his head at the memory. "The smell…the slaughterhouse smell of copper and shit… the world snapped back into focus. I was Frank Hoop again, screaming down at Rhodey to keep his eyes closed. And I'll never forget the look of him reaching up into the light like a starved, terrified child with tears streaming down his mottled face."

He drags the scrubber two thirds of the way down the playback, and pauses the image.

"A couple things that didn't make sense," Hoop continues. "One, where were the bodies? He couldn't have jettisoned them, because if he opened that hatch the pressure would've turned him into a meat cloud in a blink. So…what happened to the others?" He clicks the playback one frame at a time until a white shape of some kind freezes at the very bottom of the image, within feet of the airlock. "And two…what's that look like to you?"

I look at the playback, and a pair of wide eyes look right back, wreathed in the shadowy abyss like smoke. I look, and I feel a cold blade dragging up the length of my spine, sinking deep into the small of my back, short-circuiting my unsteady legs. In the darkness, in that impossible crushing realm, I see the hard sharp angles of a face rising up out of the depths. The face of a man so pale it's impossible that he had ever seen the light of the world. A face locked in an eternal rictus, its lips peeled back over its teeth, its mouth stretched open mid scream. At first I think it's the face of a dead man—a corpse or something, one of the drowned crewmen—but then it moves. The face twists in the blackness and opens and closes its mouth like the jaws of a dying cobra, like the wide feathery gills of a diseased fish, and it looks up toward the viewport, at the shadows writhing therein.

And the floodlights go out.

[End of excerpt]

***

Evidence item U-33 CN# 24-001387
Victor Rhodey Video Interview #62 [original video recording, pre transcription]
Master: not for distribution, under penalty of law.
August 20, 2023

Begin playback:

The recording cuts into focus and Edgerton can be seen sitting cross-legged in front of the thinner man, placing an 8x11 photograph at his feet. The photograph is of Francis Hoop pulling a blindfolded Victor Rhodey out of the Deepsea Meridian. Rhodey's mouth in the photograph is agape, full of flesh and pouring blood. His hands and arms are also covered with sleeves of brown black fluids and viscera.

"Those men had children," Edgerton breathes, tilting his head to meet Rhodey's eyes.

The thinner man draws up and refuses to look at the photograph.

"Wives, and families," he continues. "They have a right to know what happened, don't they? Rhodey? So now's your chance to do what's right...the right thing, right now...and tell me what happened."

Rhodey is silent, tucking his head between his pulled up knees.

"I mean, tell me it was self-defense," Edgerton says, opening his hands. "Tell me there was only enough oxygen for three men for 60 hours. 120 hours for two men. 240 hours for one. Tell me there was no food or water...tell me that you had no hope of ever seeing the surface again, and that you were operating on some animal instinct to prolong your life as long as humanly possible...for Christ's sake, tell me something!"

Edgerton calms himself and gently places a hand on the thinner man's knee.

"Look, I'm not your judge," Egerton says, starting over. "I'm not here to tell you what's right or wrong. I can't possibly presume to know what you went through. But I'm here to try and understand. I'm here for you to finally talk to somebody, to tell your side of it. Because if you don't get it out, I can't help you. And it'll never heal. It'll always be with you, festering inside like cancer." He bends lower, gauging whether or not he's getting through. "Do you understand what I'm saying?"

"He made me choose," Rhodey whispers, his mouth pressed to his knees as though he would gnaw his own flesh.

"Who made you choose?" Edgerton asks, "Sayvor? Goodman? Did they do something to you—?"

"The pale man," Rhodey says, lifting his face. "The man who came up out of the darkness." He stares with a deep pain in his eyes. "He made me choose between my flesh... and theirs." He stops and raises his hands helplessly, trying hard to keep from screaming. "What would *you* have done?"

Edgerton pulls back and shakes his head sadly, clenching his jaw. He stands and steps back toward the table, and leafs out another photograph from the file. He returns to his spot on the floor, and lays it down on top of the first photograph.

"Rhodey," he says quietly. "I want you to listen, because it's important and I think you need to hear it."

He reaches forward and grasps the smaller man's shoulders with both hands, pulling him gently up out of the safety of his knees.

"There was no pale man in the chasm," He says softly, looking deep into his eyes, "No monster...no leviathan...no demon...just you, Rhodey." He shrugs gently, "Just you and them, and the darkness."

Rhodey welds his eyes shut, fighting his own breath, fighting the tears streaming over his lips. We see now that the second photograph is the last image recovered from the crew capsule's SD card, captured right before the onboard batteries died. It's hard to tell at first, but we can see the silhouettes of two arms reaching out of the darkness, digging their thumbs into the pulped bloody eye sockets of another man.

End Playback.

CANNED CRAB

Nick Nafpliotis

Late afternoon had always been Joe's favorite time to walk the beach of Sullivan's Island. The waves crashed against the shore with a serene fury while the sun was set low enough so that it didn't feel oppressive. The day was done, the night had yet to arrive, and the tide was out just far enough to gently wash his unfashionable Auburn University crocs as they treaded across the white sand.

So when Joe's friend Clay suggested that they go for a run on the beach, he'd initially been all for it. Exercise wasn't really his thing, but the act of minimally burning a handful of calories (which his doctor had been hounding him to do for some time) seemed much more appealing when it wasn't on a treadmill or trudging across the Ravanel Bridge. What Clay failed to mention until the day before, however, was that their jog would be taking place at the ungodly hour of 6:00 A.M. Joe was ready to back out right then and there, but the promise of being treated to a McDonald's breakfast had been enough to make forgoing a couple hours of sleep a worthy sacrifice.

Around 2:00 AM that night, however, Joe's salvation from early morning cardio appeared to arrive in the form a freakishly strong and quick storm. For five straight minutes, lightning flashed and thunder shook his entire apartment, easily waking him along with anyone else who didn't happen to be dead. Torrential rainfall lashed against building's walls and windows, soaking the surrounding area in a way that hadn't been felt since Hurricane Gaston in 2004. Then as quickly as it started, the storm stopped, leaving a handful of fires from the lightning strikes and a small amount of flooding downtown. The eerie calm was soon broken by the sound of emergency vehicle sirens, but their incessant wailing was no match for Joe's desire fall back asleep.

When his alarm went a few hours later, he turned on the news to see if there was any information about the storm. The local media seemed to be just as perplexed about its origins and intensity as he was. The storm cell had initially popped up over Gold Bug Island, swelling to near hurricane force intensity while managing to stay localized to the Mount Pleasant and Charleston areas. Five minutes later, it was gone. The system hadn't disappeared or severely weakened in a short amount of time; it had completely disappeared off the radar all together.

Joe wasn't a weather expert, but he'd lived in Charleston long enough to have watched his share of The Weather Channel during hurricane season. What happened last night was like nothing he'd seen before. Before he could spend much time thinking about it (or make his way back into bed for a quick snooze), Clay pulled up outside and began honking his car horn. Joe hastily threw on the clothes he normally played basketball in, charging out the door without brushing his teeth or shaving. By the time he'd gotten out the door and reached the door of Clay's idling jeep, his friend was holding the horn down without pause or mercy.

"I have neighbors, you dumbass!" Joe hissed as he slid into the passenger seat and slammed the door shut. "Why the hell can't you just go up and knock on the door like a normal person who isn't an asshole?"

"Because I knew you'd pretend to still be asleep and make me wait outside for you," Clay answered matter-of-factly. Joe glared at Clay for a moment before finally turning away and fastening his seatbelt. He was normally game for putting up with his friend's abrasive personality, but that was after being awake for a few hours and fortified with at least two cups of coffee.

"It's times like these that I wish more of my neighbors owned guns," he muttered. "Let's just get out there and get this over with so we can hit up the Golden Arches before work."

"And don't forget, it's my treat," Clay said, flashing that smarmy grin of his.

The two men rode in silence at first, save for the nerve shattering cacophony of the morning DJs chattering and cackling over Clay's speakers. Joe waited for a couple minutes before reaching over and angrily switching the radio off. Clay started to protest, but thought better of it, allowing his friend to rest his head against the passenger side window in peace. "Did you hear about what happened last night?" Clay asked.

Joe kept his eyes closed, and his head resting against the window as he answered. "You mean the mini hurricane that kicked our asses in the middle of the night? I'm pretty sure everyone heard about it when the storm woke them up."

"No, not that," Clay said. "The crazy old lady who lives in that shack near the cove got arrested again.

Joe opened his eyes and sat up. The woman to whom Clay was referring was something of a local legend. No one knew her full name, although some long-time residents of the island claimed that her first name was 'Roberta.' Rumors about her being a witch had proliferated ever since he and Clay had been in grade school, with some people even claiming that they knew someone (or had a friend of a friend) who'd dared to drink one of the magical elixirs Roberta allegedly brewed inside her home. It was never the actual storyteller who'd experienced the old woman's dark magic, of course. That, combined with the fact that Joe considered anything mystical in nature to be complete crap, meant that he simply classified her as crazy old lady.

There was absolutely no debate, however, about the 'crazy' part. In addition to the large black hood she constantly wore (even in the summer), Roberta was violently territorial of her property—which was a whole other oddity unto itself. Her house had somehow managed to defy all zoning laws, sitting almost directly on the beach, and isolated from any other neighboring structures. There was no clear property line delineating where her land actually was, but Roberta seemed to consider herself the guardian of any beach area that lay within sight of the cove. This often brought her into conflict with tourists and college students. When her dust ups with these 'trespassers' made the news, it was almost always due to her exhibiting some type of behavior that straddled the line between hilariously insane and genuinely terrifying.

A couple weeks ago, a bunch of frat boys had been drinking and acting like a bunch of idiots on the rocky beach landing right next to her shack. According to witnesses, Roberta came out and began screaming at them while pointing to the cans that they'd carelessly tossed next to her house. The frat brothers predictably reacted in 'drunk bro' fashion, laughing and refusing to do as they were asked. She responded by walking back inside and retuning with a Grim Reaper-worthy, full-length scythe. Roberta then proceeded to chase them, swinging the blade at the littering douchebags, who quickly went from macho catcalls to squealing like scared little children as they retreated to their oversized trucks and SUVs.

No one was hurt, but the incident still resulted in a visit from the Sullivan's Island police department to arrest Roberta on assault charges. As the officers hauled her off, she'd screamed something about how 'The Beach will avenge this!' while pointing a boney finger at the pack of onlookers. Joe wasn't sure how a 'Crazy Roberta' story could get much better than that, but he was now fully awake and eager to hear what his friend had to say.

"So Roberta was released from jail last night," Clay began. "She went back to her home, got out a bunch of crazy witchcraft stuff, and began performing some type of ritual. People back on Jasper Boulevard called the police about weird blue flames popping up from the beach where her house is. When the police got there, Roberta had made all these symbols in the sand and lit fires everywhere."

"That is pretty weird, but I don't think it's illegal to practice witchcraft as long as its in your own yard." Joe said.

"I guess," Clay responded. "But when rich old white people get spooked about something, they tend to get their way, especially around here. The police arrested her again. But get this: As the officers were hauling her off, lightning started coming down out of nowhere all over the beach. That's when the freaky storm started last night."

"Damn," Joe exhaled. "That is pretty messed up. Was she trying to cast a spell or something when it happened?"

"Didn't hear," Clay said. "Police buddy of mine got it second hand. But he did say that the guys who went out there to arrest her were on the verge of shitting their pants when they got back to the station. According to them, the last thing Roberta yelled before they put her in the squad car was 'The Beach's reckoning will rise tomorrow!' After that, she went dead silent for the rest of the night."

"And now we're headed there ourselves. Awesome," Joe deadpanned. "Next time you decide to drive us into a mystical death trap, can we move it back to the afternoon, at least?"

"Oh please," Clay said, rolling his eyes. "If magic were real, then the hex I cast on your fantasy football team last year would've worked. And besides, the closest she's ever come to hurting anyone was slashing at some drunk frat boys who probably deserved it. She's back in jail, anyway, so you're not getting out of this."

The pair parked at their usual station and made their way out to the beach, which was bustling with people and their dogs despite the early morning hour. Pets were allowed to be off leash until 10:00 AM, so humans and canines alike were frolicking everywhere, leaving tracks of feet and paws in the tide soaked sand. The sun's golden rays helped create a gorgeously picturesque setting…if you were willing to ignore the trash and fulgurite encrusted rocks that littered the entire beach.

The intense lightning from the night before had managed to fuse portions of sand into what at first glance appeared to be glassy pieces of gnarled driftwood. While the phenomenon wasn't at all uncommon, there were usually only a few of these rocks to be found after the most violent of storms. Now there were twisted rocks to be every few feet, indicating that the ground had been struck an alarming number of times. The formations were also much larger than usual, with some rivaling the size of the smaller dogs that ran in between them.

The beach trash, on the other hand, was something that both residents and visitors of Sullivan's Island had become all too familiar with.

"Look at that," Joe said, motioning to a pile of empty Bud Light cans. "There's a freaking trashcan two stations down. Is it really that hard for these fratholes to walk a few feet and throw their shit away?"

"How do you know the litter bugs were male?" Clay asked as the pair began to jog along the shoreline.

"No wine cooler bottles," Joe panted. He was already starting to feel out of breath.

"See, this is what really chaps my ass," Clay grumbled without a trace of the fatigue in his voice. "I get why the police might have a problem with a crazy woman lighting fires and screaming like banshee in the middle of the night, but what about the tools who are constantly tossing their empty beer cans everywhere? Seems like that would be a bigger priority."

"Most people aren't too eager…to call…the police on their own…spoiled kids," Joe spit out through labored breaths.

As the two continued along the beach, the amount of cans littering the ground in front of them went from the expected handful to an alarming quantity. After half a mile, both men stopped and stared in bewilderment at the blanket of multi-colored aluminum that lay before them.

"What the hell?" Joe gasped. "There aren't even this many cans on the beach during the weekend or after a holiday. Where did they all come from?"

Clay and Joe stepped gingerly around the discarded containers, noticing for the first time that many of them seemed actually embedded into the beach itself. Others were washed up from the steadily receding tide. Some of the cans looked liked been buried under shallow ocean water for years.

Other beach goers walked between the few pathways of sand that remained amongst the garbage. Some had started collecting the cans and taking them to nearby recycling bins, while others just stood and stared in perplexed bewilderment. The dogs, however, were fascinated by the alien objects that surrounded them, sniffing and barking at the cans with relentlessly. A few of the four legged beach goers seemed scared, darting back and forth in desperate pleas for their masters to follow them back towards the marsh.

"Hey, check that out," Joe exclaimed.

Lying on the ground directly in front of them was Samuel Adams beer can. That was strange enough on its own—Sam Adams could normally only be found in bottles—but the can was also wobbling and shaking on its own. A few seconds later, eight spindly legs and two claws extended out of its top, tearing through the aluminum to accommodate the creature's frame.

"Beer can hermit crabs," Clay said. "The only cool thing about people throwing their shit all over the beach. Can blame the little guys for using whatever they can for shells."

"Little?" Joe asked. "Dude, that thing's the biggest damn hermit crab I've ever seen. Its body is practically ripping the can in half."

"I've seen them even bigger than that when I lived in Florida."

"Yeah, well, I'd prefer it if the ones around here stayed the size of a golf ball or smaller," Joe said with a shudder. "Crawly things creep me out."

"At least you'll see this one coming," Clay replied with a smirk.

From off in the distance, a loud female scream cut through the air, snapping Joe and Clay's attention from the hermit crab still toddling at their feet. A girl who looked like she was in her late teens was running away from one of the recycling bin sand holding her hand. Blood streamed from between her fingers.

"Wasn't she just picking up cans?" Joe asked.

"Yeah," Clay sighed. "I guess these little guys are feeling a bit feisty this morning.

"...or drunk," Joe added.

At that moment, a group of cans near them began to shift and roll over, exposing five more hermit crabs. After righting themselves onto all eight of their legs, the cluster of creatures began to head in the direction of the screaming girl. As Joe's eyes followed their path, another group of cans emerged from the marsh. These moved with a bit more purpose, following a middle-aged housewife jogging in the other direction.

A few yards away, a cocker spaniel puppy jumped and barked incessantly at a can cluster that had made its way towards the middle of the beach. After deciding that its attempts at intimidation weren't working, the dog reached down and bit into an empty Bud Light Lime container. Before the animal's teeth could puncture the can, the other ones swarmed on top of it. The dog's horrified yelps were quickly overpowered by metal crunching over it.

"Holy shit!" Clay shouted as he and Joe backed away.

The two friends turned toward a wooden walkway that led back to the boardwalk. Before they could retreat, Clay yelped and back spun around. A claw extending from a Coors Light can was pinching his right heel. Three more cans scuttled toward his other foot, which he used to kick them all away. They tumbled a short distance and rolled to a stop. A freakishly long, oddly textured hermit crab emerged from the opening. The creature flailed its claws and legs in the air for a moment before righting itself along with the others. Then they all charged toward them.

"Run!" Clay screamed.

The two men scrambled toward the walkaway. Behind them, the pursuing cans clinked and clattered as they picked up speed. Joe soon realized that they wouldn't make the boardwalk before being overtaken. It was time to make practical use out of his rarely worn running shoes. He spun around to face the oncoming creatures, then lifted his foot high into the air, and brought it down hard into the middle of the cans. Two of them instantly crunched flat, blue blood and yellow guts squirting out onto the sand. Another one caught the end of Joe's heel, causing it to skid behind him and roll down the beach. The occupants of the other two cans, however, were undeterred. They leapt onto the top of his foot began to climbing his leg, pinching and biting the whole way.

Joe cursed and swatted at the crabs, sending them flying through the air. They landed in a newly formed, large cluster of red and white cans. The creatures quickly regrouped and charged forward, sending Clay and Joe scurrying again towards the wooden walkway. This time, however, they had enough of a head start to reach it before their pursuers could close the distance. They climbed up on top of the railing, getting their feet off the ground just before clattering metal and pinchers could reach them. The red and white of cans, which Joe and Clay could now see were Budweisers, proceeded to ram themselves against the wooden post repeatedly with no effect.

"Good thing we got chased by the domestics," Joe said, motioning with his head down to the next station marker.

A family of four had climbed on top of a nearby picnic table. They screamed in terror as cans of Newcastle and Guinness piled on top of each other in a much more intelligent (yet ultimately futile) attempt at reaching their prey. Unfortunately, the portly father panicked and lost his balance, tumbling forward towards a small ravine in the marsh below. The vast majority of the crabs that had been harassing the family immediately turned and scurried towards their fallen prey.

"OVER HERE!" Clay yelled, frantically motioning for the father to come over where he and Joe were standing.

The father quickly got to his feet and began climbing up the tiny hill with a speed that belied his ample girth. Behind him, cans were falling over each other into the ravine. A wave of aluminum crashed down under the tall grass, spilling and piling so fast that the crabs overtook the man's left leg in a matter of seconds. The father screamed. Blood leaked through the shuddering metal as it crept up toward his waist.

"Just keep moving!" Clay shouted. "We'll pull you up!"

The father grit his teeth and continued climbing towards

Joe and Clay. The rest of the cans behind him and swarmed over the edge of ravine, moving with angry purpose as they closed in at a sickeningly rapid rate. The man reached up and grabbed Clay and Joe's outstretched hands.

"Pull!" Joe shouted.

They tried to lift him up, but something pulled even hard in the other direction, so strong that it nearly dragged Joe and Clay down from the wooden railing. Below them, the cans had now swarmed and piled around the father's other leg. He cried out as the crabs bit and pinched his pale, uncovered legs.

"Keep pulling!" Clay shouted, struggling to maintain his balance on top of the rail.

Joe wanted more than anything to try and save the man. It had started to become bleakly evident, however, that if they didn't pull him up soon, they would have to let go or risk being dragged down themselves. But before he could determine when the appropriate time was to let the man to die, the decision was made for him. The father's voice, which had been wailing like a human car alarm, went silent. At the same time, the rest of his body went completely limp. Clay and Joe nearly fell backwards as the man's torso, now free of its bloodied and partially devoured lower half, flung up onto the railing.

"SHIT!" Clay exclaimed.

They immediately let go of the father's upper half, watching in horror as it fell into the pulsating pile of cans below. The man's glassy eyes stared lifelessly up at the sky while the rest of his body was swarmed and devoured.

Back on the beach, cans of all different colors and beer brands moved across it in rapidly expanding pods. Each living creature they came in contact with, both dog and human alike, was quickly and violently overtaken. Their screams and yelps mixed with the sound of crunching aluminum, creating a lurid symphony of metallic anguish. The beautiful sunrise behind it all made the horrifying scene appear even more surreal.

"What the hell do we do, man?" Joe asked. "We can't just stand there and let this happen!"

Clay stared blankly out at the beach and shook his head.

"Well, unless you've got a weaponized trash picker or a military grade recycling program, I'm not sure there's anything we can do. Give me a flame thrower and some melted butter, though, we might be in business."

Despite Clay's attempt to make light of the situation, Joe could see that his friend's eyes were wide with a mix of fear and shock. He was also pretty sure (and desperately hoped) that they didn't know any of the beach goers being attacked by the can-shelled crabs, but watching people and animals die before their very eyes still easily ranked as the most awful thing he'd ever seen.

The crabs' initial victims were now in the process of being abandoned for fresher prey. The formerly thrashing humans and dogs had been replaced with lifeless, partially devoured corpses. Blood dotted the white sands as the ravenous creatures scuttled away, leaving red trails that crisscrossed from the marsh to the edge of the tide. Those who'd managed to avoid the first attack had attempted to escape to both areas with wildly varying degrees of success. Many had kept their heads enough to find high ground like Joe and Clay, including some of the dogs. Some had even found refuge by fleeing into the ocean. Those that simply ran straight into the marsh, however, were now disappearing under the tall grass. Their futile cries for help quickly morphed into screams before giving way to the sound of metal clinking together.

Joe looked over at older woman barely maintaining her balance atop a signpost. "Why the hell are the hermit crabs going apeshit like this?"

"You'd be pretty pissed off too if your home was a light beer can that some douchebag couldn't be bothered to throw away," Clay said. "But I'm guessing their transformation into a homicidal species has something to do with what's happening over there."

Joe looked where Clay was pointing. The crabs were abandoning the people on walkway railings and signs en mass to the middle of the beach. Cans crunched together in a gigantic, colorful metal cluster, which swirled like a vortex around a three foot tall lighting rock jutting out of the ground like tree branch. The crabs below Joe and Clay's feet ceased snapping up at them at scurried off to join the others.

"It looks like they're all circling the same place," Joe said. "Except for that pocket of Pabst Blue Ribbon cans wandering by themselves near the lighthouse."

"I guess man-eating hermit crabs can still be hipsters, too," Clay said with a smirk.

"Dude, this isn't funny!" Joe shot back.

"Neither is that," Clay said.

He pointed toward the mass of cans again, which had stopped swirling. They were now crackling with electric blue sparks. The lighting rocks around the beach all began to glow blue, acting has conduits for the electricity as it intermittently zapped over the entire the area. Seagulls that had been hovering overhead squawked in alarm and took off. Droplets of white feces plunked down onto the cans as they began to merge and fuse together into an unidentifiable mass. As the blue zaps increased in frequency, the aluminum bent and molded itself into the shape of a gigantic, unshelled hermit crab. The currents melded together in a final blue flash as metallic monstrosity groaned to life, pushing itself up on all eight legs so that it towered over the one and two story homes in the distance.

"Holy shit," Clay breathed.

The giant crab's claws, which both seemed to be made entirely of Corona Lite cans, gleamed in the sun as they flailed above its head. A pod of Pabst Blue Ribbon and Natural Lite cans scuttled over from the lighthouse to join it. The metal crab angrily swatted them aside, sending a shower of spinning aluminum and waving black legs through the air.

"Well, at least we can all agree on that," Joe said under his breath. "Let's get the hell out of here."

Clay followed him as he jumped off the railing onto the walkway. People were running past them toward the boardwalk, where curious onlookers had begun to wander forward to see why everyone was screaming. Upon seeing the giant metal crab, they began to scream, as well. The creature threw its head back and unleashed an ear shattering noise, like a lion's roar mixed with a car crash.

Joe and Clay spun around and joined the retreating masses, their feet slapping loudly on the wooden walkway leading from the beach. By the time they reached the boardwalk, the giant crab had begun to move forward, its metal legs grinding like nails on a chalkboard as it bore down on the various restaurants lining the other end of the marsh. It reached one with a crab on its sign and tore into the building, creating an explosion of wood and plaster.

The creature emerged from the haze of debris into the parking lot on the other side. Glass crunched and car alarms blazed. People screamed and fled in all directions as the crab moved onto the boardwalk with alarming speed, snapping its silver metal claws at anything that moved. Joe watched in horror as an older man who'd been jogging with his headphones on was snatched up into the air.

"C'mon!" Clay yelled, pulling Joe behind him.

The old man's screams rose above the car alarms and emergency sirens that were now wailing in the distance. The claw drew his flailing body towards a dark spot on the creature's head where the mouth should be. The area was filled with overturned hermit crabs, all writhing and wriggling with excitement as their meal moved in. Seconds later, nothing was left of the old man but a bloody skeleton. The giant metal crab lifted the man's remains and tossed them down towards an oncoming police car, causing it to swerve and crash into a street lamp Joe and Clay had just passed. The other police cruisers skidded to a stop. Officers poured out and took cover behind them while drawing their weapons. Gunshots clinked off the massive aluminum beast's hide. It let loose with another angry roar that nearly caused Joe to fall over.

Clay, who was a few feet ahead of him, turned to say something. His voice was immediately drowned out by a squad of helicopters thundering above them. He then pointed emphatically toward the Ben Sawyer Bridge, which would lead them off the island back to Mount Pleasant. Joe nodded and pushed himself to catch up. As they turned off Jasper Boulevard onto the bridge, Clay reached out and tapped him on the shoulder.

"There's a lesson here, you know," he shouted over the distant gunfire and screams. "Litter really does hurt everyone."

"Especially…when…it's…drunk…and…pissed…off," Joe added between breaths. "And running…*sucks!*"

ON ULLINS BANK

John Linwood Grant

There should have been a new moon over us, but the cloud-cover was too heavy, charcoal smears above the pitch-black waters. All around lay the midnight of the North Sea, not a wave crest to colour that vast, empty sight.

We were the only star in the darkness. Aboard the *Gull*, the searchlights glared, wardens of our filthy work. The skipper was already out of the wheelhouse, ready to pull his weight.

"Hey, hey, hey!" he sang out as the winches smoked, and the trawl net rose, the dripping, weed-encrusted otter-boards showing above the flat sea.

"High up!" said Henrikssen, grabbing one of the steel ropes.

"High up!" The rest of us gave him an echo, and hauled.

"Set back on him!" The skipper checked the winches, and the boy Charlie fed them oil from the tin. "And again. All together..."

"Oh-ho!" we gave him, shoulders tight.

We hoisted the cod-end on board, and flipped the catch into the gutting-hold as it came, kicking dogfish across the deck as we worked. Those rough-skinned buggers had a bite on them, though we saw few enough here.

This was our second day in the new fishing ground, a bank the skipper had only told us of when we were at sea. Ullins Bank, he called it, but there was no mark on the charts. A day off the coast, yet the sea seemed empty. Working as a single-boater, we'd seen no-one apart from a Swedish yacht, far away.

"We'll trawl after dark, lads. We don't want others finding

this one, believe me."

It made no difference to us, so we fished the bank at night, only using the lights when we had to, and trying to keep them down.

I slid into the open hold, where the catch was being gutted and crated. A hell of a catch it was as well, fat fish in their hundreds. I picked up my knife and began to work. I didn't need to feel my fingers, so the cold made no difference. They did their job, twenty years of memory locked in those sinews. Grab by the gills, slice and twist. Then into the crates with such as ice as we had left and roped down ready for the voyage to market.

Charlie, who was between the crates and me, took the fish as Bill Cabett and I gutted them. He was fifteen years old and skinny, some cousin of the skipper's. Now and then, he stopped to lift up a bucket of entrails and chuck it over the side for the seabirds – though I'd not seen any recently. The dogfish would be happy enough, anyway.

"Almost full, Mr Kell." Charlie whistled. "Every crate."

"Pack them down, boy, and our fortune's made."

In truth, this was the best fishing we'd had all year – a month's catch in two days. Small steam-trawlers like our *Gull* couldn't compete with the fleets. We worked on. There must have been a stench to the hold, but after so long as a trawlerman I could no longer tell. Bacon burning on the stove below, yes, but fish?

Bill paused, cod guts dripping down his smock.

"We'll be wearing silk waistcoats, Harry my lad." He grinned at me. "Never seen such catches."

"That's true enough."

"Luck at last, eh?"

I held back on that one. Bad luck is what you notice; good luck is rare and has a price. That's what my father used to say, the gloomy bugger. I had a touch of my father in me, maybe, and I couldn't grin back.

"How are your hands, Charlie?" We'd brought up turbot and cod, plus some haddock good enough for top price.

"All right, Mr. Kell."

Which was probably a lie. Trawling was hard on a body. What made it harder here was the weed, or sponge, or whatever, that came up with the gear. It was Charlie's job to pluck it from the nets and the guide-ropes, though we helped him when we could. Kelp and bladder-wrack were common nearer the coast, but out here it was sea-chervil. Except the weed wasn't that, either.

'Dead-man's fingers', Henrikssen called it. It was pale, gelatinous and slimy, in swollen lengths up to a foot long. He'd seen its kin off the Swedish coast, he said, though not quite the same, or in such quantities. No one liked the stuff, or the name. Tom Parvitt's brother had hands which looked like that when he washed up, long after the *MacDonald* foundered off Filey Brigg. The colour of a wet grave.

This stuff came up in bucketfuls, stuck to the edges of the otter-boards, which held the trawl net open, clinging to the steel ropes, tangled in the rough netting itself. We all had a touch of rash on our hands and forearms, red welts, which itched, but nothing much to worry about; Charlie had the worst of it, even when we shared the cleaning of the gear.

"Dogger Bank itch." Bill Cabett wiped his fingers on his smock. "Not more'n that."

I had seen Dogger Bank itch. A nasty rash that soon went away with calamine lotion and a week or two off the nets. The men of the trawl fleet off the Dogger had it often. This was worse, though maybe it too would pass when we'd been ashore a while.

On the way home, we off-loaded some of the catch to a Hull carrier, half full from one of the fleets. When they saw the fine, prime fish we had, they were happy for the extra weight.

"No showing off now, lads," said the skipper, as we turned for the coast. "Unload quiet when we get back, and keep the whooping down, else others will be on our tails."

So we made Filey Brigg with sober faces, took a turbot each for our wives and sweethearts, and sold some to the inns and some to the merchants.

We thought our luck was in. We were wrong, though it took a while to learn.

***

Working the new ground was hard. The skipper had us out every chance he could, always leaving harbour with the dawn and heading south east, then turning north again when the sea lanes were empty. Two days journey there and back, two days of trawling on the bank until the ship was so crammed with fish we could hardly move. It was easier on some than others.

We were on our third trip when we saw the boat. The trawl was ready to drop, the sea was calm, and there it was in the eastern gloom.

"What is that feller there?" Henrikssen squinted.

"Our marker-boat," said the skipper. "Pay no heed."

"What if he is in trouble? I do not see a sail."

"Get to your work," was the only answer.

Henrikssen, Bill and I shared a look; the boy was fiddling with one of the otter-boards, checking the links. Single-boaters didn't have markers.

"I've seen it before," said Bill. "Low and handy. Allus when we're trawling this bank, mind."

Perhaps I had as well, but I'd marked it as a shadow on the water. I went back to the job.

The catch that night was heavier than usual, the cod-end packed with wriggling brown and silver. I thought the winch would burn out as it strained to bring the weight in. Cod in abundance, but better than that—turbot, which was always called prime and fetched a rare price at the markets. Hardly a dogfish, witch or megrim in there.

"It's money dancing." Charlie grinned as he helped me pack fat turbot into the crates. The live fish flopped and slithered around his boots, waiting for our knives.

What did fish feel? Maybe nothing. Less than the pigs I'd seen slaughtered on my uncle's farm. I could never have done that.

The skipper paid us our share for that trip, prompt as

always, and said we would wait a day or so. He'd know when 'things were right' to go out again. We were glad for the break.

It surprised me that we hadn't been followed—there was plenty of talk about the weight of fish we were landing, and the quality. I'd have thought the *Sprite* or Jed Barton's *Swordfish* would have trailed us just to find the general area where we trawled, but no. We never had company.

As if thinking made it so, I met Jed next morning, coming out of the Star. He'd had a pint or two, by the smell of him, but nothing that stopped his legs from working or stilled his lips.

"Harry."

We touched our caps, mocking. We'd been close enough once, at least to share a slate at the Star. Then Jed had hired out to the fleet, and the *Swordfish* spent most of her time on the Dogger, making better money than the *Gull*. He fell in with company people, and like herring-nets, we drifted.

"Your skipper's done well."

He was testing me, I thought. There were plenty who wanted to know where we'd been.

"Aye. He knows his way around out there."

Jed nodded.

"I tried after you last Thursday, you know." he said, tugging at his moustache. "Wondered where you were fishing, doing so fine."

"Did you, now?"

"Followed the *Gull* out, and saw you turn, north nor' east."

"I didn't see you."

He frowned. "No. Couldn't have spotted a whale in that bloody fog, damn your luck. We were surprised you didn't turn back yourselves."

I forced a smile. "A good skipper and a good compass. That's all you need."

We talked shop and nonsense for a minute or two, asked after each other's families, and went our ways.

Thursday? It had been cold, with clear skies all day, not a touch of fog. It was always possible that the *Swordfish* had hit a sea-fret, coming in off the waters, but still...

Putting it aside, I went shopping. I bought Elsie a new dress, paid off the last of our debts, and peered into the tailor's window on the High Street, admiring a length of tweed. A new Sunday suit might soon be in order. With extra brass in my pockets, I stopped off the Ship Inn for a pint or two afterwards.

I hadn't expected to find anyone I knew at the Ship, but the skipper was there in one shadowed corner, sitting on his own. A bottle of whisky stood on the table, a third down.

"Skipper."

"Harry."

No invite to join him, no word I should leave. So, I sat down. I told him about meeting Jed and mentioned the fog.

"Sea-fret," he said. It was more of an echo than any thought of his, I felt.

"Ullins Bank's been good to us," I said between mouthfuls of beer.

"Aye." His eyes were redder than usual, which I put down to the drink.

"How did you find it?" I tried to sound casual.

"Find what?"

"The bank. Our pot at the end of the rainbow."

"Word came to me."

I watched the way he gripped the bottle.

"It didn't come to any of the other skippers."

He didn't like being pressed.

"I met someone in the know, all right?" He poured out more whisky.

"So the Devil walked into the Old Ship, and bought you a pint?" I laughed; he didn't.

"Weren't the Devil." A mutter, the clank of glass against tobacco-yellowed teeth.

"Then who was it?"

"Just someone who knows the waters." He looked up and smiled at me then, a smile that didn't ring true. "I've been thinking."

I waited.

"Might be time to get a second boat. There's a small steam-trawler up for auction next month. Handy enough. Thought you might skipper it. Under my watch—at first."

This had never occurred to me. I was as near as God his first mate, but on a boat the size of the *Gull* there wasn't much rank outside of him.

"You interested?" he asked, blunt.

"I…yes, like as not." I couldn't think of what else to say.

"Good."

And that was it.

Afterwards I sat outside our cottage with Elsie in the late afternoon sun. Onions and cabbage; parsnips and something else. I was no gardener, but she'd set out rows aplenty before the money had started coming in. Before Ullins Bank. She was a practical lass.

"Others'll find it soon, Charlie. The wives talk. Aggie Barton looks askance at me—her Jed's boat took mostly dogfish last time they went out."

"I saw him. They'll eat," I said, uncomfortable.

She looked at my hands.

"And this." She made to touch the sores there, but I flinched.

"That'll pass, love. The skipper's a fair man. He'll see he's working us to the bone and back off. Besides, we've probably taken the best for this season."

The sun caught her tip-tilted nose, her brown eyes.

"So you say. But what man stops when he smells his fortune."

And some of her look at that moment was meant for me.

***

We went out again a day later. The weather was beginning to bother me. I supposed that Jed Barton had started it, with his talk of fog, but the truth was, we had never had bad weather on the Ullins Bank. Whatever the sea was like going to it, or coming from it, the water there was placid and the air still. Cloud aplenty, but none of the North Sea blows, no lashing rain. I was a fool to miss a storm, but I did. This had begun to feel wrong.

The marker boat was there the evening we arrived, further east by our reckoning, and the skipper told us where to trawl. So we did. We came up with sole so big the fish-kettle hadn't been made to take them, but we were tired. Bill was cursing, not his usual way, and Henrikssen cut himself with his own knife. I took him aft to bind it, a nasty gash on one arm.

"You see it?" he said as I tied the ends of the linen.

I followed his gaze. The marker-boat, nearer than usual. With his free hand, he reached into the deck locker from which I'd had the bandages. He held out a spyglass, which must have been far older than the *Gull*.

"Go on, tell me what you see."

I shrugged and lifted the glass. It took some adjusting, but I managed to focus on our companion. Or our shadow. Moonlight and a scatter of stars caught the low shape, higher at prow and stern. It looked clinker-built and wrong. There was no mast, and no engine housing I could see. A figure stood forward, eyes on the sea, not us. A tall, thin figure, wrapped in oil-skins or a heavy cloak, with a sliver of his face visible from the side.

I told Henrikssen what I saw.

"My father came from Norway," he said, when I'd finished.

That was hardly news.

"Aye, and..."

"These men, these boats, they are not good. The Folk, my grandfather called them. Finnfolk. They are not like us."

"You mean they're foreign?"

He pulled the sleeve of his gansey down, covering the bandaged arm. "You will joke at me."

I heard the Scandinavian in his voice, always a sign of Henrikssen being serious. He was worried.

"No," I said, "I don't think I will. Not tonight."

"They are dark men. They say that each of the Finnfolk has a thing, a certain bone, marked with Godless words, which moves their boats. They can call the weather, raise or calm the waters, if they wish."

"Ullins Bank." I spoke soft, so as Charlie couldn't hear me over the engine.

"Yes." Henrikssen looked to where the skipper stood by the winches, checking them.

"It's only a story," I said, but my mind was back in the Ship Inn, thinking about talk of 'someone in the know'.

When we got back to the hold, Charlie sat on its edge, using a spike to get that glistening weed from the trawl net. It was obvious that he was trying not to touch it.

"Is it worse?" I asked, and crouched next to him, having a go at the weed myself.

He knew what I meant and held up his hands. They were blotched with red sores, and the palm of the left one was cracked open, weeping.

"Go below and get a cup of tea. We'll all have a mug, eh?"

He left eagerly, and Henrikssen joined me on the net.

"This weed, or sponge—whatever it is..." I shook my head.

"It is from them, the Folk."

"Another of your grandfather's stories?"

"No. But it is only here on this bank."

I pried free a slippery mass, about twelve inches long, and sliced into it. My blade hit something firmer inside. I twisted the knife, opening it up.

"Chalk," I said. "Like coral, inside."

My voice was steady, but my hand was not. Thin, chalky lengths formed some sort of core to the protrusions from the main stem. White fragments, each about the length of a finger-bone might be when flesh and sinew had rotted away. Which it couldn't be, of course.

Henrikssen took the weed from me, tossing it into the sea.

"Dead-man's fingers."

***

We worked the bank—we were trawler-men and didn't know what else to do. Nearly a month had passed, and we were rich, by local standards, but fit to drop. I wanted Charlie at least to set back from the job for a while, but I knew why he pressed on. Since his father had gone down on the *Swallow*, six months back, he had his family to support.

There was word among the crew, even down to Bill Cabett, a cheery soul in all weather. No one liked the black marker-boat or the stillness of the sea, however easy it made the work. No one liked the dead-man's fingers, which came up with every trawl.

Worst was the quiet. The *Gull* always had gulls, waiting for entrails and slop, or resting on the crosstrees for a moment before scudding on their way. On Ullins Bank, no seabird flew. I'd heard it told that the cries of gulls were the voices of dead sailors, watching over the living. Whatever watched us on the bank was something else.

With the new moon coming round again, the skipper wanted us out again. The forecast wasn't good; we were tired, making mistakes. We almost had mutiny, if you can have such a thing on a small trawler. One of the fore gallows was bent out of kilter, barely fit after such heavy use, and there were holes in the trawl net. Even the thick trawl-warp, steel rope, was showing wear. Bill Cabett wouldn't pledge for the engine getting us back in, even if it got us out.

The skipper took me into the cabin while we were in harbour. It was a rough morning, dawn on its way. Waves broke twenty feet high on the Brigg, where the land dared to thrust into the sea; beyond the harbour itself we could see a serious swell, enough to keep most boats moored.

"This'll be the last time on the bank. I promise you." His face was pale in the cabin lights. "Harry, I'm paying off the… marker-man. Him. It's time."

"Good."

"Tell the lads we need this last one. Please."

He'd never said please to me in seven years. I nodded.

"As you say, skipper."

It took some arguing with the lads. Word was the big fleets were out, but they had their carriers and their hospital ships from the Seaman's Mission. They watched out for each other and could take more of a blow than a single boat with no hope of quick relief. I checked the signal flares and had Bill make sure the life-jackets were sound.

And out we went, the *Gull* pitching and rolling, spray hissing on the funnel. It gave me no pleasure that the closer we got to Ullins Bank, the calmer it became. By dusk, we were there, and yet again the sea was smooth, too smooth. I thought of Finnfolk, and of ways that shouldn't be. I thought of Elsie, and her complaints that I'd missed church service too often this last month.

The marker-boat was nearer than usual, and even in the gloom, I could see the figure standing in it now. I shivered, said nothing. We fed out the gear, and crossed the bank, nice and slow. When we brought it in, it was heavy as ever.

Work took over. As we gutted, Henrikssen stood by me.

"Here." He reached under his smock and passed me something. It was a cross, a simple iron one hung on an old leather bootlace.

I frowned.

"Wear it," he said, and went back to the catch. I watched as he slid his knife up through the belly of a huge cod, almost losing his grip on it. Awkward, I slipped the thong around my neck and shoved the cross under my gansey.

We were three-quarters full after the first trawl, which would have been unthinkable a month ago. I thought the skipper would push us to one more, but this time was different.

"That's it. The bank's about done for now, and we've earned some serious shore time."

He stood by the larboard rail, his sou'wester in his hand.

"Harry, take the lads below. There's a half bottle of whisky behind the stove. We'll have hot tea, and a good measure before we head back."

I did what he said, but when the tea was brewed, I went up, quiet like, for I wanted to know what was going on. The hatch was just aft of the funnel, and it was easy to slip into cover. The skipper was by the rail, and the boat out there was coming closer. It had no lights, no sail. I listened hard, but couldn't hear an engine.

"*Gull.*" A voice across the water.

"Aye," called back the skipper.

The strange vessel came into the gleam of our own lights, its gunnels hardly above the water. A dull thud, and its occupant was onto our deck.

Elsie says I'm no great judge of men, but this one had me cold. Taller than the skipper, which was a good height, with long dark hair and some sort of oilskin wrapped around narrow shoulders. It trailed to his booted feet, scraping the deck planks.

The skipper stood uneasy, one hand on the rail.

"We're done," he said. "I have what we agreed." He held out a leather satchel, heavy by the way he handled it. "A full weight in silver."

The dark man stared. Sallow is the word for his look, I think—a lean, sallow face with thin lips, and eyes that were darker than the night. He moved to a heap of dead-men's fingers, bending to pick a handful up. They had lost their gelatinous look, and now seemed even more like their namesakes.

"And a little more." The dark man's voice was a wicked thing—like the slither of a shark from the deeps, an eel from its lair. His hand moved on the weed like you would stroke a dog—almost a caress—before he lay it down.

"Aye. I added extra good silver coin," said the skipper.

"Who have the dead-men marked?"

The skipper stared at him.

"What do you mean?"

"We take a tithe, and the dead-men know their own. There will be one of you they have marked, and he is ours. There is always one—that is the bargain. Silver and a little more, for the fair fortune we gave you."

"No." The skipper's eyes were wide, shocked. My only comfort was that at least he hadn't known. That would have been too much.

"Did we keep our word?"

The skipper shuddered. "You did, but you didn't tell me..."

"Now you are told, and now you are wiser." The other peeled back thin lips. His teeth were small and sharp and as yellow as the skipper's, but not, I think, from tobacco.

There was a scuffle behind me, and Charlie was there in the hatchway, hauling himself on deck.

"What's going on, Mr. Kell?"

The dark man turned, and I knew that he saw those hands and arms. I smelled his cold greed, like it was in the air between us, his eyes on the weeping sores that ran from fingertip to elbow. I kicked at Charlie's shoulder, and with a surprised yelp, he tumbled back down the ladder, out of sight.

"See?" It was a hiss on the night air. "He is marked, and there is the rest of the bargain. And a runtling, no loss to you. The dead-men have chosen who will join them."

"You can't have him," I said, standing forward. Even from here, the stranger smelled of mildew and sea-rot, like tarpaulin left in the hold too long.

The skipper swore, pressing the leather bag into the dark man's hands.

"I'll find more silver, if I must. Leave the lad alone."

"You break oath with us. We will have all, or you will have nothing."

If there'd been a gun on board, even a rusty shotgun, I would have grabbed for it. Instead, I pulled Henrikssen's cross from under my gansey, and held it up on its thong. It was all I could think to do.

"Take the coin and go, who or whatever you are." I said. "Leave God-fearing men to their business."

He did not flinch, but his sallow face twisted.

"Then you will have nothing," he repeated.

I made to close with him, not really knowing what I was doing, but he was off over the rail, and that long, low boat was moving away, fast. The dark man had one hand lifted, and in it was a length of something yellow-white, much like bone...

"Harry, I—"

"I'll get steam up," I said, not trusting myself to speak to him.

To the others I said something about a deal gone wrong, that the man who knew these banks had asked for more than he deserved. I ignored their questions, but Henrikssen saw what he needed to know in my face.

To the skipper I said nothing. He took the helm and bolted the wheelhouse door behind him, a bottle of whisky in one hand.

As we tried to make sure all the gear was stowed or tied down, I saw that there were other boats out there, all the same as the stranger's.

"Three," said Henrikksen, his broad face set hard. No one else could hear him. "Three to bring whatever comes. They are not a kind people, the stories say."

The waters over Ullins Bank were already choppy, such as we'd never seen them. Within the hour, the *Gull* was pitching badly, and the engine was struggling. I had Bill down there, his face black with soot and grease as he tried to keep it going.

What came was a storm, worse than the blow outside the harbour, worse than any we'd seen for a long time. If luck could turn, ours had, and with a vengeance. Charlie lay sick in his cupboard-bunk, pus weeping from his hands, as if a fever had taken him, while Henrikssen and I did what we could. I hammered on the wheelhouse door, but the skipper didn't even turn to look.

Ullins Bank was a boiling cauldron. Waves broke over the bow, the gunnels, from every direction, and only the skipper could know if we held a course or not. The deck locker with the spare compass had been ripped open when the mast went. Drenched and freezing cold, we worked on, praying we could get into deeper water.

There was no true morning. Black cloud clung to the horizon in every direction, and the gale tore at our rigging, anything that wasn't bolted down twice. The aft-mast went sometime in the first hour, almost taking the trawl net with it, and we worked like dogs, the two of us on deck. If the gear went over, empty but still wet and heavy, the boat would go with it. I cursed myself for not insisting that it was properly stowed before we set out home. We would have cut it loose at that point, but it was tangled in the aft gallows. Henrikssen almost went over with a blow from the trawl-warp, which slammed by him, but I hauled him safe.

"See to the boy!" yelled Henrikssen. I caught a billow of smoke from the funnel, and though I could hardly hear its pounding, it seemed that Bill was keeping the engine alive.

Half the North Sea went down with me into the cramped crew cabin. Charlie was out of his bunk, moaning.

"I can hear them," he said, clinging to me. His hands looked worse than ever, a pale ooze from every sore. I gave him my cross, for luck, I said, and forced him back into his cubby. Once there, I poured hard drink down his throat until he quietened a little.

When I reached the deck, my sou'wester lost in the gale, Henrikssen had found an axe, God knows from where, and was slamming it into the wheelhouse door, an old wooden thing. The planking splintered easily, and the door flew open.

"Do something!" he yelled at the skipper. "This was your deal."

"We can ride it." The skipper's voice was slurred, hardly his own. I pressed to Henrikssen's side in the doorway as another wave broke over us, taking the glass out of the side port. A sliver struck my cheek, warm blood mingling with the icy water.

"We can't." I gripped his shoulder. "We'll go down, man."

And we would, I felt in that moment. The pumps were going, but the gutting hold was full of water, and the storm was getting worse.

The three of us stood there, little good against the three who were out in the storm, calling it down on us. I believed in the old tales at that moment.

"Take the wheel, Charlie," said the skipper, and pushed past me.

I think we would have stopped him if we'd known his mind; I hope we would have. At any other time. But the wind shrieked, the helm bucked and needed strong hands on it. A loose steel rope whipped against the wheelhouse, a sound from hell.

The skipper took a long swig from the bottle and tossed it into the storm.

"Here's a little more for you, you bastards!" he cried out, and threw himself to the larboard rail. Threw himself to it, and over it.

There was nothing we could do. No line or lifebelt could have found him in that sea. We tied the broken door shut and huddled there, keeping a course for home. The wind died down within the hour, and by the time we sighted Filey Brigg, the storm might never have been.

***

With the battered *Gull* in her harbour berth, I did what I could. Charlie I sent to Scarborough, and though he lay abed in the hospital there for a week, he came out of it with no more than some curious rounds scars on his hands and arms. He remembered nothing of the storm, or any dark stranger.

To him and Bill, to the locals, the skipper had been lost in a gale, and most around those parts understood that. One life only was a good result for some families, who'd lost more than one brother or son, father or uncle, in a single stiff blow.

The skipper had no near kin, but it was a shock when I found he'd left the *Gull* to me. Not as much of a shock as when his body came in with the tide, a few days later. It was a cruel, battered sight, and everyone in port wondered how it could have found a current to bring it here, from so far out.

Everyone except the two of us who'd heard the dark man speak.

If the message needed to be clearer, the skipper's body was tangled with that weed. Dead-man's fingers, the slimy stuff caught around his arms and legs. I had it torn off, and his clothes burned, before he was laid out.

***

We are going back to Ullins Bank, Henrikssen and I, with

cold iron and a priest. There's a churchman out of Whitby who didn't laugh when I told him the story. We found heavy chain from the scrapyards, and he blessed it with his best words and all our will. The *Gull* will get us there, and God's grace may keep us whilst we seed the waters. Maybe it will cleanse them, maybe not, but Father Gyll says it will keep those other folk wary and away, for a while at least.

I'll trawl no more. Crab pots will do, line-fishing by the cliffs, and whatever Elsie can grow. Maybe I'll learn to dig. My hands look clean, the skin free of sores, and a spade would suit them better. There's no use for a trawlerman who flinches when the gear comes up and weed from the banks is tangled in the net.

Or one who watches the horizon, waiting for a long, low boat that never comes.

THE WAY WE ARE LIFTED

Aric Sundquist

Madison pried off her leather work gloves and placed them on the concrete slab. She grabbed the paracord rope firmly in both hands and leaned forward, hanging dangerously over the side of the building. Although the rope prevented her from falling over, she would still get in trouble if someone spotted her. She gave a quick glance over at the Chancellor plucking a tomato from the roof-garden. He didn't notice her absence.

From ten stories above, Madison watched the dark water shift and swirl throughout the city streets. Sunken cars resembled gigantic beetles and a single crane rusted away in the intersection like a mechanical dinosaur struggling out of a tar pit. The wind was just beginning to pick up, nice and cool and causing the edges of her dress to flap around her thighs and boots. Far below, the current rose and kicked up sediment in whirlpools, turning the water into deeper shades of blue and purple. The smell of salt and seaweed permeated the air.

Madison knew those signs well. A storm was coming.

Down the street, she saw a faded stop sign shaking in the current. She never understood how the signs used to direct traffic. She had asked Alice about it once, and her best friend explained how the YIELD and STOP and TURN LEFT signs all worked. But the explanation only confused Madison more. Alice then pointed to the wires crisscrossing the streets and told her the metal boxes used to change colors. Madison thought back hard and tried to remember what the boxes looked like before the floods, but she couldn't remember much. She remembered a few things, however, like being tucked into bed and her mother kissing her forehead. She remembered waking up early to the smell of pancakes and her dad bringing her food on a TV tray. She also remembered hot summer days and running through the park as fast as she could while the grass and dandelions blurred together into one long series of watercolors. This was by far her favorite memory—of flowers and sunshine and being with her parents. She felt safe then. She felt loved.

She had other memories from before, but they were starting to fade, replaced with newer memories—of the sun beating down on her back, of working until her hands bled and listening to the screams of the girls who went into the Chancellor's office at night.

Still grasping the rope, Madison leaned forward as far as the slack would allow, searching the sunken ruins. Sometimes the water distorted in ripples from the Deep Ones catching fish for supper. She had never seen one up close, but she knew they were dangerous. Last year a girl named Catherine had jumped off the rooftop and everyone rushed over to watch the strange fish-people tear her apart and fight over the remaining scraps like ravenous dogs. The Chancellor said it was an accident and he had his two Advisors string up the rope as a precaution. But everyone knew she had jumped off the side on purpose. Some even said she was pregnant at the time.

Madison eventually spotted the little rowboat in the water, wedged against a tall pole that used to hold light. Her heart kicked in her chest. She had seen pictures in old magazines of how boats worked, and she could read enough to figure some things out. She knew people used paddles and sails to push the boats through water. But now, with the ongoing storms getting much worse, the boat would keep moving downstream with the current. She doubted it would stay put much longer. With another storm brewing on the horizon, it was possible the boat would disappear by tomorrow morning and her life would become even more miserable.

Just then a sharp pain startled her back to reality. A hand squeezed her neck, then wrenched her away from the side of the building. She fell to her knees.

The Chancellor loomed over her with dark eyes that didn't seem to have pupils anymore, and with a sloped forehead and hair beginning to fall out at the roots. He licked lips smeared with tomato juice and put his hand on the grip of his pistol in a threatening manner. "Get back to work, daydreamer," he said.

Madison coughed and rubbed her neck and got her breathing back. She ran over to the roof-garden and knelt down, flinging up dirt with her shovel, making more of a mess than actually helping.

"You shouldn't have done that," Alice said, kneeling down next to her. "It'll draw attention." Alice was in her late thirties, tall and thin and with long brown hair just starting to turn grey at the edges.

"I know," Madison said. "But I had to see."

Alice nudged Madison out of the way and poked a seed deep into the soil with her finger. "Is the boat still there?" she asked.

"Yup. But not for long, I think."

"Okay," Alice said, pulling out another seed. "We'll leave tonight. If anyone tries to stop you, use this."

Alice pulled something shiny from her boot. Slid it over in the dirt.

A knife.

***

Madison waited until the sleeping quarters grew quiet in Upper Eden. The children usually stayed up pretty late, telling stories and playing cards by candlelight. When the room finally went dark and all the children settled into their beds, she gathered up her belongings and crept out into the main hallway.

Her boots echoed loudly on the tile floor, so she pried them off and placed them in her pack and went barefoot, sliding with her back against the walls, steering clear of the light thrown from the wall lanterns. The oil smelled like rotting fish. Some of the children joked that the oil came from the blood of Deep

Ones. But that seemed silly. Blood didn't burn like oil.

She darted from shadow to shadow, checking each corridor one at a time, hoping the two Advisors weren't doing any late night patrols.

Finally, she made it to the Chancellor's quarters. The door was closed and the window shuttered, but she could hear an adult speaking inside. Instantly she recognized Alice's voice. She reasoned that her friend was causing a distraction, so Madison gathered up courage and darted to the far door and up the remaining stairs, leading outside.

Cool air greeted her.

Thunder shook the building and caused the metal infrastructure to shutter and groan. The air held a strange mixture of moisture and electricity, energizing her body in chaotic waves. Thankfully the rain hadn't started yet.

She found a place in the shadows and laced up her boots, sticking the knife flush against her leg inside her boot, like how Alice had hidden it earlier. She threw on her jacket and checked her supplies sealed in a plastic bag: three candles, a compass, a half-full lighter, a tin cup for bailing out water from the boat, and a Swiss-army knife. Content, she placed the bag back in her pocket and waited. Her whole body vibrated with fear and excitement.

Soon, Alice emerged from the stairs, glancing around the rooftop. Madison stood and waved.

"Were you seen?" Alice said, moving over and crouching down. She wore faded jeans tucked into her boots and a black coat that fit tightly over her body. Her hair was tied back tightly in a braid and made her look different. Madison had never seen her hair like that before. It made her look older.

"Nope," she answered. "They were sleeping when I left. What about the Chancellor?"

"He's incapacitated."

"What?"

"He won't be moving for a long time."

"Oh," Madison said. "Are you sure we can't bring the others with us?"

"Yes, I'm sure. I pried a little, but they're too scared of getting caught. And we can only fit two in the boat, right?"

"Right." She hadn't thought about that.

"The Advisors do their patrols every hour," Alice said, "so we don't have much time. I have four canteens with fresh water. Now, I need you to go and get the food while I work on the rope. Okay?"

Madison nodded and immediately jumped into action. Ever since the three men had begun looking at her with uncomfortable stares, she couldn't wait to leave the rooftop colony. She wanted to be away from this place, on dry land brimming with trees and flowers. She wanted to feel safe for once, not a prisoner on a concrete island.

Madison moved quickly, wrenching out carrots and potatoes from the roof-garden, stuffing them inside her pack, to the point she could barely close the straps. Alice used a knife to cut down the paracord rope, tying the ends together and making one long coil from the pieces.

"I'm going to lift you down first," Alice said. She cinched the rope around the younger girl's waist and thighs. "I think I have enough to get you to the fifth floor. When you stop, get inside, quick. Light one of your candles and wait for me, but don't go anywhere else, okay?"

"Okay."

Madison looked over the side of the building and into the vast darkness below. For some reason her vision blurred, and she felt sick. Her body began trembling.

Alice hugged her, tightly. "Just be as still as you can and don't look down. I'll do all the work." She anchored the rope around a pipe for more leverage, then began lowering Madison down the side.

At first, Madison felt discomfort from the rope digging into her waist, almost like a burning sensation. She bobbed around like a worm on a hook, until finally finding her balance by planting her feet firmly against the building wall. The pain lessened instantly. She moved lower and lower, and it felt as if she floated through a midnight ocean with saltwater and seaweed and a hundred other smells swirling around her. She angled her head up at the rain clouds just as the first drops stuck her forehead, tickling her neck and face. She held out her arms and felt free. She felt wonderful.

When she hit the seventh floor, a sound startled her out of her reverie. Without thinking, she looked down just as the lightning lit the city in flickering bursts.

Hundreds of the Deep Ones swarmed below. Pale bodies looked like a mass of writhing flesh and fins and webbed appendages. The lightning went off again, and she saw the creatures hopping on top of submerged vehicles as if they were lily-pads. Others swarmed up telephone poles.

Fear clenched her stomach. She let out a shrill scream. From high above, Alice shouted something over the thunder, and then Madison was being lowered faster.

A new sound rose with the wind, a chorus of strange, guttural voices. Madison had heard the frog-talk before when it rained, how the Deep Ones sing to the Old Gods, but she only heard it from one creature at a time—not hundreds in unison. She felt bile rise in her throat and wanted more than anything to be inside the building, in her warm cot and dreaming away the rest of the night. She clenched her eyes shut and didn't open them for a long time.

When she finally opened her eyes, she glanced up and saw Alice waving frantically. Through the sickening amphibian song and the wind screeching all around her and the rain kicking up faster, she could make out a few select words— mainly *move* and *hurry.*

In front of her a dark rectangle led to an even darker room. She grabbed hold of the brick, and with every ounce of strength, hoisted herself onto the windowsill, putting her back against the glass. The lightning flared again and she saw herself in the glass, saw her long blonde hair and wide blue eyes that looked way too scared. The window was cracked in places and it took no strength at all to break with one well-placed kick. She climbed inside and planted her palms into something squishy.

The carpeting was soaking wet and felt like mud between her fingers. She couldn't see a thing besides basic shapes—the looming darkness of the hallway stretching in two directions on both sides and a crumbling wall directly in front of her. The smell was beyond horrible—fish and sawdust and mold.

She untied the rope and gave it a few tugs. The end of the rope flapped around like a restless snake and then lifted upward into the night air.

Madison ducked below the window and lit one of her candles with her lighter, protecting the flame with her body from the wind. She waited patiently, not moving a muscle until her friend arrived safely.

Finally, she heard labored breathing and noticed a shadow slip over to the window ledge. Alice crawled through and leaned against the wall, catching her breath. Then she untied the rope from around her waist and hugged Madison.

"I'm proud of you," Alice said. She set her pack down and lit a lantern. The light shone down the hallway like a small sun in a galaxy of dark doorways.

Alice noticed a piece of plastic on the wall holding a map. She wedged her knife behind the cover and pried until it shattered, then grabbed up the map inside and brought it into one of the offices, setting it down on a desk full of dust and dead flies. Although the paper was faded and had considerable water damage, it was still readable.

"See here?" Alice said. "It says *Fifth Floor Recovery Unit.* This is where people used to go to get better after surgery. I brought my daughter Lillian to a place like this, many years ago."

"Were there nurses here to take care of her?" Madison asked.

"Yes. They had nurses take care of her until she got better. She had cancer, Maddie. She lived a few more years."

"I'm sorry."

"That was a long time ago, before the waters rose and the Great Ocean covered the world. That was before people started worshipping the Old Gods and changing into the Deep

Ones."

Madison nodded in understanding. She knew of the Old Gods, but didn't understand much of the details. The women in Upper Eden weren't allowed to worship the Old Gods, for fear of the change coming upon them. The Chancellor had even allowed a Catholic service every Sunday in the cafeteria, although Madison hardly ever went. The hymns reminded her of going to church with her parents when she was younger. It always made her uncomfortable.

Alice pointed to the map. "Okay—we're right here, at the Janitor Station. There's a staircase on the other side of the floor, right next to the elevator shaft. We just need to find it."

"Do the stairs lead all the way down?"

"Almost. They lead to the second floor. An escalator in the lobby leads down to the first."

"That's a moving stairway, right?"

"That's right. But it doesn't move anymore."

"Oh."

"We need to move fast and quiet the whole way. If you hear anything, hide as quickly as you can. You still have that knife?"

Madison motioned to her boot, to the knife handle poking out.

"Good," Alice said. "Now let's get going."

***

Alice and Madison trudged through a maze of debris and dark hallways. High above, ceiling tiles were stained brown where rainwater had gushed through over the years. Twice they had to stop and wait for the rain to lessen, or else get drenched, possibly extinguishing their light. But they continued moving forward, winding through the crumbling corridors, using the lantern as their only source of illumination.

Madison was fine with the encroaching darkness surrounding her on all sides; she just wanted to get away from the frog-talk as soon as possible. The croaking had lessened considerably, but still, the thought of hundreds of Deep Ones chanting outside to some ancient god still creeped her out.

They traversed crumbling ceiling tiles and hopped over barricades made of concrete slabs and rebar. At one point a gigantic hole blocked their way, as if a bomb had detonated and tore through the carpeted floor. They found an alternate route through an abandoned cafeteria and continued onward.

After an hour of travel, the terrain became more hospitable, with less debris in their way, and with less dust peppering their lungs through each intake of breath. They quickened their pace and sped past hospital rooms containing bed frames and blood bags hanging from metal racks and looking like decaying jellyfish. They came to a gigantic hallway containing old desks and computers—a place Alice called a "Receptionist's Center." The entire wing of the hospital funneled toward the elevators at the opposite end of the hallway. A single closed doorway stood next to it.

Madison felt relieved. She was about to sprint toward the door, but Alice stopped her dead in her tracks. The young girl was so excited about finding the door that she didn't see what was right in front of her.

In the center of the hallway, stood a bed frame on wheels. Boards were propped horizontally on top and leather straps dangled from the sides. Dried blood and pieces of rotting meat covered the wood and straps. Flies buzzed around it in a dark pestilence. On the floor, a trail of blood led to a garbage chute in the wall. A metal lid was affixed firmly over the chute.

"What is it?" Madison asked.

Alice shook her head. "I don't know, Maddie."

Madison took a few steps closer to the strange contraption. The object looked like a portable chopping block—the kind used to clean fish for dinner, but much bigger.

To her right, moonlight slipped through an adjacent doorway. The smell emanating inside nearly caused Madison to throw up. But she held her breath and forced herself to move closer.

Alice followed her close behind, knife in hand.

Scattered throughout the room, a dozen bloated bodies

rested on beds, naked and hairless and with blistered skin starting to harden into scales. At first, Madison thought they were all dead, but then she noticed faint movement—lungs breathing, webbed fingers twitching. They were all hooked up to IV's. Somebody was keeping them alive.

The creatures were called hybrids by the girls in Upper Eden. The Chancellor and his advisors were perfect examples of this transformation; all three men were devout in their belief of the Old Gods, and one day hoped that Dagon would give them eternal life. To them it was a great reward to change into a Deep One and swim forever in the Great Ocean. To Madison it just seemed weird.

Alice put her hand on Madison's shoulder, guided her from the doorway to a corner in the hallway near a desk. "I think we're in danger," Alice said, shuttering the lantern until only a single slice of light trickled out.

"Did they see us?" Madison asked.

"I don't mean from the hybrids," she said, motioning to the room with the slumbering creatures. "They're in the Dreamlands, I think. This place looks well used, though. There's no dust anywhere."

"Oh. What are the Dreamlands?"

"The Dreamlands are a place full of ancient creatures that live beyond space and time. It serves as a testing ground for becoming a Deep One. Once the change progresses, you have to survive inside the dream for a set amount of time. The test ensures only the strongest survive their ascension and return to Earth."

Madison grew confused from some of Alice's words, but she understood the basics. "Oh," she said lightly under her breath.

"But don't worry—you can only travel to the Dreamlands if you're a believer, and you have to be on the verge of death to enter."

Madison decided to ask a question she'd wanted to ask Alice for a long time. "How come you haven't changed?"

Alice slipped her knife back into her boot and began

rummaging through her backpack. "Knowledge is different than belief, Maddie. I know about these things, but I choose to follow a different path—a different religion. I want more than anything to see my daughter in heaven, so I make that my reality."

"So, if I want to see my parents again, all I have to do is believe hard enough?"

"That's right," Alice said. "But remember—there are worse things in the world than Deep Ones. Especially those things that dwell between worlds and prey on your mind. No matter what, always remember who loves you, and who you love. That's all that matters in the end."

"Okay, I will."

Alice smiled brightly. Madison saw faint wrinkles around the corners of her eyes. She had never noticed the wrinkles before. Maybe because Alice seldom smiled.

Alice continued rifling through her backpack. She finally found what she was looking for and drew it out. Madison gasped.

A large revolver.

"Where did you get that?" Madison asked in amazement. She touched the firearm with her fingertips; it felt cold and strong.

"It's not important where I got it from," Alice said. "What matters is that I have it now." Alice opened up the gun and checked the bullets inside. Six shots.

Just then footsteps echoed down the hall. Alice shuttered the lantern fully and they both crouched underneath the computer desk, waiting.

Through a crack in the desk frame, Madison noticed two figures emerge from the doorway, each holding a lantern. They wore black robes. They stopped at the cutting board and unlocked what looked like a brake mechanism, then slid the frame closer to the room with the hybrids. Both of the cloaked figures disappeared inside for a short time, then re-emerged with one of the hybrids in tow. They placed it on top of the cart and inspected the body closely.

"No pulse," the taller figure said.

"May he join Father Dagon in the Great Ocean," the shorter figure answered. A woman's voice. From a leather satchel hanging from her side, she pulled out a curved knife and a hatchet. She handed the hatchet to her companion.

They began cutting.

Madison couldn't watch the butchery, so she turned away. The cutting and hacking sounds made her feel sick, so she glanced at Alice and held the older woman's hand. In the dim light, she saw Alice watching the hooded figures intently, her face set in a grimace.

The figures stopped when more footsteps thundered down the hallway. Someone was running. Madison resumed watching.

A third figure came into view. Madison recognized the newcomer—one of the Chancellor's Advisors, a man named Lawrence. He was dark-skinned and always dressed in camouflage. He had the same sloped forehead as the Chancellor.

"The Chancellor's dead!" Lawrence blurted out.

"What?" the woman said.

"He was stabbed to death!"

"Who did it?" she commanded.

"Someone named Alice, we think. She stabbed him and took one of the younger girls. I have the others out looking for them. We're still trying to figure out how they escaped."

"Is this woman a breeder?"

"No, she wasn't able to conceive. She's just a worker. The younger girl will soon be of age."

The woman thought for a moment, then spoke. "We'll summon a Hunter to track them down." She turned to her companion, the tall male still holding the hatchet. "Dispose of the remains and join us downstairs. We need to prepare."

He nodded to her. "As you command."

Lawrence and the woman hurried toward the doorway and then were gone. The lone figure wheeled the cart over to the garbage chute and threw the dead hybrid's remains inside. When he finished, he moved the cart back to the hallway and locked the wheel mechanism in place, then grabbed up his lantern and hatchet and exited through the doorway.

The door slid shut in a whisper.

***

"What did he mean the Chancellor was killed? Madison asked after the cloaked figure had left.

Alice sat on top of the desk and tinkered with the lantern shutters. "I stabbed him when I left, Madison. He deserved it—more than you know. His Advisors deserve it, too. I hope they all burn in hell."

"Oh." Madison didn't ask anything further.

As soon as Alice fixed the lantern, they walked cautiously past the room with the sleeping hybrids and scooted around the bed frame coated with fresh blood. Madison batted at a swarm of flies and held her nose from the smell. She thought about prying the garbage chute open and glancing down to see where they had disposed of the remains, but decided against it. She didn't want to know.

Alice stopped in front of the door near the elevators and listened. No sounds. She opened the door, and it swung open on well-oiled hinges. A rush of humid air greeted them, harboring the smell of fish and saltwater.

Madison followed Alice down a concrete staircase. At the second floor the stairs ended in a brick wall and another door, just like the map depicted. Alice opened the door, and they both peered down a lit hallway.

Before Madison could even take in the setting before her, she heard chanting. Her heart beat faster, and she grew deathly afraid. She thought about running back up the stairs and away from the horrible voices, but when she looked back up at the staircase, all that greeted her was silence and an impenetrable darkness. For some reason it scared her even more.

She swallowed hard and forced herself to enter the hallway. Lanterns were strung along the walls and vines covered the sides, dislodging ceiling tiles and wrapping around rafters. Strange bulbs grew from the ends of the vines, like closed flower petals, but much bigger and with blue veins that shimmered in changing hues. Madison thought she saw the vines shifting just slightly as they shuffled past, but she knew it was just her imagination playing tricks on her. Vines didn't move like that.

"We're gonna try to slip by them," Alice said. "They're doing some sort of magic spell. They said something about summoning a Hunter to try and find us."

"What's a Hunter?"

"I don't know."

"Can't you just shoot the fuckers?" As soon as Madison said this, she covered her mouth instinctively. The Chancellor had never liked any of his girls swearing, so she always did it in her head. But to Madison, it felt good to say it out loud for a change. She wanted to say it a hundred times.

"Guns draw attention," Alice answered. "But don't worry—if sneaking doesn't work, then I'll shoot the fuckers. Every one of them."

They glanced in a few of the office rooms that contained beds, desks, and old books with strange runes on the covers. Alice led Madison inside one of the rooms and handled one of the books, flipping through the pages one at a time.

One picture depicted a being with a face like a starfish crouched in a house of pillars far beneath the ocean. It had a strange name, one that Madison couldn't even come close to pronouncing. Alice continued to page through the book, stopping at a picture showing a cloaked figure holding up a baby to an altar while the night sky depicted stars shifting into alignment.

"What is it?" Madison asked. "What are they doing?"

"They're killing children, Maddie. That's why we were brought here after the floods. We were brought here to breed children for their rituals."

Alice threw the book down on the desk. She looked like she wanted to rip it to shreds, but she forced herself to walk away.

They continued back outside and made their way down

the hallway, past offices that had been turned into living quarters, checking each one to make sure they were empty. The chanting grew louder as they walked.

Soon they arrived at a large entrance with a motionless escalator leading down to the main floor. Alice blew out her lantern and placed it inside her backpack. They both crouched behind the wood railing and peered down.

In the center of the ground floor, a dozen cloaked figures prepared a ritual, all standing in a circle. Runes were chiseled into the floor, depicting strange patterns. Sandbags were set up along the sides, preventing the water from rising and flooding the floor. The storm had passed outside and moonlight struggled through the windows. It looked like it would be morning soon.

"What now?" Madison whispered.

"We're going to wait until they leave. Hopefully it'll be light by then."

"What if they come up the stairs?"

"Then we'll hide in one of the rooms and make a run for it when they walk by."

Madison didn't know how long they sat waiting, but it felt like hours. Finally, the morning sun filtered through the windows, and the air grew warmer. The chanting kept going the whole time, but flipped an octave lower and gained in resonance.

As Madison sat with her back against the railing, feeling the strange song wash over her in a vile seduction, she saw Alice's eyes suddenly grow wide.

Madison peeked over the railing. She wanted to see, too.

The cult had thrown back their hoods, showing scaly flesh and sloped foreheads and no hair. In the center of the summoning circle, a wind swirled like a miniature tornado. It changed hues, into every color of a rainbow, and then all the colors mixed together and became as black as tar. Madison didn't know what she was looking at, but she knew something was crossing over, and it was growing bigger, with a body like oil, and with bulbous eyes and long tentacles.

As she watched, Madison felt a wave of fear set in. She

closed her eyes and covered her ears and quietly hummed a song to herself. But it didn't work. Again, the thought of running hit her, and she started to stand, but Alice grabbed her arms and pulled her down to the floor, hard.

"Don't run," Alice said through clenched teeth.

Madison collected herself and continued to watch them summon the strange creature from some dark abyss. The cult chanted a strange word over and over again—*Shoggoth*. Then one of them dragged a man near the others. Madison didn't recognize him. He was old and haggard, his hands bounds. The female leader grabbed him by his beard and jerked his chin toward the ceiling, then unsheathed the same curved blade she had used upstairs. She held the blade to his throat. Just as she was about to slice his neck, sacrificing him to their sadistic ritual, thunder went off inside the building, right over Madison's head.

Madison's ears instantly started ringing. She glanced up and saw Alice holding the gun in outstretched hands. Smoke dispersed from the long barrel.

Outside the circle, one of the cultists had fallen over and twitched on the ground. After that, everything happened quickly.

Alice was suddenly halfway down the escalator. She fired again. And then again. The leader shouted something about continuing the ritual, but then froze, seeing the blood from her twitching brethren enter the summoning circle.

"Wait!" the leader cried in a normal language, rushing over and trying to soak up the blood with her sleeves. "We want you to hunt humans, not us! Not the Order of Dagon!"

But it was too late. The creature they had called a *Shoggoth* attacked.

Madison didn't know what to do when the screaming started. Her feet were planted firmly in place. She heard Alice yelling at her to run, but she couldn't move a muscle. And then her friend was back up the stairs and pushing her down the escalator. They sprinted across the floor toward the main door.

Madison heard a strange sound and ducked just as a body

flung clear across the room. It was the bound prisoner. She heard the sound of bones breaking when he landed. Then she was jumping over the sandbags just as three more shots went off. Glancing back, she saw the creature slither toward the cult leader. The woman was about to run, but a dark tentacle wrapped around her and squeezed, and her insides became her outsides. Her knife clattered to the ground. Others screamed and tried to flee, but the monstrosity caught them all, one by one.

Madison didn't want to see any more. She ran as fast she could, with Alice close behind. Then she was outside with the cool wind against her face. She rushed down the concrete steps toward the water.

The tide had lowered.

***

The boat had moved downriver during the night. It was now wedged inside the front window of a submerged car, the stern kicking up to the sky.

"There!" Madison said, pointing. "I see the boat!"

Alice threw the empty gun away and waded into the current. Madison followed closely behind, feeling the cold water stab at her legs, numbing her body in waves.

They made their way along the side of the hospital, moving as quickly as they could, checking each step carefully. But the current proved too strong for Madison. She slipped and went under. Strong hands gripped the back of her dress, wrenching her up.

"Be careful!" Alice shouted. "Hold on to my jacket!"

Madison held Alice tightly, and they continued moving forward, until they were crawling on top of a submerged car and catching their breath. Overhead, the sunlight struggled through the fleeting storm clouds. The warmth felt good on Madison's face.

"We just need to make it to the next car," Alice said. "Stab anything that tries to get you."

Madison had forgotten all about her knife. She slid it from

out of her boot and held the blade tightly in both hands, then nodded that she was ready.

They slipped back into the water and traveled fifty paces, to a crooked telephone pole caked with algae and mud. The boat was much closer now, only twenty paces away. Madison was about to ask Alice a question when a splash startled her. She glanced behind her. Alice was gone.

Madison screamed for her friend, but there was no answer. She was just about to dive under the water and look for herself, when Alice suddenly resurfaced, her chest bleeding from deep claw marks.

"Keep moving," Alice said, coughing. She held her chest tightly, blood trickling through her fingers and staining the water.

They traveled until the current went over Madison's head. She stood on her tip toes, angling her nose to the sky, but it wasn't enough. She went under and coughed and swallowed water. The knife drifted out of her hand, lost forever in the current. But then Alice was there, grabbing her up and cradling the girl her in her arms. She lifted Madison high in the air and placed her on top of the car roof.

They were at their destination.

Madison jumped into action and began wrenching the boat free from the damaged windshield. Alice helped, standing in the water, keeping an eye out for more attackers. The boat was a little bigger than Madison had previously thought—maybe seven feet long. But they would both fit inside just fine.

They finally wrenched the boat free. With their combined strength, they stabilized the craft in the current. Madison threw her pack inside and crawled in. Alice was about to jump inside as well, but something bumped into her and she lashed out with her knife, nearly setting the boat adrift.

"You have to go on without me," Alice said, straining to hold the boat in place. The muscles in her arms and neck began bulging from the tension. She looked like she was in a lot of pain.

"Wait—you can't!" Madison began.

"I'm bleeding, Maddie. They can smell it on me. They'll chase us through the whole goddamned city."

"But you have to come with me!"

"I love you, Maddie. I love you as much as my own daughter. Now get going and don't stop. Don't ever stop."

Alice released the boat.

Madison screamed, and tried to stop the boat, but the current caught hold and flung her downstream. She glanced back just in time to see Alice crawl on top of the car hood. Then she saw the Deep Ones attack—first one, then two, then a dozen. Alice lashed out with her weapon many times in a violent frenzy. Blood and severed limbs splattered the water.

Madison's thudded against another vehicle and stopped moving, momentarily. The bow of the boat dipped and water began rushing inside. If she didn't push off and continue moving, the water would submerge the small vessel.

Madison knew what she had to do. Grabbing up her gear, she hefted it over her shoulder and was about to jump out, leaving the boat to suffer its own fate. But when she glanced back, all she saw were Deep Ones swarming over the vehicle like mutated rats escaping a flood.

Alice wasn't there anymore.

***

Madison floated for three days throughout the ruins of the city. Once in a while something struck the bottom of the boat, but the vessel never capsized. There was a small leak near the seam, and she had to bail out water every few hours. But it didn't bother her. It gave her something to look forward to.

Eventually the days stretched into a week, and the constant sun on her body made her lightheaded. The river widened into a vast sea, and she found herself in the Great Ocean.

She knew she needed to get out of the sun, or else she would become dehydrated. So she propped up her jacket with branches fished out of the water and made a makeshift lean-to. Every morning she boiled water with the candles, breathing in the vapors to avoid dehydration. The salt collected on the bottom of the tin cup in tiny crystals, and she tapped it out into the water. She ate her food until there was nothing left.

Once, a storm hit and nearly tipped her over. But she remained steadfast and rode out the wind and rain, always watching the horizon for any signs of life, of land, of anything. Sometimes the Deep Ones swam past her in a collection of ripples, as if they were a school of fish. But they never attacked. She didn't know why, but she assumed they must have thought the boat was a piece of driftwood and decided to leave it alone.

After two weeks she began feeling tired more often. At night she stared up at the sky, at all the stars looking like tiny holes in the night. And then she looked past the lights, at the heavens beyond the far reaches of space. She thought about her parents and wondered if they were waiting for her. She also thought about Alice.

Once, when she looked into the water, she could see her best friend just below the surface, her dark hair billowing in the waves, her clothes torn and bloody. Madison tried to rescue her by reaching down into the water, but Alice sank out of reach, gone forever. Madison cried and yelled for her friend to come back. But Alice never did.

Then one day Madison jerked awake and felt something covering her body. She realized she hadn't bailed out the water in a very long time. But she didn't care anymore. She could barely move, could barely think straight. The boat lurched and began to sink just as she managed to pull herself up and glance over the side.

To her amazement, she had arrived at the edge of the world.

The boat jettisoned over a gigantic waterfall. Instead of falling, the boat glided through the sky like a midnight dove, weightless and free. She reached out her hand and touched the stars and planets with her fingertips, smeared them like acrylics across canvas. The sky distorted in ripples and smoothed back out into glass.

Throughout the spectacle, she began hearing the frog-talk echoing to her like a long-forgotten dream, beckoning her to join them. A staircase materialized out of obscurity, cloaked in mist and shadows, looming before her in monolithic proportions.

But Madison didn't fall for it. She remembered Alice's words, which now seemed like years ago, and she fought against the siren song, resisted the temptation to join them in their strange world. She concentrated on her mother and father instead. She concentrated on Alice.

Immediately the staircase rolled back into the mist and was gone. The amphibian song dissipated, and Madison's vision shifted back to the night stars spread out in front of her like glass.

She was back in her boat, sinking.

The waves pressed down on her chest and drew her breath out in gasps. But she didn't care anymore. She welcomed it this time. She held her arms open wide, like a child waiting for the loving embrace of a parent, and as the boat sank slowly beneath the waves, she felt her soul lift higher and higher and jettison throughout the cosmos like a rocket ship exploding through distant galaxies.

Familiar voices called out to her, guiding her like beacons in the night sky. The voices became stronger and everything shifted around her in a kaleidoscope of colors; it changed from the watery night spotted with stars to a summer field full of sunshine and dandelions.

She was finally free. And then she was running home, quickly.

SURVIVING THE RIVER STYX

Paul Michael Anderson

Even doped-up, Riley knew getting on an ocean liner wasn't a logical extension of immersion therapy.

His view was a pastel panorama that ran like tie-dye. Far off in the bay, the ocean liner *Queen Victoria III* squatted like a marshmallow in the steel-wool Atlantic. Voices washed over him, a meaningless tidal roar, pressing him further into the wheelchair. His arm tingled where Dr. Hogan injected him. Nothing else did, though. All numb.

Andrea and Hogan stood elongated before him, the only clear things on the crowded dock. The curls of Riley's wife's hair were rusted horseshoes; Hogan's beard a writhing hive of ants. Andrea's eyes twinkled and Riley tried to remember the last time that had happened. Before the trouble with his company, surely.

His eyes moved slowly over the ocean liner. Each incision of the various decks transformed the ship into rows of gleaming teeth. The boat that would take them to the liner bounced over the grey waves, approaching, and vertigo bloomed like a flower in the center of Riley's head. All that water.

Surrounded by all that water.

His heart pounded enough to make him hiccup.

I can't do this! How can they expect me to do this?

Riley heard a scream. He passed out before he could tell if it was him or someone else.

***

Unconscious, he felt calm; he felt *himself.* He was everything he knew Riley Christopher McCarrick, millionaire

451

software whiz-kid, to be. The quaking ruin that reality thrust upon him—too scared to be in the shower for longer than five minutes, cringing if an errant raindrop smacked his face—was banished.

Sound began to filter in, growing louder as the darkness lightened. The sounds smoothed, separated into Andrea's and Hogan's voices.

Andrea: "Can't believe how long security took."

Hogan: "Be glad they didn't take us back to the port."

"That guy tried to rip someone's throat out with his *teeth*."

A sound of a hand across fabric. Hogan rubbing Andrea's back? Riley's stomach tightened. When was the last time Andrea had allowed *him* to do that? "The man's gone. An isolated incident." A dry chuckle that sounded like dead leaves rattling. "Maybe he was aquaphobic, too."

Why is that funny? Riley thought.

Soft footsteps, then Andrea said, "He's waking up, Derek."

How do you know his name?

Hogan's said, loudly, "Are you with us, Riley?"

He opened his eyes, and Hogan's face hovered just inches above him. Riley cringed. Hogan stepped away.

"Are you okay?" Andrea asked. She stood beside the bed on his left.

"How are you feeling?" Hogan asked. He pulled an unmarked vial of piles from his blazer pocket.

Riley ignored him. Their cabin was standard mid-level hotel fare...just on the water. A sliding door led to the balcony on the right, covered by a near-sheer curtain. The smudge-line of the horizon peeked in, and he turned away, his stomach a ball of discomfort. *Who in his right mind puts a man phobic of water...?*

Hogan cleared his throat and nudged one of Riley's fists with a glass of water until Riley took it.

"How long was I out?" Riley asked.

"Roughly six hours. We've been at sea for four."

Silence fell, the kind of silence no one wants to break. Hogan watched him. Riley watched his hand gripping the glass until his knuckles whitened.

"What are you thinking?" Andrea asked.

Riley frowned. "I'm thinking who in their right mind puts a man afraid of water on an ocean liner?"

"Now, Riley, you're not afraid of *water*," Hogan said, his voice smooth and quick. You could tell he'd said this kind of thing before. "This is stress, exacerbating a *pseudo*-fear of open water. Your aquaphobia is nothing but smoke-and-mirrors. I'm trying to help you remember what's *really* important in life—"

"Shut up." Riley swung his feet out over the side of the bed and forced himself to stand. Lightheadedness smacked him and he planted his feet. "What's the term you're always throwing around— *'obfuscate'*? *Excellent* word. You're obfuscating the point. Who in their *right mind* puts a *man afraid of water on a goddamn cruise?*"

Hogan and Andrea retreated towards the alcove.

"You're obviously excited," Hogan said. He shook the pills. "Perhaps you need—"

"Get out."

"Maybe later." Hogan set the vial down on the desk. "But, really—"

"OUT!" Riley hurled the glass. Hogan and Andrea ducked, and the cup exploded against the far wall.

Hogan flung open the door and dashed out, Andrea at his heels. In the hallway, a man in a white button-down shirt sprinted past, his face a pale, shocked blur.

Riley slumped against the wall, dizziness slamming his stomach into a blender. *I can do this. I can do this.*

His gaze fell upon the vial on the desk, and he didn't know what he hated more—Hogan, the ocean, or how much he wanted those pills.

***

If he didn't look outside, his nausea and vertigo were dim annoyances. He'd taken a pill, hating himself for it, but it had slowed him down, calmed him. The pill wasn't as powerful as the shot Hogan had given him, but he thought if he took more than one at a time, it could be.

His eyes fell upon his things scattered across the bedspread, among them an issue of *Wired* with him on the cover. THE FIRST STAR TO FALL? Read the caption. *Riley McCarrick's Omega Systems the First Casualty of the New Global Economy?*

His fists clenched, his trim nails digging into the palms. He barely felt it.

Riley hadn't needed Hogan to tell him that his aquaphobia stemmed from stress, which fed on the control he lacked at work and home. It was all pop-psychobabble. What Riley needed was help *controlling* it.

Hogan began mentioning a cruise after a year of everything continuing to spiral out of control. Andrea had been for it from the beginning, showing an enthusiasm he hadn't seen in years. She'd called it a second honeymoon, a chance for renewal. He'd felt tag-teamed.

Why would they do this? A part reasoned. *Andrea could be spiteful, but you* pay *Hogan.*

Andrea might be paying him more, and maybe not in cash. Paranoid, but she knew Hogan's name when Riley had never told her. Hogan had rubbed her back when she barely let Riley near her anymore.

The cover smiled at him, a photo from before Omega went public, and his wife didn't hate him. He sneered and smacked it aside. The movement brought the vertigo back, and he sat down on the edge of the bed, breathing through his mouth. He could imagine the ship heaving this way.

"Fool," he muttered, and made himself straighten. He spied the vial of pills—unmarked, of course, my dear Watson, what better to enhance the delusions of the victim?—on the edge of the desk, and picked it up, rolling it in his hand. He'd already had one, and more might invite another acid-trip fever dream, but what did he care? He didn't know how long this cruise was. Andrea—ah, and the delusion grows roots, Watson—had set it up.

He thumbed the cap off and shook two out, setting the vial

down. The tiny white pills looked so innocent. *Alice ate the cake that read EAT ME, and down the rabbit hole she went.*

He dry-swallowed the pills.

***

The colors popped, the sound of the ocean was in time with his pulse, and he didn't know if he was asleep when the knocking started, or if he just became aware of it. It was too crisp and professional to be anyone but room service—had he ordered food? Had Andrea, working like Oz far and away, ordered it?

The knocking continued, forever and ever, world without end, amen, chunky peanut butter.

Christ, just leave the food at the door. When he was hungry, he ate pills. Didn't they understand that?

He stumbled into the alcove and nearly flattened his face into the wall. Whoopsie. Who knew they offered plastic surgery cruises? Captain, I wish to flatten this nose of mine. Money is no object. Just ask Andrea, the Great and Terrible Invisible Wife of Oz.

He slid towards the door and fell against it, pawing the handle until he could stick his head out.

The clerk on the other side looked how Riley felt; hair a crow's nest, dark bags bulging under red-ringed eyes that cut to the left and right, a mouth that twisted and writhed, two-parts sour grin, one-part anxiety.

"I don't want any food," he said. That's what he *thought* he said, anyway.

The clerk's mouth quivered like a sound wave. "So you *haven't* eaten, sir?"

"No," Riley said. "You and Andrea gonna force-feed me? Me no hungry. You go away."

He thought he heard a scream and started to dismiss it, until he saw the clerk cringe.

That was real, he thought. The hair on the back of his neck stood on end.

"Very well, sir," the clerk with the dancing mouth said.

"We've been having some issues with...food poisoning...and we wanted to make sure everyone had eaten." He shook his head. *"What* everyone had eaten. Excuse me." He looked like he wanted to giggle.

It wasn't the clerk's eyes staring at him, but the clerk's Bozo the Clown grin. Riley couldn't look away from it. That scream, he wanted to say, aren't you supposed to check on things like that?

"Me no hungry," Riley repeated, pulling his head back in. "You go away." He closed the door and latched it.

He thought the clerk might've yelled, "Everyone must *eat*, sir!" but another scream went off--or *maybe* went off. Riley was out of the alcove, and his pulse had again fallen into rhythm with the ocean current. That's the key to fear—become it. Like Batman. His blood was one with the ocean.

His eyes fell upon the vial of pills. His friends. Counting them individually—even pairs!—along with his buddies' vertigo and nausea, he had quite the shindig on his hands.

"Party down," he muttered, scooping up another two pills. He dry-swallowed them.

His feet tripped over themselves and he fell onto the bed. *The comfiest rabbit hole ever,* he thought, and passed out.

***

This time, knocking *did* wake him up, but it was not the ever-professional, ever-consistent knock of room service, but a drunken wham.

"Riley!" Andrea's voice, a near-scream. *"Riley, open up!"*

He fell off the bed, his arms and legs freshly-stitched parts of him he could barely control. *Just call me Raggedy Andy.*

"Riley, please!"

He knee-walked into the alcove. Gone was the acid-trip fever dream, but his thoughts were cotton candy, teased apart and spinning in the churn.

"Riley!"

He used the handle to heave himself up, threw himself against the door to keep his balance, and looked through the peephole.

Andrea leaned against the door, her hair a mess, mascara raccoon-circles around her shocked, red-ringed eyes. In the distorted fisheye, she looked like an alien, a nightmare *E.T.* The strap of her evening gown had fallen into the crook of her elbow and one breast, shockingly pale, was exposed. A bloody handprint painted the nipple. He couldn't see her hands.

"The Great and Terrible Invisible Wife of Oz!" he cried. "How in the hell are ya?"

She flattened her face against the peephole. "Lemme in, Riley! It's dangerous out here!"

"Which is why *I* am in here, partying down."

Her exhale fogged the peephole and he frowned. "You have to help me!"

Anger, an old, forgotten part of him, flickered in the back of his head. "Like you're helping me, right? Right, Wife of Oz?"

She pounded at the door with her invisible hands. Did he hear metal clang? Was she a cyborg? *"Help me, you bastard!"*

"Show me your hands."

She didn't move.

"Show me, you bitch!"

She threw herself off the door and weaved on her feet like a boxer about to drop. She didn't raise her hands, but she didn't need to.

She held a carving knife, bloody and dripping. "Let me in!" she cried. "People are attacking out here!"

Riley, frowning, pushed himself away. "Should've picked a better cruise. Go away."

Andrea pounded and kicked at the door. *"You bastard! Let me in! LEMME IN RIGHT NOW!"*

"Not by the hair on my chinny-chin-chin."

He fell against the wall, but didn't feel nearly stoned enough. It was still night, the lights were on, but the colors were dull, washed with gray. Vertigo and nausea had flown the coop. Where were his friends?

He went to his knees next to the desk, knocking the open

vial over, and spilling pills across the top.

Andrea shrieked and pounded. *"LEMME IN! I'LL KILL YOU, RILEY! LEMME IN LEMME IN LEMME IN!"*

Riley scooped a handful of pills into his mouth and swallowed. *What a dull party, really.* For good measure, he scooped and swallowed another handful.

"HEARTLESS BASTARD! UNFEELING PRICK!"

Darkness clouded his vision. *I feel nothing,* he agreed and fell onto his face.

***

A scream forced him awake and what felt like spun glass in all his joints forced him to scream back.

He clawed his way to the bed and thrashed himself slowly into a sitting position. He felt like he'd fought World War II, both theaters, single-handedly. His skull pulsed, heavy whams against his forehead and ears. The crotch of his jeans was bunched and cool against his skin. He'd pissed himself at some point.

His sightline met the surface of the desk, where he saw the empty vial and three lonely pills.

He massaged his forehead. "Did I fuckin' take *all* of that? How am I not dead?" He looked underneath the desk and saw a pile of crusty puke. Well, that explained *that*.

How long had he been out? The gap in the drapes, cold grey daylight fought for space against the nightstand lamps. It could've been hours. Or days.

Why was he up now, then?

Another scream erupted outside, distant, and he remembered.

He used the desk to pull himself to his feet and shambled into the alcove, a hand on the wall for balance. He collapsed against the door with a grunt and looked through the peephole.

The body of an elderly man lay in a pool of blood against the opposite wall of the hallway.

Riley jerked away from the door, the migraine shoved forcefully onto the backburner. "Christ!"

He rubbed his eye with the heel of his hand and looked again.

Same image.

He was shivering as he opened the door, but couldn't stop.

The old man looked as if he'd once had a face, but what was left resembled something shoved into a Mixmaster. This guy hadn't screamed recently. The blood he lay in had dried.

How can you be cold? A part of him scolded. *This is a body, for God's sake!*

He looked down the hall. Doors marched away to his left and right, dwindling to points on the horizon. Blood smeared the walls, dried to brown smears.

He was the only living thing in sight. The only sound was his leaden heart and shallow breath.

"Jesus," he muttered.

He stepped back inside, closed the door and went to the room phone. According to the directory, just picking up the phone connected it to the front desk.

He got nothing but dead air. He hit zero for the operator and the line rang and rang. He dropped the phone back into the cradle and didn't bother fixing it when it landed askew.

His mind wanted to drift to the corpse, and he forced it to stop. He had to think.

Where had everyone gone? Who was screaming and why hadn't anyone done something about the old man?

There's no one to *do something.*

He remembered the nightmare clerk saying people were suffering from food poisoning, and that he should eat.

He remembered Andrea, blood-streaked and raving, pounding on the door. Dream or real? Live or *Memorex*?

The body outside isn't Memorex, he thought.

What if everyone's *gone? What if they're all dead? Who's driving the ship?*

"Bullshit," he muttered.

You have to find someone.

His shivering worsened. How could he leave this for... *that*? He hugged himself, but the shivering didn't lessen.

If there's no one here, who's controlling the ship?

The potential answer—*no one*—made him shiver harder.

No, he couldn't stay here, if only to find out what *was* happening.

He changed into clean clothes, shutting his mind down, working on automatic. He forced himself back into the hall, checking the number on the door as he left. 9.040, the brass plate read. He hadn't even known what his room number had been.

He turned left, following a sign which stated that he was on DECK 9 and that elevators were this way. The silence reminded him of libraries. The carpet so thick, his footfalls were silent. Nothing but the roar of his own blood in his temples.

He came to an open door two rooms down—9.036—and made himself stop.

"Hello?" He flicked the switch plate on the left. Peeking out from around the corner were feet. He entered, recognizing the shoes, and thought of Andrea again.

He looked around and the air left him. "Jesus."

Andrea lay sprawled on the floor between the bed and the bathroom, the skirt of her evening gown hiked up to reveal cotton panties. Her head, smeared with blood, was cocked up and away.

Hogan's open mouth lay on her torn throat. Riley could see purple-gray intestine underneath his shirtless belly. The bloody carving knife lay nearby. The coppery stink of spilled blood and dried shit clogged his nose.

People are attacking out here, she'd said before screaming that she'd kill him. His eyes falling on the knife to avoid the view of the mutual murder, he thought, couldn't *help* thinking, *If I'd opened the door...*

He bolted and leaned against the hallway wall, closing his eyes. His stomach threatened, threatened...but didn't have anything to throw up. He coughed, his spit thick and disgusting, and slumped against the wall.

I don't think Andrea expected this, he thought and clapped his hands to his mouth to stifle the scream.

Breathe. Calm down. You can do this. He didn't believe that—how much could he do if he'd almost overdosed like an idiot on pills?—but it calmed the scream that wanted to jump from his mouth. Who knew who might hear?

He looked longingly down the hall, back toward his room, but it didn't even have the comfort of familiarity for him.

The rabbit hole spit me back out, he thought.

***

He came across the body of a boy of nine sprawled in an open doorway further down. His eyes had been gouged out, leaving bloody sockets crying blood. Riley glanced behind him, sure that the eye-gouger was creeping forward with bloody fingers, but he had the hallway to himself. His pulse was its own raging ocean current.

Suites named after English Queens met him at the end. Just before these was an archway opening to the stairway and lifts. Inside, another archway led to the opposite hallway, but he had no interest in seeing *that* carnage. He considered taking a lift, but God knew what he might find in them.

The ship was silent. He didn't even hear the piped-in Muzak that a lot of hotels played in the hallway. It was just his breathing, his heartbeat. His sign of life. He wondered how many rooms there were, how many people in them, all of them as silent as the old man and the little boy. His wife. Dr. Hogan.

Riley turned towards the expansive, carpeted stairs. He kept his eyes glued forward as he descended, his shoulder brushing the far wall.

The body of a young, blonde clerk lay sprawled on the landing of Deck 8, his chest cavity opened up like a peapod, his insides bulging against the ragged edges, and Riley stopped on the last few stairs.

Unlike the old man, the clerk's blood hadn't dried into the carpet.

If Riley touched him, his body would not be cold.

He glanced behind him. There was nothing up there.

He came down slowly, eyes cutting to the archways. A fire-axe lay against the bottom step, the blade wetly smeared with pieces of the clerk.

The spit in his mouth felt viscous and snotty. He swallowed, but it didn't help. He needed a weapon, but, Jesus, what if the handle was still warm from whoever had killed the clerk?

Stop the weak-sister routine and take it, a part of him chided. He crouched down, his fingertips touching wood, and his hand curled around the axe. Something wet fell off and landed with a squish.

He closed his eyes. His stomach would never forgive him.

A scream erupted, high and yodeling from the left hallway, then cut off abruptly. A cackling laugh followed it. His testicles shrunk into tight little balls.

Having a weapon didn't mean he wanted to use it. He went down the next flight two at a time, not looking back.

***

He didn't bother with the rest of the rooming floors. Although he saw no more bodies, he heard running footsteps and jerky panting. He didn't want to meet their owners. He thought of all those bodies, and his mind wanted to shut down. How? *How?*

On Deck 3, someone's bellowing roar enveloped him, and the stairwell ended with a hallway curving right. He inched forward, the sound boxing his ears, wrapped him in an audio cocoon. His skin tightened with gooseflesh. He felt like every idiot in every horror movie who goes deeper into the haunted house, but what other choice did he have?

The hallway curved outward, until he imagined it reached the perimeter of the ship. He could imagine the waves crashing into him, separating only by steel and insulation.

Keep your mind off that. You have bigger concerns. Understatement of the still-fresh millennium.

The hallway curved inward again, and the bellow grew louder in volume, but maintained pitch and tone, the words distorted nearly to fare-thee-well. A recording.

Near the end, someone had written with blood-smeared hands I LOVE YOU over and over along the wall. A body with a great chunk of throat torn away lay beneath this declaration. *I'm on the ship of the dead. This isn't the Atlantic. It's the River Styx.* Not surprisingly, this didn't make him feel any better.

The hallway opened up onto the oval-shaped Grand Lobby. The marble floors were awash with blood and bodily fluids. Torn bodies lay in piles. Some draped the circular front desk in the center like trophies. Who could've done this? A part of his mind screamed, but the bigger question was, still, *how* could someone—or someones, since a group made infinitely more sense—do this? The stench was like Hogan and Andrea, jacked to the tenth degree.

The other end of the Grand Lobby led into a shop concourse. On the left of the hallway was a darkened wine bar called Sir Elliot's. Bar stools littered the opening. On the right was a trashed newsstand.

The recording boomed from hidden speakers.

"...YOUR LUXURIANT VACATIONS," the voice bellowed. Static obliterated its sex. *"WHILE MILLIONS STARVE AND DIE UNDER WESTERN IMPERIALISM, YOU FILL YOUR FACE WITH FOOD ON BILLION-DOLLAR ROWBOATS. HOW DOES IT TASTE NOW? HOW—"*

Feedback screamed and Riley screamed with it. The recording died, and the silence deafened him with its completeness. He looked around, as if to see why the recording had ended. His heartbeat echoed in the stillness.

A diminutive man in a chef's smock staggered out of the wine bar, meat cleaver in hand, and Riley froze. Blood stained his hairy arms to the elbow. His red-ringed eyes twinkled.

"Messy," he said conversationally. He sprinted forward, raising the cleaver. *"Messy, messy, MESSY! NO WAY TO SERVE CUISINE! NOT AT ALL!"*

The man brought the cleaver down, and Riley thrust the axe out, blade turned away, as if he were bunting. The axe-head crashed against the man's inner forearm. The impact drove the cook backward.

Riley swung the side of the axe, and it slammed into the side of the man's face with enough force to vibrate up Riley's arms. The man's eyes rolled up into his head, and he dropped with a grain sack thud, the meat cleaver clattering.

Riley staggered into the front desk. The axe shook in his hands. His breath hitched in and out of his mouth. "Oh shit, oh Jesus, oh hell."

He couldn't remember the last physical confrontation he'd had, probably not since he was a teenager, and adrenaline skimmed through his blood, his nerves flashing like Christmas lights.

Anger filled him. This was ridiculous. This was all...so... *ridiculous.* This...this *wasn't right.* What in hell's name had happened here?

"Hey!" he screamed. His voice echoed back, and that only made him angrier. This was an *ocean liner,* for God's sake. *"Anyone here? Where are you? C'mon! WHERE THE FUCK ARE YOU?"*

"Everyone's dead," a woman said behind him. "Or insane."

He spun, and the boy and girl, maybe six, cringed behind the woman's legs. Their eyes ate up their pale, cherubic faces. The woman stared at him, a hand on the backs of their heads, fingers smoothing their blonde hair.

"We'd been hiding in the newsstand." Her dark hair shined in the lobby light. Blood smeared her summer dress. "He'd been looking for us."

"What *happened* here?"

"Don't you know?" she asked. Her eyes shined with shock, but weren't red-ringed. Was that how you could tell? He thought of the clerk, Andrea, this cook.

He lowered the axe. "I was...sick."

"Have you eaten anything?" Her tone added weight to the question.

He shook his head. "I haven't eaten since..." He looked at her. "...how long have we been at sea? I was unconscious. I..."

He looked away. "...I don't handle water too well."

She studied him, and he couldn't meet her eyes. "We've been at sea for five days. It started getting bad the second day." *I'm a drugged Rip Van Winkle.* "Was this an attack?"

She shrugged, a frustrated gesture. "I guess so. They did it through the meals." She shook her head. "God, you're the first person we've seen who's still sane."

"I'm Riley."

"Sheila." She looked down. "This is Dylan and Sara. I don't know where their parents are. I couldn't leave them, though."

Riley nodded. "What do you want to do?"

Sheila's face screwed up into a strange expression. "Everyone's dead and nothing's steering this monster except maybe a boat version of autopilot. The *only* thing to do is get off."

***

They went back into the newsstand while Riley kept lookout. His chest felt decidedly hollow as the main question hovered over him: *How can I get off?*

When they returned, Sheila's hands held onto the children and two bulging plastic bags.

"How can we leave?" he asked, taking one of the bags. He opened it—bottles of water, single-serving packages of pretzels. He pulled out one of each and opened them. His stomach roiled, but it roiled over a sucking pit of nothing.

"Find one of the tenders—those boats we used to cross from the dock to the ship." Her tone suggested he should know this, and he chased pretzels with water, not pointing out he'd been stoned to a fare-thee-well at the time. "There are four openings and we need to launch it without killing ourselves." She frowned, as if realizing how unlikely that last part was.

He kept his voice even. "Can you drive a boat?"

"I can try. My husband used to own a boat in the 1990s." She looked away, biting her lip. "I gotta *do* something. I can't just...*stay* here."

"Where are the tenders?"

"Deck 8. I checked the map." Sheila glanced at Dylan and Sara. "Will you hold one of their hands?"

He nodded. Sara was as unmovable from Sheila's side as her thumb was immovable from her mouth, but Dylan numbly took Riley's hand, letting Riley lead him away from his sister.

The walk back was slow. Riley looked ahead while Sheila watched from behind. He kept the bag in the hand he held Dylan's so he could keep the axe free.

Riley slowed when they reached the dead clerk, nudging Dylan behind him. Sheila looked over Riley's shoulder and gasped. She quickly swallowed and looked down at Dylan and Sara, who looked up at her with all the animation of dolls.

"Look at the ceiling, guys."

He led them around the corpse and towards the right-hand hallway. He poked his head around the corner and stared at the piled bodies further down. "This is lodging. How do we get to the tenders?"

Sheila pointed to the right. He saw signs for a beauty parlor and a bookstore. "Through the salon and out onto the decks. There are station doors inside, but..." She looked at the bodies and shook her head. "I don't wanna go down there."

Riley nodded. Every organ inside seemed to pulse.

The salon's door was metal-framed with pebbled glass. He nudged it open. One of the stations immediately to the left reflected the rest of the parlor. He saw his haggard face repeated on broken mirrors. "C'mon."

Barbicide stained the floor and the room reeked. The four perm chairs had been upended. No bodies, but a fat trail of blood led down the back hallway to the right.

"Door's over there." Sheila pointed towards the far left corner. With each glass-crunching step forward, his heartbeat grew more leaden. He had to breathe through his mouth in order to get enough air and, still, he felt light-headed.

Two steps lead to the deck door. Sheila was reaching for the knob when something crashed in the back hallway. They heard slow, squishy footsteps and something metallic being dragged.

Riley nudged the boy towards Sheila. "Go."

She took the boy's hand and the bag. "Riley—"

"Do you want someone following you?"

She bit her lower lip, then got the kids out quickly. Riley caught a salt-choked whiff of ocean. His stomach cramped, and he couldn't shrug off the insane relief he felt when the door closed.

He turned back. Two stations dominated the center of the room, obscuring his view, but he saw a bloody white shirt, a tattered burgundy dinner vest.

He circled around, axe at his chest. His pulse pushed at his Adam's apple. *Here's your choice. Deal with the open water... or stay on this ship. With this.*

The man stepped out, and it was the clerk from his acid-trip fever dream. His back was stooped, his face dotted with blood. His red-ringed eyes bulged. He dragged a fire-extinguisher by the hose, the bottom dented and greased with blood.

"Have you eaten, sir?" The muscles of his arm bulged as he hefted the extinguisher. "Gotta eat, sir, gotta eat—"

The clerk swung the extinguisher low, and it bashed into Riley's thigh. The pain was instantaneous, seizing-up his entire leg. He cried out and fell.

The extinguisher slammed into his kidneys. Riley screamed. He saw a red bulge rearing, and he tried to block with the axe. The head smacked the man's forearm, and the extinguisher flew over Riley's head, crashing somewhere.

The clerk pounced, and Riley pushed the axe-handle between them. The man was small but whipped and snapped like a downed power line. He grabbed hunks of Riley's hair and yanked. The pain peeled Riley's lips away from his teeth.

The clerk bashed Riley's head into the floor. A white light exploded in front of Riley's eyes. Riley heaved against the man with the axe handle, as if doing bench-presses. The clerk's hands left Riley's hair and moved across his face, thumbs digging for his eyes.

With a knot of strength that dug cannibal-teeth into his

kidneys, he shoved the man back. The clerk tensed against the side of the salon door. Riley swung the axe one-handed, a wide, powerless move, and the side of the axe-head collided with the clerk's jaw. The clerk jerked right, his temple slamming into the salon door's pebbled glass, cracking it.

Riley pushed himself forward, shrieking with his kidneys, and drove his weight into the clerk. The clerk's head bashed a ragged hole through the glass, the breaking shards tearing the man's throat out, transforming his scream into a choked, wet gargle. Blood flew in thick spurts.

Riley jumped, cringing, away from the spasming body. He stumbled into one of the station chairs and dropped the axe to cling to it. His entire side was an icy lump.

He looked at the door leading to the deck and thought of seeing the cobalt waves of the ocean crashing, of smelling that sea air. He fell to his hands and knees and retched yellow bile laced with threads of blood.

Nope, sorry, I can't.

A hiccup burned his throat. He thought of the magazine back in his cabin, foretelling the demise of his company. He might've been a stranger to that version of Riley Christopher McCarrick, CEO of a dying company, husband of a dying marriage.

He thought of Andrea, carrying a knife and screaming to be let in. He thought of Andrea and Hogan killing each other. It could've been him.

I can't stay here, he thought, then said it aloud. His voice was a frog's croak.

He crawled to the steps. At the top, he grasped the doorknob, his fingers grinding blood into the brass. He leaned his head against the door, taking deep breaths. He could hear the crash of waves outside, a seashell roar. Tons of open water.

Don't go out there! A voice cried. *You can't!*

"You act like I have a choice," he croaked. He turned the knob and pushed. He winced against the dull brightness, the sea wind pulling his clothes and filling his face with its nauseating scent. As his stomach clenched, he crawled out onto the wooden planks of the deck, letting the wind slam the door closed behind him.

He crawled forward, side brushing the wall, head down, breathing shallowly. His heart trip-hammered in his chest, his pulse a bass-drum explosion in his head.

But...he was doing it. He was outside, he was next to water, and he wasn't stopping. He might not survive—the idea of settling a small boat into the water with two adults and two children all but assured this—and he was starving, beaten half to death, and nauseous, but still whole. Still moving.

Doctor, I believe I've finally conquered aquaphobia.

He barked laughter in between retching, and kept crawling.

He made his way down the deck to where he hoped Sheila, Dylan, and Sara waited.

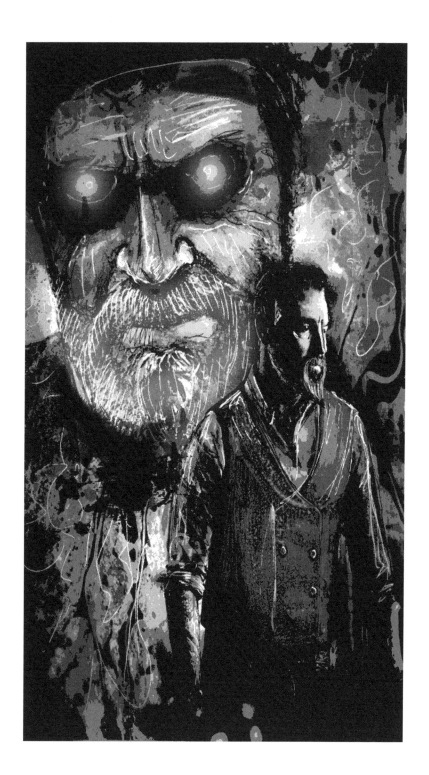

THE WATER ELEMENTAL

A.P. Sessler

Maggie Dearing sat in her wing back chair, the embroidered pattern in its fabric not dissimilar from the one she at present crocheted into a doily with hook and lace.

A collection of other doilies, sweaters, blankets and baby's clothes sat around the room on tables and kitchen counter, some with paper tags attached labeled SOLD. A series of framed samplers either hung from or leaned against the walls, some bearing the same paper tag.

She hummed a pleasant if melancholy tune, until heavy footsteps and the sound of a man heaving came just outside her door. She was at first startled, but took a deep breath and returned to her work, ignoring the door that swung open and rattled the hanging samplers.

"Maggie, love. I'm home," announced the disheveled man in a voice too loud for such a small room.

His skin was like dried leather, tanned by the burning sun. Beside deep crows' feet, cool, blue eyes with tiny, black dots for pupils flashed out of his dark, narrow face.

"Hello, Sam," she said with little fanfare.

"*Hello, Sam,*" he mocked her. "Hello to you, too."

He looked about the room littered with her handiwork and humphed, then removed his wool cap and placed it on the rack by the door. His feet dragged across the plank floor, muted by the occasional throw rug, as he made his way to Maggie and leaned over to kiss her.

When she smelled the alcohol vapor oozing from his breath and pores she closed her eyes and grudgingly accepted the wet kiss on her cheek.

He cleared his throat. "I've just come back from—"

"From the bar, no doubt," she interrupted.

"If it's any business of yours. The man that hired me bought me a drink to seal the deal. That's how we do it 'round here, if you don't mind."

"A *single* drink?"

"Yes, a *single* drink," he said, rattling his gray, bearded jowls.

"And where are you gallivanting off to this time?"

"He's in need of a pilot to show him 'round the Graveyard to the Chesapeake. Says there's a shipwreck he's partial to salvaging. He's got several men with diving gear, so I won't be setting a toe in the water this time 'round. Just guiding him through the shoals to the part the old-timers call Rhines. We'll only be out seven to twelve weeks, and it's big money this time, Mag. Really big money."

"And this stranger. He's able to pay you a decent wage?"

"The man wears gemstones and rubies the size of your fist," he said, shaking his own.

Her eyes remained on her sewing needle, not once expressing a glance of interest. "Perhaps they're glass."

"Love, you don't buy a ship like the Maiden with glass," he said with wide, truthful eyes she didn't bother looking into.

"The Maiden? So that's who I'm sending you off with? Another harlot of the sea."

"Don't be daft, Mag. She could just as easily be named the Tight-Twat Nun or the Old Hag. But it's none the difference to you, I see."

"Just so I get this straight. I let you leave me alone with all the responsibilities you vowed before God to handle for seven weeks—"

"Or twelve," he interjected.

"*Twelve* weeks, and when you come back we'll be able to settle into an early retirement?"

He half nodded and shrugged—more or less—something akin to a West Indian head shake.

"And just who is this wonderful, generous man who plans on snatching you away from me?" she asked.

"Love, don't be like that."

"What is his name?"

"DeFillipo, if it matters to you."

"It figures. And from what far corner of the world did he crawl out of?"

"I've no earthly idea, as it that mattered either."

"Certainly it does," she said, laying her sewing needle and doily on the arm of the chair and finally facing him. "I would like to know who and where to send the bills that will be piling up at our door during your absence. Or do you think I can pay all our debts with my knitting alone?"

"Mag, after this trip, our debts will disappear."

"I seem to have heard this before. Then after you injure yourself or some poor soul in one of your drunken rages and end up in jail the only thing that disappears is the money you promised to bring home. Does that sound familiar?"

"Watch it woman, you're pushing me."

"I don't see why you have to go out all the time. You have a perfectly good boat-building business right beneath us with men willing to pay you top dollar and you want to go off with every stranger who promises you the easy life."

"You think sailing across the Graveyard in the middle of a Nor'easter seasick with dwindling supplies is easy? Like sitting here knitting your doilies?"

"I didn't say it was easy. And don't mock me. My knitting puts food on the table when you're busy spending your money at the bar."

"I said, watch it, Mag."

"It's not the sailing I mind. Not even the time you spend away. It's the fact you can't spend a single day at sea without drinking yourself completely useless and wasting every penny of our money."

He saw everything go red: Maggie, the room, his own pea coat, even his own flesh. The only thing he wasn't conscious of was his own right hand, which drew back over his left shoulder like an arrow on the bowstring and shot forth.

He watched his hand strike her face. For him there was no sensation. It was as if someone else had backhanded his wife and not him. He was merely a nosy viewer looking over his own shoulder, that is until the color returned to the room.

He was back in his body. The only red he saw was the subtle hue in her cheeks, and the blood trickling from her busted mouth. He turned his trembling hand over and gazed at it.

She stared at him in disbelief, unblinking, breathing staccato breaths. She brushed the corner of her mouth with her fingers and pulled them back.

"Get out!" she shouted, staring at her own blood.

His eyes shot up. "I didn't mean to."

"I said get out, and don't come back. Sober or drunk I never want to see you again."

"Now, Maggie—"

"I mean it! Go to the one you've always loved. Maybe she'll have you back."

He took a deep breath as his hand balled into a fist and raised.

She glanced at the end table, where her crochet tools rested. She snatched the pair of sterling silver scissors up and held them before her, their twin blades facing him.

"Hit me again? Just you try it, you drunken fool," she said with gritted teeth and mad eyes.

He lowered his fist and humphed. "I'll return, to the sea I will, and leave the likes of your meddlesome kind behind me."

"I only hope she treats you as you've treated me."

"She'll treat me just fine, that much I'm sure. Good riddance!"

He stumbled for the door, pausing a moment between his staggered steps to catch his balance. He pulled it open and slammed it shut behind him. As she listened to his heavy feet stomp down the thin, plank stairs she trembled and wept.

***

With the cold nights that followed her seething anger cooled, so much that the longing for her to be rid of him became an all-consuming desire for his return. She found herself marking the calendar with each passing day, praying for and awaiting the ship's safe arrival in port.

***

She stood in the crowd of anxious wives, mothers-to-be and children, awaiting the moment the man of their house came galloping down the towering gangplank. Several faces elicited a hurried heartbeat, but when they came in focus her shoulders dropped.

Sailors took their women in arms, raised children high, and kissed them all with tears of joy and laughter abounding. In an hour's time, the crowd diminished to a handful of worried women, who at last were relieved when their lost lover appeared.

Maggie stood alone on the dock. Chatter and applause were replaced with the mournful call of seagulls. The sun was about to dip into the sea; its red, rippled reflection spread over the surface of the harbor.

With a palm over her eyes, she gazed at the weather deck for signs of movement. Six silhouettes stood at the rail, almost motionless. It appeared they were watching her as much as she watched them. A head turned to another, then another head faced another, soon all the shapes disappeared. A moment later, a lone shape approached the gangplank.

Her heart began to pound. The shape descended. Soon she would be face to face with her estranged husband. What would she say? What would he say? Had he forgiven all as she had? Surely he had, since he came skipping down the gangplank. Her bosom welled with breath and her smile grew wide to welcome him.

When the man drew close, her breath left her. It wasn't her husband. He wasn't any kind of man she wished to see. In fact, she would even say he seemed suspicious.

"Mrs. Dearing?" the man asked.

"Yes," she answered, hardly facing him.

"Would you come with me?" he said, his tone sober.

Without waiting for an answer he turned back toward the gangplank.

"Is something the matter?"

He didn't answer.

"Is Sam safe?" she tried again.

He stepped up the gangplank and began to ascend.

"Sir? Did you hear me?" she asked.

"I did, Ma'am," he said, continuing his ascent without facing her.

She stopped.

A few steps later he realized she was no longer following. He faced her.

"Are you going to answer me or should I stand here all night?" she asked.

He glanced back at the men awaiting him atop the weather deck. A man raised his arms waist high, his palms face up.

"Your husband is well--"

She took a relieved breath.

"—all things considering," he added.

"Considering what?" she asked.

He turned and continued his ascent.

"Sir? What condition?" she asked, standing still.

"It would be much easier for you to see yourself than for me to attempt to explain," he said.

A chill seized her. She raised her skirt off her feet with both hands and hurried up the gangplank.

When she reached the gangplank, the men nodded and led her toward an open ladder hatch. The man descended ahead of her. One of the remaining men motioned for her to follow.

She looked down the dark hatch to the dim light at the foot of the ladder. The man beside her held her hand until she found a secure foothold. He continued to hold her hand until she descended enough rungs to take hold herself.

Halfway down the men began to follow her, one after the other. The man who had greeted her took her hand until she set foot on the gun deck. Soon all seven of them stood at the bottom of the ladder.

Maggie gazed around the dimly lit deck. Several cannons lined the floor, all secured before closed gun ports. Few of the deck's hanging lamps were lit. The fishy, salt air above was replaced with the stale, musty smell of damp, cramped quarters.

The man spoke. "Ma'am, I am going to take you to your husband, but first—"

"First, you will tell me your name," she insisted.

"Cyril," he said.

"Are you the same man who hired my husband and led him away with promises or riches and fame?"

He ground his teeth and forced a smile. "The same."

"Hmm," she said, and sized him up from head to toe.

His ebony hair was curled and slick. A thin goatee flowed down from the corners of his mouth to his chin, and ran along his square jaw back up to his thin sideburns. In her estimate, he was flashy. A red vest over black, silk shirt with full-length sleeves, the open neck revealed a gold chain tucked beneath his shirt. His black breeches ran down long, strong legs to his black, leather shoes with silver buckles. And there were the jewels Sam had spoken of, resting on rings upon his fingers: a ruby on his left hand and a gem on his right.

"Mr. Cyril—" she started.

"It's DeFillipo, but please, just Cyril. And I should call you?"

"Ma'am. Where is my husband?"

He took a deep breath and chose kinder words. "Right this way," he said, holding his arm out.

She looked side to side, confused.

"This way, Ma'am," he repeated, flapping his palm toward the dark corridor ahead of them.

She moved forward, into the dark corridor. Old planks creaked with their footsteps and reverberated with their whispers. Light came from ahead. As they approached, she saw the open cargo hatch above and below, and beyond, the capstan.

When they came to the edge of the cargo hatch the six men stopped.

She glanced at them, but they avoided her eyes. She looked below, into the cargo hold. Several barrels stood side by side, but one was separated from the others by size and space and had a small stair beside it.

Cyril motioned toward a man in red and white striped shirt, who scaled the ladder into the cargo hold and went up the stair.

"*Ma'am,*" Cyril stressed. "Your husband is alive, and of a mostly sound mind, but something strange happened out at sea. I told you before I could not explain it, and I cannot explain it now."

He motioned to the man, who slid the head off and leaned it against the barrel.

Maggie gasped and placed a trembling hand over her mouth.

Barely breaking the surface of the barrel's liquid contents was a tiny island of pale, spotted flesh. It was motionless, so much so the men glanced at one another with bated breath.

"You pickled my husband in beer?" she forced the words out of her mouth.

"Wine, actually," Cyril corrected her.

"You said he was alive."

"Terry," Cyril called to the man in a striped shirt.

Terry looked up at his master, who nodded some unspoken command.

Terry took hold of the barrel and gave it a sharp thrust, which hardly moved it, but sent the contents sloshing side to side.

With a choking gurgle, the rising island became the crown of a head and then a face with bulging, dark eyes. Maggie wasn't sure how she knew, but somewhere in those alien eyes she saw Sam's soul, trapped inside this hideous creature.

"Maggie!" he gurgled, wine flushing out of the gills along his neck.

He stood upright, revealing only a portion more of his being. His thick, white beard, now more like rubbery strands of seaweed, showed somewhat of his appearance remained intact.

"Sam!" she answered, and rushed toward the ladder.

The men helped her descend. She ran to the barrel and, trading places with Terry on the stair, looked inside. "What happened to you?" she asked.

"I don't know," he cried and raised his hands from the wine.

His fingers were webbed, and their nails missing. She took hold of his face, but the flaring gills beneath his left ear cut her palm. She withdrew her hand and gazed at her bloodied hand.

"Quick!" Cyril shouted.

Terry took her by the wrist and dragged her to a nearby barrel. He turned the spout wide open and thrust her left hand beneath the pouring, stinging liquor.

She instinctively went to pull her hand back but he held it beneath the spout. "Why are you doing this?" she asked.

"Only a precaution, Ma'am," said Cyril. "Your husband's condition is potentially infectious, or worse, contagious."

After a moment Terry turned the spout off and released Maggie's arm. He pulled a handkerchief from a pocket and handed it to her. "Here you go, Ma'am."

She dried the wound off.

"Allow me," said Terry as he tied the handkerchief around her palm. "Better to be safe than sorry."

Shc nodded toward him and faced Cyril. "What did you do to my husband?" she asked as she approached the barrel Sam resided in.

She gently stroked Sam's brow with the back of three fingers. He leaned into her touch, the way a cat bunts to show affection.

"Not I, Ma'am. His love of drink, I'm afraid. It seems some water-bound spirit has taken possession of his body—a water elemental."

She pulled her hand back. "A what?" she asked.

"An elemental. This one thrives on and around water. Some men are more susceptible than others, and I'm afraid his endless drinking made him even more so."

"But you have him soaking in wine."

"It has enough water in it to satisfy both he and the spirit."

"He only drinks when he is at sea. That's why I prefer him at home."

"The spirit knows that. It calls to him like a Siren. That's why he always returns. He can't help himself. And when he answers it takes control of him."

She carefully brushed Sam's sad brow again, with her right palm now. "Then once he is back on land it will lose its hold and he will return to normal?"

"No one can be certain," said Cyril. "We've none seen such a case. But no matter, his fate is your decision. You can take him home, or if you choose, we'll keep him here on the ship till the end of his days, or if you think it fitting, we'll end his misery here and now."

"No!" Maggie and Sam cried out together.

Cyril nodded toward Terry, who slid the head back over the barrel. Maggie withdrew her hand to avoid it being injured as her other.

"Of course I want him home. How much do I have to pay you?" she asked, reaching into the purse hanging from her shoulder.

"It isn't necessary, Ma'am," said Cyril. "My men will take him to your home at once."

The five men nodded.

***

Maggie held folded fingers to her lips, speechless as the men rolled the large barrel through the open land-side door to the edge of the first slipway. Unable to watch, she turned and faced the bay-side overhead doors. Water sloshed just beneath the closed doors from the unseen bay.

Cyril noticed her distress but held his peace.

"I don't know why you couldn't carry him on one of your

boats, instead of rolling him around like a cask of beer," she said.

"That barrel weighs over a ton. It'd sink the wherry for sure, but no worries, Ma'am. He'll be situated soon enough."

"If he survived the journey."

After fastening a framework of ropes to the overturned barrel, the men used the block and tackle mounted to the high ceiling to pull the barrel upright and onto the slipway.

Standing on the dock, Terry pulled the nails out of the head and peeked inside to ensure their passenger was intact. He nodded and the men loosed the ropes and bowed toward Maggie.

She approached the barrel alongside the dock. "Sam?" she called. "Are you alright?"

Silence. Then a grating sound as the wood head slid aside, pushed along by slick, tube-like fingers. Hands braced against the chime of the barrel as he laboriously raised his body up enough to look into his lover's face.

"Maggie, love," he cooed.

"Welcome home, Sam," she said and smiled.

He gave a grunt as he lowered himself back inside and out of sight. In a moment, his hand reached out and pulled the head over the opening to shut out the harsh light coming through the high windows.

She stared at the barrel, wringing her hands. Cyril stepped beside her, facing the barrel as well.

"I suppose I should find him a suitable pair of breeches," shc said.

"Unnecessary, Ma'am. They'd only weigh him down. We tried to clothe him but he simply tore everything off."

"I see," she said, and looked at the floor.

"Now, your husband of course performed his duties as long as he was fit to do so. It is only right he, that is you now I suspect, should receive full payment as promised."

He had scarcely finished the words when she threw her arms around him and buried her face into his chest, weeping. He gazed down and sighed, then slowly placed his hands upon her back.

"Mrs. Dearing, you have shown extreme courage and loyalty in this, the most difficult of situations. I do not pretend to be a man of faith but I dare say God—if he is so kind and good a soul as promulgated—shall reward you well."

She mumbled something into his chest.

"I'm sorry, Ma'am?" he said.

"Maggie," she said, raising her eyes to him. "Call me Maggie."

He smiled and released her. "As you wish, Maggie."

He reached into his pea coat pocket and retrieved a small book, from which he tore a page out and handed it to her. "Should you need me, fetch for me at this address."

"I will. Thank you, Cyril."

"My pleasure," he said and bowed, then addressed his men. "Lads. Let us be on our way."

The men bowed toward her and went ahead of their master. Two pulled the landside overhead door shut and departed through the front door, followed by Cyril.

When they had left, she found a spot on the dock and sat, waiting on her husband should he have need.

***

"I brought you something to eat," Maggie called out as she approached the barrel with a small loaf of bread in her hands.

The head slid open and Sam raised himself. "Thank you, love," he said.

She leaned against the barrel and overturned her full palm, releasing broken bits of bread into his cupped hands. He buried his face in his hands and began to eat the bread.

With a loud cough, he spit the bread up and continued coughing. Maggie's heart grew weak when a trickle of blood ran from his gills. He lowered himself into the wine and a moment later bubbles rose. The floating bread on the surface of the wine was soon pulled beneath.

When it all disappeared, he raised his head above the

surface. "More, please, love," he said and just as quickly submerged.

She broke the bread into bite-sized chunks and dropped them on the surface of the wine. When they became soggy, water-logged pieces of bread they were plucked from beneath.

A knock came on the front door.

"Come in," she called out.

Cyril stepped inside. "Evening, Maggie. I do hope I'm not intruding."

"You're fine," she said and called her husband as she approached Cyril. "Sam, Cyril is here to see you."

She took Cyril's pea coat and placed it on the rack by the door. He watched as Sam's slimy hands pressed against the chime and raised his piscine body.

"Evening, Boss," said Sam.

Cyril bowed. "Sam. I see your wife is keeping you well-fed."

A loud, gurgling laugh erupted from Sam's throat. "That she is," he said and laughed again.

Maggie hid her blushing face.

Sam's laughter turned into coughing, which became noticeably painful.

"Is anything the matter?" Maggie asked.

Sam held up a finger and submerged into the barrel. After a moment, he surfaced with a smile.

"The only thing she won't give me is a drop of the hard stuff," he said and chuckled. "But I know better than to ask her. So how about you go to the corner and bring back a bottle of anything you like?"

"You should know better than to ask me," said Cyril.

Sam's laughter ended shortly. "What do you mean?"

"And how have you been holding up?" Cyril asked.

"What did you mean?" Sam repeated.

"Begging your pardon?"

"I should know better than to ask you?"

"I simply meant it would be best that you refrain from hard drink, since—well, I'm sure you know why."

"I'm afraid I don't follow."

"The drink. Remember, that is what caused your condition."

"My condition? What condition is that?"

"Sam," Maggie scolded him. "Don't start a scene."

"You stay out of this, woman," said Sam, pointing at her with a drooping finger.

"Really, Sam. There's no call for this," said Cyril.

"And you? Who are you to come into my house and tell me what I can and can't partake of? Are you a physician? Or maybe you're a ship's surgeon now? For I was certain you were nothing but a pirate masquerading as a gentleman who'd as soon stab a man in the back if there was but profit to be had."

"Maggie," Cyril turned toward her. "I think it would be best if I leave."

"Yes, I think so," she said, ashamed to look into his eyes.

"Yes. It *would* be best if you leave, Cyril," said Sam, then pointed at his wife. "Maggie. I'm not finished with you," he shouted until a fit of coughing sent him beneath the surface in search of relief.

"Come," said Maggie, taking Cyril by the arm and leading him toward the door.

"I feel somewhat at fault," said Cyril. "If it hadn't been for my offer, your husband wouldn't be in the pick—predicament he's in."

Sam raised his eyes just over the chime. He stared at his employer and wife. Sam humphed and yanked the head shut.

Cyril and Maggie faced the barrel when they heard Sam's objection.

"If it wasn't you, it would have been someone else," said Maggie. "Sam loves the sea, and that's all there is to it."

"That may be so, but I made sure he couldn't resist my offer. And now—" said Cyril, still gazing at the closed barrel. "I'd give anything to have him back to normal, if only you could have him back as you remembered. When he was human, completely I mean."

"My memories of him may not be as fond as you may imagine."

She saw his brow raise. "He was difficult I mean," she explained.

He smirked. "The sea makes a man hard. All that salt I suppose. Preserves him like a piece of pork. It makes him even tougher to swallow."

She smiled. "It hasn't made *you* too hard," she said, looking into his eyes. "Has it?"

"Each man of the sea hardens in his own way. Whether to the plight of others or the hatred of himself. One man will forsake his wife. Another will forsake conscience."

"Conscience?"

"That small bird that flutters around a man's heart, singing its song. A hard man will swat at the thing and shoo it away, til it's so far off he can no longer hear it sing."

"Which are you?"

He laughed. "Well, I'm not wed."

"Yet you regret your offer to my husband. Perhaps that bird is not so far off."

He smiled. "It's time I be on my way. I'll stop by shortly, to make sure you and the pilot are doing well."

"That would be much appreciated," she said, walking him to the door.

He reached for his pea coat from the rack and began to don it. "Think nothing of it. And if you need anything, just say the word."

As he bent his other arm to fill the limp sleeve, she took hold of it and straightened it out. He smiled and pushed his arm through the sleeve.

"Thank you," she said, her hand resting on his shoulder.

He opened the door and exited. With a sigh, she clasped her hands together.

***

Maggie sat in her wing back chair, a sampler and threaded needle in her lap. She sipped steaming tea from a China cup just above the companion saucer in her left hand before returning both to the end table beside her.

She took up her needle and pushed it through the back of the sampler when a knock came. The tea cup rattled on the saucer, its dark contents sloshed side to side.

"Coming," she hollered.

She set aside her needle and sampler, made her way to the front door and stepped outside. The salt wind blew harsh against her face on the second-story landing, but the pale, blond hair of her tightly-knitted bun hardly moved.

The bright, pale sky showed no sign of sun or rain, just a dull haze so thick it seemed to hold the airborne gulls in place. As she descended the gray, plank stairs of her two-story cedar shake home, she noticed a new bald spot exposed from the chipping, white paint.

If only Sam were back to normal. He'd put a fresh coat on the side.

She stepped off the stairs onto the small, concrete landing, and from there onto the gritty sand and seagrass, careful not to pick up a sole full of sandburs in her shoes.

She opened the first floor door to the boathouse and stepped inside. Sam was still pounding the high ceiling with the long push pole. She waited between knocks to gain his attention.

"Sam," she called.

He faced her. "Oh, hello, love," he said and leaned the push pole against the barrel. "Good idea you had, giving me this pole. I see it works like a charm."

"You're welcome. What do you need?"

"You know it's been a while. Weeks in fact. I know I shouldn't have asked last time, but I was wondering if you could fetch me a small drink."

She feigned not hearing. "Beg pardon?"

"I said I'd like a drink."

"That wouldn't be wise, dear."

"Just a small taste," he pleaded.

She sighed. "You're floating in the stuff. If you're really

that thirsty, open your mouth and swallow to your heart's content."

"*Swallow*," he mocked her with a humph. "I'm floating in my own piss and shit. What do you want, I should die?"

She paused to consider his words and gasped at the fact.

"Sam, I'm so sorry. I don't know what I was thinking. I assumed that—well, it doesn't matter. I was wrong. Forgive me," she said and marched for the front door wringing her hands.

His tone changed. "Don't leave me, love."

"I'm going to fetch Cyril. He'll know what to do."

"What good is he for?"

"He can replace the contents of your barrel with fresh wine."

Now he considered *her* words, and with a large-lipped smile of wide-spaced teeth, he nodded several times. "'Tis a splendid idea, love. Do just as you say."

"Yes, dear," she said.

He watched as she passed over the threshold and closed the door behind her, leaving him alone in the boathouse.

***

The door pushed opened with Cyril's hand. Maggie entered ahead of him. He stepped inside and let the door close. She stared at the barrel, its head drawn shut, the push pole leaning against it.

"He's sleeping," she said.

"How do you know?" he asked.

"He pulls the lid over the barrel to keep the light out."

Cyril glanced at the setting sun outside the room's high windows. His crew stepped in the door. Terry and another of the men headed for the side overhead door. Cyril raised a hand.

"Let him be," he said.

"We've come this far," said the man in sky-blue turtleneck sweater and smoke-gray toboggan. "We might as well be done with it."

"Leave the wine outside. We'll come back tomorrow,"

said Cyril.

"Boss—"

"I'm paying you for your time, Daniels, so hold your tongue lest you plan to find work elsewhere."

"Really, it's no inconvenience if you wake him," said Maggie. "He'll fall to sleep at once, and truly he would be happier."

Cyril took a deep breath and held it. Maggie waited for his answer.

Cyril cocked his head, and without a word, the men headed for the door. She watched in confusion as the men passed by to leave her and Cyril alone.

The door turned quietly on its hinges and shut. So Maggie turned to Cyril.

He placed a hand on her shoulder, and her eyes met his.

"I know you perceive you're doing well by your husband, having us change out this wine," he said. "But have you considered that the spirit that calls to him—the same that changed him so—might take even stronger a hold on him?"

She looked away. "I can't have him living in his own filth. It's inhumane."

His other hand took her other shoulder. "Maggie. Look at me," he said.

She faced him.

"Your husband. He isn't—" he sought for words. "He isn't *all* human. Not anymore. His body does things ours can't. He's got gills for Christ's sake! He inhales water. Too long outside his cask and he bleeds from the air we breathe."

With each word, she fought to shake free of his hold, but his hands only held her tighter and pulled her closer, until she found herself sobbing in his bosom.

He stroked her hair and kissed her forehead.

"Sometimes I wish I had let you have your way with him," she mumbled through her tears.

"Have my way?" he asked.

"To put him out of his misery."

His left hand ceased stroking her hair and cradled the back

of her head. His other raised her chin. Their eyes locked.

"You're a good woman, Maggie Dearing."

The tears in her green eyes sparkled like the sea. He leaned toward her. Their eyes closed and they kissed.

Within minutes they were in her bedroom, undressing.

He removed his shirt. The chain necklace she had seen only in part carried a gold coin; it glimmered in the nightstand lamplight. Another sight heretofore unseen was the myriad of tattoos covering his muscular chest.

On his right breast rested a mermaid, and over his left stood a skeleton.

"My word," she said.

"Living with a man of the sea, surely you've seen your share of tattoos."

"Never one so macabre. What does—" she hesitated before pointing at his breast. "—this fellow stand for?"

He looked at his own breast. "This fellow?" he asked, flexing his left pectoral.

"Ooh," she fluttered.

He laughed. "This is Charon. Pilot of the River Styx—the river of the dead, if you will."

She noticed the figure's outstretched palm, open beside its host's hairy nipple. "Why is his hand out? Is he a beggar?"

He laughed again. "No. He only demands his rightful wage for making the treacherous journey from death to the world hereafter."

"And what is his wage?"

He raised the coin of his necklace in one hand. "A single gold coin."

"What if you don't possess one?"

"You won't pass. You'll be stuck in purgatory or limbo I suppose. In truth, I don't much know. But I'm certain if you ever catch me dead; you stuff this coin in my mouth just to be sure."

"Let's hope that never happens," she said and took the coin in her hands.

She pressed the coin against his lips until he opened his

mouth and gently bit it. She bit the other end. They playfully tugged it back and forth for a time, then he let her have it. She opened her mouth and let the coin fall back to his chest.

They embraced and fell onto her bed.

The wine inside Sam's wooden world sloshed side to side, and soon so did he. He thrust his arms to the edge of his enclosed island to brace himself. He was still, but the wine pounded him back and forth like ocean waves.

He spit the wine out each time it ran into his mouth, even when his gills were not bothered in the least.

"Maggie?" he called out. "Is anything the matter?"

He waited for a reply.

"Maggie, girl? Do you hear me? Is anything the matter?"

He listened for an answer, but all he could hear was the sloshing wine and his own rocking world.

"Damn this barrel!" he grumbled and removed his hands from the staves to push up on the head til it popped open.

The muffled sound became crystal clear. At first, he heard her tortured moans.

"Maggie!" he yelled and reached for the push pole.

He gave two pounds on the ceiling.

"Shh!" he heard her hush from another room, but the knocking sound from above continued, and her moaning started again.

Then it grew louder, and shorter, and quicker, and soon another voice joined in—that of a man—moaning in unison as the tempo increased.

"Maggie?" he whimpered and let the pole fall from his hands to the floor.

When his mind comprehended the ugly truth in cursed epiphany, the unseen lovers exulted in their mutual and magnificent release. As Maggie caught her breath beside her exhausted steed, Sam cried the most pitiful tears he had ever known in his life.

He pulled the head of the barrel shut and submerged beneath the wine to bewail his heartbreak unheard. His muffled howls were barely audible as an ocean of lament rose to the surface in the form of popping bubbles.

Maggie rested her head on her sleeping lover's tattooed breast. She ran her fingers over Charon's fleshless frame, rubbed his outstretched palm.

Cyril smiled. She looked at his closed mouth, awaiting any further movement or word. His smile slowly relaxed. She closed her eyes and joined him in sleep.

***

It was still dark when she woke.

"Cyril?" she called.

The space beside her was empty. She reached over and felt the sheets. They were cool to the touch. She threw the blanket aside and stepped out of bed, naked; her straight hair down like a wide, unfurled sail.

"Cyril, love?" she called again.

She listened. The soft cry of gulls outside her window answered. She retrieved her undergarments from the floor and dressed, then wandered through each room, calling for him, until she heard footsteps from the boathouse beneath.

Cyril must be alone with Sam. That couldn't be good. She had also forgotten to feed him. He was probably starving by now. She rushed to the kitchen and took a loaf of bread, then descended the outside stairs to the ground level.

She pulled the door open and stepped inside the boathouse. "Cy—" she was about to call Cyril. "Sam? Is that you?"

She looked about the quiet boathouse. Where was Cyril? She had heard his footsteps.

"Sam? I brought you something to eat."

She looked over at the docks, expecting to find Cyril standing, possibly half-naked, only to see the pole. What if Sam saw him? He would be furious.

She set the loaf of bread on the dock and approached the barrel. After sliding the head off and setting it on the dock, she plucked pieces of bread from the loaf to feed her husband. Her palm had already opened to drop the crumbs when she saw the body floating belly up. Her hand trembled so greatly the bits of bread shook out of her hand onto the floor.

Her lover stared with lifeless, bulging eyes; his body a bloated mass. The tattoos on his skin were stretched out like blown-up balloons. The mermaid and skeleton on opposite breasts looked like victims of the rack—their figures contorted as much as the canvas they were painted on. The gold necklace and his precious passage to the afterlife were missing.

A scream welled in her belly like vomit, erupting through pursed lips, piercing the stillness of the room. With her mind clouded in confused terror, she turned to flee for help, when she ran headlong into a wall of wet flesh. Upon impact, there was a great squishing sound, followed by a slurping, sucking plop as she pulled away.

The foul, fishy slime stretched like unbroken cords between her and the man she once called husband; a bond between earthbound and sea bound creatures.

"How could you?" she whined.

"I had to, Mag. He was going to kill me," he said, pointing to the whaling harpoon lying flat on the dock she had mistaken for the push pole, which lay on the ramp.

"You're a murderer!" she screamed.

"And you're an adulterous whore!"

She shook her head. "No more than you. I lay with a single man. You lay with the sea, seven of them—a whole harem of harlots you could never pull yourself away from. So don't dare accuse me of breaking our vows. It was you who was to love and cherish, but you beat me like a dog and deserted me for the sea and the bottle."

"Shut up, you whiny winch!" he shouted and placed his boneless fingers around her neck.

Despite there were no bones in those minuscule tentacles, they had enough muscle to squeeze the life out her. She tried to scream, to tell him "Stop!" but no sound or air could get past the vice of his fingers.

Her head grew light and her eyes widened. She feared they would soon bulge as his did. She gazed at the gold necklace wrapped around his wrist. She stretched her hand forth and took hold of the coin that dangled from the chain.

She pulled the coin until the chain cut into Sam's soft flesh. The coin broke free as he pulled his arm back with a great howl. Blood poured from the split skin and ran down the necklace.

She closed her hand around the coin and thrust her fist into his mouth past her wrist. She opened her hand to release the coin and pulled her arm back.

Sam released her throat and grasped at his own. He tried to cough out the coin but it was stuck in his mouth as hard and fast as any fishhook.

Blood poured from his gills as he fought for air. He shoved her to the ground and hobbled for the barrel on flippered-feet. He took hold of Cyril's head and shoulder and strained to pull the waterlogged body from the barrel.

Sam managed to raise the body half way up and let it slump over the chime. With a second yank, the corpse came crashing down upon its head and falling over end-wise.

Maggie turned away at the sight in traumatic tears. In the corner of her vision, she saw his swollen hands and the jeweled rings cutting into his bloated flesh.

Sam leaped onto the chime and spilled inside like a boneless blob. With a splash, he sank beneath the surface, followed by rising, bloody bubbles.

"No!" Maggie shouted. "You won't run to your precious bottle and come climbing back into my life ever again!"

She looked about the workshop. On one wall hung Sam's tools. She ran to the wall, took an adze from its hook, and returned to the dock. She hopped down to the ramp and with a furious swing, she buried the tool's iron-head into its staves.

Sam leaped up from his violated sanctuary, gagging on the air. Maggie pulled the handle of the adze, unable to break it free. Sam leaned over the chime and took a swipe at her. She jumped back out of his reach. He made two more attempts to take hold of her before he retreated for another breath.

As soon as he sunk inside, she took hold of the handle and pulled again. The adze head broke free, followed by a gush of wine. As she stepped back to let its flow proceed unhindered, a terrified smile rose on her face.

Sam leaped up and lashed at her in a sweeping arc. Though she was well out of reach, she instinctively leaped back. When her feet landed, the wine pooling beneath her sent her slipping, reeling backward, into the air.

She fell on her back, and for a moment, was unable to move. Sam swiped at the air three or four times for no reason other than blind rage, then fell back into his diminishing supply of liquid air.

The adze lay at Maggie's side. She took hold of the handle and rose to her feet, the iron head scraping on the wood plank floor. She swung the adze a second time, planting its head left of her original strike. This time the head broke free easily when she pulled it back, creating a wider hole than before. The wine gushed out twice as fast.

She raised the adze over her head for a third strike, when the damaged staves split to pieces and Sam's slimy hand shot forth through the widening breech.

The tentacled fingers took hold of her narrow waist and squeezed. Her fingers went straight and rigid, losing their grip on the adze, which fell behind her to the floor. She felt her innards slowly being crushed in the constricting fingers' clutch.

Maggie exhaled the last breath she had when Sam's fingers went suddenly limp. His hand retreated back into the broken barrel, wine still pouring out over its fragmented staves. With a deep gasp her breath returned.

She climbed up the dock and approached the barrel, hesitant to look inside. She leaned against the chime and peeked down. Staring at her with bulging, milky eyes and the last pulses of blood trickling down from his gilled neck, Sam reached up from his inevitable grave for her hand. His slick fingertips brushed hers. She pulled away.

The soul she thought she recognized in her husband's eyes weeks before was gone now. Maybe it was never there at all. Perhaps it was lost at sea, afloat some derelict vessel captained by Death itself, looking for clear passage to another world beyond. Wherever Sam was, he was dead to her.

Maggie's face and the lamplight outside the barrel were swallowed in darkness as she slid the head into place.

THE PAPER SHIELD

James Lowder

If the professor ever knew my name, he never used it. "You there," he'd bellow. "Careful with that crate! Its contents are worth more than the hides of this whole miserable crew!" Or sometimes he'd just bark something like—"Move, you contemptible walking ballast!"—when he was stomping from one end of the ship to the other and found me blocking his path. Now, I've long considered the sea my home, and even before that fateful mission with the professor, I'd shipped out enough times to know how to keep clear of others on deck. Yet somehow, I was always in his way. We all were. The *Chelston* was better than one hundred meters from bow to stern, a sizable enough freighter, but it felt like a river punt with him aboard. In truth, it's hard to imagine any place big enough for the likes of Charles Augustus Thaxton.

There was no way to avoid him. No corner of the ship was too dark, too distant for his rounds. Above deck, he checked and rechecked the automatons and the modified heavy cranes he'd installed, or quizzed the guards stationed around the other special equipment, which remained hidden from us beneath tarps for much of the voyage. Then he'd stomp off to harangue the glow bug about the wireless or the captain about the evasive maneuvers to be used in the event of a French airship attack. Below deck, he seemed intent on inspecting every pump, valve, hatch, and seam. He even bulled into me once near the crew quarters. I turned a moment before impact to find him huffing toward me, green eyes piercing beneath the great bald dome of his head. He was too caught up in his thoughts to offer up an insult this time. He merely grunted through the mechanical

497

speaking box clutching spiderlike to his throat, before giving me a rough shove.

Startled, I dropped the magazine I'd been carrying, and old habit prompted me to try to retrieve it, so it wouldn't be trodden upon. Apart from charts and logbooks, printed matter of any sort tends to be handled pretty roughly at sea; a page from *Sartor Resartus* will make a serviceable napkin, or Bunco scorecard in a pinch. It takes considerable effort below deck to keep paper clean and dry, too, even for those inclined to bookishness, so anything brought aboard is usually seen as disposable. Me, though, I can't imagine going anywhere without something worthwhile to read—and doing all that I can to keep it safe. Respect for the word, printed or written, was something my father instilled in me. He was a schoolmaster, and in my reverence for knowledge, at least, I will always be a schoolmaster's son. Not even my awe of Thaxton could change that.

I wasn't nearly fast enough to grab the magazine. As I reached down he trod upon my hand, without malice but forcefully enough to send me back against the bulkhead. When I got my wits about me again, I was relieved to see that he'd stepped over the journal. I picked it up gingerly with my bruised hand and gritted my teeth in anticipation of a harangue that would leave my ears aching as painfully as my purpling fingers. Instead, I found the professor glowering at me. More precisely, at the old number of *Scientific Alarums* resting on my lap.

The tiny gears and pistons of Professor Thaxton's speaking box clicked and whirred as it worked. He'd designed the marvel himself after a mission in Afghanistan went horribly wrong, and a Russian scientist slit his throat. Some in the press claimed that Thaxton could have given himself the voice of an angel, but he'd chosen one that mixed the clack and rattle of a difference engine with the growls of a safari's worth of wild beasts, because the resulting metallic snarl more accurately conveyed his intended tone.

"What's that trash you're holding?" he demanded in that

awful voice. "Something for keeping down the fly population in the head?"

"N-No, sir," I said. "I was reading a piece in here on the possibility of ether-burning rockets and travel to the moon."

His expression wavered for a moment, teetering between annoyance and disappointed amusement. I'd seen that battle play out on many a master's face during my school days, and even that of the occasional first mate during my time at sea. Fortunately, amusement won out this time, and Thaxton was smirking as he replied. "No doubt the editors of that dubious publication have concluded that the moon is a mirage—or a hoax, like they did with the clockwork detective I created to solve the Enigma of the Severed Head."

I should have let it go at that—smiled, gathered up my magazine, and scurried off. Had we still been ashore, I might have done so. I've always been bolder once I've lost sight of land, though, and the chance to speak to the professor was too great an opportunity to let pass. "At least they share your disdain for Baglioni's theories on Atlantis," I offered, far too brightly.

"Those imbeciles deserve no plaudits for rejecting Baglioni's fantasies," Thaxton said. "There are foods so indigestible that even a starving rat would refuse them, but that's no reason to mistake the rodent for a gourmet." He gestured at the *Scientific Alarums*, dismissing it with the sweep of one grease-blotched hand. "Find something more substantial with which to better yourself, or at least something worthy to be trampled over. Even the flies deserve more substance from their doom than that rag offers."

Some element of that last pronouncement brought the professor up short, and whatever part of his intellect I had momentarily distracted, turned back to other, more weighty matters. As he stomped off deeper into the ship, he was muttering darkly to himself about things part of me wishes were still a mystery.

***

My assignment to the *Chelston* had been an unwelcome surprise. For a time after I got the orders, I wondered what I'd done to earn the Admiralty's scorn. The notification arrived on the heels of them rejecting me as automaton artificer on the *Terra Nova*. Instead of manning Scott's supply vessel for the First British Airship Antarctic Expedition, I would be stuck on a refitted lumber hauler bound for the Atlantic, under the command of a man notorious for losing a revolutionary self-directed and, as it turned out, homicidal clockwork policeman on London back in '03—or staging a clever deception to that effect in order to cover for the misdeeds of a friend at Scotland Yard, if you believed his critics on Fleet Street and in the British learned societies. Excited as I was about the prospect of meeting Professor Thaxton, his mission promised to be rather less glamorous than the race to establish the first permanent airbase at the Pole. In fact, it sounded a bit absurd, as all his exploits were wont to do at the start.

A disagreement over the fate of Atlantis between the professor and a marine biologist by the name of Baglioni, had set the whole thing in motion. Thaxton's plan was for a quartet of ships to trawl the waters northwest of Cape Juba, off the Continental Slope, using reinforced cranes and modified diving bells to bring up artifacts that he guaranteed would establish the truth about the fabled lost continent. Or at least disprove the theories put forth by Bory de Saint Vincent in 1803 and, most recently, Doctor Rupert Baglioni, that cite volcanic eruptions as the cause for Atlantis's demise and identify the Canaries, Madeiras, and Azores as its remnants. It was the promise of those artifacts, their potential scientific and, of course, financial value that drew bids of support for the expedition from both public and private sources.

Our government seemed enthusiastic about the venture, which was a surprise given their skirmishes with the professor over the years. No one could accuse Thaxton of being disloyal to the Crown, but he did not always share the War Office's notion that all scientific research should have an obvious utilitarian, martial goal. His grail was truth, no matter its usefulness, no matter the consequences of its achievement, and he'd been quite vocal in the past about resources directed to the military that might have instead bolstered his operations. Most famously, he'd told Lord Kitchener and the Committee of Imperial and Colonial Defense: "There was much Plato got wrong, but he was spot on when he identified ignorance as the root and stem of all evils, a blighted class which, of course, includes war. Conquer ignorance and you lot would be out of a job in a fortnight."

Still, when news of the proposed expedition hit the papers and the Royal Societies announced their support, the Admiralty was right there with a promise of several noted specialists— geologists, meteorologists, and the like—to assist the professor, as well as a score of nameless, less noteworthy sailors, such as myself, to man the lower decks. Thaxton took them up on the promise of engine room and automaton artificers, along with mechanical stokers for each of the four ships, but rejected the specialists on the grounds that he himself could provide whatever scientific expertise the mission required. If the Sea Lords took offense at that slight, they did not voice their anger, at least in public.

The press hounded both camps for a time, hoping to stir up the sort of ever-escalating row for which the professor was notorious, but no one rose to the bait. By the time we set sail, Fleet Street had turned its attention to the latest in a yearlong string of bombings and bloody assassinations across London. A few of the more radical journalists claimed that the chaos was the work of an apocalypse cult hurrying along the end of the world, but most of the papers pinned the terrorist activity on a boogeyman suited to their readers' tastes: French or Russian spies, any of a dozen homegrown anarchist groups, or immigrants of one race or another. The consensus held that the terror was meant to disrupt the start of the Festival of Empire. If that was the intent, the scheme failed. The opening at the Crystal Palace, scheduled for the night of our departure, went off without a hitch. There were fireworks over London as we set sail, but they were not for us.

I cannot speak to the mood aboard the other three freighters in our little group, but the *Chelston* was a grim place indeed. A decade waiting for a seemingly inevitable war with the French and the Russians—*sitzkreig*, as our allies in Berlin call it—had left most of the career sailors dispirited. At the outset of our expedition, a few of the engine room artificers tried to build up a camaraderie around increasingly rude jokes about the mermaids Thaxton was going to haul back for the London Zoo. There was no way such feeble efforts could compensate for the generally sour mood, and the way in which the crew had been assembled. Sailors were arriving from all over the fleet right up until we cast off, so everyone was left to size up the men working around them even as they tried to get their bearings on the officers' expectations and the ship's routines. That's a certain course to mistrust, just as the secrecy shrouding large parts of the mission guaranteed a steady swirl of rumors. Logic proved even more useless than usual against this shipboard gossip because the professor's past exploits lent even the most fantastic yarns an air of credibility. In some cases, the truth proved stranger than the speculation.

Take the rumors about the phantom passengers. Such tales are common enough when a crew is patched together on a new vessel, and the civilians on board aren't experienced enough to avoid getting lost below deck. Someone glances up from a duty to see an unfamiliar person wandering past, somewhere he shouldn't ever be, and they assume it's a stowaway. After a telling or two, it's a damned spirit prowling for revenge. The first week out, the *Chelston* was full of chatter about such things. I myself thought I'd seen some oddly dressed men creep onto the ship the night before we left, but let it go as a trick of the fog after the officer stationed on deck told me that no one had come aboard for an hour or more. Others said they'd heard eerie chanting rising from a part of the hold off limits to everyone save Thaxton. Fear of the professor's wrath prevented us from venturing down there to settle the matter.

It turned out that there really were a dozen men lurking in the *Chelston*'s hold: cultists, like the ones described in the radical papers. It was only when we'd sighted the African coast that the truth about them was revealed, at least a small part of it. Their leader was a smirking New Englander by the name of Marsh who dressed in the robes of an ancient Persian priest. I was on deck delivering a message from the chief artificer to one of the petty officers when Marsh led his people up from the hold. They took positions around the ship, praying in a language none of us recognized, as if to sanctify the work being done by the sailors and the automatons. The ministrations were not well received. The men—those not frightened by the sudden appearance of the rumored phantoms, anyway—made their unhappiness known with sharp elbows and sharper words whenever the chance arose.

It was then that Thaxton arrived, rushing down from the bridge. I expected him to grab the nearest cultist and pitch him overboard, but instead he roared at the sailors he passed, "Eyes to your work! Leave the priests to their business!"

Marsh soon fell into step with the professor. He walked not in his wake but at his side, an equal. Even the captain had not managed that feat in the days we'd been at sea. As they strode toward a hatchway, Marsh drew a thick, tattered book from the satchel slung at his hip and offered it to Thaxton, who waved it away. They were right in front of me then. The look on the professor's face was positively demonic. His eyes were wild, his teeth clenched in a mad grin.

Reeling with disbelief, I watched them disappear into the ship. I couldn't understand it. We were finally in position, readying the equipment for its first pass of the ocean floor. There could hardly have been a worse time to unleash this lot of mumbling mystics.

I wasn't the only one baffled by the professor's actions. In something of a haze, I delivered the message from the chief artificer, then made my way down to grab a meal, before I took on the afternoon watch over the automatic stokers. When I got to the galley, I found it humming with confusion and concern about the morning's events. I lingered in the passageway, wondering if I could stomach the uninformed speculation.

"I'm having second thoughts about going in there, too," said someone at my shoulder. The femininity of the voice was something of a surprise. The compulsory universal service laws hadn't been enacted yet, mind you, so distaff sailors were still a rarity in the fleet.

I turned to find myself facing the only woman aboard the *Chelston,* and the only reporter who had ever gained Thaxton's trust. "I wouldn't let the cook hear you say such things, Miss Hayes, ma'am," I noted. "He might take it as a comment on his skills, whether you meant it as such or not. After that, you wouldn't want to eat anything he'd serve you for the rest of this trip."

She tried to muster a laugh at that, but the result was less than convincing. It seemed that the concerns plaguing me, or some variation thereof, had her by the throat, too. As I took in her worried look, I found myself staring at the scars on her face and the reflective circles of her goggles, the sure signs of a former ether addict. Awkwardly I forced myself to look away. She ignored my discomfort and invited me to join her in the galley. Soon enough we were sitting together at the end of one of the metal trestle tables.

Darcy Hayes was as far from my notion of a pressman as Thaxton was from my notion of a scholar. My uncle wrote for the *Cornish Post and Mining News,* but he was a tweedy sort, bright and conscientious, and not terribly interested in anything adventurous, or even out of the ordinary. Not at all like the ambitious London rumormongers you hear about, slinking around after indiscreet politicians and harrying crime victims, then rushing back to Fleet Street with their latest scoop. Not at all like Darcy Hayes. She was a stringer for one of the most aggressive of the radical papers, *Uncommon Sense.* I could see right away why Thaxton trusted her. There was a brashness about the woman, a cheerful insolence that let you know she disdained guile. Some former aether junkies hid their scars with makeup, but she left them alone, even the blackened tip of her nose. The ugly mark suggested that her use of the distilled element had been prodigious. Without the dark goggles, she probably couldn't even see the mundane world anymore.

It was impossible not to catch fragments of the conversations going on around us. A few of the sailors hushed their voices to whispers in deference of Hayes, but many simply blurted out their opinions of the mission and Thaxton and, most pointedly, the strange priests.

"You're getting this as a proxy," I explained after the men nearest us left the table, grumbling and casting baleful looks back at Hayes. "They wouldn't dare speak so bluntly around the senior officers and they're frightened of the professor."

"Oh, this is nothing new. I've had respectable men, titled old codgers and the leaders of venerable societies, hurl insults my way that would make the saltiest seadog blush. Their anger's got little to do with me, though." She sighed and sipped her coffee. "They wouldn't know me from Eve, except for my association with Thaxton. But they aim their venom my way because they all understand that he'd brain them if they so much as looked at him cockeyed."

"I've read about those incidents."

"Don't believe everything printed in the newspapers," she said archly. "Anyway, if you're worried that I'm going to report your mates, don't be. I usually just allow his critics to have their say and let it go at that. No need to get him riled up about the buzzing of gnats. That's not to say your shipmates are gnats."

"When you're around Thaxton, it's hard not to feel like one. I ran into him below deck the other day." I held up my still-bruised hand. "The other marks are less visible."

"You should have seen me after my first meeting with him." That memory lightened Hayes's mood considerably, and she seemed to shake off whatever had been troubling her. "Look," she said, "I understand why everyone is so concerned. Those priests were a surprise to me, too. But they must have a purpose for the expedition, even if we can't see what it is just yet."

"Do you know who they are?"

"Members of a Yank religious cult that's been predicting the imminent end of the world since Fashoda set us on the brink of war with France. My editor thinks they're linked to all the trouble the lapdog press has been pinning on free thinkers and immigrants. Their leader's a nasty piece of work. Involved in some weird doings on both sides of the Atlantic. I'm guessing that book he's lugging about contains some information Thaxton needs for the search."

It seemed reasonable enough on the surface, but if you plumbed the depths of the hypothesis at all, it sounded wrong. "You know the professor better than I do, but after all he's been quoted as saying about superstition, it seems to me that he'd just call the cultists dunderheads before snatching the book from their altar, if he thought it held some knowledge worth preserving. It's not like he's tolerant of ideas that contradict his. Look at the way he went after Doctor Baglioni for saying that volcanoes might have sunk Atlantis in his lecture on—what was it again: the morphology of the squid?"

"That's right." Hayes didn't give me the look of surprise I often get when I mention some obscure fact I've picked up from my reading, but I could tell she was recasting her opinion of me. "I can guess now why you know so much about the professor: You read the science press."

"The Baglioni lecture was written up in the news section of *Beyond Nature*, though other places picked up the story of Professor Thaxton bursting in from the wings and shouting him off the stage after the Atlantis comment. What I've never quite been able to figure out is how Baglioni ended up as the nemesis on the other side of this debate. The lecture was supposed to be his last before retirement. As far as I can tell, he'd never written about Atlantis before. He's a biologist."

"And a tough old mummy," Hayes added. "Not Thaxton's equal, of course. Then again, few are."

It was time for me to report back to the engine room. Hayes offered me her hand, transparent, aether-blighted fingernails and all, as we left the galley. "It's no good trying to second-guess Thaxton on any of this," she said, grinning. "It's not just that he's blazing new trails. He's blazing them across locales not found on any maps. We'll just have to see where we end up."

"What if those trails take us somewhere we don't want to go?"

Hayes's smile wavered just a little. "That's not really something to worry about," she said. "It's not like we can stop Thaxton from taking us all with him, once he's set his mind on a destination."

* * *

The diving bells the professor created for the expedition were remarkable things. They boasted echo-mapping systems decades ahead of the crude submerged sounding devices that were in use at the time around lighthouses, with hydrophones and noise filters that allowed them to send back clear reports of the seabed. Each bell also housed two guns capable of firing six belt-fed torpedoes apiece. The torpedoes were tipped with powerful magnets and attached to spools of heavy wire of a wholly original and incredibly strong alloy. Like the professor's infamous clockwork policeman prototype, the bells and torpedoes possessed a capability for self-direction and independence far beyond the most advanced mechanical constructs of the time.

The controversy surrounding the expedition's outcome has overshadowed the astonishing nature of these inventions, and some of his colleagues still deny Thaxton his due for their innovations. That's no surprise, really. All the bells used for the mission remain shattered and sunk at the bottom of the Atlantic. There were no spares, no back-ups. The professor has refused to release any information about them directly through the usual scientific publications, instead spreading the knowledge through a network of likeminded and similarly reckless truth-seekers. He's filed no patents, demanded no payments—though several braggarts falsely claiming credit for some facet of the inventions have found themselves battered and bullied into publicly acknowledging their deceptions.

It's a shame the original bells were lost. They were magnificent. I saw them up close, saw them in action. Once the mapping maneuvers started in earnest, many of us took shifts away from our regular stations to support the operations on deck. Apart from Thaxton's marvels, the search phase itself was tedious. For more than a week, our group trawled in patterns dictated by the professor, who commanded all from the *Chelston*. He refused to supervise from the bridge. It was, he said, too removed from the actual work being done. He had the captain set up a station for him on the deck. In the final days before the discovery, he was a fixed point around which moved a scrum of men and equipment.

The doom-saying Americans lingered at the edges of this Thaxton-centric system. Their leader, on the other hand, tried to position himself close by the professor's side. Marsh was an inconsistent presence, sometimes forced away by sailors repositioning a bank of sensors, sometimes by the need speak quietly to one of his countrymen. When he managed to stay close, he created an uncomfortable juxtaposition. One moment the professor would call out sounding data for Hayes to enter into the meticulously maintained logs. The next, Marsh would crack open his moldy old book and croak out a prayer for his followers to ape back at him in ragged, broken chorus. Not even the most devout of the zealots could keep up with the professor, though. The Americans required sleep, where Thaxton, apparently, did not.

Ideal weather and a calm sea greeted us the day the search ended, all out of line with the unreal events that marked its close. We only knew that something unusual was going on when the ships were ordered to full stop, and the wireless was relocated to the professor's command post. My duty station was close enough to Thaxton that I could hear his growled orders and the glow bug repeating them to the other vessels. Throughout the afternoon, messages flew back and forth, choreographing a series of complex maneuvers to position the bells. Once they were in place, they largely directed themselves in firing their torpedoes, which in turn swam incredibly elaborate routes to ensnare the object of our quest.

Hour after hour, the work dragged on. The priests were hoarse from their chanting, the crew weary and tense before the maneuvers were complete, and the torpedoes had each locked onto a bell with its powerful magnet. By the time Thaxton finally gave the order to raise the prize, the sun had sunk to the horizon. Its dying light washed the world in stunning reds and golds.

All except for the thing we hauled up from the depths.

It emerged from the water between the four ships, pulled up by the groaning cranes and supported on a net of alloy wires strung between the diving bells. At first, it appeared to be a gigantic column resting on its side. The more of the thing that rose above the waves, the more it became clear that it was not some remnant of a lost architectural wonder, but rather something organic. Not a whale. Not a giant squid or octopus. No, we had snared a single, gargantuan tentacle, and it reeked like all the charnel houses and killing floors in England flushed out at once. Its surface was the pale white of old death. No light from the sunset lingered upon it. Or perhaps the sunlight vanished into its blotchy bulk. Looking at it was like looking into nothing, the Void made manifest.

The initial cheers of triumph fell silent, and a dread settled over the ship as pernicious as the stink from our prize. The cultists dropped to their knees, screaming praise to the ancient thing from the sea. Some of my crewmates dropped to their knees as well, but their prayers were directed at younger gods and prophets.

"You shall be exalted for this, Professor," Marsh crowed. "Your name shall be legend among the faithful. You have proved the existence of the Dreaming One!"

Thaxton had been looking out at the ghastly white limb. Now he turned. The demonic grimace was gone. In its place was a snarl of utter disdain. "Yes, I've proved the thing you worship exists." He lunged at the American and clouted him in the ear. The priestly headpiece that Marsh wore tumbled to the deck. "I've wanted to strike that blow since I first heard of the schemes you and your idiot followers have undertaken in the name of that bloated corpse—the murders and the chaos you've sown. I've wanted to do worse since I first set eyes on you, you howling buffoon. You have no idea how much self-control it takes me to hold off bashing in your brain-deprived skull every second I'm near you."

Marsh pointed to the creature. "That is the doom of Atlantis. You have proved it to be so. Now it will be the doom of England and France and the rest of the corrupt Old World!"

"That thing has no power over England. England has science and reason. With those tools, and my intellect, I've pulled that beast up into the daylight. Look at it. The object of your worship is a thing of flesh and blood." Thaxton strode forward to loom over the cringing mystic, and through his speaking box he declared, "Since it is flesh and blood, it can be destroyed. Watch."

As the professor turned to give a command, Marsh scrambled away. He dropped to all fours, scuttled beneath one of the command post tables, and got to his feet on the other side, near where Miss Hayes was standing. There he held up the ancient tome from which he'd recited his prayers. "With this I have seen the things that dwell beyond the rational world," he said. "The feeble constructs of your science and reason cannot stand against their coming."

Marsh shoved the reporter aside and grabbed whatever logbooks and charts he could hold. Crushing them and his own book to his chest, he turned for the rail. Hayes was on his heels in an instant, a dirk in her hand, but it was I who tackled the priest—or rather, who knocked most of the books and papers from his grasp before he went over the side.

As for what happened next, the official reports claim that one of the cranes on the *Caria* gave way, so that the massive, lifeless object shifted awkwardly in the net. A crane on the *Chelston* followed suit. Then the explosives inside the bells and the torpedoes went off, as Thaxton had ordered, and it was all over. The unidentified salvage blew apart and sank back into the Atlantic.

I recall those moments differently. No sooner had Marsh gone overboard than the entire ship lurched heavily to starboard. The air was filled with the blare of klaxons warning of the impending explosion, but also the teeth-gritting whine of metal twisting and the roar of sudden waves pounding the hull. The deck tilted madly. I fell upon the logs and papers, and Marsh's old book, pressing them beneath me to stop them from sliding away. The angle of the deck was so great that, for a moment, I had a clear view of the weird prize in our net. Contrary to what the reports claimed, it did not simply lay there, lifeless. It flexed and pulled down with tremendous force. Only then did the cranes and cables give way, just before the explosives went off. Then something—some tool or piece of equipment from the commend center not properly secured—crashed into my skull.

I was gazing at the thing when unconsciousness took me. The whiteness of it drew me in, swallowed me and pulled me down with it to the bottom of the ocean. There I floated, aware of terrible shapes, aspects of an ancient being's form that emerged from the surrounding darkness and then dissipated: a body like a bloated, scaly dragon; rudimentary wings; a pulpy head with a muzzle of tentacles that stretched along the floor of more than one ocean, a single strand of which Thaxton had pulled to the surface. I saw then that the beast lay sleeping among the submerged ruins of not just Atlantis, but all the great cities of mankind that ever were and ever would be. Its bed comprised their buildings and the bones of countless generations. My hands began to burn, and then my arms and my chest. I tried to hold back the shriek of pain, fearful that any sound would draw its attention, but I failed. The sound of my scream was the color of the beast. No sooner had the cry been uttered than the whiteness turned on me and took me into its smothering embrace.

They tell me that I was still screaming when they got me to the sickbay, where I was sedated, and the books and papers finally pried from my grasp. The steward bandaged the scorched skin of my hands, arms, and chest. No cause was ever offered for the burns. They healed before we reached port, so the wounds rate no mention in the reports generated by the doctors on shore.

All four of our ships limped back to London, damaged though they were, with crews shaken as badly as if they'd endured a month-long battle. "Shell shocked" is the term the Army is using now to describe the boys returning from the trenches in Alsace and Sebastopol. The doctors used other words to describe what happened to me, mostly Greek, or derived from the Greek. The scientific sound of them has provided more comfort and speeded my recovery more effectively than anything else the doctors prescribed.

On the day, the *Chelston* made port, and the expedition officially ended, Miss Hayes stopped by the sickbay to inform me that the surviving cultists were going to be set free. "Such are the professor's wishes," she noted with a shrug, then offered me a few words of advice on dealing with her fellow pressmen, who would be swarming over the story like, she said, "rats on a carcass." It was inevitable that the time she'd spent with the notoriously press-hating professor would sour her opinion of her fellows. Or perhaps she had witnessed this empty frenzy play out enough times with her own aether-warped eyes to recognize the game for what it is.

True to Miss Hayes's prediction, it was impossible to avoid reading about the professor in the expedition's aftermath. Claims of fraud, both intellectual and criminal, filled the papers day after day. The learned societies whose funds he had accepted declared that the entire misadventure was nothing short of a swindle, that he and Baglioni had staged the Atlantis debate to gain money and resources for a scientifically worthless monster hunt. The lack of hard evidence of the thing we dredged up and the confused accounts of the expedition's final day fed the fires of controversy, though they eventually died down, smothered, some say, by the government. Those looking for a reason to explain such an intervention, or for the support the Crown provided the expedition in the first place, might mark the notable decrease in the crimes attributed to the doomsayers in the months after our return.

Though I never again spoke with the professor, I did receive a communication from him toward the end of my convalescence, just before I shipped out again. My name was on the envelope, but in a different hand from the note inside. It was most likely that of Miss Hayes, who had been tasked with delivering the heavy package and this letter:

Sir—

I am told by my associate, the bearer of this message, that I have you to thank for saving the logs and charts that the unconscionable cur Marsh attempted to take with him when he rid the world of his own pernicious presence. For that, I offer thanks, though I must also point out that you would have done a greater service to me and to the world if you had let him destroy his book of credulous gibberish instead of the few papers of mine to which he clung to obstinately as he went over the rail. Since Miss Hayes has also reminded me that you and I crossed paths aboard the ship, in an incident that I vaguely recall involved you taking a blow to stop me from treading upon a publication that is hardly worth even that low treatment, I cannot express surprise at your lack of discernment. Still, I recall you claiming an interest in knowledge, so by way of providing you with something more substantial with which to better yourself, I offer the enclosed. They are flawed, every last one of them, but they demonstrate thought. I hope it proves contagious and that by taking in what knowledge these volumes contain you will become a carrier. If ignorance and superstition can propagate in this fashion, so, too, can truth and reason.

—Charles Augustus Thaxton

As for the gift itself, it comprised well-read, dog-eared copies of *The Origin of the Species*, Hooke's *Micrographia*, Newton's *Philosophiae Naturalis` Principia Mathematica*, Babbage's *Triumph of the Thinking Machine*, and a dozen more. Many have notes in the margins, in Thaxton's precise script, and a few have whole sections or entire chapters crossed out, with the word *rubbish* written across the pages. I value these books beyond measure.

Despite the challenges of keeping them safe from the grime and damp, I've carried one of the volumes with me each time I return to my home on the deep, on every ship I've manned since the *Chelston*. Some of my mates consider me a jinx because I served on the Thaxton Expedition—a venture as infamous as Scott's disastrous trek to the Antarctic—and they view the books as nothing less than tokens of ill luck. I've been told that rousing the thing, whatever it was, finally jolted the world into the war that now engulfs it from pole to frozen pole.

I see it differently. I have a mission, the one with which the professor charged me in that final letter. I am an agent of truth, a carrier of knowledge. Like the cultists he let scatter back to their warrens to describe the rough treatment of their would-be god at the hands of one lone scientist, I spread the message: *reason will triumph.*

On most nights, when we are gliding across the great shroud of the sea, my shipmates and me, I speak to them of the products of science that keep us safe from Russian submersibles and French airships. The echo-mapping system now outfitted throughout our navy would seem familiar to anyone who had seen the equipment aboard the *Chelston,* and the remarkable new alloy that has found such sudden and widespread use among the shipbuilders of Great Britain is particularly well suited for armoring hulls. But there are times when I am reminded that the enemies' weapons, too, are the product of science, and in those awful moments my mind conjures up an image of that thing beneath the Atlantic, and its vast demesne, built upon the bones and works of innumerable dead priests and warriors—and scholars, too. On those nights, I clutch the books the professor gave me a little more tightly and silently hope that they are, as he claimed, shields against chaos, and not charts setting our course toward that unspeakable kingdom of ruin.

SEASCAPE

Jack Ketchum

He rose slowly to a dim pale wavering light, crawling up through dense viscous fluid into full brightness and then finally clarity. He saw where he'd been swimming to and gasped and screamed.

***

"I'm going with you," she said.

He smiled and put down his crossword puzzle on the comforter beside him on the bed.

Outside the open window, he could hear the sea, breakers against the jetty buffeted by winter winds.

"I don't think so. What's a five-letter word for *mooed*? *Moo* as in cow. Beginning with an 'L' I think."

She was polishing the bedside table, rubbing in lemon oil. *Giving it a drink* was how she put it. "*Lowed*. And who says I'm giving you a choice, Ben." She glanced at him and nodded. "Write it in," she said.

***

Charlie Harmon had just passed by with a linen cart when he heard the scream devolve into a long low moan streaming out from 314, and he moved past the uniformed cop peering in through the doorway, brushed his shoulder as he passed so that the cop seemed to glare at him a moment, and it was only once he'd reached the old man's bed that Charlie realized the cop was only startled—and maybe even a little scared.

The nurse was Denise. One of the good ones. Denise had brains and dedication, and her voice had the ability to soothe without false cheer. She was using it on him now as she lifted his head gently off the pillow, firmed it under him, set him back down again, and then reached for a tissue on the bedstand and dabbed his eyes. *You just take it easy now you been through an a lot Mr. Sebald, you just rest up and you're gonna be fine, doctor'll be in here soon, and I'll be right back, I'm just going to get you a little chipped ice for your throat okay? And you need anything else either, Charles here or I'll come runnin' won't we Charles.*

Outside in the hall again. He walked with her to the nurses' station and the ice machine, and she sighed and shook her head.

"I don't know," she said. "Sometimes I just don't understand."

"What's with the cop?" Charlie said.

The ice tumbled down into the plastic cup.

"Suicide watch," she said.

***

There was never a time in memory when Ben hadn't loved the sea. Summers when he and his older brother John were growing up his family had rented a small wind-battered bungalow in Asbury Park, New Jersey—long before the town's slide into decay—the same place five years running. The house lay directly on the beach. The porch was always dusted and sometimes halfway-buried with sand. A boy could roll out of bed and grab a glass of orange juice and a piece of buttered toast, and five minutes later be scouting the hard wet tideline for horseshoe crabs and jellyfish marooned along the shore.

At high tide, he bodysurfed the whitecaps tumbling to the beach.

He took part-time jobs summers during his college years at a lumberyard in Cape Cod, and a greasy-spoon diner in Falmouth, just to be near the sea and the kind of life the sea afforded—so long as you didn't have to buck it for a living. A life of flesh and youth. Of tan-lines and dried white jagged salt lines against the skin, skin that glowed at night in driftwood firelight, that flaked and peeled and just below which lay a smooth new layer, fresh pink and incorruptible. He met his future wife Ruth—just twenty years old then—over lobster and corn on the cob at a clambake on the beach one night a few miles north of Portland, Maine

They slept together in the gentle susurration of that same beach the following night and with no one else ever again.

When his brother John died, he and Ruth had been living in New York City for almost thirty years. But the sea had never lost its lure for John either. Quite the contrary. He'd bought a small cape codder and set up practice directly after medical school in what was then the sleepy little town of Cape May, New Jersey long before the tourists discovered its turn-of-the-century charm—a house down by the Point where his only neighbor was a nun's retreat, St. Mary's by the Sea. When his heart failed him lunchtime one hot late-August afternoon walking out of the air-conditioned Ugly Mug into the sticky thick humidity along the sidewalk, he had just turned sixty. He had never married. He left the house to Ben and Ruth.

They'd been happy in New York, but there was nothing particularly keeping them there. Ruth had retired from the bank two years before, and Ben's illustration work came and went by mail. They had no children and two tabby cats, George and Gracie, who were only too happy to be packed up and moved to someplace where birds large and small swooped by all day long, or pecked around for bugs along the porch, where bees and dragonflies zoomed and darted into view, and moths fluttered nightly at the windowpanes.

They had all but stopped making love in the City.

The seashore was their fountain of youth.

***

"How's your Shakespeare these days?' she said.
"What?"
"Your Shakespeare. Put your puzzle down again."
"Okay."

"'If it be a sin to covet honor, I am the most offending soul alive.'"

"That's Henry something."

"That's right. The Fifth. The St. Crispin's Day speech. Very good. Now listen to me. I not only love you, I *honor* you. Are you listening? Yes? Good. And you honor me, right?"

"Yes."

"Then don't argue, dammit. The cats can stay with my sister. She adores them."

***

The shivering came in waves, and it was violent, as though he were trying to shake himself apart, and not what Ryan knew he was really doing, generating heat. But the pauses between episodes of shivering got longer and longer as they undressed, dried him down, and then wrapped him in the polypropylene, woolen blankets, and the space blankets, applied the chemical heat packs to his neck, his armpits, his groin, and the palms of his hands, yet finally, despite all that, the shivering had stopped altogether, and now Ryan was worried as hell. Because now there was no radial pulse, and only the faintest in the carotid. And that looked to be winding down as well.

They hoisted the stretcher into the rear. They were doing it by the book, but the man was slipping. His temperature was down to 86 degrees, and he was damn slow about getting it up any further.

He was looking at a guy whose body had passed through hibernation into a state of metabolic icebox here. Blue skin, muscles rigid, pupils fixed, and no discernable breathing. He looked dead. He acted dead. But Ryan knew he wasn't dead and wouldn't be for a while at least. They played possum on you. The rule of thumb with victims of hypothermia was that there was no such thing as cold and dead. Only *warm and dead.*

He shut the doors behind them. The heating unit was already blasting.

His partner Knowles had the warm dextrose drip into

him, and they were feeding him warm moist oxygen. Outer temperature was important against further heat loss, but not nearly as important as internal. They had to stabilize and try to raise his core temp as soon as possible, or they were looking at potential damage to the heart, lungs or brain. Or all three put together.

"CPR?" said Knowles.

"No way. He's still got a pulse. We stay with that for now. At this point his heart's hyperexcitable as hell. We do CPR, and he's still pulsing we risk arrhythmia. We could kill the poor bastard."

"Okay. What then?"

He heard an engine rev, glanced out the double doors, and saw their sister EV pull away awkwardly across the sand.

"Relieve him. That's what we do," he said. "I want to express his urine. He's got a bladder big as a football from cold diuresis, and he's using up heat to keep *that* warm instead of the rest of him. There are times our bodies aren't too swift about priorities."

"We ready to roll yet, gentlemen?" said Andrews from the front seat. Andrews was young and way too impatient for his own good, but he was a damn good driver.

"One second," Ryan said. "Knowles, grab me a Foley twelve. Our guy's gotta see a man about a horse."

He held out his hand for the catheter.

***

The first thing he learned about even the possibility of being seriously ill was how lonely it was. It was lonely to its very core. People could be concerned, kind, encouraging, and even loving but illness was a thing you did all on your own—something no outside hand could touch. Certainly not the doctors. The doctors were there simply in the capacity of benign detectives. Well, hopefully benign at least. To them you were a sort of crossword puzzle to be either solved, or abandoned as impossible to solve whatever the case may be. Later they might rise to the level of trusted advisors. Still later, once you damn well knew you *were* sick, angels, demons, or secular gods.

Yet even in their hands as they poked and prodded you were alone, cast deep inside yourself. Aware finally that the flesh which had once sustained you beyond any question or second of doubt was now unexpectedly falling prey to time and dissolution. That your flesh had now turned undependable—and in Ben's case, since it was prostate cancer and metastasizing like crazy—that it had turned into the enemy, was hard to explain even to yourself. Incomprehensible to anyone else.

It was your flesh, and thus your personal enemy, and yours alone. The word *alone* had never held such clarity and weight.

A caress could comfort. Sure. But it couldn't pay the troops enough to convince them to continue the battle. The troops were tired. The troops were all in mutiny.

Ruth had tried of course.

She suffered too—from osteoporosis. And osteoporosis was pain in spades god knows and a betrayal all its own, but people lived for years with it. It wasn't a hangman's noose waiting in the yard.

"Remember?"

Her single counterinsurgency weapon was their past, and she wielded it tenderly and with grace.

Remember? The antique store in England where they bought the cedar chest. The owner right out of Dickens. The climb to the shrine at Delos where the wind took her wide-brim hat and sailed it out to sea. Setting up his first painters' studio in Portland, and not a job coming in for months, Ben painting angry frustrated abstracts until finally Bantam came through with the fantasy series. He should have stayed with the abstracts, she said, which were selling in the high five figures. *Their first kitten, Agamemnon, who had hidden sulking under the bed for a week like Achilles in his tent, and then suddenly for no observable reason, decided that he was master of all he surveyed. High tea with Liz and Josie at the Plaza. Christmas dinner with Neil and Donald on Mount Desert Island.* On and on.

Her version of events was not always as he remembered them, but he supposed that was to be expected.

And that was the second thing he learned about being seriously ill.

What a strange and special repository he was.

How much sheer history you had inside you that was going to die when you did.

He realized with a kind of growing awe that his *own* version of events would simply disappear shortly as though it had never existed. What would be left would be Ruth's version, friends' or relatives' versions, or his publishers' versions. His own point of view, that which was uniquely Ben Sebald's, would pass utterly from the world's vocabulary. And his secrets—guilty personal failings, which he had tried to keep hidden from everyone all these years, even from Ruth—would ironically become irrelevant. As perhaps they always were anyway.

He told her what he wanted to do.

"What about Greece?" she said. "You always loved Greece."

"Not Greece this time."

"I'm going with you."

"I don't think so. What's a five-letter word for *mooed?*"

* * *

Charlie Harmon was on lunch break in the cafeteria, and his luck was bad again. Sorenson sat down unwelcome as always with his tray directly across from him, and the tuna salad on his plate was about the same color and seemingly the same texture as Sorenson's teeth. His brilliant hospital whites only enhanced the illusion. Charlie's appetite was rapidly swimming downstream.

"True story," Sorenson said. "We had three drunks in here from Wildwood one night couple years ago. Tail-end of a very liquid wedding party. I mean, they're loaded as hell. So they decide to jump off the pier together. Made a pact. Said they'd had it—enough's enough, right? Life sucks. Maybe they couldn't get laid that night, who the fuck knows. But see, one of them's wearing this really expensive cashmere coat, and he takes it off and puts it down on the rocks, and on their way off the pier arm in arm one of the other drunks steps on it. The guy with the coat says, you fucking piece of shit! Why'd you step on my coat? Why the fuck would I want to go out with an inconsiderate piece of shit like you? And he starts swinging. The third guy, their buddy, he gets between the two of them, and before you know it all three of these guys are in the drink, and not one of them can fucking swim. They were lucky the groom came down for a smoke. His wife didn't care for cigarettes."

Charlie looked at him.

"So your point is?"

Sorenson shrugged. "No point, Charlie. Just how fucked up is this business anyway though, huh? Just how fucked up is it?"

"Jesus" Harmon said. "Eat your lunch."

***

He held her as he always had when they were young. His arms still strong around her back as he kissed her, and then shifted his weight suddenly and toppled them off the jetty into the blaze of freezing water—black granite and weathered lichen-covered concrete already well beyond their grasp in just an instant's time should they even have thought to reach for it again as the swells moved them back and forth to sea. She gasped at the sudden blinding cold and clutched his waist.

The tide went wild only once and threw him back amid spray and foam into one of the huge granite blocks beneath the surface, bruising his hip just below where the ropes bound the two of them together, and then sent them floating free.

They went down and then up again, and he could feel them shivering almost in a kind of unison, and her eyes were wide blinking away the water, and her face had taken on an unlikely pallor. *I love you* he shouted, and she began to say the same *I love*...when they were drawn down beneath a wave.

When they rose again, he shook his head and realized in that movement of his neck how much his muscles were already stiffening. *This soon,* he thought. *Good.* His throat felt rubbed with salt. The membranes in his nostrils burned.

His eyes burned too, but he could still blink the sting away and look at her. At some version of her anyhow, one he had never quite seen before whose lips and eyelids were stained a delicate blue. With a shock, he saw that she was smiling. Or perhaps the muscles of her face were contracting into what appeared to be a smile—perhaps it was a swindle of a smile. But he didn't think so. He thought that it was real. He felt light-headed, almost drunk himself. He pulled her closer until he couldn't feel his hands anymore, and then his arms around her, and when finally the sea drew him down to darkness he wasn't sure exactly who was there with him at all.

***

When Ryan, Knowles, and Andrews responded to the call and pulled up beside the old man on the beach, he still had the rope lashed around his waist, but the other end had come free so that their sister unit found the woman several yards away, lying face-down just above the tideline with her head half buried in the hard wet sand. The two kids who'd found them couldn't have been more than ten years old, but that didn't stop one of them from having a cell phone. Times like this you could almost like the goddamn things. It had maybe saved the guy.

From what Ryan could tell the woman wasn't likely to make it.

She had eaten a lot of sand.

***

He woke and saw where he'd been swimming to, and that he was alone.

He gasped and screamed.

***

"*You're a fool,*" she said quieting him. "*I love you, but*

"Aw, goddammit!" said Charlie Harmon. "Shit!" He reached for the paddles and thrust them at her. "Goddammit!"

"Hush," said Denise. "Charlie, look at his face. Look at him. You see that?"

He looked down at the man and then at her.

Her dark green eyes were pooled and still.

"Hush, Charlie" she said. "Shhhhhhh."

CORBETT'S CAGE

Shawn P. Madison

John Corbett gasped for air as the tremendous wave washed over him. His cage slammed against the metal plating of the great ship as he hurtled against the cold, wet bars. His left ankle still bled even though the bastards nearly severed it about an hour ago. The sea heaved to and fro, and continued to smash into his cage, more often than not submerging the iron box for several seconds.

This blasted night couldn't become any worse, couldn't grow more insane, could it? The storm raged wildly, tossing the huge pirate vessel as if it were so much driftwood. With each grand swell of the dark waves, his cage would once again slam into the side of the ship, rattling his teeth, and sending him crashing against the bars. He was sure of a concussion, and the dizziness became harder to shake off.

"Damn you bastards!" He roared into the night and quickly gulped in air as another monstrous wave washed over his cage.

He emerged once again gasping and spitting out the fetid seawater. Five others of his crew hung in identical cages along the starboard side of the ship, just high enough to avoid total submersion, but low enough to keep them in water. He bet his life that six more of his crewmates suffered similar fates on the ship's portside.

"Why?!" he demanded of no one but himself, not willing to waste any more energy on the effort of screaming. Thirty-six of the original sixty-seven man crew of the cargo ship *Hargitay* had been murdered outright once the filthy band of pirates gained control, including the captain. The cutthroats made the remaining twelve men watch in shackles as they stripped the bodies of their thirty-six fellow seamen, methodically cut them up into ragged little grisly pieces, and piled them into a bloody corner of the deck. Only the heads remained whole. Nineteen other crewmen were also killed in the brief but bloody battle for control of the *Hargitay*.

The pirates came upon them seemingly out of nowhere. The strange night sky was a melee of half-raging storm clouds, crackling thunder, and half-hazy full-moon. Before the *Hargitay's* crew knew what happened, their sails blazed, and pirates had boarded their ship.

Strangely enough, the *Hargitay's* cargo remained in the holds as the pirates sank the once proud ship. The pirates removed the crew, most of them carved up, then brought out the cages, thick iron bars on all four sides, and on top with a single iron plate for the floor.

Corbett, the *Hargitay's* former second-in-command, went kicking and screaming into his. Before going in, he noticed a sliding partition in the single-plate floor with a crank underneath for opening.

He had tried for the better part of an hour to reach for that crank, stretching with all his might through the unyielding bars of the flailing cage, but nearly broke an arm due to the harsh and unforgiving seas.

With the moon for his only light, his and five other cages were hauled over the side with enormous geared winches. Corbett closed his eyes against the ghastly horror of these memories, and another wall of water slammed his cage against the ship's metal side. The cacophony of the incessant waves, mixed with the constant metallic clanking of multiple cages striking against the dull iron plates that lined the pirate ship, sheared through his brain like a spike, his mind caught in a whirlwind of confusion and pain.

In the hazy moonlight streaming in from one half of the sky, he watched in terror as the gory bits of his fallen comrades fell into the sea like so much bait. He couldn't shake the dreadful vision of Captain Charles Derry's head as it hit the ocean mere feet from the bottom of his cage, bobbing twice before vanishing beneath the murky waves. Derry's lifeless eyes seemed to look straight through to his very soul as they vanished into the ocean depths.

The rain slashed sideways, pelting his naked body. Soaked and shivering, Corbett worried only slightly about confinement in a metal cage amidst such a horrendous lightning storm. He dreaded something else much more—his impending death.

Just as another wave slammed his cage, a blood-curdling scream rang out in the night, loud enough to break through the crashing waves and booming thunder. Several screams followed, some of his own included, but that last one sounded like the slaughter of another of his crewmates.

His ankle still oozed, though much less now than before, creating a bloody trail across the iron plate floor, through the bars and into the ocean. The slightly scabbed and ragged slash at his ankle-joint was half-clotted with blood. The briny seawater caused the wound little pain compared to hat his body suffered as it jostled around the cage with each and every pounding wave.

He'd noticed, while still in shackles on the deck, that the twelve men spared from the cages were the largest men aboard the *Hargitay*. Was that to make the cage a more snug fit? Or just to show them that even their twelve largest men were no match for these pirates?

Though the pirate band uttered few words, except for the war cries and battle-whoops during their initial siege, he overheard two of the filthy maggots say that the twelve *Hargitay* crewmen ought to be enough food to give them safe passage through the night and into morning.

Were they to be eaten, then? Were these pirates cannibals? If so, why put us in cages and suspend us over the side? Questions and more questions, but no answers came, as more water filled the cage, and Corbett's teeth rattled once more upon impacting against the iron plates.

He strained to look toward the next cage in line hanging over the side of the immense ship. He swept a soaked hand across his eyes several times to try and clear away the onslaught of salty water, but the driving rain filled in wherever the ocean failed to reach.

An enormous ship, easily one of the largest vessels Corbett recalled ever seeing. Its sides seemed encased in smooth iron-armor plating. The flags, which rode high on the wind earlier in the night, were of many colors, but bore no resemblance to any he recognized.

Daggett McConnell was inside the next cage down. Corbett tried calling out to him, but it was no use, the raging seas drowned out his voice.

McConnell wasn't moving much anymore. In fact, the man hadn't moved at all for quite some time, except for his body's jostling with the slamming waves.

Better off for him, Corbett thought and railed against his bars with no effect. Another wave and Corbett held his breath as he braced for the impact. Once the water cleared the cage, he shook his head and tried to peer upward against the slashing rain. He could see their faces, looking down over the side, suddenly watching. The last time he glanced up no one occupied the deck, but now there seemed hundreds.

"What?" He screamed up at them, but to no reply. Just an endless sea of faces to mirror the endless swell of waves. No emotion, no joy, no malicious satisfaction, just a look of morbid curiosity on each and every face.

Suddenly, most of them turned to look toward McConnell. Corbett tried to clear his vision, but could only see the man's cage careening back and forth against the ship. The night grew dark again, but the moon still barely shone through the haze in its half of the sky.

Then McConnell screamed. A long and languishing scream, which pierced the raging storm so completely that it sent shivers running down Corbett's spine. Corbett gripped the bars tightly, trying as hard as he could to get a better view of McConnell.

The man still screamed, at the very top of his lungs, and looked down toward the now open floor plate of his cage. Something was there, what was it? A dark shape, a menacing figure rose from the raging gray water—reaching for McConnell's cage.

"McConnell!" Corbett screamed, but the man paid him no mind. Instead, he kicked furiously at the thing that reached through the bottom of his cage with a thick scaly arm.

"For Chrissakes, McConnell!" Corbett wailed, his face wedged tightly between two bars, and his arms straining against the cold wet iron, but it was no use.

The thing's head cleared the water then, all gleaming white teeth and beady yellow eyes. One clawed hand gripped firmly around McConnell's right ankle and pulled him out of the cage with a thick and muscular arm. McConnell tried to kick at it, but another hand rose through the waves to grab the man's left ankle.

Corbett watched in horror as his crewmate grabbed a hold of the bars of his cage, screaming as razor sharp teeth chewed off first his right foot, then his left. The thing sunk its yellow claws into McConnell's right thigh, heaved down, and half of the man's left leg disappeared into the gaping maw.

McConnell's left hand let go of the bars as he struggled desperately to remain in a cage he spent the last hour trying to escape. The man held fast to the bars for as long as he could while the dark scaly thing ate its way up to his waist. Then McConnell suddenly looked toward Corbett's cage, their eyes met, the most horrifying and helpless grimace on his former shipmate's face. The two men locked stares for that barest of moments, an acknowledgement of lost hope passing between them in that instant, and then McConnell was simply gone.

Corbett noticed that he held his breath and sucked in a huge gulp of rain-laced air. His heart seemed about to burst forth from within his chest. "What in the name of God Almighty..." he murmured and tried once again to loosen his bars.

Snick of something sharp grated across the bottom of his cage. The sea swelled up and slammed him one more time against the side of the ship, but the sound was there again almost immediately.

Looking up, all of those faces peered straight down upon

him. "Go to Hell!" He shouted at them as the grating noise grew louder, and the crank beneath his cage began to turn.

"Go to hell...all of you!" He screamed in fear, rage, and terror once more as the partition in the floor of his cage slid aside.

Corbett looked down through the gaping hole in the bottom of his cage and saw not the roiling ocean, but dozens of large teeth gleaming dully in the bare moonlight, the thing's yellow eyes so full of hunger.

He felt sharp claws grab on to his ankle.

Corbett screamed.

JONAH INSIDE THE WHALE: A MEDITATION

Jason Sechrest

Well, isn't this a fine *how do you do*? I've heard of being stuck with a whale of a problem, but this is ridiculous. For Gods' sake, could you not have just killed me?

…

…

Silence? No booming voice from the heavens above, or the bowels just below me? Well, that's fine. It was a rhetorical question anyway. You needn't bother yourself with response. Apparently, the answer is no. No, death would simply not have sufficed. It would not *do* to be merely taken in by some dastardly sea creature, to be mauled by gnashing teeth, and to have my bloody remains floating in the fearful fathoms of some ocean terrain. No, certainly not. Instead, I seem to have been swallowed whole. As if I were a valium, or some runaway tooth.

Runaway, now there's a word. One I'd dare not say, and yet here I've said it. Oh, I've said it, and what of it? Alright, so I admit it. Running away is what got me into this glorious mess to begin with. I was trying to escape my destiny. But isn't that one's right? Oughtn't it be up to the individual to choose when they rise to their own greatness? I'll decide when I'm damned well good and ready to live my life in its most fulfilled state of being, and not a moment before. It is one's right to live a life of blissful mediocrity! Well, that's my story at least and I'm sticking to it. Like an adhesive. What's that old childhood nursery rhyme? "I am rubber! This whale is glue. What bounces off me is *destiny*."

Anyway, where were we? Ah yes. Running away. The moral of my story as passed down throughout the generations will undoubtedly be that this way lies ruin. Only, it hasn't been my ruin. That's just the point, isn't it? I'm neither here, nor there. I'm in what must be God's most odious of purgatories—the stomach.

Well, it's not all that terrible I suppose. Now at first, yes, the stench of rotting fish was enough to make my poor eyes sting, but truth be told I do think I'm getting used to it.

My goodness, there are a *lot* of fish in here. So many fish, so little time. My new friends! We'll have a gay old time being slowly digested over the course of, oh who knows how many days?

Just how does one become digested anyway? Well, I suppose I'll be an expert on the subject soon enough. Something about acid breaking down food into bits of mush. Yes, that's it. That's what we learned in school. The stomach has a capacity for turning solids into liquids. I'll tell you one thing I didn't expect from this whole scenario—not that I was expecting to be swallowed by a whale at all this afternoon. But I had most definitely not anticipated the heat in here. Who knew the stomach was such a hot ticket? My skin feels as though it's been roasting on the beaches of Bermuda.

So dreadfully hot. More than hot. What is the word? Humid. A wet heat.

Sticky. Yes, that's the word any poet laureate worth his salt would use to describe this most moist of atmospheric condition. Sticky.

Oh bother Jonah, what do you care how to describe it, or how Shakespeare would deem to describe the weather in a whale's a stomach? You've got bigger fish to fry, Jonah. Like *how* are you going to get out of here? *When* will you stop running from your destiny? And *why* have you begun speaking to yourself in the third person? Yes, these are the questions you should be asking. The how, when and why of it all. Those are, in fact, the three rules of journalism I believe. I would have made a good journalist, I think. I just never had the right paper, nor the right pen. You know, it takes a special kind of desk too, I'm told, to really get those thoughts down and onto the printed page.

You're digressing again, Jonah. Digress. Digress. Digress. That's why you're here, Jonah. You have *digressed.*

You're a digresser from way back. Your parents were digressing long before you knew how to talk. And their parents before them were Nobel Prize winners for achievement in art of digression. Always wandering from that beaten path, forever tethered to absolutely *nothing.* And here you find yourself stepping away from the *plan,* well is it any wonder? You needn't Freud to tell you where the blame lies.

You know, I must say considering this accidental detour, I am much calmer here in this sticky stomach than I've any right to be. These fish, on the other hand? Not so much. In various states of distress are they. Some half-rotting while others flippity-flopping atop the water. Several dozen remain alive and well, perfectly capable of swimming past my ankles. At least, I assume those are fish. After all, what else could they be? An eel, I suppose. An ocean snake of some kind? What other aquatic creatures squirm their way through these underwater cities, only to be swallowed like good old yours truly? Fish. Yes, it must be fish.

I cannot see them here in the dark, but I certainly can smell them. Truth be told, I think it's the dark in here that *most* disturbs me. I swear I could get used to the stench. Oh, I know you must think me crazy! Jonah, how can you stand the smell of *rotting* fish? But you know, I'll be really honest with you. I think there's something almost sweet about the smell after a while.

In fact, I could make a go of this place, really. I could live here. Humbly and quietly. It's not the most optimal of living conditions, but perhaps one day Moby Dick here will swallow a candle. Maybe some throw pillows. I believe in miracles, you know. I'll just sit here and meditate, that's what I'll do. I'll sit here and believe that good things will come to me, and so they shall.

The power of positive thought, that's what I always say! You know, sometimes a single positive thought is all it takes to turn God's back around.

Yes, meditation. That's the ticket. I could *really* get into a good state of mind if only it weren't so hot in here. You see, I'm constantly having to wipe the sweat from my brow and damned if the sweat isn't getting thicker with each swipe. I'm telling you, these are more than mere beads of sweat, these are big drops, a faucet really of—

Wait. Oh, no. Perhaps this isn't really sweat at all. Is this...? Oh, dear God, yes I think it is. It's happening on my arms too. And my hands. I'm—*melting*? Oh my goodness, yes. I'm sure of it now. On my hands. Where once there was skin, now there is but a thickness. A dense puddle. Liquid flesh, I suppose. As though you had taken a human being and put him through a blender. That's what's happening to me, I tell you! Oh God, that *is* what's happening. I am being liquified. Only I'm not in a blender. I'm in the stomach of a whale. The stomach acid eating away at my flesh in a way that would be all but painful if I could *feel* anything but the numbness of my extremities.

Well now, that's a bonus I suppose. It's a plus, I must admit. If there was a pros and cons list to be made for being swallowed by a whale, the fact that it's nearly painless is one for the pros column.

What now? What's to happen next? What's to become of you, old Jonah? What happens once Moby's stomach acid eats its way through the rest of you?

Organs to juice? Mind to mush? This is what becomes of us.

Oh, dear Lord, please do not let me go this way. I promise I will be a good boy and dutifully carry out your will. Whatever is the will of God, that shall be my destiny. Let me be written in the book of life and let it be said that Jonah will rise to that greatness, that he has learned his lesson dear God, and that he will never deter from the path again. Heredity digression be damned, I tell you, the cycle stops here.

There. I've made a commitment and I'm going to stick to it. Much like my hands have become stuck to each other. You see, I clasped them together in prayer position, but what with the heat…the stickiness and the acidity of it all…it would seem my hands have become glued together.

Oh, dear God, I do believe I am being digested. Please. If there is any chance for me, any opening—

Just a minute, speaking of opening. What's this? A light at the end of the tunnel? No, *literally* I do see a light at the end of the dark tunnel above me. Of course, that could just be me dying, but I do believe Moby Dick has opened his mouth to the skies. And from the intense rocking of this belly beneath me, I would bet that myself and about three dozen fishies are soon to be spit out!

Meditation, see. That's where it's at. Positive *thinking*, and positive *living*. I'm telling you, it works every time.

ABOUT THE AUTHORS

RICHARD CHIZMAR – is the *New York Times* bestselling author of *Gwendy's Button Box* (with Stephen King) and the founder/publisher of *Cemetery Dance* magazine and the Cemetery Dance Publications book imprint. He has edited more than 30 anthologies and his fiction has appeared in dozens of publications, including *Ellery Queen's Mystery Magazine* and multiple editions of *The Year's 25 Finest Crime and Mystery Stories*. Chizmar's third short story collection, *A Long December*, was recently published in trade paperback by Gauntlet Press. Please visit the author's website at: Richardchizmar.com

BILLY CHIZMAR – his first short story was published in 2015 in the anthology, *Dead Harvest*. His essay, "The Role of God in Stephen King's *Desperation*" will appear in *Reading Stephen King* edited by Brian Freeman later this summer. Chizmar was recently named as a U.S. Lacrosse Academic All-American during his senior year at St. Paul's and will be attending and playing lacrosse at Colby College in Maine.

MARK PARKER – is the author of numerous short works of fiction, including, *Biology of Blood, Way of the Witch, Banshee's Cry: A Highland Ghost Story, Lucky You, The Darkest Night of the Year, Last Minute Shopper, Killing Christmas, The Troll Diner, Born Bad,* and *Hell's Half Acre*, which is being adapted by *Cemetery Dance Publications* as a short graphic novel. As editor and publisher, Parker's credits include *Dead Harvest: A Collection of Dark Tales, Dark Hallows: 10 Halloween Haunts, Dark Hallows II: Tales from the Witching Hour, Fearful Fathoms: Collected Tales of Aquatic Terror (Vol. I –*

Seas & Oceans, Fearful Fathoms: Collected Tales of Aquatic Terror (Vol. II – Lakes & Other Bodies), and the acclaimed novella, *Darkness Whispers,* co-authored by Richard Chizmar *(Gwendy's Button Box,* with Stephen King, and *A Long December)* and Brian James Freeman *(The Painted Darkness, Blue November Storms, Black Fire, More Than Midnight, Weak and Wounded, Dreamlike States,* and *The Halloween Children,* with Norman Prentiss).* He is also the publisher of the forthcoming Detective Marlowe Gentry thriller novels, *A Coin for Charon, The Dark Age,* and *October's Children,* by Dallas Mullican.

LAIRD BARRON – spent his early years in Alaska, where he raced the Iditarod three times during the early 1990s-and worked in the fishing and construction industries. He is the author of several books, including *The Beautiful Thing That Awaits Us All,* and *Swift to Chase.* His work has also appeared in many magazines and anthologies. Barron currently resides in the Rondout Valley writing stories about the evil that men do.

WILLIAM MEIKLE – is a Scottish writer, now living in Canada, with over twenty novels published in the genre press and over 300 short story credits in thirteen countries. He has books available from a variety of publishers including Dark Regions Press, DarkFuse and Dark Renaissance, and his work has appeared in a number of professional anthologies and magazines. He lives in Newfoundland with whales, bald eagles and icebergs for company. When he's not writing he drinks beer, plays guitar, and dreams of fortune and glory.

CAMERON PIERCE – is the author and editor of numerous books, most recently *Taut Lines: Extraordinary True Fishing Stories* (Little Brown UK) and *Crawling Darkness* w/ Adam Cesare (Severed Press). His work has appeared in *Gray's Sporting Journal, Flyfishing & Tying Journal, Letters to Lovecraft, Cthulhu Fhtagn,* and many other publications. He lives in Astoria, Oregon.

DALLAS MULLICAN – After spending twenty years as the lead singer of a progressive metal band, Dallas Mullican turned his creative impulses toward writing. Raised on King, Barker, and McCammon, he moved on to Poe and Lovecraft, enamored with the macabre. During his time at the University of Alabama at Birmingham, where he received degrees in English and Philosophy, Dallas developed a love for the Existentialists, Shakespeare, Faulkner, and many more great authors and thinkers. Incorporating this wide array of influences, he entices the reader to fear the bump in the night, think about the nature of reality, and question the motives of their fellow humans. A pariah of the Deep South, Dallas doesn't understand NASCAR, hates Southern rock and country music, and believes the great outdoors consists of walking to the mailbox and back. He remains a metalhead at heart, and can be easily recognized by his bald head and Iron Maiden t-shirt. He is the acclaimed author of the Detective Marlowe Gentry thrillers, including the soon-to-be published *A Coin for Charon, The Dark Age,* and *October's Children,* from Scarlet Galleon Publications.

BRYAN CLARK – is a lifelong horror fan and lover of monsters. He has previously published with Scarlet Galleon Publications, LLC in the *Dead Harvest* anthology, and writes about horror and exploitation movies in various locations around the web, and can be heard discussing them every other week on Attack of the Killer Podcast. Bryan lives in Iowa where he helps his father put the ground to sleep every fall.

LORI R. LOPEZ – dips her pen in poetry, prose, and art. Born in Wisconsin, she later lived in Florida and Spain as well as Southern California, where she currently resides. A vegan, mother, wearer of many hats, Lori is the author of peculiar works including *Leery Lane, The Dark Mister Snark, The Strange Tail of Oddzilla, Poetic Reflections: The Queen of Hats, Odds and Ends: A Dark Collection, The Macabre Mind of Lori R. Lopez, An Ill Wind Blows, The Fairy Fly,* and *Chocolate-Covered Eyes.* Her work has appeared on *Hellnotes, Halloween Forevermore,* and *Servante of Darkness*; in *The Horror Zine, Weirdbook,* and *The Sirens Call,* as well as a number of anthologies such as *Dead Harvest, Journals of Horror: Found Fiction,* and the *H.W.A. Poetry Showcase* Volumes II and III.

ANNIE NEUGEBAUER – is a novelist, short story author, and poet. She has work appearing in over seventy publications, including magazines such as *Apex, Black Static,* and *Fireside,* as well as anthologies such as Bram Stoker Award finalist *The Beauty of Death,* #1 Amazon bestseller *Killing It Softly,* and Scarlet Galleon's *Dark Hallows II: Tales from the Witching Hour.* Annie's an active member of the Horror Writers Association and a columnist for Writer Unboxed and LitReactor. She lives in Texas with two crazy cute cats and a husband who's exceptionally well-prepared for the zombie apocalypse. You can visit her at www.AnnieNeugebauer. com for blogs, poems, organizational tools for writers, and more.

W.D. GAGLIANI – is the author of the horror-thrillers *Wolf's Trap* (a finalist for the Bram Stoker Award in 2004), *Wolf's Gambit, Wolf's Bluff, Wolf's Edge, Wolf's Cut, Wolf's Blind,* and *Savage Nights,* plus the novellas *Wolf's Deal* and both the original "The Great Belzoni and the Gait of Anubis" and the upcoming Acheron Books version. He has published fiction and nonfiction in numerous anthologies and publications such as *Robert Bloch's Psychos, Fearful Fathoms, Undead Tales, More Monsters From Memphis, The Midnighters Club, Extremes 3: Terror On The High Seas, Extremes 4: Darkest Africa,* and others, and early e-zines such as *Wicked Karnival, Horrorfind, 1000Delights, Dark Muse,* and *The Grimoire.* His fiction has garnered six Honorable Mentions in *The Year's Best Fantasy & Horror* (one of which, the story "Starbird," is also part of Amazon's Story Front program). His book reviews and nonfiction articles have been included in *The Milwaukee Journal Sentinel, Chizine, HorrorWorld, Cemetery Dance, CD Online, The Writer* magazine, *The Scream Factory, Science Fiction Chronicle, Flesh & Blood, BookPage, Hellnotes*, and many others, plus the books *Thrillers: The 100 Must Reads, They Bite*, and *On Writing Horror*. He is a member of the Horror Writers Association (HWA), the International Thriller Writers (ITW), and the Authors Guild. Additionally, the creative team of W.D. Gagliani & David Benton has published fiction in anthologies such as *THE X-FILES: Trust No One, SNAFU: An Anthology of Military Horror, SNAFU: Wolves at the Door, Dark Passions: Hot Blood 13, Zippered Flesh 2, Malpractice, Masters of Unreality*, etc., online venues such as *The Horror Zine, DeadLines* and *SplatterpunkZine*, plus the Amazon Kindle Worlds *Vampire Diaries* tie-in "Voracious in Vegas." Some of their collaborations are available in the collection, *Mysteries & Mayhem*. The author can be reached at: www.wdgagliani.com, www.facebook.com/wdgagliani @ WDGagliani

STUART KEANE – is a horror and suspense author from the United Kingdom. He is currently a member of the Author's Guild, and co-director/editor for emerging UK publisher, Dark Chapter Press. Currently in his third year of writing, Stuart has started to earn a reputation for writing realistic, contemporary horror. With comparisons to Richard Laymon and Shaun Hutson amongst his critical acclaim, he cites both authors as his major inspiration in the genre, and is dedicated to writing terrifying stories for real horror fans. He can be reached online: www.stuartkeane.com, www.facebook.com/stuart.keane.92, @SKeane_Author.

JACK ROLLINS – was born and raised among the twisting cobbled streets and lanes, ruined forts and rolling moors, of a medieval market town in Northumberland, England. He claims to have been adopted by Leeds in West Yorkshire, and he spends as much time as possible immersed in the shadowy heart of that city. Writing has always been Jack's addiction, whether warping the briefing for his English class homework, or making his own comic books as a child, he always had some dark tale to tell. Fascinated by all things Victorian, Jack often writes within that era, but also creates contemporary nightmarish visions in horror and dark urban fantasy. He currently lives in Northumberland, with his partner, two sons, and his daughter living a walking distance from his home, a home that is slowly but surely being overtaken by books.

D.G. SUTTER – is a novelist by the wee hours of morning. By 6 AM he can be found lumping boats on the historical docks of Gloucester. He has a strong draw to the sea and loves fishing. His short fiction and poetry has been published through several print and online mediums. He is currently at work on his sophomore novel. Keep up with him at www.dgsutter.wordpress.com

BRAD P. CHRISTY – is the author of *Miseryland*, *Angel Dust*, *Krampus: the Summoning*, *T'was the Fifth of December*, *The Things We do for Love*, and *Welcome to New 'Awlins*. His poetry has been featured on Literary Escapism, and he writes for the horror blog, Ghost Night Review. He is a member of the Horror Writers Association and the Writers' League of Texas. Brad currently resides in the Pacific Northwest with his wife.

JOHN EVERSON – is a staunch advocate for the culinary joys of the jalapeno and an unabashed fan of 1970s European horror cinema. He is also the Bram Stoker Award-winning author of *Covenant* and eight other novels, including the Bram Stoker Award finalist *NightWhere* and the dangerously seductive beach tale of *Siren* (his *Fearful Fathoms* story is set in the world of *Siren*). Other novels include *Redemption, Sacrifice, The Pumpkin Man, The Family Tree, The 13th* and the spider-driven *Violet Eyes*. To catch up on his blog, join his newsletter or get information on his fiction, art and music, visit

John Everson: Dark Arts at www.johneverson.com.

ERIC S. BROWN – is the author of numerous books including the Bigfoot War series, the Kaiju Apocalypse series (with Jason Cordova), Kraken, Dropship Marines, and Sasquatch Lake to name only a few. His short fiction has been published hundreds of times in the small press and beyond including in markets like Baen Books' Onward Drake and Black Tide Rising anthologies, the Grantville Gazette, and Walmart World magazine. The first book of his Bigfoot War series was adapted into a feature film from Origin Releasing in 2014.

C.M. SAUNDERS – is a freelance journalist and editor. His fiction and non-fiction has appeared in over 60 magazines, e-zines, and anthologies, including *Loaded, Record Collector, Fantastic Horror, Trigger Warning, Liquid Imagination,* and the *Literary Hatchet.* His books have been both traditionally and independently published, the most recent being *Apartment 14F: An Oriental Ghost Story (Uncut),* which is available now from Deviant Dolls Publications. He is represented by Media Bitch Literary Agency.

DAVID MICKOLAS – David lives in Charlotte, NC, and is the author of several short stories, including "Operation Devil Walk" from *At Hell's Gates: Volume II.* When he is not writing, he is a producer for one of the South's largest ABC affiliates. He is also an Emmy Award-winning motion designer and book cover artist, and can be reached on Facebook at: https://www.facebook.com/pages/Universal-Book-Covers/1420865084863088

DOUG RINALDI – was born and raised in Connecticut, and spent his formative years exploring the woods near his home. He envisioned otherworldly scenarios that ignited his imagination, inventing horrifying tales about devious lunch ladies and world-eating monsters. Throughout adolescence and into adulthood, he loved to create. Whether through drawing, graphic design, or writing, art was his life. In 1995, he received his art degree in Computer Animation and Special Effects for stage and screen. However, writing dark fiction was his true calling. At the turn of the millennium, he bid his home state a final farewell and relocated to Massachusetts where he's been honing his writing and artistic skills ever since.

ANDREW BELL – is the author of three novels, and has appeared in dozens of horror fiction anthologies including, *Dead Harvest* from Scarlet Galleon Publications. He lives in the north of England, and hopes readers will enjoy his story, "Hallowed Point".

SHANE LINDEMOEN – is a genre writer from the Upper Midwest who's made a mark bending themes of horror with hard science-fiction. He writes humans into extreme situations, and the goal is to subvert his own fears with hope. Shane's debut novel, *Artifact* (Boxfire Press, 2013) received the Golden National Independent Book Award. "Wanderer" is his first professional attempt at short fiction.

NICK NAFPLIOTIS – Nick Nafpliotis is a music teacher from Charleston, South Carolina. He is also a television, novel, and comic book reviewer for AdventuresinPoorTaste. com. His inane ramblings on writing, weird crime, bizarre classroom experiences, and pop culture can be read on his blog, RamblingBeachCat.com. His short fiction has appeared in anthologies such as *Dead Harvest* by Scarlet Galleon Publications, *Twice Upon a Time* by Bearded Scribe Press, and others.

JOHN LINWOOD GRANT – is a professional author who lives in Yorkshire with a pack of lurchers and a beard. He may also have a family. He writes dark Edwardian tales, such as his novella *A Study in Grey,* and other weird and speculative fiction, including his *Mamma Lucy* tales of

1920s hoodoo. Published in a wide range of anthologies and magazines, he edits anthologies himself, and is co-editor of *Occult Detective Quarterly*. His collection *A Persistence of Geraniums & Other Worrying Tales* is due out Summer 2017 from Electric Pentacle Press.

ARIC SUNDQUIST – is a writer of speculative fiction. Born and raised in Michigan's Upper Peninsula, he graduated from Northern Michigan University with a Master's Degree in Creative Writing. His stories have appeared in numerous publications, including *The Best of Dark Moon Digest*, *Night Terrors III*, *Evil Jester Digest Vol. 1*, and *Division by Zero 4: rEvolution*. Being a writer and a musician at heart, he also enjoys tabletop board games, playing guitar, and traveling with his girlfriend. Feel free to visit him at: aricsundquist. weebly.com.

PAUL MICHAEL ANDERSON – is the writer of *Bones are Made to Be Broken* (Written Backwards/Dark Regions Press, 2016), and has appeared in dozens of anthologies and magazines, including *Chiral Mad 3, Qualia Nous,* and *Lost Signals.* A sometime editor and occasional journalist, his articles have appeared on sites such as Bloody Disgusting and LitReactor. He lives in Northern Virginia with his wife and daughter.

A.P. SESSLER – is a resident of North Carolina's Outer Banks, and searches for that unique element that twists the everyday commonplace into the weird. When he's not writing fiction, he composes music, dabbles in animation, and muses about theology and mind-hacking, all while watching way too many online movies. His short stories have appeared online at Human Echoes Podcast and Acidic Fiction, as well as print anthologies such as *Zippered Flesh 2, Dandelions of Mars, Star Quake 2, Cranial Leakage*, and *Dark Hallows II: Tales from the Witching Hour.*

JAMES LOWDER – is the author of the bestselling, widely translated dark fantasy novels *Prince of Lies* and *Knight of the Black Rose*, short fiction for such anthologies as *Shadows Over Baker Street*, and comic book scripts for Image, Moonstone, and DC. As an editor, he has directed novel lines or series for both large and small publishing houses, edited nearly two dozen anthologies, and currently serves as executive fiction editor for Chaosium. His work has received five Origins Awards and an ENnie Award, and he's been a finalist for the International Horror Guild Award and the Stoker Award.

JACK KETCHUM – is the pseudonym for a former actor, singer, teacher, literary agent, lumber salesman, and soda jerk—a former flower child and baby boomer who figures that in 1956 Elvis, *dinosaurs and horror probably saved his life. His first novel, Off Season, prompted the Village Voice to publicly scold its publisher in print for publishing violent pornography. He personally disagrees but is perfectly happy to let you decide for yourself. His short story The Box won a 1994 Bram Stoker Award from the HWA, his story Gone won again in 2000—and in 2003 he won Stokers for both best collection for Peaceable Kingdom and best long fiction for Closing Time. He has written over twenty novels and novellas, the latest of which are The Woman and I'm Not Sam, both written with director Lucky McKee. Five of his books have been filmed to date—The Girl Next Door, The Lost, Red, Offspring and The Woman, the last of which won him and McKee the Best Screenplay Award at the prestigious Sitges Film Festival in Spain. His stories are collected in The Exit at Toledo Blade Boulevard, Broken on the Wheel of Sex, Sleep Disorder* (with Edward Lee), *Peaceable Kingdom* and *Closing Time and Other Stories*. His novella *The Crossings* was cited by Stephen King in his speech at the 2003 National Book Awards. In 2011 he was elected Grand Master by the World Horror Convention.

SHAWN P. MADISON – the creator of the Guarder/U.E.N. Universe, currently lives in the beautiful Garden State of

New Jersey with his wife and a veritable cornucopia of kids. Although he has written in many different genres, he tends to write mostly science fiction and horror. He has published more than eighty short stories in thirty different magazines and anthologies, both electronic and print. His first novel, *Guardian Lore*, was released by NovelBooks, Inc. in March of 2002, the follow-up novel, *The Guarder Factor,* was released by NovelBooks, Inc. in November of 2003, and his collection of short horror fiction, *The Road to Darkness,* was released by Double Dragon Publishing in April of 2003. You can reach Shawn via e-mail at: asm89@aol.com

JASON SECHREST – from blogger to social media guru, Jason Sechrest has been a published writer since he was fifteen years old, when he began his career as a staff writer for Femme Fatales Magazine, interviewing women of the horror, science-fiction, and fantasy genre. In 2016, Jason Sechrest was hired by *Cemetery Dance Publications* to write the monthly column "What I Learned from Stephen King"—exploring the wisdom, life lessons, and spirituality hidden within the works of the Master of Horror. The following year, Sechrest launched the website SechrestThings.com, a blog dedicated to his own musings on the world of horror and suspense. Most recently, Jason's first work of fiction, a short horror story entitled "Orange Grove Court," was purchase by *Cemetery Dance Magazine* for publication in 2018.

TITLES BY SCARLET GALLEON PUBLICATIONS

Dead Harvest: A Collection of Dark Tales

Dark Hallows: 10 Halloween Haunts

Dark Hallows II: Tales from the Witching Hour

Darkness Whispers

Fearful Fathoms: Collected Tales of Aquatic Terror
(Vol. I – Seas & Oceans)

Fearful Fathoms: Collected Tales of Aquatic Terror
(Vol. II – Lakes & Other Bodies)

* A Coin for Charon (A Marlowe Gentry Thriller)
by Dallas Mullican

* The Dark Age (A Marlowe Gentry Thriller)
by Dallas Mullican

* October's Children (A Marlowe Gentry Thriller)
by Dallas Mullican

* Dark Hallows III: Blood Moon
(13 Vampiric Tales)

* forthcoming

35135445R00336

Printed in Poland
by Amazon Fulfillment
Poland Sp. z o.o., Wrocław